Just some of the rave reviews for J. Kenner's powerfully sensual and erotic novels:

'*Wanted* is another J. Kenner masterpiece . . . This was an intriguing look at self-discovery and forbidden love all wrapped into a neat little action/suspense package . . . Evan was hot, hot, hot! Together, they were combustible. But can we expect anything less from J. Kenner' *Reading Haven*

'J. Kenner writes a compelling erotic story about two people with many secrets . . . Whenever Evan and Angie are together, the air sizzles with tension' *Cocktails and Books*

'*Wanted* by J. Kenner is the whole package! A toe-curling smokin' hot read, full of incredible characters and a brilliant storyline that you won't be able to get enough of. I can't wait for the next book in this series . . . I'm hooked!' *Flirty & Dirty Book Blog*

'I loved this story! It had substance, lovable characters, and unexpected discoveries. And the love between Evan and Angelina was passionate, explosive, and utterly wonderful' *Part of That World*

'I don't know if I have enough adjectives to describe the hotness of this book . . . Julie Kenner writes a heck of a story and I am definitely a fan!' *About That Story*

'J. Kenner's evocative writing thrillingly captures the power of physical attraction, the pull of longing, the universe-altering effect one person can have on another. She masterfully draws out the eroticism between Nikki and Damien . . . *Claim Me* has the emotional depth to back up the sex . . . Every scene is infused with both erotic tension, and the tension of wondering what lies beneath Damien's veneer – and how and when it will be revealed' *Heroes and Heartbreakers*

'*Claim Me* by J. Kenner is an erotic, sexy and exciting ride. The story between Damien and Nikki is amazing and written beautifully. The intimate and detailed sex scenes will leave you fanning yourself to cool down. With the writing style of Ms Kenner you almost feel like you are there in the story riding along the emotional roller coaster with Dam

J. Kenner loves wine, dark chocolate, and books. She lives in Texas with her husband and daughters. Visit her online at www.jkenner.com to learn more about her and her other pen names, and to get a peek at what she's working on. Or connect with her via Twitter @juliekenner or through www.facebook.com/JKennerBooks.

By J. Kenner

Most Wanted Series
Wanted
Heated
Ignited

The Stark Series
Release Me
Claim Me
Complete Me
Take Me (e-novella)

Heated
J. KENNER

headline
ETERNAL

Published by arrangement with Bantam Books,
an imprint of Random House,
a division of Random House LLC.

First published in Great Britain in 2014
by HEADLINE ETERNAL
An imprint of HEADLINE PUBLISHING GROUP

1

Cataloguing in Publication Data is available from the British Library

ISBN 978 1 4722 1513 0

Offset in Sabon by Avon DataSet Ltd, Bidford-on-Avon, Warwickshire

Printed and bound by CPI Group (UK) Ltd, Croydon, CR0 4YY

Headline's policy is to use papers that are natural, renewable and
recyclable products and made from wood grown in sustainable forests.
The logging and manufacturing processes are expected to conform to the
environmental regulations of the country of origin.

HEADLINE PUBLISHING GROUP
An Hachette UK Company
338 Euston Road
London NW1 3BH

www.headlineeternal.com
www.headline.co.uk
www.hachette.co.uk

Acknowledgments

I want to say a huge shout-out to everyone I've met across the social media community, some only in 140 character increments on Twitter, others flashing across my Facebook pages and profile. (I mean, it's an amazing world when you actually meet and interact with folks who will later become friends, beta readers, and more only through 140 character flybys.)

Every one of you makes me laugh and smile, and the support and enthusiasm I've received is both thrilling and humbling. So here's to all of you: *#YouGuysAreTheBest*.

I also owe special shout-outs to Neil Orme, whom I found on Google when I needed a research fact (sorry—spoilers abound!) and he answered my out-of-the-blue email in less than an hour; to Dana for the reads, the enthusiasm, and the Chicago advice; and to Elle and Christie for the hashtag, emoticon, and teaser-image luv. *#YouKnowYouRock*

Most of all I have to thank the fabulous folks at Bantam, who really do go above and beyond. *#MyPublisherIsAwesome-Sauce*

Heated

one

Right and wrong.

Good and evil.

Black and white.

These are the parameters of the world in which we live, and anyone who tries to tell you otherwise—who argues that nothing is absolute, and that there are always shades of gray—is either a fool or trying to con you.

At least that is what I used to believe.

But that was before I met him. Before I looked into his eyes. Before I gave him my trust.

Maybe I'm a fool. Maybe I've lost my balance and my edge. I don't know.

All I know is that from the moment I met him, everything changed. One look, and I feared that I was in trouble.

One touch, and I knew that I should run.

One kiss, and I was lost.

Now the only question is, will I find my way back to who I was? And more important, do I want to?

Nothing is ever as easy as it should be.

My dad taught me that. He served as a special agent with the FBI for twenty years before leaving that post to become the chief of police in Galveston, Texas, an island community with enough crime to keep his life interesting, and enough sunshine and warm weather to keep him happy.

During the years I was growing up, I'd watch as he spent hours, days, weeks, even months putting together a kick-ass case against some of the vilest criminals that ever walked this earth. Thousands of man hours. Hundreds of pieces of evidence. All those little ducks lined up just the way they should be—and it didn't make one bit of difference. The defense would spout some technicality, the judge would cave, and *poof,* all that work went down the drain.

Like I said, nothing is ever easy. That's the first truism upon which I base my life.

The second is a corollary: No one is what they seem.

My stepfather taught me that. He was a fast-rising major league baseball player that the press took a liking to. They called him the golden boy, predicted he'd spearhead his team to the World Series, and did everything but genuflect when he entered a room. What they didn't report was the way he beat my mother. The way he forced me to watch, threatening that my turn was coming. His hands, his fists, a broken beer bottle. Whatever was handy. I'd flinch with every blow, and when her bones snapped, I'd feel it too, and my scream would blend with hers in some horrific, discordant melody.

Somehow none of those hospital visits were ever reported in the local paper, and on the rare occasions when the cops showed up at our house, nothing ever came of it. Harvey Grier had the face of a prince and the smile of a homecoming king, and if his fourteen-year-old stepdaughter called the cops one night with a bullshit story that could ruin his reputation and queer his lucrative deals, it must be because she was your typical bored teenager. Certainly it couldn't be that she lived with the monster day in and day out, and saw all too clearly under the pretty boy disguise.

My stepfather is dead now. As far as I was concerned, that was a good thing. The man wasn't worth anything except driving that second lesson home: There are monsters hiding under the most innocent of countenances, and if you don't keep your guard up, they will bite you. And hard.

The takeaway? Don't take anything for granted. And don't trust anyone.

I guess that makes me cynical. But it also makes me a damn good cop.

I sipped champagne and thought about my job and those two axioms as I leaned against one of the white draped pillars in The Drake hotel's cloyingly elegant Palm Court restaurant. I didn't know a soul there, primarily because I'd crashed the party, and I was doing my best to blend with that pillar so that I could simply sit back and watch the world—and the people—go by. I was looking for one face in particular, because I'd come here with a plan. And I intended to stay in my little corner, holding this pillar, until I spied my mark.

I'd been standing there for an hour, and was beginning to think that I had a long night ahead. But I'd survived worse stakeouts, and I am nothing if not determined.

I'd been to the Palm Court once before when my dad had me for a weekend and we decided to have an adventure. But tonight most of the familiar tables had been moved out, giving the guests room to mingle around the elegant fountain and massive floral arrangement. As far as I could tell, the dress code for the evening was anything that had premiered during Fashion Week, and the only reason no one was pointing a finger at me and snickering was that my off-the-clearance-rack dress was so utterly pedestrian that it rendered me invisible.

Flowing strains of classical music filled the room, provided by an orchestra tucked into the corner, but no one was dancing. Instead they were mingling. Talking, laughing. It was all very proper. Very elegant. Very festive.

And I was very much out of my element.

My natural habitat is Indiana, where I'm actually a bit of a celebrity within the force as the youngest female ever to make detective with the Indianapolis Metropolitan Police Department. I'd come to Chicago because I'd been going out of my mind while I rode out a stint on medical leave, and when one of my confidential informants, Candy, asked me to track down her former roommate who'd fallen off the planet, I'd decided to do a little off-the-books investigation.

According to Candy, Amy had been working as an exotic dancer at an upscale Chicago gentleman's club called Destiny until about two weeks ago. "She'd been there almost a month and was jamming on the tips. She even liked the other girls. And I'm pretty sure she was banging one of the owners. So it wasn't like she had a reason to just split."

To my way of thinking, banging the boss might be reason enough, especially if the boss is the one who told you to move on.

"Yeah, but she would have told me," Candy said, when I suggested as much. "She might take another job or even move, but she'd call once she got settled. Something happened."

Normally, I wouldn't worry. After all, twenty-two-year-old exotic dancers pull up stakes and disappear all the time. Maybe they're just trying to shake off the old life. Or maybe they're following a guy. Amy had been on her own since she was fifteen and knew how to handle herself. She was clean, so I didn't expect that she was laid out in a heroin den somewhere. Plus, I knew she fantasized about Prince Charming riding in and whisking her off into the sunset, so maybe she'd realized that banging the owner wasn't going to stick, and she'd set out for New York or Vegas or someplace else with a surfeit of rich, horny men.

But I didn't believe any of that. Candy had been more than seven months pregnant when Amy moved to Chicago, full of promises to come back loaded down with presents for the baby and, most important, to be there for the birth. Assuming the kid came on schedule, that was just over two weeks away.

I hoped to hell she'd just gotten carried away with a guy and would surface any day now with stories of hot nights and wild sex. But I worked homicide, and it was in my nature to fear the worst.

While I was making the drive from Indiana to Chicago, I'd put in a call to a friend in the Chicago PD, and he'd confirmed that she wasn't cooling her heels in a Cook County cage. I was somewhat relieved to know she was either staying clean or playing it smart, but I'd secretly hoped that she'd gotten arrested for shoplifting and was too proud to call Candy for bail.

I'd rolled into Chicago just after seven on a Wednesday night, and I'd made Destiny my first stop. The place was clean and classy, with drinks that weren't watered down, girls who looked happy to be there and not at all used up, and a clientele that skewed heavily toward the professional end of the spectrum. The place had a full bar, including Guinness on tap, and a decent menu that included some rather delicious cheese fries.

I'd certainly seen worse places, and as I sat at the bar and looked the joint over with a cop's eye, nothing wonky popped for me.

Enter the Second Truism: No one is what they seem. Or, in this case, no *place* is what it seems.

I learned that when I met Agent Kevin Warner, an FBI buddy, for breakfast the next morning and he laid out a whole list of badass shit that he thought was going down in that club. He tossed allegations around like candy. And when he hit the Mann Act charges—prostitution, white slavery, and other nasty felonies—my ears perked up.

"Slow down, cowboy," I'd said. "They got busted for that shit?"

"Fucking immunity," Kevin said. "They helped shut down a white slavery ring that was working off the West Coast and spreading all the way toward our fair city."

"They?" I repeated.

"Black, August, and Sharp," he said, naming off Destiny's three owners—three celebrated businessmen who were the toast of Chicago. I mean, hell. I'm not even from Chicago, and I knew all about those guys. "They're slick, those three," Kevin continued. "Slick and smart and as dangerous as sharks in dark water. Got the immunity deal to hide behind, and that cut my investigation off at the knees."

I nodded. Immunity was part of the game. The whole point was to protect a suspect from prosecution. If there wasn't guilt there in the first place, that protection really wasn't necessary. In other words, it was a rare suspect who was given immunity without being dirty.

Frankly, the whole idea of giving a suspect immunity irritated me, but I knew it was a necessary evil. Besides, I figured that justice would find a way. At least that was what my dad always said when one of his defendants pulled a technicality out of their ass and shot the finger at the law.

Karma really could be a raving bitch, and I wondered if she was baring her teeth in the direction of Black, August, and Sharp. Were they as dirty as Kevin said? Were they simply good citizens who shared their knowledge with the Feds? Or were they somewhere in the middle?

I didn't know, but I figured the odds ran toward the first or the last. "How broad's the immunity?" I'd asked.

"If I have my way, they'll wish it was broader. I'm dead certain they're neck deep in all sorts of shit. Gambling, smuggling, money laundering. Bribery, kickbacks, fraud. You name it, they're in it. But they've got powerful friends, and I'm not authorized to officially pursue any of it."

I heard the frustration in his voice. He wanted these guys—wanted them bad. I got that. There were a lot of reasons I'd become a cop, but in the end it all boiled down to protecting the innocent and stopping the bad guys. To making sure the system worked and that those who crossed that line paid for the breach.

I lived and breathed my job. It was both my redemption and my salvation. And I was very good at what I did.

"I can't push on this," he'd said. "But you can."

He was right. My mind was already turning over options, trying to figure the best way to slide my pretty ass into Destiny, chat up the girls, and get a line on Amy. Once I was in and poking around for information, there was no reason I couldn't poke around for more.

Frankly, that would be my pleasure. Immunity might be a necessary evil in the world of jurisprudence, but I was more than happy to give Karma a little push. And if I found out that those guys were into other shit, bringing them down would be a damn good way to balance the scales of justice.

All of which explained how my mission to get one missing dancer back to Indiana had morphed into a full-fledged, albeit off-the-books, undercover operation. At one point I might have considered waltzing into Destiny and boldly announcing that I was looking for a friend, but once I knew that the owners could be dirty, that plan went right out the window. I wanted to know what they were up to—and if the white slavery allegations turned out to be true, I wanted to kick a little ass.

It was that whole "undercover" thing that was my current sticking point. You'd think it would be easy for a genuinely pretty woman—that would be me—to get a job as a cocktail waitress in a Chicago-based gentleman's club, but you'd be wrong. Despite my camera-ready face, nice tits, and tight ass, the application I'd submitted yesterday had been politely declined. And that despite the fact that I have honest-to-goodness waitressing skills.

Thus illustrating that First Truism: Nothing is ever as easy as it should be.

And that brings us right back to the Second Truism: No one is what they seem.

Take Evan Black, for example. This was his party that I'd crashed. A formal affair to celebrate his engagement to Angelina Raine, the daughter of vice presidential hopeful Senator Thomas Raine.

I saw him standing across the room, a movie-star gorgeous man with his arm around an equally stunning brunette that had to be Angelina. She was leaning against him, looking giddy with happiness, as they chatted with two other couples. All clean and shiny and polished. But if Kevin was right, Black wasn't the man he appeared to be.

Or what about Cole August, Black's business partner, who received so much adulation from the press and the public for the way he'd pulled himself up out of the muck of his Chicago South Side heritage to become one of the most respected and influential businessmen in the city? He might look positively droolworthy as he stalked the far side of the room with a cell phone pressed against his ear, the very picture of the entrenched businessman.

But I happened to know that August hadn't left that shady heritage as far behind as he liked to pretend.

And then there was Tyler Sharp.

"That's the one," Candy had said when I ran the name by her. "Amy was head over heels for the guy."

"He feel the same?"

"Don't know."

"But she was fucking him?"

"Yeah. At least, I think so. I mean, wasn't like she was post-ing pictures on Facebook. But no way would she have walked away from that, and from what you're saying . . ."

We might have been talking on the phone, but I could still picture the way Candy shrugged as she trailed off. I knew what she meant. I'd done additional homework on Tyler Sharp, much of which I'd relayed to Candy. To bottom line it, he had a weak-ness for women, and I fully intended to capitalize on his wom-anizing ways. If I couldn't get into Destiny through my stellar waitressing skills, I'd get in close through the man.

In other words, I was planning a seduction.

All things considered, that was a better approach than my first plan. Waitressing only gave me access to the club. But sex opened all sorts of doors. Pillow-talk. Computer access. Who knew what else. Play the game right, and I'd have a box seat to the best show in town, whether it was gambling, smuggling, or something much more heinous.

And if it turned out that Tyler had gotten Amy involved with anything hinky, I'd castrate the son of a bitch.

First, I had to find him.

He'd been out of town for the last few weeks, so I had yet to see him in person, but I was certain I'd recognize him the mo-ment he entered this room. Like I said, I'd done my homework, and where looking at photographs of Tyler Sharp was con-cerned, that wasn't exactly a hardship. The man definitely qual-ified as eye candy.

He stood just over six feet tall with a lanky, athletic build and the kind of dark blond hair that boasts flashes of gold in the summer. I knew that his business interests were wide and varied and not always legal. And I knew that he carried an American Express Black card. He owned at least a dozen cars, but rarely drove them, preferring his Ducati motorcycle.

"You look lost."

I'd been glancing toward the entrance, but now I jerked my head to the left and found myself staring at a leggy brown-eyed blonde with hair so thick and shiny she could do shampoo commercials. She held out her hand, and I took it without thinking. "I'm Katrina Laron—Kat," she said, then hooked her thumb toward Angelina Raine. "I'm the bride's best friend, which makes me the pseudo-hostess. And you are?"

Her smile was polite, but held an edge, and I was certain that she knew damn well I'd crashed the party.

Great.

"Sloane O'Dell," I said, using my mother's maiden name and not my own last name of Watson.

"Who are you here with? I think I know everyone on Lina's side of the guest list, so you must be a friend of Evan's?" Again with the polite smile. Again with the protective edge.

"I'm actually looking for Tyler," I said, and prided myself on my ability to tell the truth and lie all at the same time.

"Oh, really?" Her brows lifted. "Friend or foe?"

"Excuse me?" I kept my expression casual and hoped that my naturally pale skin wasn't flushing.

"It's just that I know Tyler didn't bring a date, and if you're not one of Angie's or Evan's guests . . ."

Fuck. Fuck, fuck, fuck.

"I took a chance," I said, once again relying on total honesty. "I think he'll want to see me." Okay, that part I wasn't nearly as sure about.

"Listen, I don't mean to sound like a bitch, but Tyler's a pretty private guy who attracts a lot of female attention." She shrugged. "You wanna tell me why you think he'll want to see you?"

"Not really, no."

She looked at me hard, obviously taking my measure. Then she snagged a glass of wine off a passing waiter's tray and took a long swallow "All right, then. Let's go find him."

"I've been trying to do that all evening," I said wryly.

"He arrived just before I came over to politely inquire about your intentions. Hang on," she said as she lifted herself up onto her toes and waved across the room. "I see him."

I craned my neck, but as I was a good three inches shorter than Kat, I had absolutely no idea if she'd managed to catch his eye.

Time dragged, and I was beginning to think that he either hadn't seen her or had chosen to ignore her, when I saw the glint of gold as the light struck his hair. He wore a charcoal gray suit, and the fine lines and expensive material contrasted with the slightly mussed hair that he wore just a little too long for the corporate rule book. Now it was tied back in a manner that highlighted the sharp angles of his cheeks and jawline.

His cerulean eyes were the perfect contrast to the golden blond hair, conjuring thoughts of sun and sand, wild days and wicked nights. All in all he had a devil-may-care look about him, and that was only accentuated by the beard stubble. My fingers twitched, and to my horror, I found myself wanting to reach out and stroke his cheek, letting the roughness there smooth away my hard edges like sandpaper.

He eased around the fountain and jockeyed through the crowd with the kind of confidence that comes from knowing that people will move out of your way because you're just that cool.

"Tyler!" Kat called again, and I had the unreasonable urge to clamp my hand over her mouth. This was the guy I'd come here to get close to, but right then, I didn't feel prepared at all.

I'd known before coming tonight that Tyler Sharp was among the finest of male specimens, but never in a million years would I have anticipated my own tingling, visceral reaction to the man.

I wanted to duck behind the pillar. I wanted to bolt. I wanted to find some sanctuary until I could get my head together and find my center. But that wasn't an option. He'd seen us, and though he nodded to Kat, I was the one who drew his focus. His eyes met mine, and the impact of that simple look ripped through me in a way that left me weak and confused. I'd never met Tyler Sharp—had seen him only in photographs, learned about him only from articles and from chatting up cops. But in that moment it felt as though I'd known him all my life.

I wasn't entirely sure I liked the feeling—or perhaps I just liked it too much.

He stopped in front of us, and I told myself to get it together. I was not the kind of woman who lost her cool around a gorgeous man. Or, at least, I hadn't been two minutes ago.

As he looked at me, his sensual mouth curved up in the manner of a man about to sample something delicious—and the something was me. I shivered, the unexpected thought making my body tingle in a way that caught me off guard, but that I couldn't deny liking.

It took one hell of an effort, but I straightened my shoulders and met his eyes coolly, determined to take back at least a modicum of control.

"Sloane was looking for you," Kat said.

"Was she?" His attention stayed full on my face, and I thought for a moment that if I stepped closer, I would drown in those liquid eyes. "Funny," he said. "She's just the woman I want, too."

two

She's just the woman I want, too.

His words wrapped around me, as enticing as a caress, and the control I'd been clutching scattered like so much dandelion fluff.

That moment of weakness passed quickly, though, shoved aside by years of police training and the deeply ingrained cynicism I'd lived with since childhood. Tyler Sharp was a con man and a womanizer and who knew what else. He knew how to flatter. How to entice. How to make a woman feel special and interesting and, yeah, just a little turned on. But no way had he really been looking for me. He'd been out of town for weeks, and I knew that he'd returned only this afternoon. So, no. I wasn't on his radar.

I told myself that was a good thing. If Tyler Sharp was going to be looking at me, I wanted him to see only what I was willing to reveal.

As if in answer to my thoughts, he glanced down, then drew his gaze over me, starting at my newly-painted pink toenails and moving so slowly up my body that it took all my willpower not to shiver. When his eyes once again reached mine, I almost gasped at the wicked fire I saw beneath the fierce arctic blue. A wild, penetrating flame that had the power to burn away my cover and leave me naked, all my secrets fully exposed to this man.

The thought should have angered me. At the very least, it should have worried me.

Instead, it excited me.

You're off your game, Sloane. Walk away. Just walk away, get your bearings, and kick off the op tomorrow.

Good advice, actually. And why wouldn't it be? I was a damn good cop, after all.

Apparently I was also a damn fool, because I had no intention of walking away. I wasn't entirely sure if I was sticking because of the mission or the man, but I told myself it didn't matter. That the little trill of sensual pleasure I felt low in my belly wasn't a weakness—it was an asset. This was a seduction, after all. A little sizzle and pop between us would only make the job easier. And a lot of sizzle and pop would make it a hell of a lot more fun.

Still, I owed either Tyler Sharp or my hormones a thank-you. Because my reaction to this man reminded me that I needed to be careful. Tyler Sharp was a dangerous breed, and though he might not know it yet, he and I were locked in a heated battle. One that I fully intended to win—even if that meant playing dirty.

Beside me, Kat shifted. The movement caught my attention, and I turned to see her watching Tyler.

He gave her the slightest of nods, and she cleared her throat.

"Um, yeah, well, I'm just going to run and find Lina and give her and Evan another hug. Attend to my pseudo-hostess duties. Maybe cure cancer and solve that whole world peace problem. Hopefully you two will muddle along without me."

"I think we'll manage," Tyler said. "I promise to take good care of Sloane."

"Yeah," Kat said. "I just bet you will." She winked at me, then bopped away. I watched her get swallowed up by the crowd, grateful to have a moment to gather myself. When I turned back to Tyler, I saw that he hadn't taken the same opportunity. He was still focused entirely on me.

"Alone at last," he said.

I shifted my weight, not liking the way this man unnerved me. I was a detective, for Christ's sake. I ate suspects for breakfast, and my bad cop skills in interviews were worthy of an Academy Award. I'd never worked undercover, though, and I suddenly had all sorts of respect for my peers who put on the mask and held tight to their secrets.

Then again, I was no stranger to masks or secrets. I could do this. And as if to prove it to myself, I looked up at him through my lashes, hoping the effect was as sexy as I imagined. "Should I be nervous? A man like you looking for me?"

"A man like me?" His voice was low. Enticing. "Interesting. So tell me—what am I like?"

I stepped closer to him, lifted my hand as if I was going to touch him, then pulled it back with a slightly embarrassed expression. "Tempting," I said, and though the word was calculated, it was also very true.

"Am I?" He looked pointedly at my hands. "And that makes you nervous?"

"That? No." I drew in a breath as I considered my next move and, as in chess, where that move would take me. "I'm pretty good at resisting temptation."

"Are you?" He leaned in, his mouth so close to my ear I felt the whisper of his breath on my hair. "I'm not. As far as I'm concerned, giving in to temptation is one of the few true pleasures in life."

Oh, my. A hot coil of desire twisted through me, making my skin flush and my knees go weak.

If he noticed my reaction, he said nothing. But he began to walk slowly around me, as a man in a museum might circle a statue.

I started to turn as well, tracking his movement. "No," he said, the command in his voice undeniable. "Stay still. Look forward."

I stopped, hesitated, then turned my head to look out at the party, at the people floating by in pretty dresses and elegant suits. With smiles and laughter and nothing on their minds except the quality of the wine and the rhythm of the band.

I told myself that my acquiescence was simply part of the game—he was a man who wanted control, I was the woman falling under his spell.

But it was more than that, and I damn well knew it. That flutter I felt in my belly wasn't the excitement of the chase, but the anticipation of his touch.

Yeah, Tyler Sharp was dangerous, all right.

He was behind me now, and though I could no longer see him, I felt his presence as firm and gentle as a kiss. My breath caught in my chest, and I realized that I was anticipating the brush of his fingertips upon the nape of my neck, then his hand on my bare back, exposed in the halter-style dress.

But the touch never came—and my breath never came easy.

When he spoke, his voice was low, as if too much volume would break the spell. "You're a riddle, Ms. . . ."

"O'Dell," I whispered.

He was right there, but I couldn't see him. I could only breathe in the scent of him, fresh and woody, like a forest after a rain. Sexy, enticing, and undeniably male. "Sloane O'Dell," he said. "I like it."

"I like the way you say it." I kept my voice low and full of invitation.

"Do you?" he asked, as he finished the circle. "I'm very glad to hear it."

I looked at him, at that perfect face, and felt my fingers twitch with the desire to touch him, a desire that was magnified because I could see only too well that it was returned. Tyler Sharp wanted me, too. Maybe he was teasing me, playing me. Maybe he had an agenda. I didn't know. But my world centered around seeing—seeing people, seeing evidence, seeing the truth. And I saw the truth in the way Tyler's eyes were dilated. In the slightest flush of color on his skin. In the way that his pulse beat just a tad too quickly in his neck.

Yes, he wanted me—and yet there was no denying that he was playing with me, too. We were locked in a game, and though I'd initiated it, I couldn't claim to fully understand the rules.

I felt unanchored and slightly out of control. But at the same time, I felt more desperately alive than I had in a very long time.

With some effort, I managed to gather myself. "You never did say why you were looking for me."

"No. I didn't."

I couldn't help but grin. Forget chess; this was way more fun. "Am I supposed to guess?"

Instead of answering, he just smiled. Slow and easy and full of decadent promise. "Sloane," he said. Just a syllable. Just a name. But it was my name, and it seemed to drip with honey. I wanted to taste it. Taste him.

A shiver raced up my spine. My inner thighs felt warm, and my breasts strained against the bodice of my dress. It had been years since I'd had such a pronounced reaction to a man. He might be as dangerous as they come, but that was part of what made my job exciting—the more dangerous the quarry, the bigger the thrill.

Tyler took a step forward, and I took a corresponding step back, then one more just because I wanted to clear my head. I realized too late that he'd edged me back against the pillar. I might have been trying to escape, but there was no place to go, especially not when Tyler leaned forward, pressing his palm to the pillar just over my shoulder. He was right there, right in front of me, so close I could feel the air thickening from the pressure.

"Tyler." My voice was low, barely a whisper. "I don't think—"

"No," he said. "Don't think. Just wait. Just close your eyes."

I fought the urge to protest—this is what I wanted, after all. To get close to this man. To heat it up and see how far we could take it. No matter how out of control I might feel, I had to remember that this was my game, and though he might score a few points, I was the one who'd made up the rules.

"That's a good girl," he said, as I let my eyes flutter closed.

I concentrated on breathing, trying to ignore the way the tiny hairs on my arms stood up, a reaction to the electricity now swirling in the few inches that remained between us. He cupped my jaw with his free hand, then brushed his thumb lightly over my cheek. *He was going to kiss me.*

My mind was spinning so damn fast, reeling between excitement and wonder. He was a tool, a suspect, a criminal. Even so, I wanted this, and not because seduction was my endgame.

I simply wanted the man. Damn me to hell, I wanted him bad.

I felt the brush of his lips against my ear as he spoke. His voice was as soft and sensual as the kiss that I expected, but the words held the sting of a slap: "You shouldn't be here."

Ice burned in my veins, and I stood as tight and still as a statue.

He'd made me. Goddammit, how the hell had he made me?

But no. The "how" wasn't important. Now it was all about denial and damage control.

I allowed myself only a second to rein in my fear. I let confusion color my expression—not hard under the circumstances—then I opened my eyes. He'd stepped back, and I met his gaze boldly. I expected to see anger and accusation on his face. Instead, I saw warmth. "I—" I closed my mouth and regrouped. "What are you talking about?"

"You shouldn't be tucked away like this." He spoke simply, apparently oblivious to my discomfiture. "You should be the center of attention. See that flower arrangement?" he asked, nodding toward the stunning arrangement of flowers that dominated the center of the Palm Court. "You outshine it a thousandfold."

It was an utterly unoriginal line—not worthy of the man at all. I thought about telling him so, but considering my goal of getting close, insulting him probably shouldn't be my next move. Frankly, I was so flustered I wasn't sure what the next move should be. All I knew was that I'd gone on the defensive, and I needed to drop that before he noticed.

It took some concentration, but I managed to conjure a shy smile. "You're very sweet," I said. "And I'm very flattered."

For a moment, he said nothing, but I saw the inquisitive gleam in his eye, along with the way his head tilted slightly, as if he was examining something curious. "No," he finally said. "I don't think you're flattered at all."

"Excuse me?" I couldn't help the bite of temper in my voice, but it was directed at me, not at him. I should have gone for bold, not demure. Should have stepped forward instead of stepping back.

I'd miscalculated. And I didn't like to lose.

"You don't strike me as a woman who needs pretty words and flattery. I think you like a more direct approach." Once again, he closed the distance between us. Once again, the air shimmered with rising heat, this time fueled by the kind of danger that had the power to burn.

"Is that what you think?"

"It's what I know. It's who you are." He took hold of my wrist, the shock of his touch effectively silencing my lie. "Tell me why you were looking for me, Sloane. Tell me flat out."

I drew in a breath, buying time as I weighed my options and considered how to mix truth with lies. "I saw you," I finally said. "On the television, in magazines, in newspapers. You seemed powerful and a little mysterious."

"Always good to keep the press and the public guessing. It increases the mystique."

"Does it? Well, I guess it worked. I've thought about you, Tyler Sharp. You wouldn't leave my head. And I decided that I had to get close to you. I had to know if the living, breathing man was as interesting in person as he was in my fantasies."

I met his eyes. Made sure that he could see the heat in mine. "I wanted to get close. I wanted to see if you were the kind of man I wanted in my bed."

"And?"

"Now I've met you," I said as I gently pulled my arm free. But my smile was slow and easy and full of invitation.

And leaving that little bit of bait dangling, I slowly walked away.

three

I managed to keep my back straight and add a nice little swish to my hips as I crossed the ballroom toward the ladies' room. I wasn't about to turn around and check, but I imagined that he was watching me go, and I couldn't falter. Not then. Not after taking the kind of chance I'd just taken.

The moment I was through the door of the restroom, though, I raced to the closest cubicle and locked myself in. As with everything at The Drake, even the bathroom was elegant, and my little stall was a far cry from typical. Instead of simply housing a toilet, there was a marble vanity, a sink, and an upholstered stool, upon which I gratefully sagged. I pressed my elbows to the counter, stared at my reflection, and sighed.

"That was either a brilliant move or complete lunacy," I announced, but the girl in the mirror didn't say a thing, and I can't say that I blamed her. Her always pale skin seemed to glow, and the flush of excitement that colored her cheeks only made the smattering of freckles stand out more. Her tumble of wavy red hair—the other souvenir of her Irish heritage—had come loose from the messy knot she'd secured with a pair of decorative chopsticks atop her head, and now a few tendrils framed her face in a way that was undeniably flirty.

Considering the outcome of the operation was still an open question, she looked far too smug—far too excited. As if she was setting out on a grand adventure.

"Idiot," I said to her—to myself—as I glanced at my watch, gauging how long I should wait before I went back into the ball-room. I'd thrown down a gauntlet specifically because Tyler was the kind of guy who needed a challenge, but if I stayed away too long, my plan might backfire. Some other woman might slide into Tyler's arms. He might decide to cut his losses and head out. He might decide that I was just too much damn trouble.

Right. Enough with the gauntlet throwing. Time to get back in the game.

I hurried out of the stall, yanked open the door to the ladies' room, then headed back into the ballroom. I scoped out the room, searching every face for Tyler, but there was no sign of him.

Well, damn.

Honestly, I should have expected it. Nothing is as easy as it should be, after all.

I am not a party hound. Neither do I do small talk well. And my warm, comfy pillar was all the way across the room. I was making my way in that direction when I saw him standing amidst a small cluster of women. I winced when a blonde with amazing tits and the kind of neckline that was bound to cause a traffic accident laughed heartily and slid her arm around his waist, leaning against him as if she'd otherwise be knocked over by his wit.

His own grin widened, and he added something to the conversation that I couldn't hear. Everyone in that circle was enraptured by him, and to be honest I was surprised the whole room didn't turn toward him, drawn by his smooth manner and gregarious smile. In that moment, I was certain that what Kevin had told me of cons and confidence games was true; Tyler had the looks, the charm, the whole package designed to entice and steal and finagle while the mark just stood there and happily handed it over. I should know. He'd stolen my equilibrium with no effort at all.

As I watched, he cocked his head as if he'd heard something, and his eyes skimmed casually over the room. But it wasn't casual when he found me. Instead, it was a crash, and I stumbled backward simply from the force of it.

I stood there, unsteady on my feet, yet unable to look away from him. The eyes that had only moments before reflected the gentle blue of a robin's egg now danced wildly, a violent flame that was more than ready to burn.

I could see his body tense, his muscles tightening as if he were a wild animal about to spring. The hunger on his face was unmistakable, and my pulse kicked up as I fought the sudden urge to bolt.

Go, I thought foolishly. *Don't you know you're the prey?*

Maybe I was, but I couldn't look away. I was captured, locked in place by nothing more than a look. And if he intended to destroy me, I knew in that moment that I would willingly let him reduce me to rubble.

And then it was over.

Deliberately, he turned away, then whispered something into the blond bitch's ear. She laughed, the sound high-pitched and grating. It was a good thing I'd left my weapon in my glove box, because right then I had the urge to get off a few rounds. As it was, it took all my willpower to keep from stomping over there and seeing whether my best punch would shatter her overly Botoxed forehead.

Fuck.

I wasn't supposed to be this riled up. On the contrary, I'd been trying to rile him up.

Apparently, my plan had boomeranged.

Double-fuck.

With a massive effort, I got my feet to move. Since I couldn't think of a better option, I headed for the bar, figuring that wine would either help me think or help soothe my wounded pride. I was diverted, however, by the tall, gray-haired man who was heading right toward me. He opened his mouth to speak, but I shook my head once, then continued on my way to the bar. He sidled up next to me a moment after the bartender had handed me a glass of merlot and ordered himself a beer. "Nice party," he said. "You know the groom?"

"A bit," I said. "You?"

"You could say that." He stuck out his hand to shake. "I'm Tom Cray," he said, which wasn't exactly news to me since I'd known Tom almost my entire life. He'd worked under my father in the Indianapolis field office of the FBI before moving to Chicago. I'd given his office a call when I'd arrived in town two days ago, but apparently he'd moved on, and was now among the big shots in D.C.

"Sloane O'Dell," I said, and saw understanding in his eyes.

We'd been moving as we spoke, casually stepping away from the bar and away from other people and prying ears. "You're on the job," he said, his words reminding me that I hadn't come to Chicago to get knotted up about a guy. I'd come to find Amy, and I needed to get my damn hormones under control.

"Not officially. One of my CIs back home had a friend go missing. Since I'm riding out the last of my medical leave, I thought I'd help her out."

"Medical?" he asked with paternal concern.

"No permanent damage," I said, my hand automatically going to my left hip. "Took a bullet, but it's healing up nicely.

Aches a bit at the end of a long day, but I can handle it." It ached now, and the ridiculous shoes I'd put on for this shindig didn't help. Not that I shared that little fashion tidbit with Tom.

"And your partner? Hernandez, right?"

"I forgot you two had met. Bastard bailed on me," I said, but I was grinning.

"Finally retired?"

"Meredith freaked when I got shot," I said, referring to my partner's wife. "Said I was young and could take it, but at his age, he'd be laid up, incapacitated, maybe even dead if he got one of those nasty superbugs that you read about infesting hospitals. Meredith's a bit of a worrier and a lot of hypochondriac. Not great for a cop's wife. But he was ready. They moved to Wisconsin. An old Victorian she'd inherited a few years ago. They've kept it as a rental, but I think Hernandez is planning to spend a lot of time fixing it up." I shrugged. "I'd go out of my mind, but I think he's pretty happy with the plan."

"So who's filling his shoes?"

"No one yet. Captain said he'd make assignments when I got off medical."

The corner of his eyes crinkled. "And I can see you're doing your best to rest and recuperate."

I rolled my eyes. "Damn doctors. I'm perfectly fine, but they insisted I take another ten days. So I'm working off book."

He glanced around the ornate room. "And you think this missing girl might be hiding among the fancy dresses and bottles of champagne?"

"Unfortunately, she's not making it that easy for me. She was an exotic dancer," I added, and when his eyes flicked toward Evan Black, I knew he understood the connection.

"You're thinking the knights might know something about her disappearance?"

"You mean Black, Sharp, and August? Yeah, maybe. Them or someone who works at Destiny. At the very least it's a starting point." I glanced across the room at Tyler. "You called them the knights?"

He slipped a hand into his pocket. "From what I understand, Howard Jahn gave them the nickname, and it stuck. You're familiar with Jahn, I assume?"

"Sure." It was no secret that Tyler Sharp, Cole August, and Evan Black had been mentored by the late Howard Jahn, one of Chicago's most revered entrepreneurs.

That relationship, actually, made me wonder about Kevin's suspicions regarding the three men. I'd done my research, and Howard Jahn had a pristine record and had left a stunning legacy that included a charitable foundation and an endowed chair at the business school at Northwestern. If Sharp, August, and Black were as dirty as Kevin said they were, would Jahn really have associated with them?

I didn't know. But I intended to find out.

"So that's why I'm here," I said to Tom. "What's your story? Something going down I should know about?"

"I'm here entirely unofficially. I've known Angelina's father—the senator—for years, and I saw her quite a bit when she was dating Kevin. I even know the groom, too. I met him a few months ago through some task force business."

"Wait, back up. Are you talking about Kevin Warner? He dated Angelina? Why isn't he here?"

"Not the best of breakups. I think the fact that he tried to nail Angie's fiancé for Mann Act violations rubbed her the wrong way."

"I guess it would," I said, even as the low buzz of anger built in my belly. I worked hard to keep my expression bland and my voice casual. "Question for you—I know you may not be able to tell me much, but just how dirty do you think those three are? I know they got immunity on the Mann Act violations when that whole task force sting went down, but . . ."

"My take? Usually I think that where there's smoke, there's

fire," he said, echoing my thoughts about guilt and immunity deals. "But one thing gives me pause about those three, and that's Senator Raine."

"What do you mean?"

"He oversaw the Mann Act task force, so I imagine he knows as much about those men as anyone, at least as it goes to the trafficking allegations. Seems to me, he must think they're clean. If he didn't," he added, with a nod toward Angelina, "I doubt this marriage would be going forward."

The man had a point. "Kevin seems convinced they're getting away with all sorts of shit."

Tom's mouth curved into a frown. "Kevin may have his own ax to grind," Tom said. "Still, I think it's a fair bet those boys have played in the wrong sandbox a time or two. But you didn't hear it from me."

"Hear what?" I asked, innocently even as I tried to order my thoughts. I didn't know what Kevin's agenda was, but I was certain he had one, and I had no intention of being used as his tool.

"I'm going to go say hello to the bride," Tom said. "I'm only in town for the day, but if you need anything, don't hesitate to call my office in D.C."

"Appreciate it," I said, though I'll admit I was a little distracted. Both by the sudden burst of anger at Kevin, and by my general cluelessness at how to exploit that heat I'd seen burning in Tyler's eyes. What I wanted to do was shove the bimbo out of the way, and take my place at Tyler's side. But even if I could manage that without getting my face slashed in a catfight, that wasn't the route I wanted to take. Right now, I had the upper hand. Succumb to desire and go to him, and I lost that advantage.

No, I wanted him to come to me. I just wasn't sure how to entice him to do that.

And then it hit me.

"Tom!" I blurted. "Mr. Cray!"

He'd only gone a few steps, and now he turned back, his brow furrowed in question.

"Now that you mention it," I said, "there's something you can do for me right now."

four

Thirty minutes later, I was on the dance floor in the arms of Murray Donovan, a reporter who Tom happened to know had hassled some of the girls at Destiny and pissed off all the knights. Considering everything that Kevin had told me, that made Murray either a very brave man or an idiot for coming tonight.

Idiot though he might be, he was perfect for my purposes.

He was actually the second guy I'd sought out from Tom's list of potentials, the first being a real estate broker named Reggie from whom I'd disentangled myself after only five minutes. He held me too tight on the dance floor and, frankly, it was a toss-up which was more annoying—the way the beer on his breath mixed with the prime rib and asparagus he'd obviously enjoyed from the buffet, or the manner in which he pinched my ass.

Murray, at least, wasn't a pincher. But even that small blessing soon faded under the weight of his inane and ill-advised comments about women in general. And the girls at Destiny in particular.

"I'm just saying it made no sense to me," he said, referring to the way the girls had not only refused his repeated hounding for interviews, but had gotten the knights involved to end the harassment.

"Maybe the girls weren't interested in being featured in a magazine article."

"That's bullshit. The article would have gotten them some attention. Gotten them out of that shit-hole of a life, maybe. And what woman wouldn't want to be featured in a national magazine?"

"I wouldn't," I said, my back already up at the "shit-hole" comment. My first year as a detective, I'd put away a rapist who was targeting exotic dancers. That's when I'd met Candy. She wasn't a vic, but she'd been dancing the nights of two of the attacks, and she had a good eye, a solid memory for faces, and a habit of eavesdropping on the clientele.

Like several of the other dancers at the club, she was a single mom, high school dropout. She was raising a kid, studying to take the GED, and doing her damnedest to make a good life for herself.

The job was solid—paid the bills and gave her time to study and be with her little boy. In the past three years, she'd earned the diploma, then started taking business classes at the community college. She'd moved from the dance floor to management, and gotten herself engaged to the bartender she'd been eyeing since his first day on the job, not to mention very happily knocked up with kid number two. She'd carved out a life for herself—a good one—and it all centered on that job.

Sure, there were some clubs that treated the girls like shit, the customers worse, and ran a few profitable-yet-illegal side operations out of the back. But that wasn't where Candy worked, and it wasn't what she wanted. She was a dancer with dreams of owning her own club, and never in a million years would she have agreed to be the focus of a magazine article that suggested that either the club was sleazy, or that she was struggling through a life of slime. She was just a woman doing her best for herself and her kid, and I respected the hell out of her for it. Murray Donovan, I could tell, didn't.

"I wouldn't have anything to do with an article like that," I repeated, just to emphasize the point.

"Hell no, you wouldn't. I can tell just by looking at you. You've got too much class," he added, ruffling my feathers even more. "What do you do, baby?"

"I make it a habit of breaking the nose of assholes who call me 'baby.'"

He snorted. "That's what I mean. You've got too much spunk—too much drive—to whore yourself out like that."

Honestly, that nose-breaking thing was looking better and better.

"Come on, seriously. What do you do?"

"I work in a government office."

"Well, there you go," he said, in the kind of voice that suggested I'd just corroborated the theory of gravity. "Upstanding. Respectable. Honest work. You wouldn't take a job serving drinks topless or sliding up and down a pole."

"Wouldn't I?" My voice was icy. My stare even more so.

"Would you?"

"It's my body, and if I can make more in a four hour shift dancing with a pole than I can pulling eight hours behind a desk, why wouldn't I? Especially if I was working my way through school or had a kid to feed."

"Nah, you're just being contrary. I like that in a woman."

Oh, dear god, just shoot me now.

I glanced feverishly around the room, hoping to see Tyler seething in a corner, about to come and rescue me. I knew he'd seen the two of us together, because I'd caught him looking in our direction when I'd first slid into Murray's arms. But there was no sign of a knight riding to my rescue now.

Tyler Sharp either had serious willpower, or just didn't give a damn.

I really hoped it was the first.

I suffered through another five minutes, then excused myself to go to the ladies' room. I didn't need the facilities, but I dampened a towel and pressed it to the back of my neck. It was my trick for calming myself down. I can't say that it was working particularly well at the moment.

Still on edge from my unpleasant turn with Murray, I headed back out. My plan was to go home and regroup in the morning. Instead, I bumped into Reggie, aka the Ass Pincher.

Fuck.

"There you are," he said, bathing me in the scent of old beer. "I thought you'd escaped."

"I thought I had, too," I said, with a smile that was both cold and simpering. All around me people were laughing and dancing and having a good time. And here I was, stuck in my own version of hell.

"Another dance?"

"No. Thanks, but no."

He moved closer. I took a step back.

"I thought we hit it off."

"We really didn't."

He laughed as if I'd just said the funniest thing in the world, then slid his arm around my waist.

I jerked away. "Watch the hands, buddy."

"You are so fucking beautiful."

"You're going to want to take a step back," I said, somehow managing to speak despite my gritted teeth.

"What I want is to taste you."

My hand curled into a fist. "Dammit—"

"I'd do what the lady says."

Tyler.

I jerked free of the Ass Pincher even as Tyler yanked him away from me.

"I mean it, Reggie," Tyler said. The charm that had colored his voice earlier was gone, replaced by a steel-edged hardness.

"I—I didn't realize she was with you, Tyler. Honestly. I mean, she danced with me, and—"

"Sloane shares my interest in supporting charitable causes."

"What?" Reggie's brow furrowed. "But this isn't a charity event, and—" His mouth snapped shut as anger and insult flashed across his face. "*I'm* the charity? Now, you listen to me, Sharp. No way am I—"

"Yes," Tyler said smoothly. "You are going. And right now."

Reggie's eyes cut to me. "You can do better."

"Than you? Oh, most definitely."

It was a low blow, but the guy was a prick, and I felt nothing but satisfaction when I saw the angry red start to creep up his neck. "Fuck it," he said. "You two deserve each other."

Tyler turned to me, ignoring Reggie's retreating back. "First thing that man ever said that's made any sense at all."

"I could have gotten rid of him myself."

"I believe that." He glanced down at my still-clenched hand. "But I didn't think Angie would appreciate it if you laid him out. Fancy hotels like this add an up charge to the cleaning fee when blood is involved."

I laughed. I also relaxed. "Fair enough. And I suppose I should thank you for the rescue. Even though it took you long enough."

"Is that a criticism?" His hand slipped around my waist, but rather than jerk out of his embrace as I had with Reggie, I had to force myself not to press closer.

"Just an observation."

He eased us toward the dance floor, then started to sway

with the low, slow strains of music. I felt light, as if Tyler's hands were the only things keeping me anchored.

"I'm glad to hear it," he said. "Still, I suppose I lost some of my chivalry street cred."

"A bit." My voice sounded breathy, and I wanted to close my eyes and melt from the heat that his palm pressed against my naked back was generating.

I'd gotten lost in the swirl of sensations and emotions, and I stumbled blindly, trying to find some sort of rope to draw me back to myself, but failing miserably. I'm not the kind of woman who falls apart in the arms of a man, but right then, I was unraveling. And my dark and scary secret was that I liked the way it felt.

"I suppose I'll have to earn it back." His words, whispered at my ear, skittered across my skin like an electric current. They were only sounds, with no meaning attached to them at all. Just the low, sexy tones of his voice.

"Hmm?" I asked stupidly. "Earn what back?"

He chuckled, as if he knew damn well that he was the source of my confusion. "Chivalry. You said I lost some street cred."

"Oh. Right." I managed to gather myself, then tilted my face up to look at him. I saw desire behind the blue fire of his eyes, and I wrapped it around me, reveling in its warmth. "I guess you will. I mean, what's a knight without his chivalrous reputation?"

"For the record, it was worth it to make a point."

"What point is that?"

His expression changed, and I once again felt trapped in his gaze. As if he didn't just desire me, but had claimed me for his own. "I didn't like it when you walked away from me. And I'm guessing you didn't like me staying away."

"No," I admitted. "I didn't." I turned my head again, not wanting him to examine my face too closely. Not because I was lying, but because there was more truth in my words than I wanted to admit.

He stroked his hand lightly over my back as we continued to move on the dance floor. I pressed against him and sighed, my body feeling warm and melty.

"Remember that," he said gently. "And don't walk away from me again."

The meltiness hardened into steel as I came to a stop, then stepped out of his arms so I could face him dead on. Around us, other couples continued to swirl, but I barely noticed them. "Are you fucking kidding me?"

"No," he said simply. "I'm not." He tugged me back to him, then slid us seamlessly back into the mix of dancing couples.

"You're pretty damn sure of yourself."

"Very. What did you think? That walking away was going to wind me up? Was somehow going to make me want you more?" His voice, low and smooth, sent shivers coursing through me. "I'll tell you a secret, Sloane. I already want you more. I saw you, and I knew I would have you."

I licked my lips, but stayed silent. In part because I wanted to see where he was going, but also because I couldn't trust myself to speak.

He paused on the dance floor, then took a single step back so that he could look at me fully. "I don't know what kind of game you're playing, but I don't care."

I shook my head. "I'm not playing a game."

"No?" His gaze lingered on my face, and I had to fight the urge to turn away, afraid he'd see the truth in my eyes. "Too bad," he said. "Because I am. I started playing the moment I saw you."

I swallowed, not sure if I should run away or wrap myself in his arms. "I don't understand."

"Yeah," he said. "I think you do," and though his smile was

warm, I saw heat and danger in his eyes. "You're the prize, Sloane. And I'm in it to win."

"Me?"

"You," he said. He stepped closer, and the air seemed to shimmer from the intensity of my desire. "Does that excite you, Sloane? Knowing I want you? That I will have you?"

"Yes." My voice was soft. Breathy. My heart was pounding an unsteady rhythm, and even as the fact of my victory settled over me, it wasn't celebration that burned in my veins, but heat. A raw, primal heat that I'd never experienced before, but couldn't deny liking. "God, yes."

He drew me to him again, his hands at my waist, then easing up to brush the swell of my breasts. I drew in a shuddering breath, and though I wanted to simply close my eyes and let the wave crash over me, rational thought kicked in. "People," I whispered in protest. "Tyler, there are all these people."

"Do you care?"

"I—yes. Maybe."

I felt my cheeks burn as he chuckled. "Fair enough. With me. God, Sloane, with me, now." His voice sounded as raw as I felt, and as he led me to the far side of the room, maneuvering us through the other dancers, I followed willingly. Eagerly. And a little bit giddily from the simple high of knowing that my plan was in full swing, and I was about to enjoy the perks of my success.

He led me to the back of the restaurant and then through a hidden door into a concrete-walled service corridor lined with rolling tables topped with covered serving dishes. The staging area for the buffet and waitstaff, I realized, though I didn't have long to think about it. Tyler had me up against the wall, squeezed in tight between two tables, his hands cupped on my breasts.

He gently pinched my already sensitive nipples, and a hot wire of desire shot from my breasts to my sex. I gasped with pleasure even as I wanted to protest that there were still people around. The waitstaff. A few maids. But somehow, I didn't care anymore. Somehow, all I wanted was his touch.

"Shall I tell you?" he asked. "Shall I tell you exactly what I want? Exactly what I will have from you?"

His mouth was beside my ear, so close I could feel the brush of his lips as his words teased me. I didn't want to be entranced—didn't want to feel my body go soft with longing. But dammit, he was drawing me under, and soon I was going to drown in the swell of his words.

"Shall I go over in intimate detail how I will touch you? The way my fingertips will tease your nipples. How my tongue will dance over the curve of your ear. Will it make you wet to know how hard I am? How much I want to sink deep inside of you."

I made a little sound. I think I meant it to be a yes.

His hands eased lower, sliding down to my waist, then behind to cup my rear. He drew me in, nestling my sex against his thigh, and pressing so tight against me I could feel the hard bulge of his erection against my lower belly. I reached out to steady myself, and found the edges of two serving tables. I clutched at them, desperate to hold on, because I knew damn well that if I let go, I'd melt into a puddle on the floor.

"I imagine you taste like honey," Tyler murmured. "And when I slide my tongue between your legs, I'll lose myself in the sweetness of you. I want to watch your face as the orgasm builds inside you. I want to feel you tremble beneath me. And when you finally explode, I want to hold you in my arms and let my kisses pull you back together."

I trembled, my body hot and sizzling. I was aroused, my breasts heavy, my sex aching. I wanted his touch—wanted him to do all the things he was saying.

Hell, I simply wanted.

I breathed in. Once, twice. I needed to gather myself, my

thoughts. I needed to maintain at least some illusion that he hadn't completely destroyed me with nothing more than words.

"Wow," I finally managed. "You don't waste time, do you?"

His smile was slow and lazy. "As far as I'm concerned, time is the one thing too precious to waste."

He stroked my cheek, my hair. His fingers twined in my curls as he played and stroked. Tighter and tighter, not enough to hurt, but enough so that I gasped in surprise when he tugged my head back and met my eyes. There was ice in the blue now. A cold, winter storm, the chill of which laced his voice as well. "Tell me the truth, Sloane. Are you wasting my time?"

I felt the blood pump through me, the rush filling my head. Not fear—not really. This was excitement. Challenge. And, yes, a bit of frustration, too, because the victory I'd so greedily claimed had apparently been premature.

"Let go of me," I said, my voice matching the ice of his eyes. "I don't know what you're talking about."

He released his grip on my hair and took a step back. I used the motion of standing up straight to shake off my nerves. Despite my desperately pounding heart, right then, this was all about playing it cool. Just like in a suspect interrogation, I wasn't about to let him see that he'd shaken me.

"I know what my game is," he said. "I'm trying to figure out yours."

"I'm not playing a game," I lied.

"Everyone's playing a game." There was no humor in his voice.

I said nothing. I'd already denied. Repeating myself would get me nowhere.

"A lot of people want a piece of me, Sloane. What do you want? An introduction? A loan? I want to know why you're here. I want to know what you want."

Slowly, I shook my head. "I'm not gold-digging, if that's what you think. And I already told you what I want. Hell, *you've* already told me what I want." I took a single step forward, then pressed my hand over his cock, hard inside his tailored slacks.

I watched his face as I touched him, not moving, simply touching. " 'I want to feel you tremble beneath me.' That's what you said. That's what I want, too. Christ, Tyler, isn't it obvious what I want? Why I came here? I want you."

Beneath my hand, I felt his cock stiffen. He glanced down, then back at me. His face was all hard lines and angles, as if he was fighting for control. "Don't move," he said. "Don't even breathe."

"I—"

"No." His finger pressed against my lip before skimming downward. Over my chin, down my neck until he delicately traced my collarbone. Then lower, teasing my nipple with slow circles as I sucked in air and bit my lip in defense against the sounds of pleasure that wanted so desperately to escape.

The bodice was a halter, with two triangles of material attached to the waist, then rising up to tie behind my neck. He followed the material up, his finger skimming under the bow at the base of my neck.

"Shall I untie it? Let it fall? Shall I close my mouth over your bare breast right now, tease your nipple between my teeth? Tell me the truth, Sloane, would that make you hot?"

I swallowed. My mouth was so dry. I thought of the waitstaff. Of camera phones. Of the Internet and the image of us, his mouth on my breast, my head back, my lips parted in pleasure. I thought of it, and I felt the quickening in my belly. The clenching in my sex.

I thought—and I whispered the only answer I could. "Yes."

"Good girl," he said, as his hand sneaked down, leaving my dress intact. I breathed a sigh of relief, then gasped as he traced his way down my cleavage, his hand slipping beneath the material just long enough for his fingers to tease and for the heat of his palm to cup my breast.

"Tyler," I moaned when he withdrew his hand, leaving me clutching the tables on either side of me, because if I let go, I would surely fall.

"Hush," he said, as he moved closer. His hand snaked around my waist to find the zipper at the back of the dress, then slowly eased it down. "Now spread your legs," he ordered as he slid his palm inside my dress, over my lower back, and then down to the curve of my ass.

I wore stretchy lace panties, and he stroked my bare skin before finding the damp strip of material between my legs and tugging it aside. I heard the desperate sound of my own whimper as he teased me, then sucked in a gasp as he slid a finger easily inside me and my body clenched tight around him.

He groaned in satisfaction. "Christ, you're wet," he said, his voice raw. "I don't doubt you want me, Sloane. And god knows I want you, too." He stroked my sex once, twice, then withdrew his hand, and I had to bite my lower lip in order to silence my protest. "But there's something else going on in that pretty head of yours," he added, as he zipped up my dress, leaving me wanting and confused and frustrated. "And I will find out your secret."

He stepped back from me, then paused to look me up and down. I could only imagine what he saw. Clothes askew. Skin flushed. But I lifted my head, determined to hold my own.

He moved to the door, and pulled it part of the way open. The sounds of the party wafted in, echoing in the service hall. His eyes locked on mine, and for a moment I saw the true depth and power of this man who held so much of Chicago in his hand.

"I'll give you what you want, Sloane," he said. "What we both want. But think long and hard before you come to me. There are things that I like. Things that I want and expect from the woman in my bed. And I don't play by anyone's rules but my own."

five

I waited as the door closed, then let myself sag until I was seated on the floor with my back against the wall, two tables laden with dessert refills on either side of me.

He'd rattled me—no doubt about that. Rattled me, intrigued me, enticed me. I may have set out to seduce the man, but I couldn't deny the fact that he'd turned the tables on me any more than I could deny that I'd enjoyed it.

And I had. God help me, but I wasn't simply playing a part. I'd enjoyed it. I'd enjoyed *him*.

How the hell was that possible? I knew damn well the man was a con. A thief. Possibly a whole lot worse. A man who gave the middle finger to the law and the system that I'd sworn to uphold. He represented everything I fought against. Hell, he was everything I'd run from. Everything I'd fought so hard not to be.

Brutally I shoved away the rising images. The ones I fought

every damn day. The blood. The fear. The guilt. The crack of a gun echoed in my mind, and the sound swirled together with the scream of police sirens and the long, violent wail of soul-deep pain.

Tyler Sharp was the kind of man who would take the law and gleefully twist it until it broke. And there I was trying so damn hard to put it back together—to fix everything I'd once broken—and yet I was ready to slide into his bed?

I couldn't even fall back on the mission as an excuse. That may have kick-started it, but I was the one who was finishing it. I was the one who wanted it.

I drew in a breath and dragged my fingers through my hair. I didn't trust him—not even remotely. But I did *see* him. Whatever else Tyler Sharp might be, there was a hell of a lot more to him than the slick facade. He was a man who was very much alive, who took the world as it came, and didn't take shit from anyone.

Those were qualities I admired, and for one brief, shining moment I wished I was a girl without an agenda and without expectations. A woman, not a cop. A woman who knew nothing about all the black marks that marred his permanent record. Who wasn't even now trying to figure out the best way to proceed in order to get close, get in, get the info.

Because that was the crux of it—woman versus cop. The woman wanted his touch, his body. Wanted to feel that heat he generated deep inside her.

The cop knew that once you'd fucked a guy, you risked a blind spot, especially if that guy had already gotten under your skin.

I may have been using seduction as a tool, but Tyler Sharp had used it as a weapon, and he'd cut me down at the knees. He'd seen past the facade to the very real desire inside me, and he'd twisted it around. Used it. Taken control.

God, I was a walking cliché. The strong woman, knocked out at the knees by a smooth man with a hard cock.

Maybe. But I had no intention of losing sight of my endgame. I'd come to Chicago to find Amy, and right now, Tyler Sharp and Destiny were my best starting point.

Bottom line—I was going to stay. I was going to walk through that door and back into that party, and I was going to find him. I knew it, and I could tell by the way that Tyler had looked at me that he'd known it, too.

The party was still going strong when I stepped into the room. That made sense, I supposed, considering I'd been away less than half an hour. But in that time the world had shifted, and it seemed anticlimactic to go back into the room and have everything be exactly the same.

Then I saw Tyler across the restaurant, saw him looking at me. Saw the heat in his eyes.

No, I thought. *Nothing is the same at all.*

I considered playing it coy, but I wasn't certain he'd stand for it. More, I didn't want to. He'd lobbed the ball soundly into my court. Now it was my turn to return it.

I'd checked my purse with the attendant hired to work the party, so I borrowed a pen from the bartender, used it to scribble a note on a napkin. I folded it, then called over one of the waitresses and gave it to her. "Just make sure he's the one who gets it," I said, pointing to Tyler.

She flashed a conspiratorial grin. "You got it. Good luck."

"Passing notes in class?" Kat asked, walking up as the waitress walked away.

"Something like that."

"Buy you another glass of wine?" she asked, holding up two fingers to the bartender.

"They're free," I said.

"Don't let that discount my generosity." She took the glasses from the bartender and passed one to me. "To success," she said, then held up her glass to clink.

"Success? In what?"

"In whatever the hell that was all about," she said, nodding toward the waitress, who had just reached Tyler.

I watched as he took the note, unfolded it, and then—very slowly—lifted his eyes to mine. *Come here,* he mouthed, and the command seemed to fill me up, warm and enticing.

"Well," Kat said, a lilt to her voice. "How very interesting."

I barely heard her. I was already on my way across the room.

Tyler met me halfway, a small concession that pleased me more than it should. I'd expected him to drag out this little power play and make me go all the way to him. The fact that he didn't gave me a different type of tingle.

"I was very pleased to get your note," he said, pulling it from his pocket. He unfolded the napkin, then read aloud. *"I want to play."* He glanced up at me. "Are you sure?"

"I'm surprised. You didn't seem like the kind of man who would give a girl an out."

"Just this once." He took my hand, then lifted it so that my hand faced up. Slowly, he trailed his fingers over my palm. It was a simple touch, nothing even remotely erotic, and yet it swirled inside of me, heating me and fueling the desire that had been bubbling under the surface since he'd left me in that corridor.

"Aren't you even going to ask what the game is? What I want. What I expect." He bent over, then whispered in my ear. "Don't you want me to tell you exactly how I intend to touch you?"

Yes, yes, I wanted to scream. I wanted to know. Wanted to be prepared. But that wasn't part of the game—of that much I was certain. So I stood my ground and slowly shook my head. "I already told you—I want you. That's it. That's all I need to know."

"I'm very glad to hear it." He reached out for a lock of my hair and twisted it casually around his finger. "That way I don't need to waste precious time telling you how I intend to strip you naked. How I plan to stretch you out, and then taste every delicious inch of you."

I shivered. "No," I murmured. "You don't need to. But if you want to tell me, you just go right ahead."

He laughed, warm and full of life. "Tempting. But no." He took my hand and started to draw me across the room. "Let's get out of here, shall we?"

I hesitated, suddenly unsure in the face of reality.

He came to a stop, his eyes on my face. "Change of heart?"

"I—no," I said, too quickly if the smug expression on his face was any indication. "I was just—nervous," I admitted.

There was a sharpness in his eyes as he moved closer to me, his proximity both calming and rattling me. "Some say that nerves add to a moment's excitement."

I managed a wry grin. "Not possible," I said. "My excitement quotient is all maxed out."

"Sweetheart, there's always more." He took my arm. "With me. Now," he said, and continued toward the exit.

"Tyler!" The deep voice boomed out from somewhere behind us. "Hold up a minute, man."

Tyler pulled me to a stop, and I found myself standing hand in hand with him while Cole August closed the distance between us in three long strides.

"What's up?"

"Just checking. We're still on for tomorrow?"

"Absolutely," Tyler said. He glanced at me. "Sloane, meet one of my business partners. Cole August."

I held out my hand, and it disappeared into Cole's huge one. Despite the man's size, his touch was surprisingly gentle. "I won't keep you. I'm sure Tyler has plans for you."

His expression remained perfectly pleasant, but his tone held something dark, and as he released my hand, I couldn't shake the sense of trepidation.

Instinctively, I stepped closer to Tyler, relieved when his arm eased around me.

"Catch you later," Cole said, his attention shifting back to Tyler. "You're good?" he asked as his eyes flicked quickly to me.

"Five by five. We'll talk tomorrow."

"I'll pull Evan into the loop." He turned to me, and though his smile was brilliant, his eyes revealed nothing. "Nice to meet you, Sloane," he said, then turned away, leaving me feeling strangely confused. As if I was missing the subtext.

But then Tyler took my hand and raised it to his lips. He pressed a kiss to my palm, and despite the gentleness of the touch, it set off a riot of sensation inside me.

"Come on," he said, and drew me toward the exit, stopping only long enough to retrieve my purse from the check stand. Once out of the Palm Court, he led me through the lobby. It was a beautiful area. Ornate without being pretentious. Well appointed. Comfortable yet elegant.

I barely saw the damn place.

He steered me to the right and down the stairs to the entrance. We stepped through the doors, and he signaled to the valet. A moment later, a sleek black Lexus pulled up, and the valet opened the door.

Tyler gestured for me to get in, and once I did, he rested his hand on the hood, and bent down. He slid his hand around the back of my head, his fingers twining in my hair. He drew me close, then closed his mouth over mine, the force of the kiss rumbling through me, making my body clench and my pulse quicken.

"Tyler," I murmured when he pulled gently away.

His eyes were warm as he nodded to the driver. "Give Red your address and your phone number. Tomorrow," he said. "Be ready for me."

I gaped at him. If he'd tossed a bucket of cold water all over me, I couldn't have been more surprised. "Are you fucking kidding me?"

"Anticipation, sweetheart," he said smoothly. "It's the most potent of aphrodisiacs."

"Yeah?" I said, and flipped him the bird. "Anticipate this."

He laughed, which really wasn't what I was going for, and his smile was just a little too smug. "Oh, yeah," he said, in a voice that burned like slow, smooth whiskey. "I'm going to like fucking you."

Oh, holy mother of god. My body practically vibrated with a combination of desire and frustration. But dammit, I kept my cool. "You would have," I agreed silkily, "but you damn well missed your chance."

And then, before either Tyler or the valet could make a move, I grabbed the handle and pulled the damn door shut.

six

What the fuck? I mean, seriously. What the goddamn fuck just happened?

I leaned back, frustrated, against the soft black leather and glared daggers at the back of the head of the man who drove me.

Red. Tyler had said the guy's name was Red, which presumably meant he was on Tyler's payroll and not a random car company driver.

I considered letting Red do exactly what Tyler had instructed—take me home. But then I'd just have to get a taxi back to the Drake in the morning, since my car was still with the hotel valet.

More than that, though, I didn't want to go home. I was antsy and edgy and even though I knew damn well that I was feeling the effects of Tyler tossing cold water all over my raging libido, I told myself that my frustration stemmed from the fact that he had completely fucked up my plan: Get in, get close, get the story on Amy.

I drew in a deep breath, the kind that was intended to remind me why I'd come to this party in the first place. Not because I wanted in Tyler's bed—although that was most definitely a significant perk—but because of Amy.

Just because Tyler slammed the door on me didn't mean I had to slam the door on my goal.

I had a Plan B—and, although it was risky, in the grand scheme of things it wasn't any more risky than getting naked with a man who the entire law enforcement community of the Midwest believed was a criminal. With a little luck, it might even work.

We were on Lake Shore Drive, so I leaned forward and told Red to circle back to Michigan Avenue. "I'm in the mood to walk," I said. "You can just let me off anywhere."

He looked dubious, but he didn't argue, and I told myself that was a good sign. He dropped me off in front of Water Tower Place and I made a show of entering the mall. It wasn't quite nine on a Saturday, so the center was still open and busy, and I loitered for a good ten minutes before exiting and returning to the street. I held out my hand and got lucky hailing a taxi.

And then I went to Destiny.

I'd been twice before, of course. The first time to scope the place out. To get a feel for it and, I'd hoped, to chat up the girls. But the staff hadn't been open to gossiping about former employees, and I'd been just as unsuccessful when I'd tried to strike up a conversation in the parking lot.

The second time, I'd gone in and applied for a job. If the girls wouldn't talk to strangers, they might talk to one of their own. That plan, however, had crashed and burned.

Now, though, I could play the Tyler card. And the beauty of

it was that even if the whole thing backfired, I was still covered—all because Tyler left me high and dry in front of The Drake.

Still, my plan didn't entirely still my nerves, and my heart was pounding when I paid the driver and exited the cab in front of Destiny's unassuming entrance. I went inside, learned that women had no cover on Saturdays, and continued through the door that separated the alcove from the actual club.

I paused just inside the door to look around, pretending to be checking something on my phone. Since I'd been here before, I knew what to expect—the tables, each with a large, raised stage in the center. The girls dancing with poles. The men watching and drinking and tipping. And then tipping some more when the girls slid closer, giving them an up-close and personal view of either tits or ass, all in exchange for a few extra bills.

I bit back a smile, remembering how well Candy did on a good night in her dancing days. Exhausting, but in the right club, dancing could be downright lucrative.

Right then, though, I wasn't interested in the dancers, the men, or what was going on in the dark, secluded corners. Instead, all I wanted was to get to Tyler's office.

I saw a door with a single window on the far side of the cavernous room, just to the right of the bar. It had a plaque on it, and though I couldn't read it from where I stood, I guessed that it announced that what was beyond that door was limited to employees only.

I headed that way, put my hand on the knob, and pushed.

As I expected, the bartender called out to me. "Ladies' room is over there," he said, pointing in the direction from which I'd come.

"Thanks," I said sweetly. "But I don't need it. I'm just going to wait for Tyler in his office."

"Is that a fact?"

"Mmm-hmm," I said, running my fingertips lightly over my collarbone. I hoped I looked just a little bit drunk and very sexed up. I hoped I looked like someone Tyler would take to the back room.

The bartender hesitated long enough to make me worry, and so I soldiered on. "I just left him at The Drake. He had to finish something up with Cole, but he told me to meet him here." I upped the wattage on my smile. "He gave me pretty explicit instructions on where he wanted me to wait for him—and how he wanted me, um, dressed," I added. Then I shrugged. "Call him if you want, but he should be here in thirty minutes at the latest."

And then, with my heart pounding, I pushed through the door and into the hall.

I was guessing that the bartender wouldn't call to confirm—at least not for another thirty minutes. By that time, I'd have already had the chance to search Destiny's employee files. I hoped the files were in Tyler's private office—I was assuming he had one—but if not I figured the main business office was down this hall, too.

I'd get in the files, see what information—notes, address, forwarding information—Destiny had on Amy, and then escape through the back entrance. I'd undoubtedly have to deal with the fallout tomorrow, but at least I'd have the information.

Best case, I got outside clean and clear, then snagged a taxi at the nearby convenience store.

Worst case, the bartender called the cops on me, and I waited until they had me in the patrol car to tell them who I really was and beg them to give me a break for professional courtesy.

Frankly, I could live with either result. And the truth? I was looking forward to doing a little off-the-books snooping around. I wasn't on the job, and the Fourth Amendment be damned. I wasn't sure if it was because of the moment or because my blood was still humming with the memory of Tyler's touch. All I knew was that I hadn't been this revved in a long time.

I liked it.

Tyler's office was on the left, and I breathed a sigh of relief when I found it unlocked. I entered, then turned the lock behind me. Just in case.

It was decorated simply. A wall of filing cabinets. A large, serviceable desk. Two guest chairs. And a small but comfortable-looking sofa. One wall was dominated by a dry erase board covered with what looked like a rough schedule of employee shift times.

The rest of the walls were decorated with framed photos of buildings. Odd angles. Interesting arches. Skyscrapers straining toward the sky. They were all done in black-and-white, and each seemed to focus on some different architectural element. They were lovely, and though I never would have expected artwork like that in a place like Destiny, having met Tyler, I couldn't deny that the photos seemed to fit.

Honestly, I would have liked to have spent some time looking at them. But duty called, and I headed to the filing cabinets. They were vertical metal cabinets, each with four drawers, so that each unit was almost as tall as me. The drawers were labeled simply with alphabetical notations, and I said a silent prayer that these were for Destiny and not his personal files.

I tugged on the drawer for D–F, figuring that it was my best bet since Amy could be filed under D for "Dawson" or E for "employee."

The drawer, however, didn't budge, and I noticed the locking mechanism near the top.

Damn.

I hurried back to the desk, and had just started to search for the key or something to pick the lock with when I heard the doorknob rattle.

I glanced at the clock—not even five minutes had passed—then shoved the desk drawer shut and ran around the desk, moving on my tiptoes so that my heels wouldn't click on the wooden floor. I heard the rattle of a key, then saw the deadbolt turn. The door started to move inward just as I leaped onto the desk, leaning back a bit to accentuate my breasts and then plastering on a smile that I hoped would convince the bartender I'd come here only to get down and dirty with Tyler.

Except it wasn't the bartender.

It was Tyler himself.

"Well," he said, stepping into the office, then locking the door behind him. "Isn't this interesting?"

I crossed my legs, trying to ignore the cold wash of panic that had settled over me.

I reminded myself to be calm. That this scenario was covered by one of my contingency plans. But plans never felt quite the same in reality, and I was having to work hard to control my breathing.

"You pissed me off," I said, with a husky edge to my voice. "I thought I'd come here and try to change your mind."

"Did you?"

I cocked my head. "Greg called you, didn't he? Told you I was here."

"No."

"No," I repeated thoughtfully. Greg may have called, but that wasn't why Tyler was at Destiny. No way he could have made the drive in barely five minutes. "No," I said again. "You followed me."

He took two steps closer, and my pulse increased exponentially. "I told you, Sloane," he said. "I intend to find out what you want. Why you came after me. Why you told me that you want to play."

"I told you that already," I said. "Is it so hard to believe that I want you? That you pissed me off? And so I came here to make sure I would have you?"

He smiled easily. "As stories go, it has some heart. But I'm not buying it." There were only a few feet between us now, and he closed the distance easily until he was standing right in front of where I sat on the edge of his desk. He reached out and un-crossed my legs, then gently spread them.

He stepped between my knees, then cupped the back of my head, easing me toward him even as he leaned in and kissed me hard, biting my lower lip before pulling away.

"Try again," he said. His voice was light, but he was watching me intently, and I used the short span of time before I answered to remind myself that Tyler Sharp was a brilliant man who hadn't gotten where he was—in either legitimate or illegitimate enterprises—by being foolish or blind or reckless. On the contrary, he was clever and careful and ruthless. And that meant that I had to be even more so.

"Did you know I applied at Destiny?" I asked him. "Got turned down flat."

"Did you?"

"I thought it was strange, because I've done waitressing before."

"There's not a lot of turnover at Destiny," he said. "Our employees are very loyal. But I'm beginning to understand." He eased my dress up until his fingers found bare thigh.

I shivered, his touch making me feel a little drunk.

And then he slowly, so slowly, slid his fingers toward my sex.

"What were you planning, Ms. O'Dell?" he murmured as his fingers found the edge of my panties. He slipped under, and I drew in a sharp breath, then released a groan of pure, sensual pleasure. "Were you hoping to use your feminine wiles to convince me to give you a job?"

"I—yes—oh, god, Tyler." I placed my hands behind me on the desk as I arched my back, glorying in the delight of his touch.

"I do like your feminine wiles," he said as he slid two fingers deep inside me, then withdrew them slowly.

"So will you?" I barely managed to croak out the words. I wanted his fingers back. His touch. I looked up at him. "Please,"

I said, and in that moment I'm not sure if I was asking for his touch or a job.

He brushed a kiss over my lips. "Convince me," he said as he crossed the room to sit on the couch, leaving me on the desk, alone, turned on, and more than a little frustrated.

I looked at him. At that gorgeous face, that wide, kissable mouth. I let my gaze travel down to where his erection strained against the folds of his slacks. I knew what he wanted—and damned if I didn't want it, too.

For just a fraction of an instant I thought about what I was doing. About what I was. About lines that couldn't be crossed and rules that shouldn't be broken.

If this were anything other than an off-book operation, I'd be sanctioned six ways to Sunday. And if I tried to use anything I learned in court, the defense attorney would try to get the evidence tossed by arguing a due process violation and backing it up with buzzwords like "outrageous conduct" and "shocks the conscience."

But this was my own private op, and I wasn't on duty.

Tonight, I wasn't even a cop. I had no authority, no rank. My badge wasn't worth shit in Chicago.

This wasn't about the law. It was about bargaining and desire. And the bottom line was that I wanted him. Wanted the man—and I wanted the information he could give me.

I slid off the desk and crossed to him. Slowly—deliberately—I knelt in front of him, positioning myself between his legs just as he'd positioned me. Then I reached for the buckle of his belt and began to unfasten it. "I can be very persuasive," I said, then flipped open the button of his trousers.

Slowly, I eased the zipper down. "Very," I repeated, as I slipped my hand inside his pants and freed his hard, perfect cock. I lifted my head, just for a fraction of an instant, and saw the heat in his eyes.

Then I closed my hand around him and guided the tip of his

cock into my mouth, feeling the strong tug of desire and power cut through me as he drew in a low, shuddering breath.

He tasted of salt and musk and male, and I teased him with my tongue, relishing the sounds of pleasure he made, the low groans of satisfaction. I drew him in deeper and his body stiffened beneath me. All that power and passion, and it was bottled up tight, right there at my command, just waiting for me to release it.

I sucked, taking him in long, deep thrusts, desperate to take him further, to pull him right up to the edge, and when I felt the first shudders—when I knew he was so very close—I slowly withdrew and peered at him through my lashes, my mouth slick with him as I whispered, "Will you give me a job?"

"Yes," he moaned. "But not at Destiny."

I stared at him. And then—though my body was hot and prickly with desire, though all I wanted in that moment was to feel that gorgeous cock inside me—I laughed.

"Bastard," I said.

"Christ," he said, his voice tight with control. "This isn't how I planned it, but I have to have you. Now."

"Planned it?"

"You came out of nowhere and knocked me off kilter," he said, as he reached into the drawer of a small table beside the couch and pulled out a condom. "I will have you properly in my bed, Sloane, make no mistake. But I'm going to fuck you now."

"I—"

"No. Don't say a word," he said as he rolled the condom on. "Just lift your dress, take off your panties, and come here."

"I should go," I said, even as my sex clenched in anticipation and my nipples tightened painfully. "I should just turn around and leave."

"But you won't."

I hesitated, and part of me wanted to leave simply to keep

him on edge. But that wasn't happening. I wanted this too much. Wanted Tyler too much.

"No," I whispered as I reached up under my dress and slid my panties off. "I won't go." I left the panties on the floor and walked slowly to him.

"That's it," he said, as I climbed onto the couch, my dress spread out wide around us. I was on my knees, my shoes still on, my sex slick and wet. I reached down and found his cock, then positioned myself right over it so that the tip was barely inside me. He locked eyes with me, and then, before I could react, he grabbed my hips and thrust me down, impaling me on him.

I cried out even as he did, his body arching up as he buried himself inside me and I arched back, taking him deeper.

He moved one hand from my hip to my clit, stroking me even as I rode him, sparks of pleasure building inside me, spiraling up, faster and faster.

"Christ, you're beautiful," he said, as he stroked and teased me. I reached out, my hands to his chest. Even under the shirt, I could feel the beat of his heart.

His eyes were open, locked firmly on mine, and I could see the storm rising inside him.

"Tyler," I murmured as one of his hands reached up and found my breast, stroking and teasing my curves before lightly pinching my nipple and sending shocks of pleasure shooting through me.

"That's it, baby," he said as my body clenched around him. His fingers continued their dance on my clit, teasing and tormenting as I soared higher and higher.

"Hands on my shoulders," he said. "That's it. I want to watch you ride me," he demanded as I did as he said, impaling myself on him, feeling him go deep, so deep, and with every thrust I could see the explosion building in him, and feel the matching rise in me.

"Come on," he said, his voice tight and on the edge. "Explode with me. I want to watch you come."

As if his words were an incantation, I shattered into a million pieces, my body clenching tight around him as if he were the only thing holding me to this earth.

"Yes," he said, his clever fingers keeping me aloft even as he thrust into me again and again before finally reaching release himself, and then collapsing against the back of the couch, his arms going around me to pull me down on top of him.

"Wow," I said. I lay limp on top of him. When I found the strength, I lifted my head. "All that and you still won't let me work at Destiny."

He flashed a lazy grin. "That's not the job for you. I'll help you find something, though. But I'm curious, of all the strip joints in all the towns in all the world, why do you want so desperately to work at mine?"

I had to grin at the bastardization of the Bogart quote, but I also knew I had to give him an answer. Another lie. And though that reality hadn't bothered me at all just a short while ago, now it made my stomach twist.

"A friend told me that Destiny's a good place to wait tables. Good tips. Good management. Decent customers."

"And?" he asked as I moved off him to curl up on the couch beside him.

"And when I arrived in Chicago, it turns out she doesn't work here anymore. I tried to track her down, but nobody's heard from her. I'm worried." And that, at least, was the truth.

"What's her name?"

"Amy. Amy Dawson, but she may not have used her real name."

He nodded pensively. "Early twenties? Blond? Tattoo of a daisy?"

A ribbon of jealousy curled through me. "On her ass. Yes."

"She turned in her costume and moved on."

"Costume?"

"School girl uniform," he said. "A bit clichéd, I'll grant you. But very popular with the clientele."

"I'll bet. So she got a new job. Where?"

"Vegas, I think. But I don't know for certain. I was her employer, not her parent."

"What about lover?" I asked.

He looked at me for a moment, and I swear he could see the jealousy brewing in my eyes. Then he shook his head. "No. She had a bit of a crush. Made a move once, but I deflected it."

"Blond, pretty, ass nice enough to take a peek at now and then. Why'd you turn her down?"

His brow rose ever so slightly. "For one thing, I don't date the employees. Did that once, a long time ago, and realized it's not good for business or my sanity. For another, she was too young. I like my women to have at least a few years of drinking age under their belt. Seasons the palate." He cast a long, slow look over me. "Makes things more interesting."

"Oh. All right, then." I cleared my throat. "Anyway, that's how I ended up at Destiny. And now I want to find Amy."

"I believe you."

"Why wouldn't you?"

His laugh was low and humorless. "So many reasons. Mostly, I don't trust easily, and yet despite everything I find myself wanting to trust you. It's a bit unsettling."

"Despite everything?"

He reached over and stroked my cheek, effectively deflecting the question. "It's possible she left a forwarding address when she moved. She would have been paid in full, so we didn't have to mail a check. But we try to get addresses for tax purposes. In this kind of business we rarely have a current one, but I can check for you."

"I'd appreciate it," I said as he adjusted his slacks, then stood and fastened his belt.

As he walked to the filing cabinet, I retrieved my panties and put them on, then followed him. He opened the D–F drawer, which made me smile, then pulled out a file on Amy Dawson.

He flipped it open, scanned it, then handed it to me.

There wasn't much. In addition to the usual things like phone number and social security number, the employee form listed Candy's address in Indiana as her permanent address and a local address that had been crossed out with red pen. In the margin, someone had written, "Vegas" along with a date two weeks prior.

I looked at Tyler. "Guess you were right."

"But you're still not satisfied."

"She's not here. All that means is I need to keep looking. I need an address," I continued. "I'll do an Internet search on Amy Dawsons in the Vegas area and start looking there, but those are going to primarily be Amy Dawsons with traditional phone service, and my Amy wouldn't bother with anything but her cell phone."

"Which she isn't answering."

"Thus the worry," I agreed. "She could have lost it. Run out of money to pay for it. Have run off to Mexico with a hot guy and is ignoring it. But . . ." I trailed off with a shrug.

"Have you talked to her old landlord?"

"No," I admitted. "Amy is a text and email kind of girl. She never got around to sending her friends an actual mailing address." I sighed. "And tracking her isn't easy. She didn't subscribe to magazines, doesn't have health insurance. She doesn't own a car."

"Easy for a girl like that to fall off the grid."

"Very," I said. I started to once again ask for a job at Destiny—I wanted to get to know the girls who had been Amy's friends—but Tyler spoke first.

"Well, come on, then," he said. "Let's go take a look at her old apartment."

seven

Her apartment was just a few blocks away, and Red—who must have picked Tyler up three seconds after he dropped me off—drove us there.

It was just past eleven at night now, but that didn't give Tyler pause. The apartment was a crappy converted house, in which the original foyer had been converted to a lobby of sorts. At the end of the foyer, a new wall had been installed, and beside the single door was a small, yellow buzzer beside a speaker.

Tyler pushed the button. Waited. Pushed it again.

"What the fucking hell," crackled a voice. "It's the fucking middle of the fucking night."

"Has Amy Dawson's room been rented?"

"You interested?" The voice was now much more conciliatory.

"Possibly."

The speaker went from static to dead. A moment later, the door opened and an old man with eyebrows that resembled caterpillars opened the door. He wore a ratty flannel bathrobe and gestured us inside.

"First floor. Back here." He led us back, opened the door.

The room was about as depressing as I'd ever seen. Not much more than a converted closet with no windows. "Cheapest unit we got," the old man said.

"Did she tell you she was moving?" I asked. "Leave a forwarding?"

"No forwarding. Just said she'd got a job in Vegas."

I looked around. There was nothing in the place, not even debris. "You clean?"

"Nah, she did. Wanted her deposit back. Gave it to her, too, so don't start giving me shit."

I stared him down. "I wouldn't dream of it." I met Tyler's eyes. "So she packed up, cleaned up, and hit the road. But she didn't tell you where?" I asked the old man. "Did she take a taxi to the bus station? Rent a car?"

"No idea. 'Cept someone was driving her. Saw that much at least."

"Who?"

"Saw the car, not the driver." He glanced into the room. "You're not really interested, are you?"

"Sorry," Tyler said, then handed him a twenty. "Sorry for waking you."

"Someone went to Vegas with her," I said. "Or at least drove her to the bus stop. The girls at Destiny might know who."

"They might," he said as we walked back to where Red stood holding the door open. "But we'll talk about it later. That's enough for one night."

He was right, I thought, as I slid into the backseat beside him. My worry for Amy was fast fading, but as I shifted in my seat to look at Tyler, I couldn't help but think of Kevin's allegations—that these guys were into all sorts of shit. And, for better or for worse, I wanted to know if it was true.

We drove in silence for a while—Tyler received some texts that he needed to answer, and I took the opportunity to email Candy and tell her that it was looking more and more like Amy was alive and well and kicking up her heels in Vegas. Then I used the browser on my phone to start searching for Amy Dawsons in the Vegas area. There weren't many, and I'd start making calls in the morning.

When we finally reached the part of Chicago I recognized—down by the Magnificent Mile—I tucked my phone away and frowned at the scenery. "We're going the wrong direction," I said.

Tyler put his phone down and followed my gaze. "No," he said. "We're not."

"This is the way to Pilson?" I asked, mentioning my neighborhood.

"It's one way," he said. "But we're not going to your apartment."

I raised a brow. "No? What happened to telling Red my address. Me being ready tomorrow. All that big production about putting me in the back of this car?"

"One, it's now past midnight so it is tomorrow. And two, things have changed," he said, glancing meaningfully at me. "And I've changed my mind."

Amused, I leaned back. "So where are we going?" I asked, but I didn't really need to. Red was already maneuvering the Lexus in front of The Drake.

"What if I just want to go home," I asked, as he opened the door for me.

"I'd say no."

"Oh." I considered that. Considered my very visceral reaction to his words. We'd thrown each other off kilter at Destiny. But now . . . now Tyler was most definitely the one in control.

He held out his hand for me. I hesitated only the slightest of instants, then took it and allowed him to lead me inside the hotel and up the stairs toward the lobby.

"I hope your room's close," I said lightly, determined to steady myself. "It'll be nice to kick off these heels."

He glanced down toward the foot I had helpfully extended to show off the seriously uncomfortable strappy sandals and shiny new pedicure. "Lovely. But I might prefer you keep them on," he added, and there was no mistaking the heat in his voice. "Everything else can go."

Oh, my. So much for getting steady. He'd very soundly knocked me off balance again. I licked my lips. "Is that a particular fetish, Mr. Sharp?"

"A rather common one, I believe." We were near the lobby's plush couches, and he gestured for me to sit. When I did, he took a seat next to me, then lifted one of my legs and rested my ankle on his thigh. My hem hit just above my knee, and I wore no stockings. Fingers of cool air crept under the folds of my dress, soothing my already overheated skin.

Not that Tyler was helping to cool me down. Just the opposite. Slowly, he traced a path along my hemline, his fingertip burning a trail along my bare thigh. "It's not, however, one of mine."

"Tyler." I couldn't manage any more. I was surprised I'd managed that much.

"Hmm?"

"You really should stop."

"Perhaps. But I don't want to." His attention turned to the back of my knee, his clever fingers stroking a spot so delicious the sensation pooled between my thighs and I actually moaned. "I've had you," he said. "But I haven't yet savored you." I looked at his face, and the pure, open desire I saw there was as deep and vivid as my own.

"Please," I whispered. I meant to say *please stop*. At least I think I did. But it didn't come out that way.

His hand cupped the back of my leg and stroked down my calf slowly, slowly, so painfully slowly.

"Please," I said, trying again. "People will stare."

"People might. I don't believe you care much. I know I don't."

I closed my eyes. He was right.

Finally, his fingertip brushed lightly over my ankle, then skipped over the leather of my sandal before finding the arch of my foot and gently tracing the edge. On any other day, I might have cringed from being tickled. But right then I wasn't remotely ticklish. I was too damn turned on.

"No," he murmured, as he carefully returned my foot to the floor. "I don't have a foot fetish. But if I was going to develop one, I would surely start with yours."

"So you have no interesting proclivities?" I teased, trying to sound bold so that he wouldn't see how well he'd twisted me up. And, yes, trying to get a sense of what he intended for me once we reached his room. "No fetishes of your own?"

"I didn't say that." He stood, then held out a hand to help me up.

"If not feet, then what?" I asked, appreciating the firm way his fingers closed around mine.

His gaze skimmed slowly over me, the inspection both unnerving and very, very erotic. "You'll know soon enough."

My stomach fluttered as he led me toward the elevator.

The doors snicked open, and Tyler released my hand, only to replace it at the small of my back as he directed me into the well-appointed car. More like a little room, actually. A floor to ceiling mirror dominated the back wall, flanked on either side by wall-mounted light fixtures. At the base of the mirror, and directly in front of us, was a charming little couch.

"A fainting couch," Tyler said as I met his eyes in the mirror, my own brows raised. "A throwback from the days of corsets and minimal air-conditioning, I assume. But it certainly raises some interesting possibilities in our modern world."

"There aren't that many floors in this hotel," I countered, looking over my shoulder at the man rather than his image. "We don't have time for that many possibilities."

"A valid point." He stepped around me and moved to sit. "But it's a sad fact of our society that we don't ever seem to enjoy the time that we do have." He held out his hand, palm up. "As I mentioned, I believe in never squandering time."

I looked at his outstretched hand, and my mouth went dry, my knees suddenly weak. His lips curved up in the kind of smile that promised long kisses and slow hands, and I think I melted just a little bit right then. My only saving grace was my reflection in the mirror. At least I didn't look as unbalanced as I felt.

Why was I so twisted up? He'd already touched me intimately—already made me come. I'd already fucked him, taking charge of the moment. Riding him, watching pure passion on his face.

So what about now was keeping me so unbalanced?

But it was a foolish question, because I knew the answer. I'd surrendered to this man despite having no idea what was coming, what he wanted. How far he would go.

This was no longer about Amy. No longer about getting inside Destiny or about Kevin's accusations.

Right now, this was about nothing but me.

And that simple fact excited me as much as it scared me.

I still hadn't taken his hand, and now he crooked a finger. "Come here, Sloane," he said, and there was nothing left of the light banter or even the sharp tones of the man who refused to be played. This voice was sensual, commanding. It was a voice designed to make a woman wet, and to ensure that she obeyed.

I did.

One step, then another until I was standing in front of him. I looked down at him, not wanting to catch my own eyes in the mirror. Not wanting to see the anticipation and desire that I knew colored my face.

I felt like a rookie, unsure of what would happen next. And I was acting like a teenager, craving that first brush of his lips on mine.

Slowly—achingly slowly—his eyes roamed over me. He said nothing, but I could almost hear the low thrum of his approval vibrating in the air. He stood, the motion filled with both grace and power. And then, with unfailing gentleness, he reached out and brushed the edge of his thumb over my cheek. "I wonder," he murmured, then trailed off into silence.

"What?" I asked, when I couldn't bear the quiet any longer.

"I still haven't kissed you," he said. "Not properly, anyway. Not so hard and deep you feel it all the way in your sex. I wonder what you'd do if I didn't try to kiss you again at all."

My breath hitched in my throat, and I had to bite my lip to keep from crying out in protest. Instead, I managed to collect my thoughts, then tilt my head as I openly studied him. "So is this your fetish? Tormenting innocent women?"

"No," he said simply. "And you're not innocent."

"No, I'm not." I pressed my palm to his chest, then reveled in the way he drew in air, as if he needed to gather strength. "And I don't want to be teased."

"In that case, we have a problem." He placed his own hand over mine, capturing me against him so that I couldn't have pulled away if I wanted to. "Because I have every intention of teasing you. Fully. Mercilessly. I'm going to make you beg, Sloane. And only when I've taken you far enough will I make you come."

My mouth went dry and my skin tingled. Beneath my dress, my nipples were as hard as pebbles. I wanted more, so help me I did, and I think the only reason I didn't press myself shamelessly against him was that the doors behind us hissed open, and the gentle wash of cool air was as potent as a bucket of ice water. Especially when I saw the elegantly dressed couple waiting to enter.

I cleared my throat and, with my head high, stepped around them and off the elevator. Beside me, Tyler chuckled. "Shocking to think that they must know where we're going and what we're planning to do."

I shot him a sideways glance. "They couldn't possibly," I said. "I don't even know what we're planning to do."

He laughed. "You make a good point. But isn't the anticipation delicious?"

I kept my mouth shut, deciding that silence was the wiser course, and followed him down the narrow ninth-floor hallway. I'd never been on the guest level of such a fancy hotel, and I was just as impressed by this simple space as I had been by the Palm Court downstairs.

"It's beautiful," I said, letting my fingers stroke the molding and cream-colored wallpaper as we walked past door after door.

"It was built in 1920, and no dollar was spared. Did you know that Peter Ustinov once said that walking in The Drake was like walking on diamonds?"

"The actor?"

"Mmm. The list of people who have stayed here would make a gossip rag drool. Actors, royalty, even criminals."

"Oh, really?" I said, working hard not to sound too amused. "Like who?"

"You ever heard of Francesco Nitto?"

"The Enforcer?"

He lifted his brows, then nodded with approval. "You know Chicago history."

"I know about the Outfit," I said, referring to Chicago's infamous organized crime ring, the most famous leader of which was probably Al Capone. "Nitto stayed here?"

"Lived here," Tyler said. "Kept his office and a suite of rooms. That was in the '30s and '40s. Later—" He cut himself off with a laugh. "Sorry. The Outfit is one of my obsessions."

"It's interesting stuff," I said, filing that tidbit away for future reference. Not that it was very telling. All you had to do was look at Hollywood to know that most of the population was fascinated with organized crime.

"Architecture and real estate are my other obsessions," he continued. "Put them together and I'm known to get carried away. The Drake is like a perfect storm. But that's also one of the reasons I decided to stay here. This way," he added, pushing open a door and revealing a hidden set of stairs. I eyed him curiously, but didn't ask. And when he headed up the stairs, I obediently followed.

We emerged onto a landing for the next floor. As I followed him down the hall, I was going to ask why the elevator didn't go this far, but he'd already unlocked the door to our destination and pushed it open. The moment I got a look inside that room— although the word "room" didn't do it justice—all other thoughts left my head.

"Good god," I said.

"Spectacular, isn't it," Tyler said, the appreciation clear in his voice.

"That pretty much sums it up." The suite was decorated in shades of white and cream. The furniture looked old, and I assumed it had been selected to complement the hotel's heritage. Or, for all I knew, maybe it was original. If so, it had been incredibly well maintained.

Fresh flowers dotted all the surfaces. Artwork—mostly portraits and landscapes—hung in decorative groupings on the walls. Everything was rich and opulent, yet nothing seemed overdone.

"Wow," I said.

Tyler nodded. "To be honest, it's not my style. The architecture, yes. But my taste in furniture and interior design is more contemporary. But I can't deny this works."

"Yeah. It really does." I stepped farther into the living area, trying not to be overwhelmed. Growing up, my dad's idea of a fancy hotel for vacation was the Holiday Inn. And although my stepfather had money, I felt lucky if he remembered to give my mom cash for groceries.

Now I earned my own money, but I rarely had a reason to stay in a hotel, and when I did, I usually defaulted to the Holiday Inn. I was Daddy's little girl, after all. And considering my skimpy cop paycheck, the price was right.

That's not to say I hadn't been in some pretty fancy apartments and hotel rooms. I worked homicide, and murder wasn't picky about the price tag. But this room was beyond anything I'd ever seen. As far as I was concerned, I wasn't standing in a hotel room at all. Instead, I'd been transported to an alternate universe.

I allowed myself one long, low whistle before turning to Tyler. "Let me guess. You're really a foreign prince traveling incognito."

"I'm not," he said. "Nor would I want to be. I made my own way in the world. Family had very little to do with it."

I heard the hard edge in his voice. "I'm sorry," I said sincerely. "I didn't mean to push a button." I knew better than anyone that discussions of family could spiral down into unpleasant and unwanted territory.

I saw his chest rise and fall. "No, I'm sorry. My childhood should have been idyllic. It wasn't."

I nodded. I knew the feeling.

"It's taken me a long time to cut loose from all those threads. But that has nothing to do with you and nothing to do with this room." He took an appreciative look around. "It really is over the top, isn't it?"

"Just a bit."

He gestured toward a pristine white sofa that I realized was upholstered in silk. "Would you believe me if I told you a prince really did live here once?"

I let my gaze linger on the various small treasures. Vases. Paintings. Fancy bric-a-brac. "I think he left behind some of the royal treasure. Wait, you're serious?" I added, seeing the smug expression on his face.

"Cross my heart. A prince and a princess. They had a long-term lease, but decided not to renew when it came due about a year ago. The rumor is they're going to spend a few years in a similar property in Paris."

"So you decided that you needed to crash here after the engagement party? Soak up a little of that regal buzz?"

"Oh, it's much worse than that," he said. "I live here."

I gaped at him. "Come again?"

"I needed a place to stay. And this was available. I love the convenience of living in a hotel. I love The Drake. And you have to admit, it's got a stunning view."

I glanced toward the window where Michigan Avenue's lights twinkled like Peter Ustinov's diamonds. "Yeah. It does."

"Besides," he added with a boyish grin, "it was too fucking cool to pass up."

I laughed. "Can't argue with that. But I thought you ran more contemporary. You don't strike me as the kind of man who compromises on what he wants."

"No," he said, looking at me so intently I wasn't sure if we were still talking about the room. Then his face cleared and he smiled. "But I'm only leasing the place for another six months."

"And then?"

"Then I'll see where the wind blows."

"Away from Chicago?"

"No. I love it here. I grew up here."

"Then surely you already have a house?" From my research, I knew he owned several properties across the city, and his current residence was listed in Old Irving Park. I was curious, though, what he was going to say.

"I did," he said. "An awesome Victorian that I refurbished."

"Did?" I repeated. "You sold it? Like a flip?"

"I still own it. But I won't be living in it."

"No?" I moved to the couch and sat down. I leaned back, feeling more comfortable and at ease than I'd anticipated, all things considered.

"Sounds like there's a story there. Care to share?"

"Let's just say that I'm a sucker for a woman in need."

"I'm intrigued. Tell me the rest."

For a moment, I thought he would. Then he slowly shook his head. "No," he said. "I don't think so. I rather enjoy being the dark and brooding man of mystery."

"You don't seem dark to me," I said, and I meant it. Oh, I had no doubt he had his hands in a number of illicit pies. And he definitely had an edge. I'd seen it myself when he'd rescued me from Reggie. But Tyler Sharp was a charmer at the core. Sophisticated. Smart. A hustler, not a thug.

"Everyone has a dark side," he said. "Some people just hide it better than others."

"That's a rather pessimistic view of the world," I countered.

"You disagree?"

I thought of my own dark side and the things that I kept hidden. I thought of my stepfather, and how the world had seen a hero when I had seen a monster.

"No," I admitted. "I don't."

"And that sounds like a story as well. Don't worry," he added, "I'm not going to ask you to reveal your secrets." His mouth curved up in the faintest of smiles. "Not yet, anyway. But I am going to ask you to do something else for me."

He'd taken a step toward me as he spoke, and his voice took on a low, commanding quality. "Stand up, Sloane. Stand up, and take off your clothes."

eight

I had to take a deep breath and replay the words back in my head. "My clothes," I said stupidly. "You want me to take off my clothes?"

"Oh, yes," he said, as his gaze drifted over me with the same gleam of anticipation as a man about to unwrap a present. "I want it very much. But first things first. Stand up, Sloane."

He held his hand out, gesturing for me to rise. I complied, though my legs were a bit unsteady, and once I was upright, he turned away from me and picked up the house phone. I heard him hit the button for the operator and then speak to someone, but the conversation was too fast and too low for me to make out.

Throughout it all, I simply stood there, a little shocked, a little frazzled, and, yes, more than a little aroused.

When he turned back, his eyes were flat, and his mouth

curved down in the slightest of frowns. "My rules, Sloane. And though we got a little sidetracked, you did say that you wanted to play."

I swallowed, but I lifted my chin. My body was flush, my skin hot. My fingers twitched as if reaching for my weapon, but at the same time I could imagine the dress sliding to the floor. Me stepping out of it, going to him, and folding myself in his arms.

Could imagine it—the touch of his mouth upon my breast, the caress of his fingers over my sex—and wanted it.

I was nervous. I was overwhelmed. But god help me, I was desperately turned on.

But we were playing a game now, and I wasn't ready to concede victory quite yet.

For a moment, we just stood there at an impasse. Then he took a single step toward me.

"There are consequences for breaking the rules."

I shivered as memories sliced through me, potent enough to cut me to pieces. *Consequences.* Yes, there damn sure were. But I wasn't a child anymore. And I wasn't hiding. Not now. This wasn't about pain or about fear or about monsters who hid in the dark.

"Sloane?"

That was all he said, just my name. But I heard the worry underneath it. I didn't want that—didn't want him wondering about the secrets I held close, and didn't want him backing off now, afraid that he'd pushed too far. That I'd changed my mind.

I hadn't.

No matter what else, I wanted this. And not because of Amy. Not because I'd planned an op. But because I liked the way he made me feel, and because I wanted more. Break the rules? Yeah, where Tyler was concerned, I think that's exactly what I wanted to do.

I lifted my head, managed a teasing smile. "Consequences?"

I repeated. Slowly, I dragged my teeth over my lower lip. "Are you going to punish me?"

The corner of his mouth twitched. "I'd say that's a fair assumption."

His eyes roamed over me, the worry gone, replaced by control and anticipation. We were playing now, and knowing that sent swirls of heat reeling through me.

"I wonder if that sweet ass of yours has ever been spanked."

Oh. I felt an unexpected tingle at his words, but I wasn't about to admit that. Instead, I casually lifted a brow. "So *that's* the fetish."

"No. Just a delight."

The dark intensity of his voice kicked casual out the window, and that tingling increased to a low vibrato. "I wouldn't know."

"Wouldn't you?" He closed the distance between us, then stopped in front of me, so close I caught the scent of him. The fading earthiness of his cologne was overpowered now by a sensual musk that made me want to lean closer and taste him.

"Interesting. And I like knowing that mine will be the first hand to redden that sweet backside," he continued, as he reached behind me to briefly stroke my rear through the thin material of the dress.

I gasped, the sound both pleasure and surprise, and when Tyler smiled, I knew that I had lost this round.

"There's another rule you broke," he said. "Don't lie to me about what you want. About what makes you hot."

"I didn't—I've never—"

"Maybe not. But you know you'd like it. You may not have been spanked yet, but I see the flush on your skin, the way your nipples are straining against your dress. You can imagine the sting, then the warmth after. You can almost feel the heat spreading through you. The way your body clenches with desire. You can imagine being naked across my lap, not knowing if I'm going to spank you or fuck you, but simply desperate for my touch."

He paused, and I gulped in air, realizing with some surprise that I'd forgotten to breathe. "Jesus," I murmured.

"Tell me I'm right. Tell me you want that."

"Yes," I whispered, because how could I lie when he'd already seen the truth?

"Then you'll have it. But not now. Now you're going to strip." He pulled the folded napkin with my note out of his pocket. "You said you wanted to play."

"I did. I do. But I also expected you to keep your promises."

He lifted a brow. "I see. And what promise have I broken?"

"In the corridor. You said you were going to strip me naked." Desire cut across his face, and I took a step toward him, emboldened by victory. "You said you were going to stretch me out," I said, as my blood burned with the memory of his words. "You said you were going to taste every delicious inch of me."

I was right in front of him now, my head tilted up to see his face. His hands were in his trouser pockets, and he still wore the suit. He looked commanding and powerful and incredibly sexy, and I craved his hands upon me.

His eyes locked on mine, full of heat and power, and I drew in a breath, certain that he was just as turned on as I was. "I have a very good memory," I added.

He cocked his head in acknowledgment. "So I see. And you're right. I said all of those things. I meant all of them. And I'm looking forward to doing exactly that. But first," he added, in a voice that brooked no argument, "I'll watch you strip for me."

"I—"

"I want to see you," he interrupted. "Want to see you so much I can barely breathe." He moved across the room to a floor lamp, then adjusted it so that the beam shone like a spotlight. He nodded at the circle of light on the carpet in front of me, then moved to casually sit in an armchair. "Strip for me, Sloane."

My breath hitched as my pulse increased. The tiny hairs on my arms and the back of my head seemed to stand up. Electricity fizzed through me. I was scared—as riled and as jacked up as I'd ever been before going through a door. Then I didn't know what lay on the other side. Death? Blood?

Now I knew exactly. There was Tyler. A man who saw more of me than I wanted to expose. And that small truth was both terrifying and oddly comforting.

For a moment, I considered refusing. Telling him that if he wanted me naked he could take care of that himself. But when I saw his face, the words died on my tongue. He was looking at me with such a mixture of lust and adoration that it seemed to not only fill me but to spur me. It felt like a challenge. Like he was taunting me even as he was worshipping me.

This was the game. And the only way I could win was to watch the flame in his eyes burn even hotter with every bit of flesh that I exposed.

Slowly—so very slowly—I lifted my hands to the back of my neck. My fingers found the ties that held the halter in place, and I pulled at the bow, releasing it. I eased the two sections of material down, slowly revealing the swell of my breasts, the tight brown of my areolae, the hardness of my nipples.

I dropped the material, allowing the halter portion to dangle at my waist. The air felt cool against my heated skin, and my breasts seemed heavier, as if they were begging for the support of his hands.

I heard Tyler's sharp intake of breath, saw the way he shifted in his chair and the way his fingers tightened on the armrest, as if he was working hard to hold himself back.

"You're so fucking beautiful," he whispered.

"That's what the guy downstairs said."

"Shit." The curse was low, almost inaudible. "I didn't mean to put that in your head."

"No . . . no, it's just . . ." I drew in a breath. "He said it and I wanted to bolt. You say it, and—"

"And what?"

"And I want you to touch me."

His face was cast in shadows, but I could still see the way his features tightened, as if he was putting up a fight. "I will," he said. "Dear god, I will. But right now, I want to look at you. Go ahead," he said with a nod. "I want to see every inch of you."

My body thrummed with nerves and excitement, and my hand shook as I reached behind to the zipper. I tugged it down, then gave the dress the tiniest of shoves. The material spilled off me to pool around my feet, leaving me clad only in the pale pink panties and bright red shoes.

I licked my lips, then met his eyes. Then I carefully stepped out of the dress and stood still again. I was only a few feet closer to him, but the air seemed thicker, full of power and promise.

"Do you have any idea how lovely you are?"

My cheeks warmed from the compliment. I knew I was pretty, some would even say beautiful. But once I decided to become a cop, it wasn't pretty that mattered, but strong. Now my body was tight and lean. Feminine, yes. But powerful, too.

"I want to see the rest of you," he said. "Take off the panties. But leave the shoes on."

I swallowed, strangely shy. I was practically naked already, but there was something about stripping completely except for a pair of high heels that seemed so bold. So decadent.

I looked down, concentrating on the floor as I hooked my fingers in the waistband.

"No," Tyler said. "Eyes on me."

"Tyler."

"Shhh. No arguing. Just do."

I did. And though I expected to feel even more shy, more exposed, in fact I felt just the opposite. I felt bold. Wild. I saw his desire plainly, and I knew that right then I was the one who held the power.

I was no stranger to power—I wielded it every day in my work. But this was the first time I'd felt truly powerful as a woman.

I liked it.

I let the panties fall with a little hip shimmy, then carefully stepped out of them as well.

"Now, that is a pretty picture," Tyler said, slowly taking me in. His smile twitched when he got to my neatly shaved and trimmed sex. "And you're a natural redhead."

"Did you have doubts?"

"Nice to have confirmation. Do you have the temper that goes with it?"

"Cross me and find out."

"A fiery temper often translates to fire in bed." He stood, then slowly moved to stand in front of me. "I'm looking forward to finding out if that's true."

He reached out then to cup my breasts in his palms. His skin felt hot against mine, and I closed my eyes with a small moan of satisfaction that turned into a gasp as his thumbs flicked over my nipples. Then he released me, and I opened my eyes to see him circling me, his focus so intent that I had the feeling he was memorizing every inch of me.

I twisted, wanted to keep him in sight, but kept my feet planted. When he had circled me completely, I met his eyes as he smiled in approval. "You're perfect," he said. "And you're already aroused. I like that—I like knowing that you want me touching you, stroking you. That you already crave me deep inside you again."

I started to shake my head—to protest simply for form. But it would be a lie. And I knew that he could see the truth in the color of my skin. In the way my pulse was pounding, the beat obvious in my neck and in the rise and fall of my chest. My eyes were surely dilated. And those natural redhead curls between my thighs were damp with the evidence of just how turned on I was.

So instead of protesting, I simply looked at him, my own gaze dipping down to his crotch—and the pants that were doing very little to hide just how aroused he was. "I like knowing it, too."

He chuckled. "I'm tempted to throw you back on that couch and take you right now."

"Yes, oh, please, yes."

He stepped closer, and though he still didn't touch me, every atom in my body buzzed and hummed in anticipation and want. *Please*. The word seemed to scream through my mind. *Please touch me*.

"Soon," he said. "What's that saying? All good things come to those who wait?"

"Fuck waiting."

At that he laughed outright. "For the record, I feel the same way. But I'm having too much fun tormenting you to stop."

"At least you're honest."

"I can be," he said. "I'm often not."

I grinned. "And again, with the honesty."

"Apparently you bring it out in me. Interesting." He took a step closer, then slowly touched his finger to the red and angry scar that marred my left hip. "Bullet," he said, his eyes flicking up to mine in an unspoken question.

"A mugging," I said, managing the lie smoothly. "Not one of my better days."

He eased around me, his finger tracing over my skin as he moved from the entrance to the exit wound. "Clean, or at least it looks it."

"It got some of the bone," I said. "It hurt like a bastard, but it's healing. Just twinges now. I don't like to talk about it."

He nodded, then kissed his fingertips before pressing them to the wound. "Then we won't. Instead, we can talk about how beautiful you are. How hard I get just watching you." He tucked a loose strand of hair behind my ear. "And I do like to watch."

He dipped his gaze to my breasts, and my nipples tightened in response. A small smile touched his lips as he lifted his eyes back to mine. "I like to see the subtle changes in your body as you become aroused. I want to memorize the expression on your face when you come," he added, taking my hand and slipping my fingers between my legs. I was hot and slick, and a tremor ran through my body as my finger barely grazed my clit.

"Oh, god, Tyler, please." I wasn't sure if I was begging for him to let me stop or to demand that I continue. Confusion swirled around me. I wanted to turn away. To pull my hand free. To hide. But at the same time, I didn't want this feeling to end.

"It's not about fetishes, it's about pleasure," he said, then gently drew my hand away, making me whimper. "And it's about pushing limits to find the ultimate. I intend to push those limits with you. Soon," he said, reaching down to lightly stroke between my legs, as I silently screamed in frustration at the gentleness of his touch when I desperately wanted to be ravaged. "Right now, I want to keep you on edge."

"You're doing a damn good job of it."

"I know," he said. "I also know you like it. Just as I know you liked our encounter earlier at Destiny. The thrill of getting caught. The excitement of what came after. Tell me," he said. "I want to hear."

"I—I did," I admitted. "I do." I straightened my shoulders as I let the truth settle over me. "I've never—It's not the world I live in," I finished lamely.

"No? That's a shame. Everyone should feel alive. Should smash up against passion and danger, against temptation and anticipation. You have to push the envelope sometimes, because otherwise how do you know what your limits really are?"

I opened my mouth to respond—to tell him that I got that thrill in my job, chasing and catching men like him. But I couldn't go there, and I swiftly bit back the words.

"What?"

"I know I have an answer to that, but it's gone." I managed a wisp of a smile. "You steal my thoughts, Tyler Sharp."

His grin revealed a dimple. "I steal a lot of things."

There were many responses to that, but before I could organize my thoughts, the bell sounded at the door. I jumped, my arms going immediately across my body as if that would somehow hide my nakedness.

"No," Tyler said, with a firm shake of his head. Whatever playfulness had been between us evaporated. This was the man in control again. The man who had told me to come here tonight only if I understood that I had to play by his rules. This was the man who had meant it.

"Sit," he said, nodding at the couch.

I froze, my skin suddenly clammy. "What?"

"Sit," he repeated, then led me to the couch and nodded for me to sit. Then he put my knees together and my hands on either side of my hips. The bell rang again. "Just a minute," he called.

"No," I said "No way."

"Oh, yes," he said, then gently cupped my breast. His thumb flicked over my nipple, and I sucked in air. "You're smart, Sloane. You understand the game."

"I'm not sure I understand anything anymore."

"I said I would win. You're my prize, Sloane. To tease, to touch, to pleasure. But mine, nonetheless. Tonight, I own you. And that means that there are rules."

Something that might have been fear riffled through me. Might have been—but I think it was really excitement. "I have to obey you."

"If you're here, you do. But you have the choice. You can put your dress back on. You can walk out that door. But I don't think you're going to do that."

"Why not?" My mouth was so dry I could barely speak.

"Because I saw your face when I touched you in the corridor, the two of us surrounded by the waitstaff, pretending like they didn't see. That they didn't care. There's a thrill in being exposed. In being just a little naughty." He held my eyes, and I thought in that moment that I had no secrets from this man. "You may not break the rules, Sloane, but I'd bet good money that you'll stretch them as far as you can."

I felt my pulse kick up, and knew it was from the truth of his words.

"It excites you, doesn't it? Knowing that you're mine. Knowing that by surrendering to me, you're capturing me as well."

"Yes." The word was a whisper.

"And you have captured me," he said. "Because this isn't about what I want, but about what you do to me. And dear god, Sloane, you have driven me to the edge."

He drew his fingers through his hair and I could see the truth on his face. The heat, the lust. The intensity of his self-control. He was like a spring wound tight, I couldn't wait for him to come undone.

"Tyler." His name felt ripped out of me, and so help me, I wanted him to keep pushing, to spread my legs wide and to finally touch me and release this sweet, relentless pressure.

"So I think you're going to stay," he continued, almost conversationally. "I could be wrong. It happens on occasion. You might storm out of here and never look back. You might slap my face and tell me to go to hell. It is within the realm of possibility."

"I might," I said. I sure as hell should.

But I knew that I wouldn't.

nine

He turned, and without another word stepped out of my line of sight and into the foyer. I sat there, my heart pounding. My skin tingling. I was aware of every tiny hair on my body, as if I'd gotten lost in an electrical storm. Tiny beads of perspiration rose on the back of my neck. I wanted to bolt—and yet I wanted to stay.

I told myself it was because of the op—because I had to get close to the man, and how the hell could I do that if I walked out on him? But that wasn't true.

I wanted to stay because he wanted me to. Because I'd seen the promise in his eyes of what was still to come.

And because, god help me, he was right—I wanted to bend the rules.

He came back into the room, just steps ahead of a waiter in a trim, black uniform who stumbled a bit before making a surprised little noise, then continuing on. I'm sure I made quite the picture, naked on the couch, my face turned toward the entrance, my hands on the cushions, and my breasts exposed.

I didn't slouch, though I wanted to. I had too much pride. But neither did I look at the waiter. For the first time since I'd graduated from the academy, I purposefully didn't look at a face. Instead, my attention was entirely on Tyler—and his was entirely on me. I saw heat in his face. Heat and passion and possessiveness.

Raw desire burned in his eyes, and in that singular moment, I knew that I held the power. That I'd turned him on, wound him up. Not because I was naked and on display, but because I was naked and on display because he wanted me to be.

And that desire—that primal, sensual hunger—cut through me as well. I felt warm, alive with a feminine power. I wanted to be touched. To be claimed by the one man who had brought me to this point, to this sharp apex of desire.

Tyler.

As if he could hear my thoughts, the corner of his mouth lifted ever so slightly, like a subtle promise of things to come.

Blood pounded in my ears and I barely breathed as the waiter hurriedly parked the cart and converted it to a small table. I heard the rattle of dishes, the distinct pop of a champagne cork.

Then Tyler was signing the check, and the waiter was gone, moving like a streak toward the door. The moment I heard the click, I gulped in air, watching as Tyler's coolly composed expression softened a bit. "You see? There's a thrill in being naughty—no, don't say anything. I can see the truth on your face. And you gave him a bit of a thrill, too, I think. If nothing else, he has a story he'll be telling his buddies into his old age."

"I hope you tipped him well," I said, surprised I could form words, much less conjure sarcasm.

"I think you were the best tip. But yes. I upped the standard gratuity considerably."

I started to stand, but he gestured for me to stay seated, and

I was glad that he did. As juiced as I was, I couldn't be certain that my legs would support me.

"You did well." He'd moved to the cart and now he took a bottle of champagne from its bucket. He poured a glass, then brought it and a small plate toward me. There was a coffee table directly in front of me, and he used his foot to push it to one side, then placed the drink and the plate on it. The plate, I saw, held a selection of chocolate truffles.

I glanced up at him, and he met my questioning look with a smile. "Time for your reward. Tell me, Sloane, what do you want?"

You. Oh, god, only you. The words seemed to press against my lips, begging for release. But I bit them back, perhaps foolishly wanting to keep some piece of me hidden despite sitting naked before him.

Slowly, purposefully, I glanced at the coffee table. "I'm very fond of chocolate."

"Is that so?" He plucked up a round truffle, gleaming with a shell of dark chocolate and topped with a tiny star of white icing. "Whatever the lady wants."

He knelt in front of me, one hand resting on my knee as he leaned forward and trailed the truffle gently over my lower lip.

"Open for me," he said, and as I slowly opened my mouth, he gently spread my legs. Cool air swept between my thighs, teasing my overheated skin and making me even more aware of how wet I already was.

I whimpered, but the sound was muffled by the candy. "That's a girl," he said, as he eased the truffle into my mouth. "Now bite down." I did, then moaned in surprise and pleasure as sweet cherry juice eased over my tongue, a stray bit catching at the corner of my mouth.

As I swallowed my half of the truffle, he took the rest and slid it over his own lips, his gaze never leaving mine as he swallowed. I saw it there—that storm in his eyes. A tempest of fire and need that would surely capsize me, send me reeling. I wanted it to. I so desperately wanted his touch, his kiss. His everything.

"Delicious," he said, and the sensuality in that single word had my body clenching. It took everything inside me not to yank him close and beg him to please, please just fuck me because nothing else could douse this building heat and bank the fire that was threatening to turn me to ash.

"But this," he said, as he used the tip of his finger to dab at the stray juice on my mouth, "this is even more delicious."

I swallowed, anticipating the pleasure of watching him slide his own finger into his mouth and then sucking the juice off. Or, perhaps he would surprise me and slide that finger into my mouth, and I could curve my lips around his finger and lose myself in the cherry-coated taste of him.

That, however, wasn't what he had in mind.

Instead of pressing his finger to my mouth, he brought it to my clit, sliding his hand down between my parted thighs. I gasped as thought abandoned me.

And then, as he slowly—so devilishly slowly—teased and played, all rationality and reason escaped me as well. I was nothing but sensation. A human-sized collection of atoms that existed solely to shimmy and buzz in pleasure.

Then he pulled away. I whimpered, desperate for him to finish what he'd begun.

"Shhh," he murmured, as he placed his hands on my hips to keep me from writhing in silent demand.

"Tyler—" My voice was raw, ripped from me. "Don't. Let me—"

"Hush," he said again, keeping me motionless. Worse, keeping me unsatisfied. "I think there's a bit of cherry juice in a very sweet spot." His eyes flicked up to mine, hot and hungry, and my sex clenched in anticipation of what was coming. "And I want just a little taste."

Yes, yes, oh sweet Jesus, yes.

As if he purposefully set out to torment me, he trailed kisses up the inside of my thigh, driving me just a little wild. I wanted to writhe, to twist my body in time with the sensations that were pounding through me, but he held me fast. I couldn't move. And somehow my immobility made the pleasure that much keener.

With the tip of his tongue, he teased the soft skin at the juncture of my thighs. I drew in a shuddered breath and arched back, trying to breathe as sparks of pleasure shot over my body, so delicious and yet at the same time not enough. I wanted the explosion.

"Please," I begged, then cried out in triumph when he shifted his attention to my clit, his tongue finding that most sensitive part of me. His tongue laved me, teased me, and my body trembled with the pressure of a building explosion that never quite seemed to come.

I arched my back, my eyes squeezed tight, as if by sheer force of will I could make myself go over. I was close, so damn close . . .

"Tyler," I murmured. "Tyler, please . . ."

Gently, he pulled away, then tilted his head to look up at me as I fought back a cry of protest. "As I said, delicious." He leaned over and picked up the glass of champagne. "Drink," he said, and I gratefully took the glass, gulping down a swallow of the cool liquid that was painfully insufficient to quell the heat that raged inside me.

"Save a bit for me," he said, then gently took the glass from me. He sipped too, then used his hands to ease my thighs even wider and then—thank god—lowering his mouth to my sex once again.

I'd expected the pleasure. I hadn't expected the mind-blowing delight that came from the combination of his hot mouth, clever tongue, and the cool, sparkling champagne. The bubbles fizzed against my already sensitive clit, the sensation almost too much to bear. A million little pops and trills, all promising something bigger, something wilder and hotter.

And yet none of them were quite enough to take me there. I needed his touch, his tongue. Needed it right *there,* but though I shamelessly shifted my hips, he never quite stayed on the sweet spot long enough to take me that final distance.

"Please," I begged.

But he wasn't interested in my demands. Instead, he shifted his attention, trailing kisses along my trimmed line of pubic hair, then up to tease my navel with his tongue.

Every touch was erotic, sending heat swirling through me. Only it wasn't the heat I wanted but the explosion, and as I moaned in both pleasure and protest his mouth closed hard over my breast and his teeth teased my erect nipple.

"You're tormenting me," I whispered, when his hand slipped between my thighs. I gasped as he slid a finger inside me, then stroked me in long, slow movements designed to let the pleasure build and build—but never quite reach the pinnacle. "You bastard," I moaned. "You're doing this on purpose."

"Clever girl." He cupped his hands over my breasts, then brought his mouth to my neck. His kisses along my neck were a different kind of torture, and I instinctively tilted my head to one side. "But is it really torment?" he murmured, his lips brushing my skin with each soft word, and sending shock waves rippling through me. "Or is it heightened pleasure borne from anticipating what's yet to come?"

"Torment," I said firmly, making him laugh. "And here I was starting to think you were a nice man. You're not."

He eased back so that I could see his face. Desire and heat and a feral ruthlessness that cut straight through me. "You're right," he said. "I'm not."

While I worked hard to keep myself from whimpering, Tyler rose to his feet. He held out his hand, and I took it with both curiosity and anticipation. I hoped he was leading me to the bedroom; I hoped he intended to finish what he'd started. I feared that he had something else in mind, though—and, damn the man, I couldn't help that sizzle in my blood that came from the mixture of curiosity and, yes, anticipation.

Without a word, he led me into a short hallway, then through yet another formal room.

To be honest, I was swimming in such a sensual haze, it's a wonder I noticed anything at all. But small things jumped out at me. The paintings. The molding. There were antiques tucked into every corner, yet the room still looked elegant, not cluttered.

We moved down yet another hall, and I entertained the insane idea that all he was really doing was walking me in a circle. More torment. More anticipation.

When I said as much, he laughed. "I'm not that cruel. The place is just huge. You could get lost in it. I do sometimes."

"Really?"

"No, but it makes a good story."

"Is that what you do? Make up stories when the truth isn't good enough?"

The corner of his mouth twitched. "Absolutely."

"Well," I said. "That's a conundrum."

"What is?"

"You're being honest about being dishonest."

"Maybe I'm just trying to keep you interested," he said, a hint of heat returning to his voice.

I didn't quite meet his eyes. "I don't think you have a thing to worry about there."

We'd reached the open door to the master bedroom, and I was surprised to see the contrast between its interior and the rest of the penthouse. This room contained the modern furniture that Tyler had said he preferred. Sleek lines that accentuated function over form, but nonetheless suggested money and taste.

Interesting. It told me that he was a man who was willing to compromise—but not on the things that were personal and important to him.

There was a pair of closed French doors on the far side of the room, behind which I assumed was a bathroom. A huge bed dominated the space in front of the windows, beyond which the lights of the city twinkled like surrogate stars.

I expected we'd move to the bed, but instead Tyler led me across the room toward those double doors. As we moved across the space, I focused on the details, looking at the room as I might examine a crime scene, trying to discern whatever I could about the man who occupied this space. The dresser—with his personal items laid out precisely on top—suggested organization even while the clothes tossed carelessly across the back of an armchair showed that he didn't take it to the level of obsessiveness.

There were no photographs, no books, nothing personal in the room. Nothing except a handmade quilt folded neatly at the foot of the bed. And that one item stirred more questions in me than all the intelligence I'd dug up on this enigmatic, powerful, and potentially dangerous man.

I must have hesitated, because I felt a tug, and when I looked over to him, his expression was cloudy. He tilted his head toward a set of double doors on the far side of the room. "Not the bed," he said simply. "Not yet."

"I was looking at the quilt," I said, inexplicably speaking in a whisper. "An heirloom?"

"Yes," he said simply.

I started to ask more, then stopped myself. This wasn't a date, and no matter how much I might be enjoying this night, I needed to remember that this was a mission. Knowing the bits and pieces might help me paint a better picture of the man, but I couldn't imagine that a quilt had any connection to Amy.

I didn't need personal details. And I damn sure shouldn't want them. I knew Sharp was dirty. Maybe not in trafficking women—god, I hoped not—but in the way he lived, the way he operated his businesses, the way he looked at life. Tyler Sharp thumbed his nose at the kinds of rules I'd dedicated my life to enforcing.

And yet in just a few short hours, he'd managed to twist me up. I told myself that was understandable—you go into an op planning to seduce, and seduction is going to happen. And, yes, Tyler Sharp had well and truly seduced me. He'd revved me up, made me want. Made me need. He'd pushed me further than I'd ever gone before, and I couldn't deny that I liked it.

But this little field trip through the penthouse had given me the chance to gather myself together, and that was good. I still wanted his touch—oh, god, did I ever—but the sensual mist that had clouded my thinking had evaporated, and I was focused on my mission.

Sex with Tyler might be damned entertaining, but at the end of the day, sex was just sex.

And it was going to have to remain that way.

ten

I think it was the candles that did me in.

He pushed open the doors, and I saw the room bathed in the golden glow of at least two dozen candles. They were on the floor, on stands, on small tables near the oversized bathtub. The room smelled of lavender and vanilla, and I breathed in deep.

"How?" I asked. "When?"

"I sent a text to the hotel from the car."

I couldn't help but laugh—he looked so incredibly smug.

He took my hand and guided me to the two steps that led up to the deep marble tub already full of lavender-scented bubbles. "Go ahead," he said. "Get in."

I stepped out of the shoes, then paused and turned back to him. "I don't understand you," I said plaintively. "You make me strip. You bring in that waiter. It's racy. Raw. I don't know—dangerous maybe. Hot, definitely."

"You forgot wild."

"Wild," I agreed. "But this . . ." I swept my arm to indicate the candlelit room. "This is wild, too. Wildly romantic. Sensual. Calm and serene and wonderful."

"And that bothers you?"

"It confuses me," I admit.

I see humor light his eyes. "Maybe I want you confused. Or perhaps I'm trying to prove a point."

"What point?"

"There are a lot of ways to pleasure a woman," he said, and his tone suggested we hadn't even begun. "Hard and raw, soft and sentimental. How can I know what she wants until I see how she reacts?"

"Oh." I swallowed. "And what is it that I want?"

"You? Sweetheart, you want everything," he said in a tone that made me go weak in the knees. "And I'm looking forward to giving it to you." He nodded to the tub again. "In."

I didn't argue. Merely moved carefully on the cool marble up to the edge of the tub. I tested the water and found it to be the perfect temperature, a little on the hot side, but nowhere close to scalding. With a sigh of absolute pleasure, I slid in.

Tyler tucked an inflatable pillow behind my head and I smiled up at him. "Joining me?"

"No," he said, as he started to take off his watch, a beautiful instrument that looked to my eye like an antique. "I'm not."

He set the watch carefully on a nearby table, and since he then started to unbutton his shirt, I decided that he must be teasing.

I watched, enjoying myself thoroughly, as he stripped off his shirt. His body was deliciously perfect, tan and lean, with the kind of defined arms and chest that you'd see on a swimmer. I wanted to reach out and touch him. To discover for myself if the smattering of chest hair was as soft as it looked, and if the muscles were as hard. I wanted to run my lips over every inch of him.

Mostly, I wanted to tumble him into the tub with me.

Instead, I settled for watching him sit on the edge, still in those elegant gray trousers. He looked like something from a pin-up calendar, all easy sensuality in slacks with no shirt and his hair slightly tousled.

He was exceptional, and I couldn't help but wonder how many women he'd brought to his room, touched, bathed, taken to bed.

I wondered—and wished that I hadn't let the thought enter my mind. I had no right to jealousy. Tyler wasn't mine—couldn't be mine—and whatever connection I might fantasize that I felt tonight was just an illusion. How could it be real when we were both clutching tight to our secrets?

"Deep thoughts?" he asked, stroking my hair.

I smiled up at him. "Just thinking how gorgeous you are."

His brows lifted. "I'm flattered."

"Like hell. You know you're amazing."

"And in so many ways," he said, with a cocky grin.

I laughed, then started to splash him. He caught my hand. "Hands on your knees," he said. "I'm going to bathe you."

I opened my mouth to—what? Complain? Question? In the end, I said nothing, just leaned back on my pillow with my hands on my knees and let him take charge.

He started with my legs. Gently, he lifted each leg in turn, putting my heel on a little step inside the tub that I guessed was made for that very purpose. He stroked my skin with scented soaps, then slid his slick and slippery hands along my feet, my calves, my thighs. When he reached the juncture, he stroked my sex lightly, sending trills of pleasure dancing through me. And then his hand was gone again, as if he'd intended nothing more than a preview of what was to come.

He moved on to my torso, then my arms and hands, sensually massaging each individual finger until I thought I would go mad with the desire for more, so much more. Then his attention turned to my breasts, caressing and stroking until I could feel every touch in every cell of my body, and my nipples were tight with need.

To my regret, though, he took it no further.

"How do you feel?" he asked, and I blinked my eyes open to see him smiling down at me with a kind of sensual satisfaction. "Relaxed," I said. "Turned on."

I saw the flicker in his eyes, but if stroking and touching me had aroused him equally, he didn't say. Instead, he simply lifted a spray nozzle and gently began to wet my hair.

His hands, both strong and sensual, massaged my scalp as the shampoo he chose—full of mint and eucalyptus—saturated my senses. I began to float, eyes closed, this man taking care of me.

I don't know how long I floated there, lost in that sensual place that Tyler had taken me. I only knew that when my eyes fluttered open, my hair was rinsed and the tub was draining—and instead of feeling cold as the water swirled away, I felt the hot pulse of desire inside me.

Without a word, Tyler held out a hand. I took it gratefully. I wasn't sure I could have managed without his support.

I padded carefully down the stairs, then toweled myself dry as he stood in front of me, just stood there watching me with the air crackling wild around us. I reached out—I had to—and slowly trailed my fingers over his bare chest.

I felt the beat of his heart beneath my hand, and pressed my palm there. I lifted my head, found his eyes, and almost stumbled from the force of the desire I saw looking back at me.

"Yes," I whispered. "God, yes."

He didn't move. Didn't speak, but as I slid my hand down, exploring the shape of him, I felt his muscles tighten with barely contained control. I smiled, liking that I was the one making him quiver, and I got slowly to my knees, thinking that I'd like to make him quiver even more.

But when I reached for his fly, he gently stopped my hand. "No."

I looked up. "I know you like it."

"Very much. And I can think of very little I'd like more than to see your lips around my cock. But not now."

"Why not?"

He held my hand and eased me to my feet. "Because the rest of tonight is about you."

"Oh."

He went to a closet and came out with a white silk robe. He helped me into it, the material as soft and gentle as a kiss. I tightened the sash, then drew my hands over the material, enjoying the way it felt against my skin.

"I do like watching you," he said softly. "I like seeing the way your body reacts to my touch. The way your eyes flutter when you come close to the edge. There's an honesty between us that's—well, I like it."

"I'm not doing anything except reacting to you," I said, my voice soft though the words were entirely true.

"Good," he said, and in that moment our eyes locked. I felt that clench in my belly, the strong tug of need. My lips parted, and I rose onto my toes, my hand reaching for his shoulder as I moved closer, craving his mouth, his kiss—

But he stepped back, and suddenly there was nowhere to go. I glanced down to the floor, embarrassed.

"I'm sorry. I didn't mean to—" To what? To kiss him? Hell yes, I'd meant to kiss him. More likely, I didn't mean to make an ass out of myself, but I was hardly going to tell him that.

And then I realized. "It's what you said in the elevator. Despite all of this. Despite making me feel like this, you're not going to kiss me. You're still tormenting me, aren't you?"

His smile was slow and sexy and undeniably charming. And

he didn't say a damn word in answer to my question. Instead, he reached for a strand of my hair and wound it around his fingers. "Christ, you tempt me." He held out a hand. "Come with me."

I was irritated, but I was also both amused and turned on. Plus, the only place to go was back into that bedroom, and that meant he was finally taking me to bed.

"Do you remember what I told you?" he asked as he led me into the room. "The things that I like?"

"Watching me, you said."

"Very good. A gold star to the prize pupil. And yes, I've liked that very much. I've liked it all—pampering you, touching you. I liked watching your face when the waiter came in. And I liked knowing that you were doing that—sitting there, exposed for him—because you wanted to please me."

He took a step closer, bringing him into the doorway, but not over the threshold. "I got hard watching you then, did you know that?"

I shook my head.

"Knowing how far you were willing to go to please me—it made me hard. Made me want you even more. And made me wonder how much further you'd go."

I licked my lips, but I didn't say a word.

"That's what you want, isn't it? The adventure. The thrill. That's why you sent me a note saying that you wanted to play— and why you got pissed when I sent you away."

I nodded.

"And you're here with me now because you crave something. Tell me, Sloane. Tell me what you crave."

"You."

He shook his head. "Me, yes, but it's more than that. You want me to take you the rest of the way. You want to find out just how far you can go." He reached out and stroked my cheek. "Why me, Sloane? I want you to tell me that."

I forced myself not to take a step back, because how could I answer that question? *Because you were right there, the focus of my investigation? Because I still want to get close; I still want inside Destiny; I still want to know what you are up to, and if Kevin is even close to right, I still want to shut you down.*

That was all true, but it wasn't the truth.

The truth was more raw, more scary. Because Tyler Sharp was dangerous. He was edgy. He was not the kind of man I should let under my skin.

Yet I had, and that truth cut deep inside me. And what scared me was the certainty that if I spoke it aloud, I could never take it back.

Even so, I couldn't keep silent. So I drew in a breath, gathered my courage, and told this enigmatic, dangerous man the deepest, most essential truth. "Because you saw me. Because you see me. Because nobody else ever has."

He held my gaze, then slowly nodded. A moment later, he moved to the bed, then sat on the edge. "Come here," he said, and I moved forward to stand between his knees. He reached out for the sash on the robe, then gave it a tug to release the bow. The robe fell open, exposing me to him.

I stayed perfectly still, though my blood was pounding so hard in my veins it was a wonder he couldn't hear it. He stood, his body so close to mine I could feel his heat. Then he reached with one hand and pulled the sash free from the loops of the robe. Next, he lifted both hands, placed them on my shoulders, and eased the robe off my body.

It pooled at my feet, leaving me naked and warm and frantic for his touch.

Slowly, his gaze skimmed over me, and with each moment that passed, I felt the need inside me grow. I didn't know what to expect—all I knew was that I wanted it, and now.

"Beautiful." A single word, but it might as well have been a touch. My breasts tightened, my nipples hardening so much it was almost painful. And my sex ached with a throbbing need that could only be satisfied by his touch.

I wanted to beg for it. To take his hand and place it upon me. Instead, I simply said, "Please."

"Give me your hand." His voice was sensual, yet commanding, and I complied without hesitation.

He held me gently, then slowly trailed the end of the silk sash over my arm, my wrist, the back of my hand. I'd never considered hands particularly erotic, but the sensual allure of the silk against my skin was undeniable.

"Please," I said again, and watched his mouth curve into a smile.

"Please, what?"

"I don't know," I said honestly. "Just, please."

"Whatever the lady wants." He twisted the sash around my wrist, then knotted it. As he did, I felt something cold rising slowly inside me, fighting through the heat. I bit my lip, resisting the urge to pull my hand back, and forced myself to simply breathe.

"There's a sensuality in being bound," he said, as the cold thing began to twist in my belly.

"No," I whispered, but I didn't withdraw my hand. The cold had frozen me.

His smile seemed almost amused. "You came to me, Sloane, remember? You came because you wanted to see how far I can take you."

But not this far, I wanted to scream. *You should know. You should see. Not this far.*

As if he heard my silent plea, he released my hand, and I almost cried out in gratitude as the ice in my veins began to melt.

Crisis averted. Horror stymied. This will be okay. This is fine. Just breathe, and everything will be fine.

I told myself that. Repeated it like a mantra as I lowered my arm, the silk still dangling from my wrist, relief flooding through me, so powerful it left me weak and a little dizzy.

"We'll go far, I promise you." Slowly—so frustratingly slowly—he stroked his fingertip along my collarbone. Then headed downward, lower and lower in a straight line between my breasts and to my abdomen.

My muscles contracted with the touch, my breath coming in little gasps. Then he moved lower still until his fingers found me wet and ready and even the slightest brush of his touch against my clit sent shivers coursing through me and made my body go limp.

"Not yet," he said, withdrawing his hand with a devious grin, then drawing me to the bed, and easing me down so that I was on my back with Tyler looking down at me from above.

"Lovely," he said. "Now spread your legs. I want to see you open wide for me. Ripe for me. I want to see your body glisten." With deliberate slowness, he slid his hands up my legs, then eased them apart. I closed my eyes, my head turned away, both aroused by his touch and embarrassed by the desire that I knew he could so plainly see.

"You look delicious," he said, and as he spoke he trailed a finger up my thigh, then over my hip and up the curve of my torso. He lifted my arm, and I felt the brush of his lips as he trailed kisses up it. "I want to touch you, to take you as far as you can go, and I want to make certain that you can't squirm away from the pleasure."

The cold thing was back, twisting in my gut, and I jerked upright, my eyes flying open as the fear crashed over me.

But there was nowhere to go. The sash was still around my wrist and though I wasn't sure when he managed it, I was attached quite firmly to the bed. "No." I'd meant to scream the word, but it was only a whisper.

"No? You came of your own accord, Sloane."

He reached for my other hand, and I tried to breathe. Tried to be a cop, and not a fourteen-year-old girl. Tried to swim up through this black ocean of fear. But I couldn't. He'd thrown me off center—yanked open the door to the abyss—and I was falling now.

"You know the rules." His voice undulated, as if filtered through the ocean of fear that was pounding in my head. "You had the chance to leave—more chances than I should have given you. And yet you came to my bed, aroused and wanting me."

"But not this." I forced the words out. "Not this. Dammit, Tyler, let me go."

I was struggling now, my heart beating wildly. The room that had been bathed in golden light was now as red as blood. As hot as death.

I could barely see him through the haze, could barely hear him through the maelstrom in my head, the memories, the fear, the pain, all tied up together like some horrible, violent monster that was intent on swallowing me whole.

"Just relax," he was saying as he began to twist what looked like a curtain sash around my other wrist.

No, no, goddammit, no!

I'm not sure how I managed it, not sure how I made my body move the way it did. But somehow I lashed through the pain. Somehow, I caught him across the face, my fist plowing hard against his temple.

"Goddammit!" His curse was filled with pain, and he reared back, and I took advantage of the movement to thrust my knee up. A one in a million chance, but it worked, and I heard his low, guttural groan as I caught him hard in the balls.

I tried to bolt off the bed, but my arm was still tied fast to the headboard. And as I tried to steady my breathing—tried to *think*—I saw Tyler lift his head, and I saw the heat and danger flash wildly in his eyes.

Before, I'd been afraid of the memories. Now, I was afraid of the man.

This is it, I thought. *Dear god, this is it.*

"Stay away," I snarled. "Just stay the fuck away."

"Sloane." He said my name and then dropped his head, his body hunched over on the floor beside the bed.

I twisted, trying to loosen the knot with my free hand.

"I'm sorry." Regret laced his voice, and when I turned my head and looked at him, the anger I'd seen in his eyes was gone. Instead I saw only tenderness—and endless pools of regret.

I felt my body sag with relief. "Let me go," I said. "Just let me get the hell out of here."

"I'm sorry," he said again as he rose slowly to his feet. "I didn't know. I thought you—I didn't know," he repeated, but I didn't understand what he meant.

He reached for me, and I flinched. He froze, his face as tight and hard as if I'd hit him.

"I didn't know," he said yet again, and though I still didn't understand, I wasn't about to ask. Right then, I didn't care. I just wanted out of there.

I felt a tear escape to track down my cheek, and I turned brutally away. "Please," I said. "Just untie me."

"Of course. Of course, I will."

He did, and I sat up, feeling fragile and confused. I started to reach for the robe, but he bent to get it before I could, and handed it to me.

I stood, then shrugged it on.

"Stay," he said, but I just shook my head. I moved to the living room, feeling a bit like I was in a dream. I didn't see my panties, and I didn't really care. I shimmied into the dress, then tied the halter behind my neck. I was already zipping the back when Tyler came in.

"Sloane. Please. Don't go."

But I could only shake my head. I couldn't stay. Not for Candy. Not for Amy. Not even for myself.

"I'm sorry," I whispered. And then I snatched up my purse and ran barefoot into the hall.

eleven

I stumbled blindly down the hall, then yanked open the door to the hidden staircase that led to the ninth floor and the elevator that would take me back to the lobby.

At each turn I looked behind me, making sure that Tyler wasn't back there. I told myself I didn't want him to follow, and since he apparently wasn't, I also told myself that was a good thing.

Somehow, though, I didn't believe it.

The fear was fading now, the memories slipping back into the dark where they belonged. Exhaustion dogged me, physical and emotional. The whole night had been a whirlwind—of fear, of pleasure, of danger and desire.

In the end, the fear had overshadowed it all, but I couldn't deny that these hours with Tyler had been so much more. More than I had expected. More than just the job.

He'd taken me to places I'd never been, and I'd felt a heightened desire that I'd never before experienced. But I couldn't stay. I couldn't give him what he wanted.

I knew damn well that Tyler was dangerous in so many ways, but I didn't fear him in bed. No, it wasn't the man I feared, but the door that he could open. A door that kept the memories and the dark things at bay.

A door I was determined to keep locked tight, and through which I dreaded even the smallest crack.

I waited impatiently at the ninth-floor elevator bank, shifting my weight from foot to foot until the elevator finally arrived and I could collapse on the fainting couch and bury my face in my hands.

The ride down was quick, and no one else got on. I wasn't surprised. I didn't know the exact time, but I knew it was very late, and the only people wandering around a hotel at this hour were those, like me, doing a walk of shame.

I stood as the elevator doors slid open—then immediately stepped back in shock when I saw Tyler standing right there.

"But—how did you?"

"Service elevator," he said, then stepped into the car, blocking my exit.

"I need to get out. I need to—"

"Sloane." That's it. Just my name, but it was so firm and so vibrant and so full of apology that it sounded to me like a seal of honor.

I melted a little. "Please, Tyler. I'm tired."

He nodded to the couch. "Then sit."

I thought about arguing, but wasn't sure I had the strength. I felt sapped. Exhausted. And I wasn't even entirely certain I was firmly rooted on the planet anymore.

I sat, and as soon as the doors closed behind Tyler, he casually hit the button for the ninth floor, then immediately hit the button to stop the car from moving.

Only then did he turn to look at me.

"You should know that I'm a man who takes what he wants," he began, as I looked down at my fingernails. "I always have, and I always will. No regrets, and no exceptions. No exceptions, that is, but one."

He had my attention, and I lifted my head to find him looking hard at me. "And what is that?"

"I will never take from a woman what isn't freely given, no matter how tempting that woman may be."

"Don't try to pretty it up for me." I kept my voice low and dangerous. "You told me flat out there were things that you wanted in your bed." I met his eyes. "Things you were more than willing to take. And, Tyler, you did try to take them."

"Yes," he said simply. "And no."

"I'm tired," I said. "I'm not interested in games or in riddles."

"Neither am I." He moved toward me, then dropped to his knees so that we were almost eye to eye. "It wasn't me you were afraid of, was it?" he asked gently. "You weren't even seeing me."

I looked away, not wanting him to see the truth in my eyes.

"I am so sorry," he said, and I understood that he wasn't apologizing for what had happened between us, but for what had happened to me all those years ago.

"It doesn't matter."

"It does," he said. "I thought at first that you—" He cut himself off with a sharp shake of his head. "I thought you were playing the game. A little fear mixed with sex can be an aphrodisiac, Sloane, especially with two people like us."

I blinked up at him, confused. "Like us?"

"I don't know you. You don't know me. Not really. And yet I've touched you, so very intimately. You've gone further with me than with anyone, Sloane. We both know it."

"Yes," I whispered.

"And I intended to take you further. There's always fear at the precipice. Always terror before you fall off into the unknown." He reached forward, cupped my face in both of his hands. "I thought that's where you were, standing at the edge of something new and terrifying and thrilling—I thought that was where we were." Gently, he used his thumb to brush away an errant tear. "I was wrong."

He drew his hands away, then stood, moving slowly back to the corner of the car to stand by the doors.

I drew in a shuddering breath, realizing as I did that I missed the comfort of his hand upon my cheek.

"Tyler."

"Wait." He held up a hand. "Let me finish. I meant everything I said to you. And I won't lie to you now. I do want to tie you down. I want the freedom to touch you. I want you completely open to me. I want to look at you, bound to my bed, and have complete power over you. I want you in a position where I could do anything to you. Pain. Pleasure. Even a little fear. But of the moment—of the unknown. Not of me. And certainly not of a ghost from your past."

My breath hitched and I blinked twice to quell the sting of unshed tears.

"I want to know that you trust me to know how far to go. That you trust me not to exceed your boundaries. I want that—but I won't push you. Not if you're not ready. Not if you don't want it, too."

I managed a tiny smile. "The couch? The waiter? Wasn't that pushing me?"

He simply stared at me. I felt my color rise, because I understood. He hadn't pushed me on that—not really. Instead, he'd seen deep enough inside me to know that I wanted it, too.

What he was saying now was that he wouldn't push me over the precipice. Not, at least, until I was ready to jump.

"Stay," he said. "Come back to my room and stay with me tonight."

I licked my dry lips. "Because you feel bad? Or because you want me?"

Instead of answering, he turned to the control box and hit the switch to put the car back in motion. Then he came to me and took my hand. He pulled me to my feet, and I didn't even have time to think before his mouth closed gently over mine. The kiss was soft and I thought I might melt simply from the sweetness of it.

When he pulled back, his eyes were warm. "Because I want you."

I nodded, breathless, my lips still tingling. "You didn't make me beg for a kiss."

The corners of his eyes crinkled. "I'll beg if you don't kiss me again."

"Tempting," I said. "But I'll be kind." I rose onto my tiptoes and brushed a chaste kiss over the corner of his mouth.

He laughed. "Fuck that," he said, then gripped my shoulders and pressed me back against the wall. I gasped, not expecting the motion, and he closed his mouth brutally over mine. Gone was the sweetness of that first kiss. This was hard and wild and demanding. Teeth and tongue and the violence of possession, the cacophony of passion. Relief swept through me even as wild thoughts clanged about in my head, unable to form into anything more coherent than a vague plea of *more, more, oh yes, more.*

We broke apart when the doors opened, and Tyler took my hand, then drew me down the hall to another elevator, this one with a plain metal interior, covered on two sides with moving blankets.

"It will take us to the service entrance," he said, and I nodded.

I felt giddy. Light. A small part of me tried to argue that my giddiness was because my operation was back on track, but that was bullshit. This was all about me. About the way he'd made my body tingle and thrum. About the heat he'd sent coursing through me and the way he'd pushed my boundaries. Even to the point of breaking.

He'd made me feel things I had never experienced, and for better or worse, I wanted to walk with him to that precipice. I wouldn't go over with him—how the hell could I ever trust a man like Tyler Sharp that intimately?—but I could damn sure enjoy the ride.

I had no idea where this was going, but for this night, I was his. Tomorrow, I would think about the job.

We were back in the penthouse, moving through the hallway by his office to the living room. Neither of us spoke, and though the silence was a comfortable one, I couldn't deny the flutter of nerves in my stomach. I knew he wouldn't bind me—but beyond that, I didn't have a clue.

"Tyler?" I began, when I couldn't take it anymore.

We'd reached the living room, and he paused near the huge window that looked out over Michigan Avenue. "Yes?"

"What are you going to do with me?"

His lips twitched. "Nervous?"

"And excited."

"I like your honesty, so I'll tell you that I'm planning something we're both going to enjoy." He moved to stand behind me, then pushed me gently forward so that I was closer to the window, and I could see both our reflections in the glass. "I'm going to fuck you, Sloane. Very hard, and very thoroughly." His eyes met mine in the glass. "If that's all right with you?"

"Yeah," I said breathlessly. "Yeah, I think that'll be just fine." I swallowed, kept my eyes on his. "Is that all?"

He laughed, and the sound made my smile bloom wide.

"No," he said. "No, it's not."

I waited for him to say more, and when he didn't, I frowned.

I saw my own brow furrowed in the reflection, and saw his expression grow more amused in turn.

"Shall I give you a clue?" he asked as the fingertips of his right hand trailed feather light over my arm. The sensation was both sweet and erotic, and it was all I could do not to turn in his arms and claim his mouth with my own.

"I could entice you with words," he said. "Someday, I want to touch you only with my voice and tease you only with my words. I want to watch as you quiver with longing, as your body goes soft and slick. I want to watch the fire build inside you, and I want to make you explode before I even brush a finger over your skin."

I trembled, knowing with full and humbling certainty that he could do exactly that.

"But not tonight," he whispered as he gently brushed his hands over my shoulder blades. "I don't have the strength tonight. Tonight, I need to touch you."

As if in illustration, he slid his hands forward so that his fingers brushed the edge of my halter. I gasped, then stopped breathing when his hands continued to ease beneath the material and over my bare skin. Then his fingers found my nipples, hard and tight and so damn sensitive. "Yes," I breathed. "Oh, god, yes."

He pinched my nipple, and I gasped as hot wires of pleasure shot from my breast all the way down to my sex.

I had to bite my lower lip as I watched our reflection in the window, and the image of us standing like that—of his fingers inside my clothes, of me leaning back against him, of the soft and sensual expression on my face—just about pushed me over the edge.

His fingers paused in their magic, and I almost sobbed in protest as he pulled his hands away, leaving my flesh cool and bereft in the wake of his touch.

"You like this," he said as he untied my halter, then unzipped the dress. It fell to the ground, leaving me completely bare. "You're like a goddess in the window, bathed in golden light. Does it excite you, knowing that someone might be looking in? Might be across the street looking out their window? Might see how lovely you are?"

I didn't answer, but it didn't matter. His hand slipped down to dip between my legs. "Yes," he murmured, finding me wet. "Yes, I think it does," he said as he trailed the fingers of his other hand over hips, my waist, my breasts.

I closed my eyes, reveling in the feel of him.

"You're too beautiful to hide away," he said, "but I'm the only one who gets to touch you."

"Yes," I murmured. "Now. Please, I need you to touch me now."

Without a word, he moved around me so that his back was to the window. He knelt in front of me, his hands on my thighs, his thumbs achingly close to my sex. Slowly, he eased my legs apart, and I felt the cool, sweet air.

"I will always give you what you need," Tyler said, then pressed a soft kiss on my pubis before rising, his hands following the movement of his body so that when he brushed his lips over my cheek, his hands gently cupped my breasts.

"Close your eyes," he said, and I did, then lost myself in pleasure as he touched me everywhere, a series of strokes and kisses and caresses teasing every inch of me until my body was so aroused I wasn't sure I could take it anymore.

Finally—oh, thank god, finally—he took hold of my hips and slid his tongue over my clit, teasing and playing as I tried to writhe in time with the pleasure but couldn't—he was holding too tight, concentrating the delight on that one perfect point.

My knees went weak, and I had to reach out, one hand clutching the wall and the other his hair, as he took me closer and closer to the edge and then—when I didn't think I could stand it any longer—the world exploded around me. A firestorm engulfed me—and I lost myself to the desperately erotic sensation of Tyler's mouth against me, of his hands upon me, of his arms around me.

He was carrying me, and I snuggled close, suddenly spent.

Gently, he took me through the penthouse, then laid me in his bed. He stood at the side, and then slowly toed off his shoes and unbuttoned his slacks. He wore briefs, and I could see the bulge of his erection behind the gray material. He stripped those off, too, and I found myself staring at the most perfect male I had ever seen.

He pulled open a drawer beside the bed and drew out a condom. I watched, awed by how hard and perfect he was, as he took it out of the package and then rolled it on.

"I'm going to fuck you now," he said as he moved to the foot of the bed. "Because I really can't wait."

I nodded, then gasped as he gripped me behind each knee and tugged me toward him so that my ass was right at the edge of the mattress. The move was bold and wild and a little violent—and I moaned in delight, lost in the pleasure of submitting to him.

"Legs up," he said, lifting my legs until my heels were at his shoulders. "Christ, I like that view."

My legs were parted, and I was wide open to him, so aroused that even the brush of air over my sex made me tremble with need. Wet and aroused and very much on display.

I twisted my head to the side as I felt the blush hit my cheeks.

"No," he said. "God, no. You're beautiful. And so wet," he said as he slid his fingers over me, thrusting two inside.

Immediately, my body clenched around him, drawing him in. But that wasn't enough. Wasn't nearly enough. I felt wild and wanton and so very empty. I needed him inside me. Was pretty sure I would shrivel up and die if he didn't fuck me right that very second. "Please," I whispered.

"Please what?"

"I want you," I said. "I want you inside me. Now."

He tugged my legs so that I slid even closer to him, and I gasped with the motion, then cried out in pleasure as I felt the tip of his cock press hard against me. "This?" he asked, slipping inside me. But not enough. Not nearly enough.

"You promised me hard," I said. "Dammit, Tyler, I want you to fuck me."

"Whatever you want," he said, then ripped a scream of pleasure, of pain, of absolute satisfaction out of me when he thrust hard into me, pulling my legs up as he did, so that he sank deep inside, then again and again as our bodies slapped together and I reached to the side to claw at the bedsheets.

"Look at me," he demanded, and I opened my eyes and found his gaze, hot and hard, pulling me. "That's right, baby."

Our eyes stayed locked as he moved rhythmically, and I felt spirals of pleasure twisting through me, rising higher and higher like some magnificent crescendo just waiting for the final triumphant burst.

I released my hold on the sheets, surrendering my body entirely to him. Concentrating on the glorious sensation of him filling me, the rhythmic pounding as he claimed me, the tight grip he kept on the back of my thighs as he drew me closer with each thrust.

I watched his face, wanting to memorize him, to learn everything about him. I moved my hands to my breasts, pinching my own nipples, and feeling a rush of satisfaction at his whispered moan of, "oh, Christ, baby, yes."

I saw the pressure building inside him, recognized the rising storm in those amazing blue eyes.

"Come with me," he said, his voice raw.

"I'm not—I can't—" I was close—the friction on my clit from his thrusts making everything inside me coil tight—but it wasn't enough to release.

"Touch yourself," he ordered. And then, more gently, "Do it, Sloane. I want you with me."

I hesitated only a moment, then slid my hand down until my fingers found my clit, then moaned in response to the first tiny stroke. He'd brought me so close. So very close, and now I touched myself—touched him too, when my fingertips brushed his cock. It was intimate, wildly sensual, my fingers right there as he thrust into me. His orgasm growing as my body clenched around him, and my own hand working to bring me over with him.

"Jesus, Sloane. Now," he said, and before I could react, he'd exploded, his body shaking as the climax ripped through him. My own orgasm came fast, and I clung to him, body to body, skin to skin, wanting nothing more in that moment but to lose myself in the scent, the taste, the everything of this man.

Slowly, sweetly, my body calmed, and Tyler pushed me back up the bed, rolling over, drawing me close to him. "You are exceptional," he murmured, as he gently brushed his lips over my shoulder.

"You make me feel exceptional," I said, fighting to keep my eyes open. But my lids were heavy, and his body was warm, and I drifted off to sleep in the arms of this man I shouldn't want, but so desperately did.

twelve

The moon shines down on the low stone wall, making the lime-stone glow and the bits of quartz shimmer. A ruin now, mostly rubble, but this part of it still stands on the hill looking down at the house.

I kneel behind it, looking over the rocks. Looking across the field.

Looking at the house where he lives. Looking at him moving around inside, so sure that he's safe behind the glass.

"You don't have to go to the academy. You don't have to become a cop."

I turn my head and face the balding man with the gentle blue eyes.

"I do, Daddy," I say. "I have to make it right. I'm the only one who understands why it's so important to make it right."

"You can't," he says. "See?" He reaches for my hands, and I see that they are slick with blood. "How can it ever be right?"

Fear slices through me, and I look to the house again.

He's not walking anymore. He's prone. He's dead.

And the blood flows and flows, filling the field, climbing the hill, reaching for the wall. Reaching for me.

I start to scream and reach for my father, but he isn't there.

Run, *I think.* Now is the time to run.

I race forward toward the house, screaming for her, searching for her.

She has to be there. Now that he's dead, she should be there.

But she's gone.

And as the force of the dream thrusts me upright and out of sleep, I scream for my mother . . . but I can't even remember if she was ever there at all.

My eyes fluttered open, the dream still clinging to me, gray and cloying.

Tyler's arm was around my waist and he was breathing soft and evenly. I didn't want to disturb him, but I also wanted to move, to shake off the last wisps of the nightmare. Carefully, I slid from his embrace, then scooted to the edge of the bed, taking care not to disturb the mattress too much.

Once up, I padded to the elegant bathroom, trying my best to stay quiet. I didn't know what time it was, but since the drapes were open, I knew that it was still dark out.

When I returned to the bed, I noticed that there was no clock. Automatically, I reached for my phone, but it was still in the living room, safe inside my purse. I almost went to get it, but then I saw Tyler's watch on the bedside table. I sat on the edge of the bed and picked it up, then tilted it to try to see the face in the ambient light from the city.

I frowned, realizing that the second hand wasn't working, and when I held it up to my ear, there was no ticking.

"It doesn't work." Tyler's voice skimmed over me, rough with sleep.

I turned to face him. "I didn't mean to wake you."

"It's okay." He sat up, then reached for the watch. "It's been broken for years."

"Oh." Maybe I was tired, but I didn't understand. "Can't it be repaired?"

"It can," he said. "It's not time yet."

He put it carefully on the table, then laid back down, pulling me with him.

I reached for the sheet, bringing it up over both of us. "You're being cryptic," I said.

"I suppose I am. It was a gift from a friend. A mentor, really. Hell, he was practically a father to me. He passed away about six months ago."

"I'm sorry," I said, propping myself up on an elbow and facing him. "Will you tell me the rest? Why haven't you had it repaired?"

"Well, that depends. Maybe it's a secret. Are you prepared to tell me yours?"

"My secrets?" I felt the quick stab of fear. What the hell did he know of my secrets?

"Not that," he said gently, and I realized that he'd seen my fear and worried that I was recalling my terror of being bound. "But there are things you're holding back. Admit it. You haven't told me the whole truth, have you?"

A cold chill swept over me. "No," I admitted. "But I don't know all your secrets, either."

His smile was thin, but there was mirth in his eyes. "Sweetheart, you don't know any of my secrets."

"No? Then why don't you tell me."

"I don't think so."

I realized that I'd tensed up, my body ready for battle. I breathed in and out and told myself to relax. "I thought you said you trusted me."

"No. I just said that I wanted to." He reached out and stroked his fingers lightly down my arm. The gesture was sweet and casual, and I doubted he even knew he was doing it. Somehow, that made it all the sweeter.

"The truth is, I haven't felt this way in a very long time," he continued as he tugged me close and curled his body against mine. "Not since I was young and didn't really understand what I had—and what I lost." He spoke softly, the words holding even more intimacy than his touch. "Now I think I understand, and I recognize it."

"What?"

"That click," he said. "That connection. It's passion, Sloane. And it's promise."

My back was spooned against his chest, and I closed my eyes, then told myself to remember to breathe as he gently stroked my hair. I couldn't deny how good it felt to be in his arms, but I also couldn't forget that he'd spoken of trust.

And I didn't trust him. Hell, I didn't trust anyone. "Don't make this more than it is," I said.

"It already is more."

I rolled over, opening my mouth to protest.

"Shut up, Sloane. We're not going to come to any sort of agreement with words. But in the silence, in the dark, I think we'll come together just fine."

He kissed me then, and as his warm hands slid over my naked skin, I had to admit he was right—we came together just fine.

thirteen

I woke to the gentle caress of the sun streaming through a small gap in the blackout curtains. I blinked, trying to focus as the events of the night came back to me. And not just any night, but one of the most decadent, erotic, amazing nights of my life.

I pushed myself up and propped my back against a wall of pillows. The space beside me was empty, but there was a small envelope perched on the pillow.

AT THE GYM.
DIDN'T HAVE THE HEART TO WAKE YOU.
COFFEE AND CROISSANTS IN KITCHEN.
I WANT YOU AGAIN. HARD AND WILD.
SOON.
T

I read the note twice, feeling like a teenager who'd just found a mash letter in her locker. All giddy and sweet and a little unsure of what to do next.

As I'd been swimming up from the depths of sleep, my mind had been filled with images of me spooning against Tyler. Of him waking me with kisses, with his hand stroking down my belly to ease the ache between my thighs.

I was wet from the night and from the erotic dreams that had followed, and I couldn't help but be a little disappointed that Tyler hadn't been in bed to make my fantasies a reality.

He'd done a number on me all right—or maybe I'd done the number on myself.

With a sigh, I sat up, the sheet wrapped tight around me. I leaned over and thrust my fingers into my tangled hair and tried to figure out what the hell I was doing. Because I damn sure wasn't being a cop. Yes, it's true that I'd gotten close to Tyler—mission accomplished there—but if I was in cop mode, shouldn't I have awakened with an agenda, all ready to jump in and move on to phase two?

Instead, I was hot and horny and frustrated the man wasn't around to cuddle. I wasn't entirely sure when I'd let go of the last strands of sanity and reason, but I knew damn well that somewhere along the way I had. Because right now, I wasn't thinking about Amy or the knights' laundry list of sins. I was thinking about last night, and about the man in whose arms I'd spent it.

Tyler Sharp had sparked something deep inside me. Something wonderful, but a little bit scary. Something that made me feel tingly and girly. That made me want to have a pedicure and pay attention to my makeup.

Something I damn well needed to guard against. *Nobody is what they seem.* Not me. Not Tyler.

I'd do well to remember that.

"Well, fuck."

My words clanged against the silence of the room, their impact like a slap. Time to wrap my fist around those threads and yank my sanity back. I needed to find out if he had any information on Amy. And I needed to watch my step.

I could fuck him, but I couldn't trust him.

With that invigorating but rather depressing pep talk, I slid out of bed and gathered up the clothes that were still lying in a heap near the door. I didn't bother with the shoes, and after a moment's debate I didn't bother with the underwear, either. I might be wary, but I wasn't stupid, and if Tyler wanted a repeat of last night's extracurricular activities, I was more than happy to oblige.

Barefoot, I padded out of the master suite and headed toward the kitchen. Tyler was as good as his word, and I poured myself a gallon-sized cup of coffee and drank it while I leaned against the counter and scoped out the kitchen. Not typical of hotels, not by a long shot. It was huge, fully stocked, and had both an island and a small workstation with a laptop and a careless wash of papers.

That was, I thought, a good place to start.

Since I didn't know how long Tyler would be gone, I moved quickly to the workstation and pulled open the drawer. Pens, pencils, sticky notes, and at least a dozen take-out menus. All of which were entirely unhelpful.

I eyed the laptop, which was open, its screen nothing but black. If there was something relevant in this suite, there was a good chance it was on that laptop. And it would be so easy to just take a peek . . .

I hesitated only a moment, then tapped the space bar. The screen blinked, then came to life, revealing an image of Lake Michigan over which an electronic notepad appeared, with six things itemized on a list:

~~Evan party~~
Jahn Foundation—board meeting, when?
Postpone Nevada, 2 weeks
Michelle—soon
~~Re: A—discuss options w/ C & E~~
~~Call Q re SW~~

The notes were primarily nonsensical, but in light of the reference to the party, I assumed it was some sort of to-do list. The kind of random list that people keep before transferring notes to a calendar or project list.

Nothing nefarious caught my eye, but I'd be lying if I didn't feel a little ping in my gut upon seeing the woman's name. Especially in such close proximity to the word "soon." I frowned. I'm not the jealous type, especially not with regard to a man I barely knew and shouldn't want. But there was no denying the evidence of my own reaction.

Apparently the man had bewitched me, because right at the moment, I was desperately hoping that Michelle was his dog.

I cocked my head, uncertain if I'd heard the front door open. My finger hesitated over the trackpad. I wanted to click on the list and see if it linked to more detailed information. If Kevin was right, who knew what kind of racketeering-related details I might find on Tyler's laptop. I might not be interested in being Kevin's personal research bitch, but I did want to satisfy my own curiosity.

But if Tyler had returned . . .

I waited, heard nothing else, and navigated the cursor to the list. After all, I might not get this opportunity again.

I clicked.

Nothing.

Nothing, that is, except the password box. I exhaled, mildly irritated but not terribly surprised. I considered trying "knights"—or even "Michelle" because I was still feeling jealous and petty. But I was confident that Tyler wouldn't be that obvious. For that matter, it was possible he had some sort of keystroke monitor and would know I'd been snooping.

I considered the computer a bit longer. The notes might mean nothing now, but maybe they would make sense later. I weighed my options, hurried into the living room to find my purse, then returned with my smart phone and snapped a picture of the screen.

It wasn't much, but at least I'd done something.

With no other plan of attack for the kitchen, I decided to see what else might be in the penthouse. I already knew there was no workstation in the bedroom, but I sincerely doubted that a man like Tyler would be willing to live without a desk, even for only a few months.

With luck, I'd find either a dedicated office or a bedroom that Tyler had set up as one. With even more luck, I'd find something interesting.

I poured a second cup of coffee and took it with me as I set out to find and search his office. I had personal knowledge that Tyler was not only well muscled, but had serious endurance. So I assumed he spent a significant amount of time at the gym. What I didn't know was where the gym was located or how long he'd been gone. If he used the fitness center at The Drake, his travel time would be minimal.

No matter what, time was of the essence, and me and my coffee hurried down the corridor that led off the south side of the living area.

The hallway angled sharply, and I'd just made the turn when I stopped dead. *Tyler.* His voice. I couldn't make out the words, but I was damn sure that was his voice.

Shit. Holy fucking shit.

He was here. In the penthouse. And he must have been here the whole damn time.

I said a silent thank-you to Saint Christopher—the patron

saint of cops—who'd apparently been watching out for me, preventing Tyler from popping into the kitchen to freshen his coffee while I poked around on his laptop. With any luck, good old Christopher would stay on the job.

The voice was coming from behind the first door on the left. Probably a gym—it occurred to me belatedly that a penthouse this large would have a private gym—and I put my coffee on a nearby table and then eased that way. I couldn't snoop while he was on the premises, so I might as well tell him I was awake.

But as I lifted my hand to knock on the door, I realized two things. First, the door was cracked just slightly. Second, Tyler wasn't alone.

The woman in me felt a twinge of guilt, but the cop didn't even hesitate. I edged quietly up against the door, tilted my head, and listened.

"Franklin showed up late for the party," said a deep voice that I recognized as belonging to Cole August. "Said to tell you that Lizzy's a gem. Guess her first couple of days went well."

"Glad to hear it," Tyler said "She works hard, and she's sharp. I figure he's lucky to have her. At least that's good news. Bentley's turning out to be a liability."

"My neck's clear on this one," a third man said, and I assumed it was Evan Black. "But if you want my advice, you don't want to waste any time getting a protection plan in place."

"Agreed," Cole said.

"I think Michelle's our best option," Tyler said, and my ears perked up at the name. "Okay by you?"

"Shit, man," Cole said. "I just fuck her. I'm not her keeper. If we need her, we'll use her. You know that."

"Fine," Tyler said. "I'll set it up. What else?"

"Lina noticed your date for the party," Evan said in a voice that sounded just a little too smooth. "Asked me if I knew who she was."

I froze, wishing I could see as well as hear.

"What'd you tell her?" Cole asked.

"The truth," Evan said. "What do you think? But, dammit, Tyler, you know damn well I'm not one to question your end-game, but you should have talked to us before fucking a cop—"

I gasped—barely a sound, but I knew in that instant that they'd heard me.

Instinctively I reached for my weapon, only to remember that I wasn't wearing it. I turned to run—because no matter what bullshit Hollywood throws at you, one unarmed, petite female detective was no match for those three—but the door was open and Tyler flew through it, catching my arm before I'd even reached the end of the hall.

"You bastard! You goddamn, mother-fucking bastard." I hurled the words at him, even as I tried to yank my arm free. No go there; he had me tight. Which left me no option but to lash out with my free hand and smash my fist into his sanctimonious face.

He anticipated the punch, so I got him in the jaw instead of his nose.

What I didn't get, was free. I was still trapped tight in his grip. Only now, he was surely even more pissed off.

"You son of a bitch." I wasn't shouting. On the contrary, my words were cold and measured, but that ice was balanced against a white hot rage.

"Jesus, fuck, that hurts," Tyler said, tightening his grip on me as he reached up with his free hand to massage his jaw.

"Tyler." Cole stood frozen in the hall, Evan behind him. They both looked as intimidating as hell. And in that singular moment, I understood how they'd risen to become such fierce and feared businessmen. Who the hell would dare cross them?

Me, apparently. *Shit*.

I considered struggling, but I wasn't going to give them the satisfaction. Instead, I stood perfectly straight and perfectly silent, willing my pulse to calm down as I watched the situation and analyzed my options.

Not a long process—considering Tyler held me tight and the fact that it was three against one, I calculated that my choices were limited.

Tyler's eyes stayed firmly on me, but he was talking to the other two men when he said, very softly and simply, "Go."

Evan took a step forward. "Listen, Tyler. I'm—"

"Later." Tyler's eyes never left my face. "Go out through the back entrance. We'll talk tomorrow. I have this under control."

I saw the doubt in Cole's and Evan's faces—and I knew damn sure they could see the fury on mine—but they did as Tyler asked, and moved down the hall to a service door.

The moment it clicked shut behind them, I yanked my arm again—and once again he held me tight.

"Goddammit, Tyler. Let me go." I was tense. Tight. And I was searching the hall, doing a visual check for anything I could use as a weapon—if I ever got free and had the chance to grab it.

"Do you know why I pushed you last night?" he asked, and I heard the danger in his voice, sharp and clean like the blade of a knife.

I met his eyes, but said nothing. I felt the tiny beads of sweat rise on the back of my neck, though, and my skin went clammy. I tried to push down the fear, tried to control the beat of my heart. But there was no denying it—and I was certain that Tyler could see it.

"Because you were a goddamn cop who had slid into my bed and I wanted—*wanted*—you to be afraid."

My mouth was bone dry as he took a step closer, and I moved back until I was pressed up against the wall, his body only a hairsbreadth from mine, and I was bathed in the heat of his fury.

"I wanted to make you wonder," he continued, his voice low

and harsh and deadly. "Wonder if you'd made a mistake playing me. Make you wonder if maybe I was the kind of man who could hurt a woman."

"Are you?"

I saw his hand rise as fury marred his face. And then, before I had time to react, to do anything, he lashed out. I winced, but he wasn't aiming the blow at me. Instead, he punched the wall behind me, setting it to shake and rattling the sconces that lined the hallway.

"I'm not," he said, his low, even voice a stark contrast to the man who'd just exploded in front of me. "Last night, I thought I was pushing a cop. A bitch cop who'd stuck her nose in where it didn't belong and was afraid that maybe, just maybe, she'd fucked with the wrong man."

He reached out, as if to stroke my cheek, but I flinched, and he paused, then slowly withdrew. "When I realized that it wasn't me you were scared of but your memories, I wanted to kick myself. I never meant—" He drew in a breath. "I never meant to hurt you that way."

"I believe you." It was true. Whatever else was between us, that fundamental point was true.

He met my eyes, his full of disappointment, and then he released me. I debated running, realized I couldn't get past him, so I decided to stay and let this play out. Besides, I wanted to know what more he had to say.

For a moment he just stood there. Then he moved across the hall and leaned against the doorjamb. Gone was the earlier fury and the regret. Instead, he looked relaxed and calm and perfectly in control.

"What is it you think you know about me, Sloane?"

I debated how to answer, then decided that some truth was the best approach. "Not much. Not much that's concrete, anyway."

"Tell me."

"I know you were given immunity for Mann Act violations," I said, watching his face carefully.

His expression didn't change at all. "That's interesting," he said. "Especially when you consider that the immunity deal was confidential."

I shrugged. "If you know I'm a cop, you probably know that my dad was in the FBI. I have a lot of resources." All true, and yet all deception. But it kept Kevin's name out of it. I might be pissed at him for pulling me into his vendetta against Evan Black, but I wasn't about to let Tyler know that an FBI agent still had eyes on him.

"What else?" he demanded.

"Nothing specific," I admitted. "You three play it close to the vest. There are rumors, speculation. Word is you bump dirty against all sorts of shit. Smuggling, illegal gambling, fraud. As far as I can tell, no one has any solid evidence."

"And that's why you're here."

"No." I caught myself taking a step toward him, and stopped. "I'm an Indianapolis homicide detective," I said reasonably. "You really believe I'm here to find out if you're smuggling cigarettes?"

I waited for him to reply, but he simply stayed silent, watching me. "How?" I finally asked.

He cocked his head in question.

"How did you know I was a cop?"

"You're not dealing with idiots, Detective. Or with men who ignore their assets."

I let his words sink in, then remembered the sign in the reception area at Destiny that plainly announced that the premises were under twenty-four-hour video surveillance.

"Remote video feed," I said.

He reached into his pocket and pulled out his smart phone. "I can play back the footage on my laptop, my phone. Like I said, it's important for me to keep an eye on the place."

"Thousands of people must cross in front of your cameras. Why notice me?"

"You intrigued me on two counts." He winced a little, then ran his thumb over the rising bruise on his knuckles. "One, I liked the way you looked. For another, we don't get many walk-in applicants. Those things combined to catch my eye."

"And you learned I was a cop? How?"

"Hardly tricky. Like I said, you caught my eye. And I find it useful to have as much information about people as I can. So I had a buddy lift your prints from your application. After that, it was no trouble at all. Sloane Watson, on medical leave from the Indianapolis Metropolitan Police Department. And that," he added with a nod toward my hip, "wasn't from a mugging."

He waited, obviously expecting me to tell him what happened. I stayed silent.

His shoulder lifted almost infinitesimally. "I told you I don't trust easy. I meant it."

I ran my fingers through my hair, trying to process all he'd told me while at the same time figuring out my next move.

My goddamn prints. It had never occurred to me that they'd run the prints of someone applying for a waitress position. And it had never occurred to me that Tyler would watch the security feed when he was out of town.

Two mistakes, and knowing they were out there—that they were on me—only riled my temper more. "You knew, and yet you brought me to your room, stripped me, fucked me?" I thought about the couch, the waiter. About the way the erotic thrill had ripped through me, like some intimate new secret that he'd shared with me.

"You played me," I said, my voice low but trembling with anger. "You fucking played me."

"Hell yes, I played you. I already told you. I pulled you in, step by step. I had every intention of using you and being done with you."

He moved away from the door, taking a single step toward me. "Nothing but one big con—or at least that's the way I planned it. Because nobody plays those kinds of games with me. Not and get away with it."

"Well, hooray on you," I said. "You win. Happy?"

"Not really, no."

"Yeah? Well, good." I tried to make the words sound cavalier and uncaring. But dammit, I did care. And now that my fear was gone and the anger was settling, I felt hollow and lost.

Goddamn me for letting myself get twisted around by this guy—this fucking asshole who didn't want a goddamn thing except to use me. And I'd gone and let myself believe that part of it was real. His talk of trust and passion. Of feeling a connection.

I'd let myself forget that he was a grifter at heart, and who better to see your weak spots than a con who manipulated emotions to make a fast buck?

Well, fuck him.

I started to turn away, but he took my chin. "No," he said, his voice soft yet firm. "I know what you're thinking, and no. I pushed you because I thought you were a cop. But when you ran—when I went after you—it was because I wanted the woman."

"Please," I said, as a brutal wave of exhaustion swept over me. "Please, will you just let me leave?"

He said nothing for so long I thought he was going to simply ignore the question. "Is that what you want?" he finally asked.

Is that what I want?

Wasn't that a loaded question? I wanted to start over. I wanted him to be squeaky clean. I wanted to not be a cop.

Except, I didn't. Not really. I liked who I was. And—though I would admit it only to myself, and even then only in the smallest, darkest parts—I also liked who Tyler was. Would he be the same man if he'd grown up all corn-fed and innocent with a homecoming king crown on his head? I didn't think so.

But it didn't matter, because this was the end. There was nothing between us now but memories, and even those were tainted, tinged with the bloodred stain of deceit.

"I don't want anything," I said wearily. "I meant what I said last night. The only reason I came to Chicago—the only reason I did any of this—was because I want to find Amy."

He arched a brow. "Aren't you afraid I sold her to some sick fuck on the other side of the world?"

"No," I said, and though I meant it sincerely, I was cop enough to know that I couldn't entirely dismiss the possibility.

He nodded his head, and I thought I saw relief in his eyes.

"So can I have the job?" I really did want it. Not only did I hope that one of the girls would know how to contact Amy, but I also wanted to find out if Kevin and Tom were right, and the knights played in a dirty sandbox.

"I told you last night," he said. "No."

"Why the hell not?"

"Those girls have been through a lot. They don't need a cop poking around in their personal business."

"They don't need to know I'm a cop."

"And I'm not going to be the one to deceive them."

"You sure as hell didn't have a problem deceiving me."

Temper flashed in his eyes. "Don't go there. Do not even start to go there."

Frustrated, I kicked the wall hard, then again for good measure. "Dammit, Tyler—"

He held up a hand. "Enough. Neither one of us is clean on that score, so let's just drop it."

"Fine."

"But even if I was willing to keep what you are a secret, Evan and Cole wouldn't go for it."

That I knew I couldn't argue with.

"You can come in," he said. "Sit down with the girls. Ask them if they know anything. It's the best I can do, Sloane. Take it or leave it."

It wasn't good enough. It wasn't even close to good enough. But unless I could figure out a way to convince Tyler otherwise, it was going to have to be.

"Fine," I said. "I'll take it."

fourteen

"Well, at least we know that she got another job," Candy said. It was just after ten in the morning, and I'd called her as soon as I'd arrived back at my apartment. Now I was wishing I'd called from the car. The cell phone connection inside my place was terrible, and she sounded so far away, making me feel even more alone. "Vegas, huh? Just the kind of place she'd get a kick out of. I just wish she would've let me know."

"Me, too, but we both know Amy's a little bit of a flake. She's probably just working twenty-four/seven. Either that, or she's quit this new job and took off with some guy to party. She'll call. More likely, she'll just show up on your due date."

"I hope so," Candy said.

"Just chill," I said. "I'll tell you if you need to worry. And right now, there's nothing to fret about."

I told myself I should believe that too, but somehow couldn't quite manage it. For now, I was willing to believe Tyler. But that didn't change the fact that Amy had fallen off the planet right when Candy's baby was due. And that just didn't sit right with me.

Dammit, I wanted inside Destiny. I wanted to talk to the staff and the customers and see if I could figure out where Amy had gone, if for no other reason than my friend's peace of mind.

Tyler's offer to let me talk with the girls might seem generous on the surface, but it wasn't going to do me a damn bit of good. People clammed up when questioned. But when they're chatting casually, memory flows, gossip flies. Chat with someone, and you get the story. Interview them, and you get facts.

More than that, I wanted a closer look at the man who'd gotten under my skin. And I wasn't going to get that by sitting down with a bunch of girls he'd handpicked who'd tell me he was the best boss ever.

Shit.

I tried to pace the small apartment I'd rented for the op, but there wasn't even room for that. I had a whopping two hundred and fifty square feet in the up-and-coming Pilson neighborhood. The kitchen was a joke, the pullout sofa doubled as a bed, and I should demand that the unstoppable bathroom mold pay rent.

As a model of taste and style, it failed miserably. As a place to park my ass while I was working, it did the job just fine.

Currently, my ass was parked on the end of the bed, which I hadn't bothered to convert back into sofa form.

"Thanks for doing this," Candy said. "I know I shouldn't have worried, but I'm blaming it on these damn hormones. They're making me crazy. Plus, I'm the size of a whale."

I lay back on the bed, smiling. "I haven't been gone that long. You were maybe the size of an elephant when I left. That's a long way from a whale."

"Bitch," she said with a laugh, which was exactly what I was going for. "I mean it," she added when the laughter bubbled away. "It's solid of you. Taking the time, I mean."

"It's what I do."

"Yeah, well. I'm just—I'm sorry about the stuff with the guy. That's a real kick in the gut."

I shrugged, then grabbed one of the pillows and curled myself around it. "It's fucked up," I said. "I never expected them to make me as a cop."

"That's not what I meant," she said gently.

"Shit," I said, but the word was soft and without malice. I'd told her nothing but the basics—that I'd gone into the op with a plan to seduce Tyler. That the seduction part of the equation had chugged along just fine. At least I thought so until it boomeranged on me and turned out to be nothing but one big con, with me wearing the neon target sign.

What I hadn't mentioned was how intimate the seduction had become—how far I'd let him go. Hell, how far I'd wanted him to go.

And I sure as hell hadn't said anything about how deeply the truth had cut me.

I should have known Candy would dig it out anyway.

"I didn't want to get you all caught up in my personal crap," I said, though the words sounded lame.

"I'm all about the personal crap," she said. "I drag you into my personal crap all the time. That's sort of the point of the whole friendship thing, right? Celebrating the good, bitching about the bad, sharing secrets?"

I supposed it was. Not that I had oodles of experience in that regard. I hadn't had any close girlfriends growing up. For that matter, I hadn't had any close friends, period. Like Candy said, friends shared their secrets. I, however, didn't share mine.

As far as BFFs went, Candy was as close as I came. It probably qualified as pathetic that my closest friend was also my CI. Then again, when did I have time to meet people other than cops, lawyers, victims, and suspects?

Not that we had a frilly-pink girly relationship. We didn't sit around discussing men and painting our toenails—and though I'd let her glimpse a few bones here and there, she'd yet to see the skeletons in my closet. But we went out for drinks and pizza sometimes, and whenever I hit her up for street gossip we usually ended up sharing a beer on her fire escape and talking about life and television and stuff. As far as I was concerned, that must put us somewhere on the friendship spectrum.

"Sloane?" Her voice held wariness now. "You wanna talk about it?"

"There's nothing to talk about," I said.

"Fuck that."

"Jesus, Candy, what do you want me to say? I didn't realize he was playing me, and I got burned—end of story. But it's only my pride that got wounded. It's not like I'm drowning my sorrows in chocolate ice cream and writing poetic love notes to him in a pink diary. It wasn't real—how the hell could any of it have been real?"

"I'm so sorry."

It was the gentleness in her voice that undid me. "Bitch," I whispered. "You're supposed to just let me wallow."

"You really liked him, huh?"

I started to say no, then stopped myself. "I liked the man I saw—I liked him a lot. But beats the hell out of me whether that man even exists. *Shit,*" I added, as I pushed myself up and ran my fingers through my hair. "It doesn't matter anyway. I'm not looking to get involved, and even if I were, a Chicago-based criminal wouldn't be my first choice."

"No, I guess not. You know what you should do?" she asked. "Go get a pint of that chocolate ice cream."

Since friends rarely steer you wrong, I took the advice to

heart. Fifteen minutes later I was cross-legged on the floor, my back to the bed and the TV on in front of me. The pint of double chocolate chunk ice cream I'd bought at the corner market was still frozen, and I was scraping the spoon along the top, grateful for every tiny little bite I was able to chip off.

I'd turned the television on in a brutal and obvious effort to knock all thoughts of Tyler, Amy, the whole damn thing, from my head. But since the only program worth watching was *Law & Order,* I was doing a piss poor job of getting clear.

I wanted Tyler. Irrational and stupid and complicated and dangerous, but damned if I didn't want him anyway. And even though I kept trying to bury any thought of him down deep, they were as relentless as the man himself.

The shrill ring of my phone made me jump, and I wanted to kick myself, because my very first impulse was to check and see if it was him.

Apparently, I'd never left high school.

With my pulse pounding, I checked the screen. Just a number, but I knew it was him. I could feel it, and I took a deep breath to steady myself before I answered.

But it wasn't Tyler's whiskey-smooth voice I heard. It was Kevin's.

"You got a minute?"

"Actually, no." Not exactly a warm and fuzzy response, but I wasn't particularly feeling warm and fuzzy toward Kevin at the moment.

"I talked to Tom," Kevin continued, undeterred. "He said he saw you at Evan Black's engagement party. Sounds like you're making progress."

"Hard to make progress when I don't know all the facts."

"Excuse me?"

"I'm just a little irritated that you somehow forgot to mention that you were dating Angelina Raine before she went and got herself engaged to Evan Black."

"*Fuck*." The word was a sharp whisper, but it came across the phone just fine.

"Yeah, I'd say so. I don't like being used for your private vendetta."

"Dammit, Sloane, I wasn't—"

"Wasn't what? Wasn't being a lying, manipulative sack of shit? Got news for you, Kevin. You were."

"I wasn't lying. I'm not manipulative. And I'm not using you."

"Color me unconvinced."

"Look, just come meet me."

"Forget it, Kevin. I'm sorry your girl ditched you, but I'm not your personal payback bitch. You have a battle to fight? I'll let you be the one to fight it."

"Dammit, you're not—"

"Listening? No, I'm not. Goodbye, Kevin," I said, then ended the call. And although it felt good to hang up and take control, I was still antsy. Stewing. Kevin's allegations about the knights stirred in my head, getting mixed up with my thoughts about Amy, and those thoughts were doing a tango with the confused mishmash of emotions I felt simply from the mention of Tyler's name.

"Dammit," I muttered, then jammed the lid back on the ice cream.

Kevin's call had pumped my edginess up exponentially. I needed to move. Needed to clear my head. Needed to figure out how the hell I could get into Destiny—because for better or for worse, my curiosity was piqued now. Tyler Sharp had shown me the man he wanted me to see. Now I wanted the chance to peek behind the curtain.

I just needed to find a way inside.

Without even realizing it, I'd moved toward the small closet that held a hanging rod, two plastic drawers, and the water heater. My running shorts, bra, and tank dangled from a coat hanger I'd hooked to the heater. I ripped off the pajama bottoms and Dr. Who T-shirt I'd tossed on, dumping them in the top drawer. Then I pulled on my running clothes, found my last pair of clean socks, put them on, and shoved my feet into my shoes.

I pulled my hair into a high ponytail, grabbed my phone, jammed my earbuds in, and set out to run.

What I would have preferred was to go to the gym and do a few rounds with a punching bag. Or, better, with one of the other officers. Cavanaugh was always up to spar, and we were pretty evenly matched. But when I was on a tear, I could beat the shit out of her and we both knew it.

No, I wanted Lieutenant Barrone. Up against him in the ring, I didn't have time to think about anything except dodging jabs and keeping my face from getting bruised. *That would be good,* I thought. *No thinking. Just doing.*

Not an option today.

My studio perched above a Mexican bakery, and I breathed in the delicious air as I stretched in the narrow alley between my building and the next. I had my earbuds, with music from my dad blasting in my ears. Some rockabilly Texas band that represented the latest in his kick to be a naturalized Texan now that he'd moved to the Lone Star State.

I liked the beat—it was fast and rhythmic and easy to run to, and I let my mind get lost in the music and the scenery. In the passing restaurants and bakeries, apartments and markets. I'd already found a circuit, and I went slow until I reached the shopping area on Eighteenth Street, then made my way back at a quicker pace, taking a few twists and turns so that I could pass by some of the neighborhood's murals.

I saw it all, the way cops do. But I wasn't looking. I was in my head. In my music. Focusing only on the rhythm of my feet and the feel of the pavement beneath my soles until it was just me and the motion. Me and the wonderful sensation of being alive, of breathing, of working muscles and knowing that I was strong. Dammit, I *was* strong. Strong enough to not give a shit about Tyler Sharp. Strong enough to block out the pain.

Strong enough, maybe, to believe that lie.

I rounded the corner to return to my apartment, not sure if I'd accomplished anything on my run other than tiring myself out. What I needed was to convince Tyler to let me into Destiny. But damned if I could think of a way. Maybe if I was as adept at pulling a con as he was I could figure out how to beg, borrow, bribe, or steal, but as it stood, I had nothing to bargain with, no one to help me, and no way into that club.

Or did I?

I stopped dead in front of my building, forgetting all about cooling down with a slow jog. Hell, forgetting about everything except this one, slim possibility.

It just might work.

A long shot, but it was all I had at the moment—and with a fresh burst of excitement I sprinted up the stairs to my door and hoped like hell that all the pieces I needed would fall into place.

fifteen

Rihanna's "S&M" blared out of the speakers, all confidence and fire, singing about how good she was at being bad. About sex. Attraction. Excitement and heat.

And there I was, my white-gloved hands sliding provocatively up and down the steel pole, my stocking-clad leg hooked as high as I dared for fear of losing my balance, and at least high enough to show off the garter that held the stocking in place.

I'd come to Destiny armed with a plan, and now I was one of six other women who'd taken the stage during the club's Saturday night Amateur Hour. Initially, I'd been nervous that the girl at the front desk would recognize me, or that Tyler would be monitoring the feed and wouldn't let me on the stage.

Now I was nervous that he wasn't even there, and that all this would be for nothing.

When the lights had first gone up—when the first strains of

music had pulsed out—my blood had beat so loudly in my ears I was certain that all the men around my stage could hear it. I'd moved slowly at first. Tentative, maybe even a little fearful. Now I had to admit I was getting into it.

I'd been in and out of enough strip joints to know that as gentleman's clubs go, Destiny was pretty damn upscale. It had a casino-style feel, with a huge main room, a long bar, and comfy tables surrounding a number of performance stages, each with their very own pole.

There were also darker areas, where a customer could take a dancer to a comfortable chair for a lap dance or, if he was really unusual, a bit of conversation.

The overall look was classy, but at the end of the day, Destiny was like any other gentleman's club. The dancers ended up completely bare. Well, completely with the exception of a tiny G-string that served only as a repository for tips, not as any sort of attempt at modesty.

Still, unlike some clubs, the dancers didn't start out that way. At Destiny, it really was a tease. A process. A seduction.

The end result, however, was the same. And I'd begun the evening feeling more than a little twitchy.

Sapphire, one of Destiny's regular dancers who was in charge of wrangling the six of us who'd entered the amateur night contest, had given us a pre-performance pep talk. "If you're nervous, just draw out the seduction. You'll want to take it all off eventually—at least if you want a shot at the prize. But you can take your time with the stripping until you find your rhythm. Just keep it hot and sexy."

Good advice, and though it had taken some time—as in, the entire length of The Georgia Satellites' "Keep Your Hands to Yourself"—I'd finally managed to kick it up.

I might have started out wanting to forget that those men were there, but as I saw the way they looked at me, I couldn't deny that I was getting into it.

I remembered the heat I'd seen in Tyler's eyes when I'd stripped for him. The tightness in his jaw as he'd fought for control.

I drew on the memory of how much he'd wanted me—of how much I'd wanted him, of how much being on display for him, of slowly stripping off my dress, my panties, had turned me on, so that I wanted each movement to be as sensual as possible. So that each glance was filled with heat and promise.

And I remembered the way he'd touched me in front of the window. *Does it excite you, knowing that someone might be looking in? Might be across the street looking out the window?*

It had—oh, dear god, yes, it had. And I couldn't deny the thrill I got doing the same in a roomful of men. The heat and the rush of knowing they could look, but not touch. That even though I would end up naked on that stage, I was the one with the power.

It was a different kind of power than I had as a cop. Different and personal because it came from me, not from the badge and the gun.

But though there was a thrill and a power that came from knowing that these men desired me, their interest didn't have the same impact on me. I wasn't dancing for them. It wasn't these men who made me want to put on a show.

For that, I had to imagine Tyler.

Tyler, sitting in the dark.

Tyler, watching me as I slowly peeled my clothes off, and getting harder and hotter as each garment was removed.

He wasn't really there—not yet. I knew, because every few minutes I let my gaze sweep the place. And with each look, I grew more disappointed. I wanted him to see me up here. Wanted him to know that I was doing this for him as much as for the job.

So help me, the man had truly gotten to me. He'd gotten under my skin, and this was as much punishment as it was tease. Except he wasn't there to see any of it.

It frustrated me that I cared—that I wanted. That all I had to do was think of him to feel my body flush. Tyler Sharp was like a flame that heated me all the way through, making me weak. Making me melt.

I was a fool to toy with that man. He was dangerous. Distracting me, when I wasn't the kind of woman who put up with distractions. Tempting me, when I wasn't the kind of woman who was tempted.

He was everything I shouldn't want and couldn't have, and yet right then there was no denying that he was exactly what I needed. Tyler Sharp in my head, in my memories, in my imagination.

I clung tight to that fantasy, using it to fuel my moves, because I had to prove that I could do this. Had to convince him I could dance in a club like Destiny. That I could make it look real.

I'd spent the afternoon shopping, trying to imagine what Candy would say to every item I picked out. In the end, I settled on a naughty executive look, all stiff and proper, but sexy underneath. I'd come onstage in a tailored white blouse, a stern gray jacket, and a pencil skirt, its hip-high slit the only indication that there was something saucy about this buttoned-up executive.

Underneath it all, I wore a red lace bra, stockings held up by a garter belt, and a pair of flirty skirt-style panties, which probably have some formal lingerie name, but since my traditional undies run to Jockey hipsters or Maidenform lace thongs, I wasn't tuned in with the underwear vocabulary.

I'd started slow and edgy, my moves jerky. But it wasn't long before I understood the pull of the music, of the lights. They were hypnotic, taking me away to a place where there were no men staring up at me. No scantily clad waitresses serving drinks to guys who were lusting for a lap dance. No bartenders. No other dancers. Just me and the music . . . and the man in my mind.

I'd already tossed the jacket aside, and now I moved with a rise in the music, sliding my hands up my body, stroking my breasts, remembering the way his mouth had teased my nipples. The way his kisses had covered every inch of my body.

"Oh, yeah, baby!" an anonymous male voice yelled when I grabbed the shirt and pulled the halves apart, sending buttons flying. I shimmied out of the sleeves, then bent down to tease that voice with my lace and silk-clad breasts. I let the shirt I still held fall on his head, then leaned in closer so he could tuck a twenty dollar bill into my cleavage.

Not bad for a day's work, I thought as I straightened and strutted once around the stage and then returned to my pole.

I glanced toward the next stage, curious as to how much my neighbor had stripped so far. She was down to her G-string, and I realized that I was moving far too slow.

Time to step it up a notch.

The idea sent a flutter of butterflies twirling in my stomach, but the nerves were edged with excitement—and that excitement kicked up exponentially when my eyes scanned the room and I finally caught sight of Tyler.

He wore jeans and a simple black T-shirt under a gray sports coat, and even dressed so casually he put every other man to shame. He held a folio, the pages of which he peered at through dark-rimmed glasses that complemented his face and somehow made him even sexier.

He passed some sheets to Greg the bartender, then walked the length of the bar in long, arrogant strides that made it clear that he belonged there. More, that he belonged anywhere he deigned to go.

He hadn't even looked at me yet, but it didn't matter. Just his proximity fired my senses, and I felt that electricity, that spark. *Twisted up,* I thought. *He's completely twisted me up.* And, yeah, I wanted to finish this dance. For better or for worse, I wanted to finish it for him.

I continued to move with the music—continued my show for the men—but I kept my attention on Tyler. He greeted customers, chatted with the waitresses, then took a seat. The bartender slid two drinks in front of him, and I frowned when I realized the second one was for a stunning brunette who sat next to Tyler.

She smiled, all casual familiarity, as tight threads of jealousy twisted in my stomach. He leaned closer, said something in her ear. And when she laughed, then leaned forward to press her hand against his arm, I had to fight back the overwhelming urge to leap off the stage and toss the bitch back.

As if he heard my thoughts, his attention shifted, passing over the brunette and zeroing straight in on me. I was doing a shimmy with the pole, one hand provocatively stroking the steel as I slid down it, the other hand unzipping my skirt.

I saw the heat in his eyes—and even in the dim light of the club, I saw the way his body stiffened as I let the skirt fall over my hips, leaving me clad only in my silky panties, my stockings, and the racy push-up bra.

And, of course, my four-inch black fuck-me stilettos. Which were, frankly, a bitch to dance in.

I saw him stand. Saw his expression tighten. Saw him reach up to pull off his glasses and toss them carelessly on the bar.

And as I reached back and unclasped my bra, I saw him start to walk toward me.

I turned away, not wanting him to see the victory in my smile, and disguised the maneuver by doing a quick tour around the stage, strutting my stuff and making sure all those men got a nice look at what they couldn't touch. Then, with a flourish, I tossed the bra to a balding man who looked ready to drool.

Stockings next, I thought, as I slipped out of the shoes. I kicked up, resting my calf against the pole. Then I stroked my fingers up my own leg, unclipped the garter, and tugged the stocking off.

The men in the audience were holding out bills and, not being stupid, I took a little time to make a circuit around the stage and collect my tips before moving on to the next stocking.

I tried to keep my eyes on the men. To keep that eye contact that I knew dancers used to make sure the tips were stellar. But I couldn't do it. I didn't care about these men or their money. All I wanted was Tyler, but he'd disappeared. No matter where I looked, I couldn't find him or the brunette, and something hard and tight knotted in my belly.

I felt a little sick, but I kept on, moving in time to some song I didn't recognize.

I kicked up my other leg, getting ready to start the same show all over again, but as soon as I did, there he was.

I froze as a psych book full of emotions pummeled me. Relief, excitement, desire—and irritation.

"What are you doing?" I asked, as he stepped up onto the stage, to the hoots and catcalls and general grumbling of the men below.

He didn't answer, but he didn't need to. He tossed his jacket over my shoulders, grabbed me around the waist, and hauled me bodily offstage. I didn't shout and didn't fight back—I was too damn shocked. And from the silence that had settled around my stage, I think the customers felt exactly the same.

"Go," Tyler said, and it took me only a second to realize he was talking to another girl, who I recognized as one of the waitresses. Her eyes were wide, and I had a feeling that she was getting an unexpected promotion. But she scurried up the stairs and wrapped her body around the pole.

The men who'd been looking shocked in my direction turned to her, and I was all but forgotten.

"What the hell do you think you're doing?" I asked, as he held my arm in a vise grip and led me toward the back. Across the room, I saw Evan standing beside Cole, their expressions unreadable.

I drew in a breath, and hoped to hell this had worked.

I relaxed just slightly as he led me into the employees-only area. Tyler said nothing as he dragged me down the hall to his office. He shoved the door open. "In," he said, that single syllable managing to convey a whole menagerie of emotions.

I complied.

"I'm sorry," I said, when he shut the door and stalked toward me. "I wanted—"

I didn't get to finish. His hands fisted around the lapel of his jacket, and he yanked me toward him, then crushed his mouth over mine, effectively silencing me. Not to mention making me forget what the hell I was trying to say anyway.

He twirled me around, then slammed us both up against the wall in a violent, wild claiming.

The kiss burned frantic and hot and had my head spinning and my body humming, although that might have had more to do with the fact that he'd spread the jacket wide and his hands were over my breasts, touching and stroking as if he couldn't get enough of me.

I knew damn well I couldn't get enough of him.

I closed my eyes, my body melting beneath him, as my mouth claimed him, as our tongues tasted each other, teased each other.

He robbed me of thought, of reason. And as I stood there, trapped between him and the wall, I could barely remember my name, much less why I'd come to Destiny. In that moment, he was my entire world, and even as something in my mind screamed for me to get a grip, to remember that he'd conned me—that he was a criminal—all I wanted to do was lose myself forever in this moment.

And then he pulled back, leaving me gasping and, dammit, very turned on.

"I already said no," he said. "So why exactly are you dancing on one of my stages?"

I didn't trust myself to speak quite yet, so I concentrated on buttoning his jacket before lifting my head. "I came to negoti-ate," I said. "But a negotiation is only as good as the informa-tion on the table."

He moved to the small sofa where he'd fucked me, then sat down, his arm stretched along the back. "This isn't a negotia-tion," he said.

"Everything's a negotiation. You're a businessman."

"And you're a cop."

"I negotiate all the time. Plea bargains. Immunity deals." I smiled prettily as I settled myself behind his desk. "You know all about immunity deals."

He chuckled. "And there's the cop," he said. "Control. Con-fidence. Determination. It was always there, but now it's in con-text. So tell me, are you good at what you do, Detective Watson?"

"Yes. I am."

"I believe you. You were good on that stage, too," he added, with a bolus of heat seasoning his voice. "Sexy. Confident. A woman with a mission."

"I *was* on a mission. I want to dance at Destiny. And now I've proved that I can," I rushed to add when he opened his mouth to reply. "I can dance, I can satisfy the customers. I can blend. Bottom line, I can be one of these girls."

"I've no doubt that you can."

I cocked my head, wondering at his game. "Really?"

"I'm more interested in why you want to."

"I told you. I want to find Amy."

"Mmm." The sound was thoughtful, and he stood up, then moved to stand behind the chair I was sitting in. He put his hands on my shoulders, then slowly slid one down, under the material of his jacket to brush my chest.

My breath hitched as the stroke of his fingers on the swell of my breast sent fresh desire coiling through me. "There's some-thing I want you to see," he said, bending down so that his mouth brushed against my ear.

I trembled, squeezing my legs together as I imagined his hand traveling lower and lower.

But that wasn't what he had in mind. Slowly, he withdrew a card from the interior pocket of the jacket, letting it trail teasingly over my nipple before he pulled it fully out and tossed it on the desk.

He brushed a soft kiss over the top of my head, then moved to sit on the edge of the desk, his thigh right beside my hand. "Take a look."

I picked it up, saw it was a postcard from Caesar's Palace. It had a Las Vegas postmark and was addressed to someone named Darcy, care of Destiny.

D—
Couldn't say no to Vegas!
XXOO
Amy

"I talked to the girls today," he said. "Most didn't know where she'd gone, but apparently she told Darcy she'd been offered a desk job here—Chicago, I mean."

"So she changed her mind at the last minute," I guessed. "Probably a guy involved—and sent Darcy a postcard so she'd know." All in all, it seemed clear cut. Though it still bugged me that she hadn't gotten in touch with Candy, too.

"You're welcome to talk to Darcy tomorrow. She worked the lunch shift today, so she's already gone. But I don't really see the need for you to play undercover operative. Unless you're thinking about it in a bedroom role-playing capacity, in which case we can keep negotiations open."

"Funny," I said, turning the chair slightly so I could see him better. "But I still want to dance."

"Why?"

Because I wanted to learn the truth about who Tyler was and

what he did. But I didn't say that. Instead, I turned to a different truth. "Because I liked it."

"Did you?" He slid off the desk and put his hands on the arms of his chair, caging me in. He pushed it back, giving him room to kneel in front of me.

My pulse kicked up in anticipation of his touch, but all I said was, "Tyler."

"I liked the way you looked up there," he said, then moved his hands to rest them on my bare knees. "I liked the way you looked at me.

"All those men," he continued, his voice low and intimate as he gently spread my thighs, making me just a little crazy. Making me just a little wet.

"Watching you. Wanting you. And you wanted me."

"Yes. Oh, god, yes."

One hand began to gently stroke my thigh, teasing me, but moving no higher than where the hem of the jacket brushed my skin. With his other hand, he reached for the jacket, and cleverly flipped open the top button.

"That's your opening offer, isn't it?" He popped the other button open. "The deal you came to negotiate? I let you dance at Destiny, and you let me touch you?"

He used both hands now to push apart the lapels of the jacket, revealing my breasts, my abdomen, and those pretty silk panties. "Isn't that like making a deal with the devil?" he asked, as his hand trailed down, making me tremble, then over the panties to find me so very, very wet.

"Or maybe you just like playing with the bad boys," he said, as he slipped a finger deep inside me.

I arched back, gasping.

"Hook your legs over the chair's arms," he ordered.

"Tyler, no—"

"Do it."

I did, and he lowered his mouth to my sex, using one hand to pull the panties and G-string aside, and the other to tilt the chair back until it seemed like I would fall. I was head-down, completely at his mercy, open and wide and essentially helpless.

And I was desperately, hopelessly, turned on.

He ran his tongue the length of me, and I shook as a storm of sparks rocketed through me, the sensation all the more spectacular because of the way the chair rocked with my arousal.

"This won't work," Tyler said.

"No," I moaned. "Don't stop."

But he was opening the desk drawer, pulling out scissors. "I need both hands to keep the chair from toppling," he said, then cut the panties right off me before tossing the scissors onto the floor with a metallic clank.

I laughed, the sound a burst of shock and pleasure. He met my eyes, his grin mischievous and deliciously sexy. "You taste good," he said, then once again sank between my legs.

His hands stayed on the chair, so that he was touching me only with his mouth. He teased me, licking and sucking, playing and tormenting.

And with each touch, each stroke, the pressure inside me built and built.

I was open to him—wide and open and I wanted this. Wanted whatever he had to give. Wanted to lose myself in whatever pleasure he could share, whatever wicked, sensual torment he could devise.

In that moment, I think I would have done anything if only he would swear that this feeling would never stop.

Little tremors shot through me, making my body shake, the chair tremble. Precursors of an explosion that was close, so close, so close—

And then the world shattered, the chair rocking, my body clenching. I cried out for him to stop because I didn't think I could take it anymore, but he was relentless, taking everything from me, pulling every drop of pleasure out of me, taking me so high I was breathless, then crashing me back down to earth again where he scooped me into his arms.

"Wow," I murmured, finding myself curled against his chest, my body bare against his shirt, the jacket hanging open around me. "Wow."

"Very wow," he said, as he carried me across the room and laid me on the couch. "I may have to put one of those chairs in every room."

I laughed. "I wouldn't object."

"Tell me you liked that," he said, as he sat on the edge of the sofa beside me.

"Yes. God, yes."

"I knew you were a cop, Sloane. I knew you were a cop, and I fucked you. I played you. And you were so damn pissed at me."

I squinted at him, unsure about this change in direction. But his expression was still soft. Gentle.

I propped myself up on my elbow. "Yes," I said. "I was."

"Would you have preferred me to have you removed from the party? To have never touched you? Never put my tongue on your cunt, my hands on your breasts? Would you rather I'd never made you come, and never felt you explode in my arms?"

"No," I whispered, my body hot and needy.

"Or what about the waiter? Do you regret that? Sitting bold and naked and open and turned on, so desperately aroused, not because of him but because you knew that watching you made me hard?"

I wanted to lie. So help me, I did.

But I couldn't bring it to my lips. "No."

"I know it," he said simply. "I know you."

I tilted my head to him. "Tyler," I said, not even certain what I wanted, what I was asking. I simply needed the sound of his name on my lips as some sort of proof that this was real.

"Shhh." He gently pressed his fingertip to my lip. "I started out just watching you. I must have watched the damn security video a dozen times. Then at the party. I couldn't take my eyes off you, even though I knew what you were. What you are."

He stroked me gently, and I closed my eyes, rolling on a wave of pleasure so intense I thought I would surely drown in it. "By everything I know, you are not the woman I should want," he said, as he trailed his finger over the wound on my hip. "Detective Sloane Watson, with just over a week of medical leave remaining. A cop, of all things. And I find myself in the unexpected position of wanting you desperately. Of wanting to stoke this fire that rages between us, hot and wild and so very combustible."

He traced his finger along my collarbone, then over my side, along the curve of my waist, following my silhouette all the way to my hip.

"I want to burn with you, Detective. And, Sloane, you should know that I make it a point to get what I want."

He smiled at me, slow and easy and full of confidence. "So this is the deal I'm offering you. While you're on medical leave, you'll dance at Destiny, you'll have free access to the club. But during that time, you are mine."

"Yours?" I repeated.

"Completely," he said. "With everything that entails. To pleasure. To punish. To tend. I won't hurt you and I won't scare you. But I will use you," he added, as he slipped his hand between my legs and slid two fingers inside me. "For my pleasure and for yours."

I squeezed my legs around his hand, my body clenching tight, drawing him in farther.

"Agree, and you can dance at Destiny. Say no, and you walk away tonight."

"I'm at a disadvantage here. I'm naked. Your fingers are inside me."

"You're the one who took off your clothes, Sloane. That was

your move, remember? I'm only playing the game. And now it's checkmate."

He thrust deeper inside me, and as he did, he leaned forward to lightly bite my breast. I gasped in surprise, but also in pleasure.

"I know you like risk," he said, and there was seduction in his voice. "You like excitement. And, my darling detective, you like the way I make you feel."

I licked my lips. After what I'd done with him, I could hardly argue.

"You came freely to my room. You stripped when I told you to. You stood naked in a window while I touched you." His voice, low and hot, swirled around me, teasing and tempting. "And tonight, you took off your clothes in front of other men, but you thought of me."

I'd been holding his gaze, hot and hard and defiant. But at that last, I looked away. God help me, he was right. Even now, I was having to fight the way he made me feel, the way he heated me up, so that every cell in my body burned for his touch.

But the truth was, I didn't want to fight it. I liked the way he looked at me. Liked the fact that my nipples got hard when his gaze dipped to my breasts. Liked the fact that the tone of his voice could make my body weak with longing. I'd known lust before; I'd known attraction. But until Tyler, I'd never experienced this wild burning, this desperate, uncontrolled passion that left me hot and needy and alive.

I felt a bit like Pavlov's dog—one look from him, and my body was primed. One touch, and I all but exploded.

It was unfamiliar and a little unnerving. But I liked it. Christ, how I liked it.

"If I told you to go back to that chair right now, you'd do it." He spoke matter-of-factly, but I saw the challenge—and the mischief—flash in his eyes. "You'd sit in that chair and spread your legs. And if I asked you to touch yourself—to stroke and tease while I got hard watching your body grow wet and slick, so desperate to sink myself inside you that I couldn't stand it anymore—if I told you to do that, I think you would."

My mouth went dry, my body limp.

"Tell me the truth, Sloane. Would you do that for me?"

"Yes," I whispered, because I already knew he would see a lie.

"Then take the deal."

"You told me you don't date the girls who work at the club."

"I break all kinds of rules, Detective. But not in this case."

I looked at him, confused. "What do you mean?"

"I'm not going to date you. I'm going to fuck you."

A shiver ran through me, one I didn't even bother to hide. "What exactly do you have in mind for me?" I asked.

"If I told you, it wouldn't be as fun."

I licked my lips. "Before, you talked about pleasure and passion and even a little fear."

"I remember."

"Did you mean it? Or were you trying to shake me because you knew I was a cop?"

"But you are a cop. You must know all about the impact of adrenaline. Of fear. How it heightens sensation, even the sensation of pleasure."

"I don't want to be tied up—"

"No," he said, and the word was infinitely gentle. "I won't. But I will take you to that edge, Sloane. And if you are willing, I'll take you over."

Our eyes locked. I'm not sure how long I stayed lost in the clear blue of his eyes. Then he spoke, softly but firmly. "That's it. That's the arrangement. Take it—and make me a very happy man."

"Arrangement?" I repeated. "That sounds so polite and proper."

"Are you suggesting I'm neither polite nor proper?"

"Not at all," I said, then grabbed his collar and put my lips to his. "I'm saying flat out that I hope you're not." I kissed him hard, then leaned back. "When I agree to something, Mr. Sharp, I go all in."

His brow quirked up. "I'm very pleased to hear it."

He stood, then gave me his hand and helped me up. Slowly, he closed the jacket that I still wore, carefully fastening each button. Then he went to his desk and picked up his phone. "Greg, bring me Ms. Watson's shoes. I imagine they're still by Stage Four."

sixteen

Tyler went into the hall to meet Greg and, I presumed, to fetch the rest of my clothes as well.

But when he stepped back into the room, all he had were the shoes. "Let's go," he said. "Put these on and button that up."

"Um, I kind of need my clothes."

He leaned against the closed door. "No. You really don't."

I stood and buttoned the jacket, my eyes narrowed. "You're really going to make me cross through The Drake in this?"

"One, you agreed to the terms."

"I didn't realize it applied to wardrobe," I grumped, making him laugh.

"And two, we're not heading to The Drake." A touch of mischief lit his face. "Not yet."

"Oh." Fingers of dread—and, yes, of excitement and anticipation—curled through me. "Should I even ask?"

"You can," he said. "But I won't tell."

He moved back to his desk and picked up the phone again. "One more thing, Greg," he said into the handset as he tossed a ring of keys onto his desk. "Tell Cole the keys to the Ducati are in my office. I need to take the Buick tonight."

He hung up and looked at me. "I'd lent him the car," he said. "But I think you'll be more comfortable in it than on the back of my bike."

"I wouldn't mind the bike," I said, then glanced down at my outfit—or lack thereof. "But I'd need my clothes back."

"We'll have to put that on our overall to-do list." As he looked at me, I saw the flicker of something hot on his face. Then he circled the desk and moved in front of me. I stood just a bit straighter, my body once again primed for his touch, going soft and ready simply from his proximity.

Without a word, he led me to the desk, picked me up by the waist, and sat me on the surface, my legs together and my feet dangling. I held my breath, already craving his touch.

"I think I'd like burning down the highway with your arms around me," he said, as he took my thighs in each hand, then roughly spread them apart, sending sparks of anticipation shooting through me. Before I even had time to gasp, he'd tugged me closer, so I was barely on the table, and my sex was right there, open and ready for him.

"I wonder," he said, as he cupped me with his hand. I drew in a shuddering breath, arching back, still so sensitive, so ready. "Would the bike's vibration get you hot? Get you ready for me?" Slowly, he eased a finger inside me, then two, then three. I was so wet, so wanting, and my body clenched tight around him. His groan of satisfaction swept over me, and I almost melted with pleasure.

"I'm always ready for you," I whispered, then thought *God help me, it's true.*

"Look at me," he said, and once I did, I couldn't look away.

"That's how I always want you from now on," he said. "Hot and wet and always ready for me. I want you so wet from the thought of me that I can bend you over, tug your jeans down, and slide into you anytime I feel like it. I want to simply brush my hand over your cunt, and have you explode for me. I want your breasts to ache in constant anticipation of my touch. I want you so primed that I can take you over the edge with a single word. Do you understand?"

"Yes," I said, though my body was so hot—my mouth so dry—that I didn't know how I managed to form even that simple word.

"Do you want that, too?"

"Yes," I said, my response little more than a moan.

His fingers were still inside me, teasing and playing. He withdrew, then brushed the pad of his thumb over my clit and—oh, god, yes—the orgasm burst through me. A small storm this time, but enough to rattle me, to flush my skin, to make me weak with both satisfaction and the desire for more.

"You're trying to keep me unbalanced," I whispered.

I saw the flash of masculine victory in his eyes before the smile hit his lips. "Is it working?"

"Yes," I admitted.

"Don't worry. If you stumble, I'll catch you." He took a step back from the desk, then held out his hand to me. "Ready?"

I considered saying no, but it wouldn't be true. I'd stepped into Wonderland, and I wanted the whole of the adventure. "I am," I said, then took his hand and followed him through the door.

I followed him down the hall, frequently tugging down the hem on the jacket even though it was long enough on me to wear as a short dress.

He led me to the parking lot and then to a classic red convertible. My dad would know the year and the make, but all I knew was that it was as big as a boat and as stylish as the day it came off the line. It had a mix of soft curves and hard angles, giving it a totally retro look that I loved. "Wow," I said.

"Yeah. She's a beauty." He opened the door for me, and I slid onto the bench seat, the leather warm on the back of my thighs.

"Nice," I said, as he settled himself behind the wheel.

"Nineteen-sixty-three Buick LeSabre," he said. "I fixed her up myself, although to be fair, she was in decent condition when I bought her. And," he added, as he peeled out of the lot, "she drives like a dream."

He proceeded to prove that point by opening her up once we hit the highway, so that I was squealing in surprise and delight as my hair went flying in the warm night air.

"Nice," I said. "And although it's got less of a vibration thing going than your motorcycle, I think we could make this bench seat work for us." I gave the red and white leather seat a pat.

He took his eyes off the road long enough to glance at the seat—and then at me. "Interesting information. And good to know. Especially considering where we're going."

"Oh." I waited a beat. "And where are we going again?"

"Nice try. But you'll just have to wait and see." He gave the seat a pat of his own. "You know the nice thing about bench seats? You can slide right over and get cozy."

"Is that an invitation or an order?"

"Take your pick," he said. "Whichever one gets you here faster."

I grinned and slid closer. He kept his left hand on the steering wheel, but his right went to my thigh—high enough to keep my blood pumping and my body primed, but not enough to touch. All of which effectively drove me a little bit crazy.

"I'm practically naked," I said. "I think you could take a little bit more advantage of the situation."

"Is that what you think?"

"Or maybe you're just not as clever and resourceful as I'd thought. Or maybe I've just worn you out already. Stamina," I said with a sad shake of my head. "Some men just don't have it."

"Careful, or I may have to spank you."

"You teased me with that possibility before," I said, squirming a little at the thought. Would it hurt? Would I like it? "So far you haven't made good on the threat. So tell me, Mr. Sharp. How does a girl have to misbehave to be punished by you?"

"Oh, we'll figure something out," he promised.

"Really? I'll have to remember to misbehave."

"Don't worry," he said wryly. "I'll remind you."

Ten minutes later, we'd arrived at a redbrick building that, as far as I could tell, had no windows and no signs.

There was, however, an intercom by the set of double steel doors, and when Tyler gave a membership number, the lock released.

The doors opened into an alcove that reminded me of the entry to Destiny. A woman in a black latex bodysuit smiled at Tyler. "Welcome back."

"Thank you, Tricia. This is my guest, Ms. Watson. If you could take her coat? And I was hoping I could use one of the collars."

"Sure," Tricia said, then winked at me. "Lucky you," she said, but I barely heard her through the Klaxons ringing in my suddenly fuzzy brain.

"Collar?" I said to Tyler, as the girl disappeared through a door in the back. "You said 'collar'? For me? And what exactly do you expect me to do once she takes my coat?"

"I'll expect you to follow me," he said, then smiled, slow and easy and seductive. "You recall our arrangement, don't you? You're mine, remember? You know what I want from you."

"A collar," I repeated, as my gut twisted with nerves. But even as it did, I couldn't deny the prickles of heat building be-

tween my thighs, or the way my now erect nipples rubbed provocatively against the silk lining of the jacket.

A collar.

And nothing else.

Oh, my fucking god.

I let it all sink in. We were in a dungeon, a playroom, a
BDSM parlor, whatever you wanted to call it. He wanted to take
me inside, and I didn't have even a clue what he intended to do
in there.

I was nervous. Hell, I was terrified.

But I was also wildly turned on.

"Yes," Tyler said, as he watched my face. "I think we're
going to have a very good time."

Tricia came back and handed him a black leather collar with
a single silver ring onto which was attached a leash.

Tyler took it, then crooked a finger, beckoning me forward.
I went, tentative, then held my breath as he brought the collar to
my neck.

"Wait," I said, then paused until he was looking me in the
eye. "Just for here, right?"

He brushed a gentle kiss over my lips. "Just for here."

He hooked the collar behind my neck, loose enough that
breathing was comfortable, but still tight enough to stay in
place. "The jacket," he said. "Give it to Tricia."

I considered arguing, but I knew I wouldn't win. And though
I'd teased in the car about misbehaving, at the moment, I really
didn't want to test the spanking waters.

I shrugged out of the jacket, folded it, laid it on the counter
in front of the girl. Her eyes skimmed over me, then she turned
to Tyler. "Lovely. Do you share?"

"Not tonight," he said, leaving me wondering what might
happen on some other night. "I want the circle. Unless it's not
available."

"Nope, you're good," she said, then pressed a button that caused another set of doors in front of us to swing inward. "Have fun."

"With me," Tyler said, and tugged gently on the leash, leading me down a dim hallway lit only with sporadically placed candles. After a few twists and turns, I started to see alcoves off the hall, some with plush furniture like a Victorian sitting room, some with much more interesting paraphernalia like sex swings and latex beds and tables crisscrossed with leather straps.

In one of the more plush rooms I saw a tall brunette dressed in black leather gently stroking the cheek of a petite blond woman with the end of a riding crop. We passed quickly, but I knew where I'd seen her before. Destiny. She was the woman who'd been with him at the bar.

"This place," I said to Tyler, tamping down an unwelcome rush of jealousy. "Do you come here a lot?"

"I don't, no."

I frowned, something in his voice sparking my curiosity.

"We just passed a woman," I said. "I saw her earlier. At Destiny." I hesitated, then added, "You were talking with her."

"That's Michelle," he said, and the name rang in my memory.

"Michelle." I remembered the note on his computer and the conversation in his office. "Wait. Isn't she Cole's girlfriend?"

He stopped, then turned to me with a questioning expression. "You were in the hall," he said, remembering.

"She's his girlfriend, right?" *I'm fucking her,* Cole had said.

"No," he said, with a touch of amusement in his voice. "Cole doesn't date."

"Oh." I considered where we were and what that meant. Cole didn't date, so what exactly did he do? "So, um, is Cole here now, too?"

"He's not." Tyler lifted a brow. "Do you want me to call him?"

"God no!" I had no issues with whatever arrangement he had with Michelle, but I really wasn't keen on him seeing me naked. Or, at least, with seeing me naked when I wasn't dancing on a stage.

"Good," he said, then started walking again.

We soon reached the end of the hallway, and I found myself looking into a cavernous room dotted with several distinct areas. Most were shadowed, though some were more well lit. Some were occupied by only one or two people, and some seemed to have gathered a crowd. In one, a woman was on her knees, sucking the cock of a leather-clad man who stood in front of her. In another, a woman stood nude, her wrists bound and her arms stretched high above her, held fast by a chain. Another woman was lashing her with a flail, breasts, belly, sex, as the bound woman cried out in pleasure for her mistress to please let her come.

I was looking at scenes, I knew. Sexual play that ran the gamut from simple to hard-core. And I had no idea where Tyler intended us to fall on the scale. I wasn't certain if I was terrified or excited, but I did know that Tyler wouldn't push too far. On that point at least, I trusted him completely.

I started to ask Tyler what he had in mind for me, but decided to keep my mouth shut. He'd be expecting the question, after all.

A giant metal circle mounted on a dais stood against one of the walls. It was lit from above by a soft glowing light. There was a table near the circle that had a variety of thin leather strips. Otherwise, there was nothing.

"I liked watching you dance tonight." Tyler spoke softly as he took my hand and led me up the dais to the circle. "I liked watching you enjoy it." He took my hand and put it on the circle's rim.

"Tyler." His name was a protest. Yes, I'd walked naked to this room. But now, to be standing so boldly . . .

"It's okay," he said, then brushed a kiss over my lips. "Do this, Sloane," he said, and I knew that my choice was simple—stay with him or break our arrangement and go.

I stayed. I wanted our deal—wanted him. And I would do a lot more than stand naked in a circle of light if that's what it took to stay in Tyler's bed.

"Good girl," he said. He took my opposite hand and put it on the circle as well, so that my body formed a Y within the circle. "I even liked the other men watching you, wanting you. Do you know why I liked that?"

I shook my head.

"Because I like owning what other people covet. And those men tonight, they coveted you." He tapped my legs, indicating that he wanted me to spread them.

I licked my lips and sucked in a breath for courage, and complied.

"What I didn't like was that those men at the club didn't know you were mine. Here, anyone who walks by knows."

The circle was bathed in light, and beyond it, I could see only shadows. But there were people in those shadows, I knew, and I imagined them coming over, looking at me, wanting me. I turned my head away, not because I was ashamed to be up there, but because I was aroused. Despite his words, despite being on display, all I wanted right then was to lose myself in Tyler's touch.

Despite? I scoffed at myself. *You're turned on because of it. Because of Tyler. Because of who he is and where he takes you.*

And it was true. So help me, it was true. I'd been aroused from the moment I met him.

"Here, I can touch you." Tyler moved behind me, his voice smooth and seductive. "I can stroke you. I can fuck you. I can claim you completely. Do you want me to?"

"Yes," I whispered.

"So do I. But not now. Not here."

I twisted my head, trying futilely to see him.

"I'm going to make you come, Sloane," he said. "I'm going to get hard watching you. Watching your nipples tighten. Watching your cunt grow slick and wet. I'm going to watch you lose yourself to pleasure, sweetheart, and I'm going to know that I'm the one who pushed you over the edge."

"Yes," I pleaded, as I closed my eyes. "Touch me. Please touch me."

"I am," he said, though it was only his voice that caressed me. "Can you feel my lips on your ear, trailing down your neck? Can you imagine my mouth closing over your breast? Can you feel me teasing your nipple with my teeth?"

My nipples tightened as I imagined him touching me, sucking me.

"You can," he said, still behind me, his breath the only thing that was actually touching me. "I can see how much it's turning you on.

"I'm caressing your belly now, my hands sliding down your abdomen, my lips and tongue tasting you as your skin quivers with each touch."

I shuddered, tightening my hands on the metal circle out of fear that I would take them off and touch myself in desperation. I felt everything he described, as if his words were a caress sending trails of fire down my body.

"I'm moving lower now, using my hands and lips to brush ever so softly over your hip, your thigh. I can see how wet you are. How open. I press my mouth to your sex and blow, just slightly, so that my breath teases your sex, cools your heat. Do you feel it?"

I nodded.

"I know you do—I can see it. The way your lips are parted. The way your pulse is beating more quickly. There's a flush on your skin—you're aroused, your body tight, your cunt aching with desire, your skin begging for my touch."

"Yes, god, yes."

"I'm touching you now," he said. "My fingers sliding over you, feeling how slick you are. I'm teasing your clit—stroking and teasing you, then sliding my fingers deep inside you. Can you feel me, baby? Can you feel me inside you, your body tight around me as if you don't want to let me go?"

I made a sound. That was the best that I could do.

"You're so close now. It's building, growing in you. Pleasure, need, like steam under pressure you're so close to exploding, and I'm right there, touching you, relentless, taking you closer and closer."

"Yes," I said, my body on fire, like a mirror of his words, I was there, I was closer, I could feel every word, every syllable, every whisper of sound as sweetly as if his hands were on me.

"I can see it, Sloane. I can see how close you are. I'm hard, baby, so damn hard, and it's all because of you. They're here, too. Watching you. Watching us. Wanting you, but you're mine, Sloane. You're all mine."

"Yours," I whispered. I tried not to think about the eyes in the dark, afraid that if I did the embarrassment would push aside this feeling, this rising, spiraling pleasure. But I couldn't keep them out—couldn't block the thought that I was his, and that they knew it and watched and wanted.

And thinking that, another tremor ran through me. An undulating wave, like a new layer of pleasure.

"That's right, baby," he said, knowing me as intimately as I knew myself. "They're out there, Sloane, in the shadows. They see the way your body flushes, the way your nipples go dark and tight. They can see how wet you are, how much you want this, how close you are. They look at you and see beauty, Sloane. And you like that they are looking. Like that they want you, but can't have you. Like that you're safe here with me, teasing them even while you know that I'm the only one who can have you."

"Yes. Yes," I said, because it was true. I'd never known it before, but it was so damn true.

"You're already wet, you're already trembling. You're so close now, baby. Imagine me kneeling in front of you. Can you feel my tongue on your clit? My finger teasing your ass. Your body is clenching, desperate for me, wanting me, and I'm sucking and licking, lapping up the sweet taste of you as it builds inside you. As you go up and up, tighter and tighter."

I moaned in time with his words, because I did imagine it, and he was bringing me closer. I was lost, battered, and as I opened my eyes—as I saw him looking at me, his face bathed in light and longing—I lost my hold on reality, and went spiraling out, over the shadows in the distance, beyond the warehouse, and into the night until finally, sweetly, drifting back to earth and into the arms of this man who'd touched me so deeply without even touching me.

"You're amazing," he said as he held me on the dais, stroking my skin, pressing light kisses to my temple, my hair.

The others were gone; there were no more shadows past the light, and I curled into him, feeling almost as if the whole thing was a dream. But it wasn't. It was real. Tyler was real. And what I felt was very, very real.

"How did you know? How did you know I would like it that much?"

"I look at you," he said. "Somehow, I can't seem to look away. And I see you."

He helped me to my feet. "Time to go," he said, and led me back toward the entrance and then out the door to the world.

"Look at you," he said, once we were back in the car. "Fire and beauty, and mine to control."

"I feel wonderful," I admitted. I turned to him and flashed a wicked grin. "I'm glad you cheated, you know."

Surprise flickered in his eyes. "Cheated? What are you talking about?"

"This arrangement. It was a con." I licked my lips and tilted my head as I examined him, this incredible, sensual, enigmatic man. "That's twice now. Our first night when you pretended not to know I was a cop, and now this. I'm right, aren't I?"

He'd started to back the car out, but now he tapped the brake. "What makes you say that?"

"Because you'd already planned to let me dance at Destiny. I didn't have to agree to your deal to get in."

"Is that so? How do you figure?"

"You didn't ask Evan or Cole. That tells me you'd already talked to them."

He met my eyes, held them as if considering something. Then he nodded. "Well done, Detective. If you hadn't shown up at Destiny tonight, I would have gone to you tomorrow."

"But you were so adamant back in the penthouse. Why the change of heart?"

"First of all, we don't have a thing to hide at Destiny, so it's not really an inconvenience having you inside."

"At Destiny," I repeated.

"Second," Tyler said, as if I hadn't even spoken, "it occurred to me that I have a few social obligations coming up where it will be handy to have a woman on my arm. And even handier if that woman is a cop."

"Oh, really? Like what?"

"Like you'll find out tomorrow night. Did you bring an evening gown to Chicago?"

"Sure," I said. "I packed it with the diamonds and furs."

"We'll shop tomorrow." His mouth curved up in a slow, lazy smile. "That may be the highlight of my day. At any rate, those were my practical reasons."

"And the impractical ones?"

"Mostly, Detective, I just want to fuck you. When I want, how I want, and where I want."

"I see."

"Sore loser, Detective?"

I regarded him for a moment, then slid across the bench and put the car in park. Then, before he could react, I took his face in my hands and claimed his mouth with my own in a long, deep, sensual kiss.

When I pulled back, he stared at me, and I almost laughed at the pleased surprise I saw in those brilliant eyes.

"I'm not a sore loser at all," I said. "And if we're playing this game, I'm damn well going to enjoy it."

seventeen

I was expecting to go straight back to The Drake, but Tyler surprised me by pulling up in front of a bright yellow building with a red and white awning.

"Hungry?"

"Ravenous," I said, then smiled. "You helped me work up quite an appetite."

"I'll remember to restock the fridge. In the meantime, Jim's will do just fine."

I peered out the window. It was right around midnight and the place was hopping. "Doesn't look like fine dining to me."

"That depends on your definition of 'fine,' " he said. "Amazing hotdogs twenty-four hours a day. You've never been before?"

I shook my head, my mouth already watering. "French fries?"

"Even cheese fries, if you want them."

"You do know how to seduce a lady."

He brushed a quick kiss over my lips before sliding out. When he returned, he handed me a bag with six hotdogs, along with French fries, cheese fries, and two Diet Cokes. "What?" he asked when he saw my amused expression.

"Hotdogs in The Drake hotel," I said. "Talk about a contrast."

"Ah, but we're not going to The Drake."

"Where are we going?" I asked warily. "Because, hello?" I gestured to the jacket of his I still wore. A jacket under which I wore no panties. Or anything else. "Not exactly up to most dress codes."

"An interesting point," he agreed. "Probably wouldn't matter, but better to be safe." He nodded toward the backseat. "Check my gym bag. Should be a T-shirt and sweatpants in there."

I gaped at him. "Unless they belong to your petite lover—in which case, we're going to have another problem—any clothes I find in that bag will swallow me."

"The T-shirt will cover you," he said. "And the pants have a drawstring. Don't worry. There won't be any fashion police around. We're going on a picnic."

"A picnic?"

"It seems like a good night for it," he said. "There's a full moon, after all. Go on. Change."

"What the hell?" I laughed and turned to rummage for his gym bag, then dragged it back into the front with me.

As he'd said, I found a black T-shirt with the Destiny logo and a pair of plain, gray athletic pants. I put the pants on first, then tied them as tight as possible. Even then, I had to roll the waist over a couple of times, and then do the same to the legs, so that I wouldn't trip when we walked.

"I don't have shoes," I pointed out.

"More's the adventure," he said, and I rolled my eyes.

I shrugged out of his jacket, then raised an eyebrow when I saw Tyler paying more attention to me than the road.

He focused on driving as I tugged his T-shirt on over my head, breathing deep his familiar, woody scent.

"Just for the record," he said, casting a sideways glance in my direction as he broke the silence. "I haven't had a lover in a very long time. A lot of women I've fucked, but no lovers." He turned his head and held my eyes. "In case you were curious."

"Oh. Okay." I glanced down at the bags of food at my feet, and realized that I couldn't quite suppress the smile that was blooming.

I cleared my throat. "So, you do pick some interesting surprises. First the, um, place," I said, and had him chuckling. "Now hotdogs. I haven't had a picnic with hotdogs since I helped my dad move to Texas a few years ago."

"They're big on hotdogs in the Lone Star State?"

"Probably," I said. "But Daddy moved to Galveston—it's an island. And there was a festival with a bonfire. So hotdogs and marshmallows were the thing. It was fun. The kind of stuff we used to do all the time, but now . . ." I trailed off with a shrug.

"Texas is a long way from home," he said.

"Yeah." I flashed a quick smile. "Sorry. A brief moment of melancholy. I miss him."

"Your mom not big on hotdogs?"

"My mom died a few years ago." The words hung flat, and I turned to look out the window. I really didn't need her in my head. Not right now.

He reached over and gently took my hand. "No one else?"

I thought about it, but there really wasn't. I loved my partner, Hernandez, but picnicking with him and his wife wasn't exactly the same. And Candy would rather scrub toilets than sit outside if she wasn't in an amphitheater with a hot band playing onstage.

"I guess not," I said, turning to look at him. "Tough break, huh? No one to picnic with."

He took his eyes off the road long enough to meet mine. "There's someone now," he said, making my heart melt just a little.

We rode in silence, through the darkened city dotted with lights, until he finally pulled over near the intersection of Michigan Avenue and Roosevelt, then killed the engine.

"Can you park here?" I asked, but he only grinned.

"Let's walk," he said.

I recognized Michigan Avenue and I knew we were near the museum campus, so I assumed this was Grant Park. But it wasn't anyplace I'd been before, and I squinted at the odd shapes that rose up in the distance as we crossed over the grass.

"All right," I finally said as the forms became clearer in the moonlight. "Why are we walking toward a crowd of headless men?"

"I'm not entirely sure they are men," Tyler said. "They're the *Agora*. You haven't seen them before?"

"Indiana, remember? I've been to Chicago a few times, but mostly for work. Once for tea at the Palm Court with my dad for my sixteenth birthday. A few times to the museums. Other than that, no tourist stuff."

"One hundred and six headless and armless men," Tyler said. "The city brought them here just shy of a decade ago."

I cocked my head to look at them. They were interesting, I thought. Interesting, and maybe a little scary, what with the moonlight and their height and the shadows.

I shivered, and focused on Tyler rather than the creatures.

"So you would have been, what? Twenty?"

"Not quite," he said, reminding me how close we were in age. And making me remember how young he was to have already acquired so much. "I used to come here at night with Cole and Evan."

"Okay." I frowned. "Why?"

"One, it's a little spooky in the dark, which we thought was fun."

"On the spooky, we're in total agreement. And?"

"And something about the statues drew us, I think. Kind of summed up our view of the world—most people aren't thinking. They're not using their heads. They're not *doing*, thus the lack of arms. And that means that those of us who do think, who do act, can make our way through the world while the rest stumble along."

I'd stopped walking to look at him. "I'm not sure if that's cynical, astute, or simply the mind-set of a man who'd easily slide into a shady kind of lifestyle."

"I'm a pillar of the community, Detective," he said with a broad, charming grin. "If you've heard otherwise, you've been talking to the wrong people."

"Maybe so," I agreed, because that was a subject best left alone. "So is that what the artist actually meant?"

"I don't know. Cole might—art's his thing. But I never wanted to find out. As far as I'm concerned, art is what you make of it. How it reflects back on you."

I considered his words. "Doesn't that make the artist irrelevant?"

"I don't think so. I think it makes him a mirror. It's one of the reasons art is often spoken of in the same tone and with the same vocabulary as music or poetry or love. Or even sex."

"What do you mean?"

"Passion, Sloane," he said, and there was a heat to his voice now that hadn't been there before. "There's no way to experience it without discovering something about yourself, too."

"Oh." It was the only word I could safely manage, because his words had impacted me more than I had anticipated. Had cut through me with their unexpected truth.

"Walk with me," he said. He took my hand, still swinging our picnic bag from his other.

"This isn't what I expected," I admitted, when I'd gathered myself back together. "Philosophy, genteel conversation, and a picnic in the park. Not what I thought you had in mind after our, well . . ."

He chuckled. "Yes?"

"Our sex-a-thon," I said with a saucy grin, and turned his chuckle into a full-blown laugh.

"Disappointed?"

"In the hotdogs? Hell no." As if to prove the point, I reached into one of the bags and helped myself to some cheese fries. "In spending time with you? No." I aimed a glance at him. "These are great, by the way. But that doesn't mean I couldn't handle more of the sex-a-thon part."

"I do admire a woman who knows her own mind." The roughness in his voice sounded like a promise. And in the moonlight, his face was all shadows and angles, making him look even more sexy. Even more dangerous.

"I'm very glad you're enjoying our arrangement so far," he continued. "I'd hate to think you were disappointed."

"You know I'm not," I said. I paused as I gathered my thoughts. "I don't know what you've done to me, Tyler Sharp. Sometimes it feels like you've turned me inside out."

"All I've done is looked at you." His low voice sent shivers through me. "And gone after what I've seen."

"Don't get me wrong, I've never been a prude or a wallflower. But until you . . ."

"What?"

"Sex was just scratching an itch. A very nice, satisfying scratch, but still just an itch."

"And with me?" He trailed his fingers up my arm. "What is it with me?"

"Exciting," I said, and saw the pleasure bloom on his face.

"And you do like an adventure."

"Yeah," I said, thinking about the night. "I guess I do." I liked him, too. And more than just for sex. He felt like he fit, and the feeling was somehow both scary and very, very sweet.

He hooked an arm around my waist and pulled me close. "But that's not too much of a discovery for you, is it? No one becomes a cop for the paperwork."

"Excitement in the field isn't the same as excitement in bed."

"Point taken. I know how I got you in my bed. How did you get in the field?"

I cocked my head, not understanding.

"I mean, Detective, why did you become a cop? And don't just tell me you wanted to serve truth, justice, and the American way. I want the deeper reason."

"It's in my blood," I said, giving him a true answer, though not the real one. "My dad's been in law enforcement since he got out of high school—me, too," I added.

"All right. I'll buy that. But what else?"

"What makes you think there's something else?"

"I don't think," he said. "I know."

"Oh?"

He held me close as he looked at me, his hand sliding beneath his T-shirt to stroke my back. "I know how to see into people, Sloane. It's a skill I learned a long time ago. How to know when they're telling the truth. When they're lying. When they truly care about something, or when they're just faking it. It's an art, reading people, and it's one I'm especially skilled at. One that's paid off for me over and over. And when I say that someone is holding back on me, I promise you can take it as gospel."

"Those sound like the kind of skills a grifter would develop. A con artist. A swindler."

"Or a businessman who wants to read his competitors. To

judge their offers and have an edge in negotiations." The corner of his mouth twitched. "Or are you saying that all businessmen are swindlers?"

"I'm saying that you're very good at what you do. Whatever you do."

"I'm flattered. And I'm still curious." He pulled away from me, making me feel cold and suddenly alone, then took my hand as we continued walking through the park.

"What are you not telling me? Please," he added gently. "I would really like to know."

I drew in a breath. The truth was, I wanted to tell him. Yes, I knew that I would have to walk away from this man eventually. And yes, I knew that it would be all the harder if I shared my secrets, my fears, my emotions.

But it didn't matter. It wasn't a question of smart, but a question of heart. And I wanted Tyler to see into mine.

"Have you heard of Harvey Grier?"

It took him a moment, and then he nodded slowly. "I think so. Baseball player, right? Found shot right as his career was really taking off."

"He was my stepfather."

"I see." Two simple words, and yet they suggested so much. And I both feared and hoped that he really did see. "Did they ever find who killed him?"

"No," I said. "No, they didn't."

"He beat you," Tyler said softly, and I saw understanding bloom in his face. "Tied you up and beat you."

I looked away, not ready to see the pity in his eyes. "No, not me. My mother. Well, he tied us both up," I explained, my voice flat. "But he never beat me. He just made me watch. He said my time was coming."

"You must be very glad he's dead." Tyler's voice was low and hard. "If I'd known you then, I would have killed him myself."

I drew in a breath, thinking that was the most perfect thing anyone had ever said to me. And also thinking that I couldn't say those words aloud. Not and continue to be the person I thought I was. The cop I thought I'd become.

"I am glad," I said instead. "But he's dead because the system messed up. I tried to get that bastard arrested, but the cops were too starry-eyed." I dropped down to the grass and stretched out my legs. "I would have kept trying, but someone blew him away first."

"So you became a cop to fix the system."

"I became a cop because I believe in the system. Harvey Grier should be spending a long life rotting in jail. Dead, and it's just over."

He joined me on the ground, his hand on my thigh. As always with Tyler's touch, I felt the heat of connection. But this time it was warm and calm and gentle. "I'm sorry," he said. "I'm sorry you had to live through that."

"But I did live through it," I said. "So I guess that's a win."

"What about your mom? She must have been relieved to be free of that asshole."

"Yeah," I said. "I would have thought so. But she shut herself off. Closed herself up. And—" I shook my head. "She just sort of checked out of herself. Just drifted. Never really settled." I licked my lips. "And then she died. Two years ago. Cancer."

"I'm sorry."

"Me, too. I thought—I thought that once he was gone she would have been happy, you know? Alive again. But she never was."

I ran my fingers through my hair and turned away, not wanting to see his face through the red curtain of my memories. "Sometimes I think that if they'd arrested him instead, if there had been a trial, she would have been able to deal with it. They'd have gotten her counseling for the abuse, right? As it was, she was just a minor celebrity's widow. She never told anyone about the abuse, and no one helped her. I tried, but I was still just a kid. If the system had worked the way it was supposed to, then maybe she—"

I cut myself off, biting my lower lip. "She was a good woman. Fragile, but good. She didn't know how to get herself out of a bad situation, and she did everything she could to protect me from him. But after I—after he was killed, she rolled into herself. I lost her."

He tucked a finger under my chin and turned my head to face him. "I've never seen you in action, but I've asked enough questions to know that you're a good cop. So you have to know that the system isn't perfect. It isn't even close."

"It evens out," I said. "Justice finds a way."

"Does it?"

I smiled. "That's what my dad always says. And my dad is a very smart man." I drew in a breath and ran my thumb under my eye, catching an escaping tear. "Sorry." I managed a teasing smile. "I guess your motto is the opposite? 'Screw justice'?"

As I'd hoped, he laughed. "There you go, assuming things about me."

"Is that what I'm doing? Maybe I want to know how you started down the dark path. Come on, Mr. Sharp. I've revealed all. Why don't you tell me why you became a criminal."

"Such a loaded question, Detective. What makes you think I am?"

"Because I'm not an idiot," I said.

"Cute, but I'm serious." He leaned forward. "I admit I like to live dangerously. I love the thrill of acquiring something through my wits. Isn't that the defining core of every successful businessman? But what crimes have I committed? What evidence do you have?"

"Never mind. Just drop it."

"No," he said. "I want to know."

I sighed. I wanted to know, too. But I couldn't deny that I feared his answer. Even so, I pressed on. "Evidence, no. But there's a lot of talk about you and your friends. A lot of specula-tion."

"Sticks and stones," he said.

"Dammit, it's a conversation. I'm not wearing a wire. I'm not even a Chicago cop. And I'm sure as hell not playing a game. Christ, Tyler, I'm—"

I'm falling for you.

I blinked, shocked by the intensity of the thought. And I didn't look at him. Instead, I looked everywhere but.

"I'm—I like you," I finally said. "I like *us*. But I don't even know you."

"What if I told you I was squeaky clean?" His voice was so very gentle, and in that moment I feared that he'd heard past the words to the truth in my voice. "What if I said that everything you fear is in the past?"

I turned now to look at him, and those stormy blue eyes were clear and warm. "That would be nice," I admitted, realizing as I said it how much I wished it was true.

I tried for a smile. "Will you tell me about your past, then? How you met Evan and Cole? The misadventures of your youth? You told me once your childhood should have been idyllic. What went wrong?"

He raked his fingers through his hair, then stood up and glanced around the moonlit park. He reached a hand down for me. I took it and let him help me to my feet, and fell in step be-side him. I assumed we were done, that he was keeping his child-hood secrets locked away, and I told myself that was good.

I didn't have a future with Tyler. Despite his protests—or maybe because of them—I knew damn well he was dirty. But for these last few days of my medical leave, I could ignore that. Pretend it wasn't true. Tell myself I was taking a vacation from myself and sliding into adventure.

I didn't need to know his secrets, didn't need to see his heart.

After all, I'd already given him too much of mine.

We'd been walking in silence for at least fifteen minutes when he said, softly and simply, "My parents live in Florida now. We don't really talk. We've never really talked."

"I'm sorry."

"Yeah. Well." We'd reached a hill atop which there was a statue of a man on a horse. The moon shone down around us, illuminating the area. It was late, probably after three, and right then it felt like we were the only two people on earth.

I sat on the side of the hill, then laid back in the cool, damp grass. Above me, Tyler smiled down, and I held up a hand. "Join me."

He did, stretching out beside me and taking my hand, and when he spoke, it was as much to the stars as to me. "I grew up in Rogers Park," he said. "Up north where Lake Shore Drive turns into Sheridan Road. Near the lake. On the Red Line. Solid middle class. Decent house. Decent neighbors. My dad managed a gas station. My mom stayed at home."

"Sounds nice."

He made a sound that might have been a snort.

"She drank. He gambled. Not just at cards or in weekend jaunts to Vegas, but in everything. Any get rich quick scheme you could think of. And he was damn stupid at it. Never once got on top of it, not that I could see. And I saw a lot."

"He talked to you about it?"

"Hell no. Neither one of them talked to me at all. The three of us lived in that house, and it was like we were three strangers. When I was very young, I'd make up stories as to why. I thought maybe I had an older brother who'd been kidnapped, and they were so lost in their grief they couldn't see me. Or that they weren't my parents at all. My parents were actually spies, and they'd send for me as soon as they were safe. Then I quit making up the stories and just figured it was me."

"Tyler, no," I said, my heart breaking for the little boy he used to be.

"No," he agreed. "I realized soon enough it wasn't me. It was them. My parents were—are—two broken people. And they didn't give a shit if they broke me, too."

"I'm so sorry."

"They paid the bills, kept the roof over our heads. But there was never dinner—I lived on cold cereal and scrambled eggs. And there was never conversation."

"Jesus," I said, though I'm not sure I spoke aloud.

"I started doing stupid shit to get their attention, but they never noticed. So I ramped it up. Stole a car when I was thirteen. Started breaking into people's houses when I was fourteen—used to steal leftovers, so that was a plus, and about the only way I got a decent meal. Stole a car when I was fifteen. Smashed it. Got arrested. My dad bailed me out, and I didn't even get grounded. Just told me to get my shit together and not be a stupid fuck." He glanced at me, his expression dry. "That's an exact quote, by the way."

"What did you do?"

"Needless to say, I didn't follow dear old Dad's advice. I did not get my shit together. On the contrary, I think it's safe to say I spiraled down. I started dealing drugs—stupid, but the money was good, and money bought me freedom and food."

"You didn't stay in drugs," I said, my voice tight. God, don't let him be dealing drugs; I'd seen the effects, and that was something I knew I couldn't deal with on any level.

"No." The word was fast and harsh. "I knew from the moment I got involved that it was all wrong. But this group of kids at my school—I clung to them because I wanted a family. Needed, even. And I went along."

He stood up, obviously needing to move, then ran his fingers through his hair. "Anyway, I had a girlfriend. Amanda. High school sweetheart, you know. Smart, pretty, sweet as she could be, and totally clean. When she learned what I was doing, she said I had to get out. That if I didn't, she was going to call the cops."

"Did she?" I asked, propping myself up on my elbows.

He cocked his head. "I told her not to. That she needed to trust me. I had a way out, but I needed to go through with a deal we had set up. We'd scored over a pound of coke at a bargain price, and we'd arranged a sale to some kids from the South Side—stupid—and if we didn't go through with it, my buddies and I knew damn well they'd hurt us. Or worse."

"Go on."

"So we went to the meet." He closed his eyes and drew in a breath. "And Amanda showed up—god*damn* her." His voice hardened with emotion and memory. "She showed up, told me to just walk away, but I couldn't, of course. She was living in some fantasy that these gangbangers would just let us go. So I stayed—and she stayed—and then—"

He clenched his fist, then punched it hard into the air. "And then the cops came and it turned into a clusterfuck. Someone pulled a gun, and then there were shots fired and I looked over, and she was on the ground, her white blouse stained with blood. She was dead before I got to her."

He closed his eyes, the pain of the memory almost palpable.

When he opened his eyes, they were full of anger and grief. "She was shot and she died and *goddammit,* if she'd just trusted me and not betrayed me to the cops, she would still be alive. Probably have a boring husband and three kids, but she'd be alive."

"It wasn't your fault," I said gently, because that is what you say when someone is grieving.

His eyes were flat when he looked at me. "You know better than that. I didn't have a gun, didn't pull the trigger, but the law says it was my fault. And the law is right."

"Felony murder," I said under my breath, referencing the

legal theory that holds culpable all participants in the crime. "I'm so sorry."

"So am I," he said. He tilted his head back, drew in a long gulp of air. "Anyway, I got sent to a scared straight camp. I met Evan and Cole there—which was about the only thing good the camp managed. That camp gave me the only real family I ever had."

"I'm guessing you weren't scared straight?"

"No," he said, he drew in another breath, obviously calmer now. "But I realized I liked a cleaner approach to my adventures. I like puzzles and playing by my wits. And as I believe I already mentioned," he added, with his eyes on me, "I like owning things that other people covet."

"You did well, and you didn't play by the rules."

"That's a fair statement." His grin was all charm. "And I should probably make clear that for everything I'm talking about, the statute of limitations has long run its course."

"I've no doubt," I said dryly.

"At any rate, we played that game, the three of us. Mixing the legitimate and the not-so-legitimate for a while. We were still very young, and then when Evan started at Northwestern, he met Howard Jahn."

"The entrepreneur."

Tyler nodded. "An amazing man. Brilliant mind, exceptional businessman. He took us under his wing. Mentored us, really. And he completely turned our lives around."

"You're saying that you're clean now?"

His smile was thin. "That's what I've been saying all along."

I looked at him, certain that he was telling me the truth . . . even while holding back. Even so, I was grateful for the glimpse into the child he was, as it told me so much more about the man he'd become.

I stood up and kissed his cheek. "Thank you for telling me,"

I said. "I look at you and I feel like I've known you my whole life, when I barely know you at all."

"You're wrong," he said. "We do know each other. We know what matters."

"Do we?" I thought of the secrets I still kept. The ones I was certain that he was holding fast to as well. But at the same time, those secrets seemed small compared to everything I felt for this man. So much—and so much more than just sex. And that was both comforting and terrifying. "We're moving so fast."

"No," he said gently. "We're just moving at the speed of us."

His words melted me a little, especially when he took my hand and pressed it to his heart, then pressed his palm over mine. I saw hunger in his eyes, but it was banked by a tenderness so profound it made me want to cry. "You move me, Sloane. Like no woman I have ever known."

"Tyler—"

"Don't talk," he said. "Just kiss me."

I did, and it was slow and deep and tender, and when he broke the kiss, it took me a moment to find my equilibrium.

"Our food is going to be a congealed and greasy mess," I whispered.

"We could eat," he said, but his voice promised something more delicious. "Or we could continue the—what did you call it—sex-a-thon? Your choice, Detective."

"That's not even a contest," I said, my pulse already kicking up. "Where are you going to take me now?"

"I like this spot," he said. "The moon, the statue. The world wide open around us."

"You like the chance of getting caught," I countered.

"No. I like *not* getting caught. And as we have already established, you, Detective, like excitement."

"I'm pretty sure there are laws against what you're thinking about."

"Probably. But in the world that exists between me and you, for the next few days, I am the law."

"Oh, really?"

"My rules, remember? My way." He eased closer to me, making the sizzle that had been running under the surface snap to life.

"Someone might come by."

"They might," he said. "I think the odds are low considering how late it is, but they certainly might." He grabbed the hem of the T-shirt and pulled it easily over my head. He tossed it on the ground. Then he gave a quick tug to the drawstring of the pants, making them immediately slide off my hips.

I licked my lips, then stepped out of the sweats, now completely naked in front of him.

"I hope someone does come by," he said, his voice low and easy. "Just imagine what they'll see."

"Tyler—"

"You, naked. Under me. Trying not to scream as the stars fall down around you. Tell me you like it."

"Yes," I said. Already I was wet. Already my nipples were tight. Already I craved his hands on me.

"I thought so," he said, stepping closer and sliding his fingers between my legs, then arching a brow when he felt my slick heat. "So tell me, Detective. Doesn't it feel good to be bad?"

"Yes," I whispered. "God, yes."

"I want to be inside you now."

His words were a seduction, a promise, an enticement.

"We can't. We shouldn't." But my body was already thrumming, and it was all I could do not to writhe against his hand.

He drew me close, kissed me softly. "We can," he said. "And we probably shouldn't. But we will anyway."

"How do you do this to me?" I whispered. "I've never felt— never done—"

"Because I see you," he said, reaching out to lightly tease my breasts. "And because I told you what I saw. Lay down, Sloane."

I did, resting my head and shoulders on the discarded clothes. My heart pounded, and I could see the way my pale skin glowed in the moonlight. I glanced around, afraid I would see some person peering out from the shadows to watch us.

But there was no one, only Tyler, looking at me with such fierce desire that my body fired even more, my breasts tightening, and my sex throbbing with the need for his touch.

"Jesus," he said, "you make me hard."

"Then fuck me," I said, reaching for him. He knelt over me, and my fingers found his fly, tugged it down. I slipped my hand inside and found his cock, so hard, so ready. "I want you dressed. I want you like this. Here. Now." I met his eyes. "I want skin on skin, Tyler."

He tilted his head, the posture casual, but there was heat—and understanding—in his eyes. "Do you?"

"Desperately. I'm clean," I said. "Tell me you are, too."

"I am," he said.

"Then fuck me," I begged, then closed my mouth over his, the kiss hard and wild. He'd cast a spell over me, but I didn't care. I wanted this. Wanted him. Wanted the night sky above us.

"Fuck me," I repeated as I tugged his hand, tumbling him down on top of me.

"Fuck me," I cried, as he drove himself into me, deeper and harder, taking everything I had to give and then some. My body was open to him, wild for him. I'd never known anything like this. Freedom mixed with fear, wildness tied to desire, lust keyed on just one man.

"Tyler," I moaned, as the building orgasm whipped over me, pulling me up and out of myself, and then—finally—spiraling me off into the night, and into the stars that rained like a firestorm down upon us.

eighteen

I awoke to the aroma of coffee and the sensation of something soft brushing over my naked abdomen. I opened my eyes, only to find that I still couldn't see.

Blindfold.

I shot up, spurred into motion by the burst of fear. My heart was pounding, and my fingers grappled at my face—then were suddenly stopped by strong warm hands gently pulling my fingers free before I could rip the blindfold away.

Tyler.

"Tyler, please."

"Shhh. You're not tied up. You're safe. You're still in bed, and you're safe." He brushed a kiss over my lips. "I want you to leave it on. If you have to take it off, I won't stop you. But if you can do this, I know that you'll enjoy it—and I'm damn certain I'll take you places you haven't gone before."

I swallowed, still edgy, but I trusted him, and I was calmer.

I wiggled my arms and legs as if to reassure myself that I could run.

"Anytime? I can rip it off anytime I want to?"

"Of course."

I managed an ironic smile. "Last night you wanted me to see the stars, and now you won't even let me see the room?"

He laughed, obviously understanding that my words were my acquiescence.

"Sight is an amazing thing, Detective. It makes it so much easier to appreciate a woman's lovely curves." I heard him move around the bed, could almost feel his eyes upon me. "To see more vividly all of her delights . . ."

Gently, he took my ankles, then spread my legs.

I squirmed, still so easily embarrassed, despite everything we'd done. But it was different somehow since I couldn't see his face, could only imagine his expression and the heat in his eyes.

"Don't," he said gently. "Do you have any idea how lovely you are? How hard it makes me just knowing that you want me? How incredibly exciting it is for me to see just how much you want me?

"Sight," he continued, and I gasped as his finger stroked slowly over my sex, dipping inside me just enough to tease and make me squirm again, this time in a silent demand for more. A demand he ignored and instead withdrew his finger. Withdrew his touch altogether.

"And taste and smell," he added, his voice now near my ear and his finger brushing my lip. "That's it. I want you to know just how sweet you taste to me, how much I crave the scent of your arousal." He traced his finger over my lip, then under my nose.

"There are words, too. The sound of my voice, telling you soft things. Or maybe my words are rough. Hard. Telling you I'm going to stroke you with a featherlight touch or fuck you until you scream."

I could feel my sex clenching, and knew by the change in his tone that he saw it.

"Keep your legs spread for me—arms, too," he said, and I whimpered in protest, certain that if I could rip off the damn blindfold I would drown in his expression of smug satisfaction.

"Please," I said. "What about touch? It's a sense, too."

"So it is. Is that what you want?"

"I want you to touch me," I said. "I want you inside me."

"Soon," he promised. "But until then, I think we can make you want it just a little bit more."

I felt something wispy and soft graze my skin.

"What is it?" I asked. "A feather?"

"There are feathers," he said. "And little strips of leather all bundled together like a flower at the end of a flexible stick."

"Um . . ."

"Technically, it's a cat toy." He trailed the feathery end over my sex, making me arch up with surprise and pleasure. "I find playing with this kind of pussy much more interesting."

"Meow," I said, and made him laugh.

"Good kitty." I heard the tease in his voice, and then felt the tease of the toy's touch. He trailed it all over me, the feathers barely touching my skin, from the soles of my feet all the way up to the curve of my ear. Everything stroked and teased and aroused, and when I was wet and hot and ready to beg him for more, he had me flip to my stomach and started on my back.

"Please," I said. "Tyler, please."

"Please what?"

"I don't know," I said honestly. I was on fire. I wanted release. I wanted him. "Everything, I think."

"Whatever the lady needs. On your knees, then. Arms on the bed, ass in the air."

"I—" I shut off my words when I realized I had no idea what I'd intended to say. So I shifted my position, did as he said, and moaned with pleasure as he thrust his fingers deep inside me—

And then cried out in surprise when the toy smacked hard against my ass, the sting both shocking and sweet.

"Oh, yes," he said as my vagina clenched tight around him. "The lady likes that."

"Yes," I whispered, as the sting seemed to spill warmth through my body, and my clit throbbed in a demand for attention.

"You're incredible," he said. "I love the way your body responds. I could tease you and play with you all day."

"That works for me," I murmured as he stroked his hands over my rear in slow, sensual circles, then surprised me again with another smack, this one just a little harder, the pain just a little sweeter.

He pressed his palm to the site, then stroked in easy, soothing circles as the fire that the first strike had sparked spread through me, like warm fingers to light me up and turn me on.

Behind the blindfold my eyes were closed. I'd never expected—never even imagined—such a heightened sense of pleasure coupled with anticipation—of his hand, of his cock, of just one more sting.

I'd thought that the rush I'd felt in the dungeon—naked and collared—had been the highest peak. But this was more.

I'd gotten a thrill from being on display, subject to Tyler's every whim. But that was an excitement that stemmed from breaking the rules, from being just a little bit naughty.

This was different, and the thrill came not from being naughty, but from being intimate. From being his.

"Again," I whispered. "Please, Tyler. Again."

Gently, he pressed a kiss to the curve of my ass. And then, just when I was beginning to think it wouldn't, that sweet sting came once more.

He used his mouth to soothe it this time, and I moaned as soft kisses started at the point of pain, then spread out, as if he was lining the threads of pleasure with kisses.

"You like that." It wasn't a question, and I didn't bother to answer. "I like watching you. The way your body quivers. The way your pale skin flushes. I like seeing you go to the edge, Sloane, and I like knowing that I'm the one who brought you there."

He trailed the feathered end of the toy between my legs, and I writhed shamelessly against it. My body was primed, ready.

He chuckled, as if recognizing my distress. "What do you want?"

"More," I said. "Everything. You."

"Good answer. Spread your legs more. That's it," he said when I complied. "Just a little bit wider."

He was still behind me, and I was on the bed, my knees near that edge, my feet just over it. I could imagine the way I looked, legs spread, back bowed, my head tilted up. I was desperately wet, a fact he confirmed when he used his thumb to tease me, sliding it over my labia and slipping it ever so shallowly into me. "Is that what you want?"

"More," I said.

"How about this," he asked as he danced the feathered end of the toy across my navel, then drew it back, so that the feathers tickled over me, over my clit, my vagina, my ass, sending sparks of indescribable sensation shooting through me and making me gasp in delight—and pushing me so close to the edge of need that I thought I might cry if he didn't take me right then.

"Please," I murmured. "Now, please."

I was close to desperate; thankfully, he didn't torment me long.

I arched up as I felt him thrust just inside of me, then I cried out when he pistoned his hips to bury himself all the way. He held me steady as he moved in and out, slow, and then faster as the crescendo built.

He spoke to me, his smooth voice like a soundtrack, telling me how good I felt, how tight I was, how much he wanted to watch me come. And there, behind my blindfold, I clung tight to the colors and lights and spinning electrons that were the only things anchoring me to this reality, knowing damn certain that when the climax came, I'd spin off into a pleasure so intense it would surely destroy me.

He kept up his rhythm, but released his grip on my hips and drew one hand down, sliding between my ass cheeks to tease the rim of my anus. Like the sting of the toy, this new sensation shocked me, taking me even higher. Incredible, yes, and so intimate that it pushed me over, deeper and harder and higher until everything was too much to bear and I cried out in the sweet, unrelenting agony of pure, glorious pleasure.

He held me as my body trembled, then tucked me gently against him and pulled me close. "Wow," I said, as he gently pulled off the blindfold. "Thank you."

"Sweetheart, I'll wow you anytime."

I lay still in his embrace until I finally—sort of—felt recovered. Then slowly rolled over in his arms. "What time is it?"

He glanced toward the dresser and the clock that sat there. "Almost ten."

I sat straight up. "Shit. I'm going to be late. And I don't think sleeping with the boss qualifies as a good excuse."

"It's okay," he said. "I changed your schedule. I have some places I want to take you first."

I lifted an eyebrow. "If that's a metaphor for more sex, you're going to have to put a pin in that."

"No," he said. "This is about Amy."

I frowned. "What about her?"

"You're still looking for her address or employer, right? I know some people who might be able to help. And then, my lovely cop, we have some shopping to do."

"Shopping?" I repeated, but he just stood up and held out his hand for me.

"Let's get dressed."

In fact, showering came before getting dressed, and despite

the very real risk of shower sex throwing us off schedule, I agreed to share the stall.

"Don't make me regret it," I said when he reached down to tug at my pubic hair. "And don't do that."

"I think we may have one more task this morning," he said, picking up a razor. "Not that I don't love this deliciously neat triangle, but all the other dancers are bare."

"Oh." I swallowed. "I'm not sure I can manage to shave there."

His grin was full of mischief. "Baby, I'm more than happy to help."

He positioned us so that we were out of the spray, but close enough that he could grab the handheld nozzle. And then, as I spread my legs and gripped the walls of the shower in both fear and an effort to steady myself, he went to work.

First, he lathered me. And then—slowly and very gently—he drew the razor over my flesh again and again. I was, I realized, getting more than a little turned on. Not from the sensation— though there was something about the pressure of the blade that felt amazing—but from the thought of him taking such intimate care of me.

"There," he said, after he'd finished and rinsed the soap from me. He pressed a kiss to my newly shaved skin, and it was all I could do not to beg him to take me back to bed.

Amy, he'd said. And he was right. If I wanted to make sure she was back home for Candy's baby, I needed to follow up.

But I couldn't deny myself one slow, deep kiss. And as my tongue sought his, I couldn't help but think of the days that were ticking away, inexorably pulling me from this man who, with every passing moment, seemed to draw me closer.

Afterward, I bundled myself in one of The Drake's plush robes, then headed back into his bedroom to hunt up my clothes. "This room is different from the rest of the place." I'd noticed the contemporary decorations and furniture the first time I'd entered, but had never said as much to him. "You did it, right? Not the hotel staff."

"It's all me," he said, stepping into the room with a towel wrapped loosely around his hips, and making me regret very seriously that whole getting-to-work thing.

"Why this one? Why'd you take the time, I mean?"

"I'm particular about my bedroom." He'd been looking past me, at the decor, but now he shifted his gaze to me. "Nothing goes in that I didn't select."

I swallowed, suddenly unsure if we were still talking about the furniture.

"So what do you think?"

I blinked. "About what?"

His eyes crinkled at the corners and, damn the man, I was certain he knew the direction of my thoughts.

"About the room."

"I like it. It's attractive and interesting, what with all the hard edges and angles. But it's inviting, too. And somehow warm and comfortable." I hesitated, then took the plunge. "It reminds me of you," I admitted, because I simply couldn't deny the truth in the words.

"Comfortable?" he repeated, his brows rising in mock horror. "I'm not sure I like that. *Inviting* works for me, though. So does chivalrous and desperately sexy."

"Are we still talking about the room?"

"What else?" His smile was all innocent.

What else indeed.

I tossed him a saucy smile, bent to retrieve the pants and T-shirt I'd worn in the park. "Thanks for the loan," I said, "but the shirt has grass stains—and I'd rather have pants that fit. Do you think The Drake's gift shop has clothes?"

"While I'm tempted to just keep you naked, you have clothes there," he said, pointing to the dresser. "Top left drawer, I believe."

I narrowed my eyes. "And how exactly did my clothes get here?"

"You left your address on your application."

"Yeah. The address to my locked apartment to which you don't have a key."

He waved my words away. "It wasn't any trouble. Cole is exceptionally skilled in two areas. Art and lock-picking. The second he has no occasion to use anymore."

He said the last so piously I had to laugh. "But he used to?"

"His misspent youth," Tyler confirmed as he fastened his broken watch to his wrist.

"With you?"

"More or less. I told you. We both did a lot of misspending before we became tight." He nodded to the clock. "We should get going," he said.

"Right." I hurried to finish putting on my shoes. I didn't bother with makeup. For one thing, I rarely bothered with makeup. For another, I'd seen the setup in the dressing rooms at Destiny. I could get fixed up before my shift.

"How do you feel about donuts?" Tyler asked.

"I'm a cop. Take a guess."

"Then we'll eat on the way."

He'd meant it about the donuts, and before we got on the highway, he pulled into a bakery and got four dozen, but only shrugged when I asked him why so many.

Then we were on the road again, and I was about to drool from the incredible aroma of dough and sugar.

"We're heading north?"

"More or less."

"To where?"

"My house," he said.

I turned to him. "I thought you said it was about Amy."

"About your search for her, yes."

"How?" I asked, a little bit wary, a little bit concerned, but mostly curious.

"Don't get your hopes up, but there are some people she may have confided in."

"Oh. Who?"

He turned to me long enough to grin. "Girls," he said. "Quite a few girls."

I saw some of those girls when he pulled into the driveway of a gorgeous mansion—house, manor. I wasn't sure what to call it. I did, however, remember what year it had been built. "Eighteen fifty-six, right? And this is Old Irving Park?"

He glanced sideways at me before he killed the engine. "You did your homework on me."

"I did. But I never imagined this." The place was stunning. Huge and grand, yet somehow still comfortable, it sat on a lot that had to cover at least three acres, maybe more. It was painted an inviting yellow and had a wraparound porch and a lovely portico.

I also hadn't imagined the girls. "Who are they?" I asked of the women who were lying out on the lawn sunbathing, sitting on the porch reading, and even working on a car that was on blocks near the back of the house.

"The residents," he said.

"Come again?"

"Why don't you come inside and I'll explain it to you."

I followed him into the stately place that managed to combine a modern flair while still keeping the feel of centuries past.

"Tyler!" A woman in a bathrobe stood on the massive staircase, her grin wide. She had a trim figure and hair that fell in ringlets. She wore no makeup, and looked one hell of a lot better than I did.

I considered hating her on sight, but decided to withhold judgment.

"Maisie, this is Sloane. She's a new dancer at Destiny."

Maisie's brow furrowed and she looked sharply at Tyler. "I thought you said it was over." Fear filled her voice.

"It is. It's done. It's over. And they aren't going to hurt any of you again. Sloane came to Destiny through the traditional application process. And she's not moving in here."

"Oh." Her tentative smile widened. "Oh, well, that's great. You're going to love it there, really." She glanced back at Tyler. "I didn't say anything wrong, did I?"

"No. Sloane knows everything," he said, looking hard at me.

"Everything," I agreed, wondering what the hell "everything" was.

"Maisie's living here while she attends community college," Tyler explained. "She's hoping to apply for a four year program next year."

"The Tyler Sharp scholarship program," Maisie said with a grin. "Listen, I'm starved. I was just heading toward the kitchen."

"Take these," Tyler said, passing her the donut boxes. But before she went, he asked if she recalled Amy. She did, but didn't know where she'd landed in Vegas. For that matter, none of the girls in the house—eighteen of them—had a clue.

"It was a long shot," Tyler said. "The girls who live in the house are pretty tight. From what I've seen they don't hang out as much with the other girls—like you and Amy—who come in through the front door."

"Is that what I did?" I said wryly.

"Compared to them, yes. But I thought they might have heard something in passing."

"So what am I missing?" I asked. "How did these girls end up at Destiny? What was Maisie afraid of?"

"I'm surprised, Detective. I thought you would have figured it out."

"The trafficking?"

"Got it in one."

I shook my head. "Actually I didn't," I said. "Explain."

"How much do you know about our immunity deal?"

"Very little," I admitted. "Just that it exists."

He nodded. "The situation's complex—lots of years, lots of people. But what it boiled down to was that Evan and Cole and I stumbled onto a white slavery ring. It was big. It was pervasive. And it was very, very dangerous."

I nodded. I hadn't dealt with any interstate prostitution rings, but I knew enough to understand the breadth—and danger—of what he was talking about.

"What did you do?"

"We wanted to shut it down, but that's easier said than done. We started gathering evidence and got it to the Feds—we did it anonymously."

"Why anonymously?" I asked, though I had a feeling I already knew the answer.

"We're private men, with sensitive business operations. We all wanted it stopped, but we didn't see the necessity of putting ourselves under the microscope."

Which, I assumed, meant that they were protecting their own illegitimate enterprises.

"Those tips resulted in the creation of a federal task force."

"The one Angelina's father oversaw."

"Right. And while the task force started working to eliminate the heart of the beast, we did the only two things we could—we continued to gather intel, and we pulled out as many girls as we could."

"Pulled out?"

He nodded. "Their network worked a bit like the Underground Railroad, only taking the girls to slavery rather than out of it. They would move them from location to location, sometimes under false pretenses—telling them they were going to be an actress, a model, something. When we got intel on a girl or group of girls, we slid in. The three of us, some of our security staff, it depended on the situation."

"But didn't that blow the whole operation? They'd know they were made before there was sufficient evidence to convict."

"That's why we couldn't get out all the girls. We had to play it safe. Go in as if we were clients. Or representing some foreign royal who was looking for a mistress. Sometimes we just initiated a car wreck and otherwise made it look like the girls simply escaped. Point is, we were creative."

"And you got the girls. That's wonderful," I said, meaning it.

"Not all of them," he said, his voice heavy.

"You made a difference," I countered, reaching out to brush my hand over his. "And you brought them here?"

"Most. Some had homes, but most were lost already. Runaways, homeless. Wannabe actresses who got sucked into the seamy side of the dream. If they didn't have a place to go home to, we gave them one, and we gave them a job. Dancing if they were able. Waiting tables if they weren't."

"And more," I said. "Maisie said something about a scholarship?"

"She's exaggerating, but yes. If they stay clean and keep their grades up, we help them get an education. And if they need help finding a job, we help them with that, too."

"You three are amazing," I couldn't keep the emotion out of my voice. It felt a little like pride, and a whole lot more like respect. "Thank you for telling me. For bringing me here."

We were standing on the front porch, looking out at the beautiful lawn and the graceful old trees and the women who were making a better life there.

He hesitated before speaking. "It was important to me that you see it."

"Why?" My word was so soft, I feared he couldn't hear it. And I held my breath, waiting for his reply.

"Because I'm proud of it. And because I wanted to share it with you." He reached for my hand, then twined his fingers through mine.

"Thank you," I said softly, and squeezed.

Behind us, the door banged open. "Tyler! Hey!"

I turned to find a twenty-something girl with a pixie haircut and dancing green eyes.

"Caroline, what are you doing here? I thought you were living on campus these days."

"Yup," she said. "Loving it. But it's Sunday, right? Maisie and I are gonna take in a movie." She blew a pink bubble and popped it.

He nodded, then turned to me. "Caroline used to live here."

"Loved it, too," Caroline said. "But the dorm is super convenient. So you're looking for Amy?"

She said all of that without taking a breath as far as I could tell. "I am," I said. "Do you know her?"

"Not well, but I'm friends with Darcy, and she and Amy hung."

My stomach twisted with disappointment. "Tyler already talked to Darcy. Amy sent her a postcard from Vegas. I'm trying to figure where in Vegas she landed. A friend's having a baby. I want to make sure she comes back in time."

Caroline shook her head. "Don't know. But the guy with the other job might know."

I met Tyler's eyes. "What other job?" he asked.

"A customer. One of the guys who gets a lap dance every once in a while. Big guy. Handsome, but gray at the temples. He does all the Cokes and stuff."

"Big Charley," Tyler said, then glanced at me. "Vending machine sales, rental, and maintenance. Cole and I contract with him for some of our properties, actually."

"Yeah." Caroline smiled. "That's him. She told me he'd offered her a job. Guess she ended up going with another offer—I figure there was a guy—but maybe she told Big Charley where she was going instead."

"Thanks," I said. "That's really helpful."

She nodded, then glanced at Tyler, her expression turning sad. "Emily and Amy were pretty tight," she said. "They only overlapped for a few weeks, but they totally hit it off."

"I remember," he said.

"Any news?" she asked, before I had a chance to ask where I could find Emily.

"None," Tyler said. He turned to me, his face grave. "Emily's one of ours. She quit a couple of months ago, and then was found dead not long after."

"I'm so sorry."

"What they're saying is bullshit," Caroline said. "Emily wouldn't turn tricks." She turned to me. "The cops said that a john messed her up. Left her for dead."

"You don't believe it?"

"No way."

Tyler shook his head. "It's hard to fathom. She was strong-willed and smart. I never thought she'd turn tricks. And if she was down on her luck, she knew she could come to me. But it's possible she hooked up with the wrong guy. Someone who thought that because she was a dancer he could take what he wanted." I heard the tight edge of control in his voice. "Bastard."

He gave Caroline's hand a squeeze. "If I hear anything more, I'll tell you. Promise."

We followed her into the house, where the conversation turned from Emily to advice about how to milk the customers for the best possible tips. When we returned to the car an hour or so later, I was full up on donuts and coffee, and overloaded with information about dancing at Destiny. But despite the passage of time and the many conversations in the interim, my mind was still on Charley.

"Do you want me to call him?" Tyler asked.

"Not yet. Caroline said he was a lunch customer. So if he's not at the club today, maybe I'll have you call. But I'd like to chat with him first."

"Fair enough."

"In the meantime," I added, "I'm going to see if I can't find her in Vegas the old-fashioned way, the detective way."

As he maneuvered the streets and highways of Chicago, I pulled out my phone and hit the only speed dial number I had programmed. Two rings later, my dad answered.

"Hey, daughter o' mine," he said, in the kind of gravelly baritone that could be either soothing or scary depending on whether he was helping a victim or interrogating a suspect. "How's the hip?"

"Hey, yourself. It's fine. They're idiots for keeping me off the job."

"No argument there. To what do I owe this call?" I could hear the clatter of the station behind him, and imagined him in front of a battered desk covered two feet thick in paperwork. "You just wanted to hear your wonderful father's voice, or do you need something?"

I laughed. "If I said both, would you see right through my ruse?"

"Pretty much."

"Okay, then I need something."

"And I'm happy to help. If you can answer one question."

"Shoot."

"What the hell are you doing working when you're supposed to be recuperating on medical leave?"

I leaned back and rolled my eyes. Beside me, Tyler's mouth quirked up. I knew he couldn't hear my dad's side of the conversation, but I supposed the one-sided version was amusing on its own.

"Saving my sanity," I said dryly. "And helping out a friend." I gave him the quick rundown on Candy and Amy.

"What do you need?"

"I've already prowled the phone listings and I'm getting nowhere. Do you know anyone in the Vegas PD?"

"I'm insulted you have to ask. I know everyone. That's what makes me invincible."

"You're not as funny as you think you are, Daddy. Seriously, I was hoping you could ask someone for a favor. Maybe she's been cited for speeding or something. Can you get someone to run a search? See if her driver's license has come up? Maybe get a current address?"

He said he would, of course. "But you have to promise not to run yourself ragged. Like it or not, you're still recovering. And more than that you need to take a step back. You go at this like a bat out of hell, but you're going to burn out."

"Daddy . . ."

"I'm serious. Go find a guy. See a movie. Take two hours off being a detective to be a girl."

My eyes were on Tyler. "Thanks for the advice, Dad. Believe it or not, I'm working on it."

nineteen

"Wow," I said as we stood in front of the vibrant purple facade. I tilted my head up to look at Tyler. "There are dresses in there?"

"Many," he said.

"If you say so."

We'd walked down Michigan Avenue from The Drake to Tonic, this Gold Coast boutique that, to my mind anyway, more resembled a child's Lego construct than an actual retail establishment. The building appeared to be made of plastic blocks, though Tyler assured me it was more solid than that. It consisted of multiple levels, like a wedding cake that had gone horribly wrong or, again, like a child's toy, if that child was trying to use up every Lego he owned.

The doorway was in the shape of a triangle, and various geometric shapes made up the row of windows that lined the second story. It was tucked in tight between two classically ornate buildings, and the contrast only made it look more, well, purple.

About the only thing the purple building had going for it, at least in my opinion, was that it couldn't be overlooked.

Then again, it had no signage at all. Presumably if you wanted to shop at Tonic, you knew how to find Tonic.

Normally I wouldn't want to find Tonic, but according to Tyler we were attending an event that night. And apparently jeans and a T-shirt weren't going to cut it.

I must have been gaping, because Tyler laughed and took my arm. "Come on," he said. "I promise you this will be fun."

I'm not entirely sure "fun" was the word, but the trip to Tonic was definitely educational. Whoever designed the place was clearly as passionate about purple as they were about haute couture. Every wall, every tile, every surface was either white or some shade of purple. I presumed the white was supposed to provide contrast, but there wasn't nearly enough of it. And though the purple was charming at first, after a while I felt a bit like I was engulfed in a giant bruise.

Bizarre sculptures descended from the ceiling, and the mannequins turned out not to be mannequins at all, but instead were live women who spent the day wearing the designs and standing frozen in place.

I really didn't see the point.

The one thing I couldn't argue with was the clothes. Everything shined and swirled and was designed to flatter.

Zelda—the sales associate who materialized the moment we entered the store—led Tyler and me to the evening gown section, where she proceeded to show us dress after dress. Each was more fabulous than the one before—and each was summarily rejected by Tyler.

"Not even close to worthy of her. And the color—it can't clash with the fire of her hair."

"I have just the thing," Zelda said, in a thick accent that

sounded Eastern European, but was probably fake. Just more window-dressing for the clients. "Arrived today. I go look, yes?"

She was gone only a few moments before returning with a simple dress that somehow managed to put all the fancier ones we'd seen to shame. It was a backless sheath, the front piece held in place by a thin strip of material over one shoulder.

The entire dress, including the skirt, was designed to hug a woman's curves, but the skirt was slit so that the woman could actually walk.

Best of all, it was the color of the sky on a clear summer day. In other words, it perfectly matched Tyler's eyes.

"I love it," I said. "Can I try it on?"

Zelda led me to the back of the store and the dressing room, which was about the size of my Chicago apartment. It had a chaise lounge, a vanity with a mirror, and a full array of toiletries so that the customer could emerge refreshed and primped. There was even a small refrigerator with bottles of Chablis and sparkling water.

I gaped a bit when Tyler joined me in the room. Zelda, however, seemed completely unruffled. Clearly, she knew who would be paying the bill for today's excursion.

As soon as she closed the door, I turned to Tyler. "I usually shop at T.J. Maxx. I think this is a step up."

"Just a bit," he said, taking a seat on the chaise. "Let's see how it fits."

I slipped out of my shoes, then pulled off my T-shirt and wiggled out of my jeans. Clad in only my bra and thong, I took the dress off the padded hanger. The material was thin, clingy, and as soft as a cloud.

"Take your bra off," he said. "The dress is backless."

I did, then inspected the dress for a way in, finally deciding that I was meant to unfasten the single decorative button at the shoulder and step in from the top. The button seemed too minuscule to be up to the task of holding the dress up, but considering how little dress there actually was, I imagined it could probably handle the job.

"Sloane," Tyler said once I was wearing it, and there was something almost reverent about his voice.

"You like?"

"I like," he said, making a turning motion with his finger so that I would turn and look in the tri-fold mirror behind me.

When I did, I saw a woman who looked like she should be on a red carpet. I stood up on my toes and the effect was even better. "I'll need the right shoes," I said.

"Of course."

"And this is a problem." I pointed to the back, where the top band of my thong showed in the deep dip of the back.

Tyler stood. "Take them off."

"Commando?"

"This dress is made for it. Take them off," he repeated.

I did, shimmying out of them and tossing them on the pile with the rest of my clothing.

I walked toward the mirror, sexy and vibrant and daring. Maybe too daring. "I love it, Tyler, but I don't know. The slit up the thigh is so high. If it were over my hip, maybe. But . . ." I trailed off as I took more steps and then turned. You couldn't actually see my crotch, but it was high enough that someone might imagine they could.

"Let them," Tyler said, when I told him that. "What's life without a little imagination?"

"Tyler . . ."

"You're beautiful and sexy, Sloane. Even in your jeans and T-shirt. But in this, you're breathtaking. Enjoy it. Better yet, let me enjoy it."

I frowned at my reflection. I did look seriously hot. Hotter than I'd ever looked before, that was for sure, and I couldn't deny that it was tempting. So very tempting.

"Besides," he said, standing and coming to me. "There will

be dancing, and this dress was made for it." He drew me into his arms, one hand holding mine, the other at my back. As he hummed something smooth and classical, he led me around the room, and even there, in a dressing room with no real music, it was almost magical.

"You see?" he said, his grin just a little bit wicked as he dipped me, making me cry out, then laugh in surprise and delight. My back arched, my leg extended out, and he pressed a kiss to the side of my neck.

He pulled me straight again, running his hand along my bare thigh as he did. "That slit is a very important selling point." His fingers continued along the length of the slit until he reached my sex. I was slick and wet, and I groaned when he thrust his finger inside me. "Definitely a selling point," he murmured.

"Tyler . . ." My protest was thin and weak.

"Hush," he said, dropping to his knees. He lifted his hands, pushing the material up on my hips so that the top of the slit framed my sex. "I have to taste you," he said, then laved his tongue over me once before tilting his head up to face me. "Don't make a sound."

Oh, dear lord . . .

I reached out, steadying myself with the side of the mirror as he drew in close once again, his hands now inside the skirt, holding tight to my thighs, his tongue so intimately stroking me.

He teased my clit with tiny, fluttery strokes, then stroked me, gloriously hard, before sucking and teasing.

My knees were weak, and I had to take one hand off the mirror to bite the soft pad at the base of my thumb simply to quell the need to scream in both pleasure and frustration. Pleasure at the riot of sensations he was sending through me. Frustration that I could do nothing more than stand there biting my lip when I wanted to cry out and beg him for more, beg him to lay me down and shove the dress up and bury himself inside me.

His tongue continued its sweet torture, and I clung to the

side of the mirror, feeling the climax build, knowing I was close, so close, and any moment I would completely shatter.

And then he backed away. "I think that's far enough."

I gaped at him. "Excuse me?"

He stood up, then kissed me, long and deep. I tasted my own arousal and moaned against his mouth, my hips crushing against him as I writhed, shamelessly seeking my release.

"Mine, remember?" he said as he broke the kiss and backed away. His expression was smug and very devious. "I want you wanting. I want you desperate. I want you so ready for me you'll come with the slightest of touches, and then again and again when I fuck you."

My body trembled from his words. "Bastard."

He laughed. "I've been called worse."

"You know I'm going to make you pay."

He bent down to pick up my bra and shirt, then unbuttoned the shoulder. "Sweetheart, I sincerely hope so."

Since there was no winning this battle, I got dressed, stifling a frustrated moan as the jeans rubbed provocatively against me. I glanced at Tyler, certain he was aware of this new distress, but he very wisely didn't meet my eye.

I picked up the dress, turning it over to look for the tag. "There's no price," I said.

"Trust me. There's always a price."

In this case, the price was five digits, and I about had a heart attack.

"For a dress? And you spent it?" We were back on the street, heading toward Michigan Avenue so we could catch a taxi back to The Drake. "I could buy a car for that."

"Not a very good one."

"How the hell am I going to wear it? I'll be afraid to breathe on it."

"You'll wear it because I want to see you in it. And later, I want to see you out of it."

Such is the irony that had become my life, because just two short hours after spending over ten thousand on a dress, I was wearing next to nothing as I moved through a strip club doing the pre-performance mingle-and-chat routine. The kind of chatter that had me saying simpering nonsense and them mostly staring at my tits.

I wore short-shorts that revealed the curve of my rear and a push-up bra that accentuated the curve of my breasts, and in a few minutes, I'd replace that with my naughty executive outfit—which, once I took it off, showed everything.

The thought made me long for Tyler, and I paused in my conversation with a Philadelphia businessman to scan the room for him.

I found him by the bar, going over what was probably an inventory with one of the two bartenders. As if he could feel my eyes on him, he looked up, and his smile held such warmth that I felt it all the way to my toes.

He shifted his gaze to a far corner, then nodded at a solitary man sitting in one of the plush chairs, nursing a drink. The lunchtime crowd tended to sit at the stage, so this man was unique simply by virtue of being alone.

Charley, Tyler mouthed, and I nodded.

I said something polite but dismissive to my man from Philly, then swung my hips to give him a little show as I moved across the room to where Big Charley sat.

He was aptly named. A huge man with dark hair except for silver sideburns, he was ruggedly handsome, like a Hollywood version of a lumberjack. He looked up as I approached, his eyes going to tits then crotch in a way that I was starting to get used to.

"Hi, sugar," I said. "You're all alone over here."

"Just enjoying the scenery," he said. A glass half-filled with golden liquor sat on the table next to a money clip that was thick with bills.

He lifted his glass and I caught the scent of bourbon. He tossed it back, then smacked his empty glass down on the table. "I have to say, the view is definitely improving."

I laughed. "You're sweet." I cocked my head, studying him. "Wait a sec, you're Charley, aren't you?"

For a moment, he looked startled. "I know I'd remember you, darlin'. So how do you know me?"

"Oh, I don't," I said. "But my friend Amy said you were the sweetest thing. She said Big Charley always sits off by himself and he's just as nice as he can be and handsome as all get out. That's you, right? You were one of Amy's most favorite customers."

"That's me," he said. "How is she? Moved to Vegas, didn't she?"

"Yes, and the mean thing hasn't called me since she got there. I can't remember where she said she was working. Did she mention it to you?"

"Afraid not." He held up his glass to one of the passing waitresses, indicating he wanted a refill. "I'd offered her a job, actually, but she turned it down. Said she was going to dance in Vegas instead."

"Dance? Well, that narrows it down, doesn't it?" I said, then laughed.

"Why are you looking for her. Worried?"

I shook my head, not inclined to delve into Candy's worries or my concerns with a stranger. "Not worried so much as frustrated. She promised a friend she'd come by and see her, but Amy tends to flake out, so I'm guessing the lure of Vegas was too much for her."

"It is alluring," he said. His eyes did another swoop over me, and I fought the urge to cross my arms over my chest. "Speaking of alluring . . ." He pulled a fifty from the money clip that sat on the table beside his empty drink. "How about a lap dance, honey?"

The thought made me vaguely ill, and I realized that although I was fine with the dancing part of the deal I'd made, lap dances were technically also part of my job.

Well, damn.

I leaned over and lightly pressed my finger to his forehead. "Hold that thought, sugar. I have to go do my thing onstage, but you're the one I'll come to after."

Lust flared in his eyes as I started to walk away. And then, just because I was getting into the part, I turned around and winked at him.

The other girls for the upcoming set were already in the dressing room, and we chatted while we got ready. I asked them about Amy, but no one said anything I didn't already know. At one point, I glanced at a snapshot, one of many on a bulletin board. The girl had blond hair, bangs, and a dimple that highlighted a friendly smile. I did a double-take, then realized it was only another girl who looked a bit like Amy.

"That's Emily," Sapphire said when I asked. "Weird, huh?"

"What?"

"Well, you're right. They look a bit alike, and they were both heading to Vegas." She exhaled, a sad, lonely sound. "Sucks that Emily never got there. You know, it seriously pisses me off that the cops haven't learned shit. It's like she was just a dancer in a strip club and they just don't care."

"I'm sure they care," I said, but I know I didn't convince her, and I made a mental note to call my friend in the Chicago PD and check on the status of the investigation.

I did my own makeup—and didn't mess it up too badly—and then the intro music was blaring and it was time to head out.

This time, I knew right where Tyler was when I climbed onstage. A nice little perk, as that lessened my nerves considerably. I danced and swayed and flirted with the customers and the pole, all the while keeping my eye on the man at the bar—my man, who was leaning back, his expression bland except for the heat in those blue eyes that never once left me.

I added an extra shimmy just for him, and reaped the reward in tips from nearby customers. Not a bad deal, really.

When the set ended, I headed straight for the bar, but was waylaid by one of the men, who flashed a hundred dollar bill, then tucked it in the band of the G-string I wore. "I'm looking for a little quiet conversation, sweet thing," he said as I took a step back, suddenly feeling very naked and wanting a bit of distance from the panting way he was looking at me. "Why don't you come with me to the back?"

I was running through my options for saying no, when Tyler approached, then plucked out the bill. He handed it to the man. "Sorry to disappoint, but this lovely lady has a private engagement in the VIP room."

I almost sagged in relief. "Sorry, sugar," I said. "Maybe next time."

"There won't be a next time," Tyler said when we were out of earshot. "You dance on the stage. Nowhere else. Not unless you're dancing for me."

I feigned shock. "But what about the man waiting for me in the VIP room?"

"Change of venue," Tyler said as we entered the employee section. "He'll see you in my office."

He had me inside and pressed up hard against the wall as soon as the door closed behind us. I gasped, breathless from his long, deep kiss, as he slipped a finger inside me, even while easing down to take my breast in his mouth.

He suckled me, making me feel wild—making me feel *aware*. So that I seemed to know every hair, every nerve ending, every tiny burst of sensation in my body.

"You're so ready for me," he murmured.

"I was ready the first moment I saw you. That night at the

party, when I saw you walking toward me, I wanted you so desperately it was almost painful." I turned my head away, not wanting him to see my eyes, suddenly afraid that I'd revealed too much.

He cupped my cheek and eased my head back so that there was no escaping his gaze. "Yes," he said, and that simple word seemed to hold a world of meaning.

I sighed. "You do something to me, Tyler. I look at you and . . ."

"And what?"

"And I want."

His smile was slow and painfully sexy. "What do you want, Sloane?"

You. "Exactly what you're doing," I said instead.

"I can't get enough of you," he said. "You're like oxygen. I crave you, I need you, I can't live without you."

"Oxygen's explosive," I teased.

"It most definitely is," he said as he lifted me. I hooked my legs around him, and he carried me to his desk. "Lay back," he ordered, and I complied without argument.

"Oh, yes," he said, his voice filled with heat and appreciation. "I like the way you look. Stretched out, naked and flush, like an offering to a god."

"Would that be you?"

He chuckled. "It might be."

"What are you going to do?" I couldn't help my whisper, or the hint of anticipation that stole into my voice.

"I could just stand here and look at you. Your skin is so pale that I see every subtle change, every flush when you become aroused. I like knowing how much you want me. How much you like me looking at you. Me wanting you."

He slowly stroked his hands up my legs. "And this is the rest. Touching you. Feeling the way your muscles tremble. Hearing how you draw breath when my fingers graze ever so gently over your skin." As if in illustration, he drew a lazy fingertip over my thigh. "Turn over now," he said.

I turned, lying flat on the desktop, my legs together, my head turned to one side.

"No," he said, "Ease down. Feet on the floor. Legs spread. Bend over and hold on."

I moved as he spoke, then realized I was biting my lip, a reflection of both nerves and excitement.

Slowly, he stroked his hand over my back, tracing the curve of my spine, the swell of my rear. "Yes," he said, in a voice heavy with lust and heat. "You're perfect, Sloane, so fucking perfect."

I said nothing. I wasn't perfect. But in that moment, I felt like I was.

He leaned over, his clothes brushing my naked flesh in a way that made me shiver almost as much as his words. "I'm going to fuck you, Sloane. Fast and hard. I'm going to lose myself inside you, and I'm going to hold tight as I feel you explode."

I couldn't speak. I couldn't move. I could only wait in breathless anticipation as he took off his jacket, then folded it and gently placed it between my belly and the edge of the desk.

I drew in a breath—Tyler's hands, his touch, his words all made me wet with longing. But that one tiny courtesy had me close to crumpling with desire and respect and something that, in another place and time, just might be love.

He touched me, using his fingers to open me wide, make me even more aroused, so that I was whimpering with need by the time I heard the distinctive sound of his zipper.

And then—oh, thank god—I felt the thick head of his cock push against me, gentle at first, teasing me, and then with one solid thrust he buried himself inside me, and I cried out as the warmth of his body pressed up against my ass, trapping me between him and the desk.

I leaned forward more, stretching my arms so that I could

clutch the far side of the desktop. "Hard," I said. "I've wanted you inside me since that damn dressing room. Fuck me hard, Tyler, please."

He didn't answer in words, but his hands tightened on my hips and the pounding rhythmic thrusts were all the answer I needed. Again and again he entered me, burying himself deep inside me until I was swirling outside myself, lost in the sweet heat of it all.

I heard myself crying out in pleasure. Heard the slap of his body against mine. And then, when he slipped his hand between our bodies to stroke my clit and bring me even higher, I lost everything except the brilliant, burning glow of the orgasm, building and building until it threatened to send me shooting off into some other plane of existence, where only Tyler could find me.

He came after me, his cry of release so wild and masculine and loud, I was certain that everyone still in the club knew exactly what we were doing. Right then, I really didn't care.

"Sweetheart," he murmured, then curled me into his arms and laid me gently on the desktop.

I smiled lazily at him. "That was seriously awesome," I said.

His answering grin was smug and very male. "Oh, yes," he said. "I do like our arrangement."

"Mmm," I murmured in agreement as I stretched like a cat, as if this desk was as comfortable as the most plush of beds. "Right now, I'm a very satisfied customer."

The jacket had fallen to the floor, and Tyler bent to pick it up. Then handed it to me. I slipped it on, breathing in the scent of him that clung to the material.

I was starting to button it when the door burst open.

"Goddammit," Tyler began, but he stopped when he saw Cole, his expression a mixture of anger and fear.

Cole's eyes darted to me, then focused on Tyler.

"Lizzy" was all he said.

twenty

Tyler caught the attention of the first nurse we came across as he, Cole, and I barreled into the ER at Cook County Medical. "Elizabeth Rodriguez," he said. "Car accident. Where?"

"Just one moment and I'll find out for you." Her words were calm and her manner efficient, and it was clear that she was used to handling crises. She crossed to a workstation and typed something into the computer. "Exam room A. Down the corridor and then to the left."

Neither man ran, but I still had to in order to keep up with their long strides. I'd changed in a hurry, and when I couldn't find my shoes, I'd snatched a pair of flip-flops that someone had left in the break room. The flip-flops were a size too big, and slapped at the polished tile floor as I ran.

I still didn't know exactly what had happened other than

that their former employee, Lizzy, had been in a nasty car accident that afternoon. She'd been unconscious for over an hour, which had worried the doctors, but had otherwise gotten away with only severe bruises and lacerations.

The car, apparently, had been completely totaled.

When she'd regained consciousness, she'd asked that the nurse contact the owners of Destiny.

She was asleep when we came in, and in the dim light of the various machines, the mottled purple and red bruises and welts on her face stood out gruesomely.

I hung back as Cole and Tyler approached the bed, and I saw the way their shoulders straightened, saw their posture go rigid with anger over this offense to the human body.

And then—though I hadn't seen it coming—I saw Cole lash out and smash his fist through the thin, pressboard wall.

I jumped in surprise, but beside him, Tyler didn't even blink. "Calm down or take it outside, man. She doesn't need to see you breaking shit."

"Fuck." Cole rubbed his hands over his shaved head, and as he turned back toward Lizzy, I caught a glimpse of a dragon tattoo on the back of his neck, the bulk hidden beneath his conservative suit jacket. "Jesus, fuck, just look at her."

He stepped closer to the hospital bed, then took Lizzy's hand. I edged farther into the room, and moved down toward the foot of the bed so that I could see everyone, but still be out of the way.

Even with two black eyes and a nasty bruise rising on her cheek, I could tell she was pretty. Her blond hair was matted now, but I could tell she wore it in the same style as Amy, shoulder-length with bangs. Her arm was in a cast, and I had no idea about the state of her legs.

At the bedside, Cole gently stroked the fingers of her uninjured hand while Tyler ran a gentle hand over her hair.

"Hey, Lizzy girl," Tyler said. "You in there?"

When there was no answer, he glanced toward Cole. Their eyes met, and I saw so much pity and concern between the two of them that I wanted to cry.

"She worked for you?"

"Used to dance at Destiny," Tyler said. "Earned her GED a few months ago, and just got her first office job. She's one of ours," he added, with a quick glance to me.

I nodded, understanding that she'd been pulled out of the trafficking ring. Poor girl had been through more than anyone should have to endure.

At her bedside, Tyler shook his head as if to clear it. "I'll need to call Franklin. Get a temp to fill her slot."

Her chart hung at the foot of the bed, and I flipped through it. I'm no expert, but when you work homicide, vice, or sex crimes long enough, you see the inside of a lot of hospitals and have the occasion to look at more than a few charts. As far as I could tell, Lizzy looked like a woman who had gotten supremely lucky. She'd be in some serious pain for a while, but in the end, bruises would fade and broken bones would heal.

I told them so, not sure if my words would give any comfort or not. To my surprise, it was Cole who turned to look at me. He nodded, one quick motion. "Thanks."

"You're welcome."

I'm not sure what compelled me, but I moved from the end of the bed to Tyler's side. "Do you want me to get you guys anything? Some coffee, maybe, while we wait?"

"No," Cole said. "I'm good. Appreciate it."

"Stay," Tyler said, and as he spoke, he reached for my hand.

I took it without thinking, and as Lizzy stirred, Tyler's fingers tightened around mine.

"Lizzy. It's Cole. Wake up, sweetheart."

At first, she didn't react, and I feared that she'd fallen back into a deep sleep. Then her eyes fluttered. The left one blinked open, the swollen right one remained glued shut.

"Hey there, kid," Tyler said, softly. "You're going to be just fine."

"Tyler?" I could barely hear her thin, fragile voice.

"Cole's here, too. Evan's on his way."

Cole clutched her hand. "What happened?"

She licked her lips. "Water?"

While Tyler found the water for her, Cole fiddled with the bed. "Do you want to sit up?" he asked, then raised the bed in response to her affirmative nod.

She scanned the room, her eyes stopping on me.

"I'm Sloane," I said. "I'm a friend of Amy's."

"Sloane's with me," Tyler said. "Go on. Do you feel up to telling us what happened?"

"My fault—ran a red light." A tear trickled down her cheek. "The guy I hit?"

"Fine," Cole assured her. "I asked when I got the first call. Treated at the scene. You didn't hurt him."

She nodded, then winced, as she reached again for the water.

"I'm sorry," she said. "I shouldn't have—" Her eyes drooped. "Medicine. I'm sorry. So sleepy."

"Go back to sleep. You don't have anything to be sorry about," Tyler said. "It was an accident. And I'll get a temp to cover for you. Just take your time, and you can go back to work when you're well."

"No." Her eyes fluttered open. "Franklin . . . please . . . shoulda taken . . . pop job . . . I don't . . ." Her eyes drifted closed, and sleep took her.

Cole tilted his head up to meet Tyler's eyes.

"Poor kid," Tyler said.

Cole glanced at me. "You two take my car. You go on to the benefit. I'm going to stay with Lizzy for a while."

"You sure?"

"Hell, yes."

Tyler hesitated, then pressed a kiss to Lizzy's forehead before leading me out.

"It's horrible," I said. "She's lucky, though. It could have been worse."

Tyler nodded, his expression pensive.

"Did you arrange that job for her?"

"Got her in with Eli Franklin. Solid job for her. Second assistant to Franklin himself. He's into real estate, and damned successful, too. We were lucky to add him to our client list. Lizzy's the first placement with him."

"You mentioned helping the girls at the house find jobs, too," I said.

He nodded. "I own a placement agency. Knight & Day staffing. I bought the company for a song, and still probably paid too much."

"I think I remember reading that you owned an agency." I grinned wryly. "You own so many things it got lost in the list."

"You could say it's a pet project. The entire organization was a mess, but I changed the name and put in a hell of a lot of man-hours. In the end it was worth my time, and my investment. It's turned out to be profitable. And worthwhile."

"Doesn't really seem sexy enough for one of Chicago's leading businessmen," I teased as we exited the hospital and headed for the emergency parking area where Cole had parked his Range Rover.

"The press is interested in sexy. All I care about is profit and functionality. In this case, I was looking at function. But because I'm a goddamn miracle worker, we're also turning a tidy profit now."

"What kind of function? I mean, job placement, obviously, but . . ."

"The girls," he said. "The ones you met, of course, but the

other staff at Destiny. Waitresses, dancers. A lot of women turn to exotic dancing because they don't have the money for school. Because they ended up with a kid but no husband. They don't have the education to make more than minimum wage. K&D helps them out. Placement, tuition assistance, job training." He lifted a shoulder. "It's working."

"K&D helps them out," I repeated. "You mean *you* help them out."

"I do what I can." We'd arrived at the car.

"Why?"

"Because they deserve better," Tyler said, opening the door for me. "And if they're willing to work for it, then I'm willing to help."

Good pay, good benefits, good policy regarding customer interaction with the girls. A semi-charitable boardinghouse. And a protective attitude toward those women that melted my heart. It wasn't the kind of thing I expected a criminal mastermind with a swindler's heart to say. It wasn't what I'd expected when I'd made the drive into Chicago.

But I was looking at Tyler with my own eyes. And not the eyes of a woman who'd been soundly and thoroughly seduced. I was seeing the man with eyes trained to see evidence and nuance. And I had to admit that I liked what I was uncovering.

This Tyler was a man who'd raced to the bedside of a girl he employed. A man who had not only rescued women, but had built up an entire support system for them.

Maybe he did have some seedy side businesses, but at his heart, the Tyler I'd seen and touched and fucked was a different breed of man than the one Kevin sought.

Assuming, of course, that I was really seeing the man. *Nobody is what they seem.*

The possibility that he was showing me only what I wanted to see gnawed at me, but I pushed it away. Both my instincts and the evidence said that I'd seen the real Tyler.

And when you got right down to it, what else was there to look at?

"You're a good man, Tyler Sharp," I said softly, once he was seated in the car beside me.

"No, I'm not." He drew in a long, tired breath. "But I have my moments."

twenty-one

"I don't think I've ever dined with the fishes," I said, as Tyler took my arm and led me to one of the cash bars set up under the watchful eye of a sleek, Bonnethead shark.

The event was in the Shedd Aquarium's Caribbean Reef rotunda. During the day, clusters of schoolchildren and tourists wandered this room. But now it was filled with over two hundred men and women gathered in small groups, chatting and drinking and watching the underwater world float by in the giant tank that sat like a centerpiece in the middle of the stunning room.

"I feel a little like Ariel," I said, referring to *The Little Mermaid*.

"Does that make me your Prince Charming?"

I grinned up at him. "Maybe. It depends on if you find me wine."

"A quest," he said, "for the fair maiden Ariel. Come, my princess, let us be off."

I laughed. "Okay. I take it back."

"I'll admit I'm no prince," he said, "but you are as beautiful tonight as any princess ever was." He hooked a finger under my chin and tilted my head up so that he could press a gentle kiss to my lips.

I sighed, feeling soft and girly and romantic, and when I took his arm, I realized I was smiling.

"What are you thinking?"

"That this feels like a date," I said. "Considering how we've spent our time together so far, that makes the night a standout."

He lifted my hand, then kissed my fingertips. "Disappointed?"

"No," I said softly. "Not even a little bit."

We continued on to the bar, where he got a Scotch and I got a glass of white wine. "I prefer red," I said as we moved back into the throng. "But I don't usually get this dressed up, and I'm currently suffering from the rather overwhelming fear that I'd get red wine all over my gown."

"Then I'd just have to strip it off you," he said, with a cocky, sexy grin.

I rolled my eyes. "Down boy. Fancy dress function, remember? Best behavior."

We were continuing the circuit around the coral reef tank, and arrived at a series of tables topped with a variety of baskets, each with a clipboard and paper. "So what exactly is the purpose of this function?"

"It's a fund-raiser to benefit pediatric neurology research," he said. "Evan and Angie should be around here somewhere. They're both—along with the Jahn Foundation—patrons of the event."

"Which means they made huge donations?"

"Pretty much. In fund-raising, the donations often go to pay for the event, which then tries to recoup that money and earn more through table fees, silent auctions, that kind of thing." He nodded toward the table with the baskets. "See anything you want to bid on?"

"I doubt I could afford anything, but we can look."

We were heading that direction when Tyler stopped. "Wait. That's Franklin. Eli Franklin," he added, pointing to a tall, thin man with deep-set eyes and a heavy brow.

"Lizzy's boss?"

"I should tell him what happened. Not wait until the morning."

"Sure," I said as he veered in that direction. We didn't make it there, though. Instead, we were waylaid by another man, this one white-haired and distinguished.

"Tyler!" he said, holding his hand out to shake as he patted Tyler soundly on the shoulder with his other hand.

"Mr. Danvers," Tyler said. "What a pleasure. Did you get the revised proposal for the security system?"

"Yes, yes. Of course. But we'll talk later. No point in boring your lovely companion."

"Oh, I'm so sorry," Tyler said, pulling me to his side. "This is my date, Sloane Watson. Sloane, this is Gregory Danvers, the CEO of Covington Investments, one of the most influential financial companies in the world."

There was something about his tone and manner that caught my attention, and I was damn certain that he'd forgotten to introduce me on purpose. I just wasn't sure why.

"It's a pleasure," Danvers said, as I extended my hand. "Tyler's given you my life story. What do you do?"

"Sloane's a detective," Tyler added, and suddenly all the pieces fell into place. What was it he'd said? That he had social engagements planned where it would be useful to have a cop on his arm.

"Is that right?" Mr. Danvers said. "What kind of crimes do you investigate?"

I ignored the unpleasant twisting in my belly and smiled at Danvers. "Homicide primarily, though I've worked vice and sex crimes and even a bit in the white collar division. Excuse me," I added, because I needed to get away and get my head clear. "I see Angelina. I'm going to go say hi and leave you two to talk."

I left before Tyler could object, ignoring the way his brow furrowed as I made my escape.

I really had seen Angelina over by the raffle baskets, but considering we had yet to even be introduced, I had no intention of actually going over there. Instead, I planned to finish off my wine and down another glass, just to take the edge off.

That plan, however, was foiled when Angelina joined me in the line for the cash bar. "I'm Angelina Raine," she said. "Angie. And you're Sloane Watson."

"Yes, I am," I answered, making her laugh.

"I saw you at my party but didn't come over on purpose. I was . . ." She trailed off, tilting her head from side to side as she considered her words. "Let's just say I was waiting to see how it panned out." She glanced across the room toward Tyler. "Looks like it played out better than anyone expected."

I cleared my throat, feeling too fragile at the moment to go there, and irritated with myself because of it. "Listen, I owe you an apology. I'm not sure how much you know—"

"Everything," she said. "Evan told me the whole story."

"Oh." I frowned, thinking of my arrangement with Tyler. Just how much of the story did Evan know?

"He told me you're a detective from Indiana, and you're looking for one of your friends who used to work at Destiny. Turns out she moved on to Vegas, right?"

"Looks that way."

She nodded. "Some of the girls do. I guess good dancers can make a nice living there."

"I'm sorry about crashing," I said.

"It's okay. And it turned out for the best. You're seeing Tyler now, which I think is very interesting. And working at Destiny, too."

"Yes, as to Destiny, but not because I have an overwhelming desire to leave the force and go into exotic dancing. I'm hoping Amy mentioned where she was going to one of her customers."

"You're still worried about her?"

"Not overly. But we have a very pregnant mutual friend, and I know Amy wanted to be there for the birth."

"Maybe she met a guy," Angie said. She glanced across the room at Evan. "The right guy can make every other thought leave your head."

I laughed. "You've got that right."

"And it's such a perfect segue I don't even have to be rude when I ask how it's going with you and Tyler."

"Oh." I shook my head. "We're just—" I wasn't sure what to say. We had an arrangement, and while I may have forgotten about it in the thrill of being with Tyler, tonight had very firmly reminded me. "I'll be going back home soon," I finished lamely.

She nodded slowly, as if considering me. We'd reached the bar, and she ordered us each a glass of wine, then turned to me as the bartender poured. "That's too bad," she said. "Kat and I were watching you at the party. And I've been watching tonight."

"Watching me?"

"Well, watching both of you. Tyler mostly."

"Have you?" I paused, knowing I shouldn't push this— knowing it didn't matter because all I had with Tyler was a snapshot in time, and whatever I thought I was feeling didn't matter. Couldn't matter.

All true—but I still wanted to know. "What have you seen?" I asked.

"More than I've seen before," she said. "I'm speaking out of turn, I know. But I've known him forever and I love him to death, and I've seen him go through a lot of women." She took a sip of wine. "They buzz around him, like moths to his light, you know?"

I nodded. I understood exactly.

"But I've never seen him actually pursue a woman. And I sure as hell have never seen him look at a woman the way Evan looks at me."

Oh. I felt my stomach do a little flip. "I—" I stopped. I didn't know what to say. But in that moment I felt strangely, absurdly grateful to this woman who was practically a stranger to me.

"I'm not sure why I'm telling you this. I mean, I know you have a job to go back to, and not even in this state. But I guess I wanted to let you know that you're different. If that matters to you."

Tears pricked my eyes, and I looked down to stare into my wineglass. "Yeah," I said. "It matters."

After Angie left to find Evan, I moved to a corner and watched Tyler finish his conversation with Danvers. It looked easy, jovial, and I could see that Tyler had charmed the man.

When Danvers departed, Tyler turned, his gaze scouring the room and landing on me. Immediately, he smiled, and the heaviness that had settled on me lifted somewhat. Apparently not completely, though, because as soon as Tyler reached me, he pressed a kiss to my temple and asked me what was wrong.

"Nothing," I said. "Tired." I tilted my head and grinned at him. "I haven't been getting much sleep."

"Who needs sleep when there are better things to do?"

I rolled my eyes and fell in step beside him as he extended his arm.

I knew I should stay silent—that I was being a fool. Hadn't Tyler himself said that we weren't dating, we were fucking? And didn't I know damn well that whatever this was would end the day I returned to Indiana?

Dammit.

How had this man gotten so entwined with my heart so quickly? How had he snuck in around all my defenses?

I knew how, of course—he'd seen a part of me no one else had. A part I hadn't even seen. He'd peeled back the hard shell, exposing what was inside. And while it felt nice to be free, that also made me vulnerable.

Now, though I hated myself for wishing it, I was craving some sort of acknowledgment that what I was feeling for Tyler—what I thought he was feeling for me—was real. That it wasn't one big elaborate con for some endgame I hadn't yet seen.

Beside me, Tyler was chatting with passersby and nodding at friends. But his eyes kept returning to me, his expression inquisitive. Finally, he pulled me aside. "Did Angie say something to upset you?"

"What? No. She was great. I like her."

"She is great," he said vaguely. "But you—"

"I'm fine," I said, then rose up on my toes to kiss him. "Really." I cleared my throat. "So you're trying to get a security contract with Danvers? That company you own? BAS Security?"

He nodded. "So far we've kept the client list small and local. But Covington's international. It would be a big coup."

"I'll bet. And having a cop on your arm probably gives the right impression. Projects confidence. Not to mention legality. Almost like an endorsement."

"I see." He slid his hands in his pockets.

"I'm sorry," I said. "I didn't mean to suggest—"

"Suggest? You flat-out said. And you know what, Detective, you're right." His voice had taken on a hard note and I cursed myself, wishing I hadn't brought it up because I had a feeling it was about to all come crashing down.

"Were you not listening when I laid out the reasons for this arrangement?" he continued, still in that hard, businesslike voice. "Because I thought I was clear. There are events where it would be beneficial to have a cop on my arm. Well, Sloane, this is one of them."

"Yes," I said curtly. "I figured that out."

"*Dammit,*" he said, loud enough to have people turning and looking at us. "Shit," he muttered, then took my arm. "Come here."

He led me out of the rotunda, around one of the rope barricades, and into an empty gallery.

"Do you really believe that?" I heard the rise of anger in his voice, but there was something else, too. Something that sounded like hurt. "Christ, Sloane, is that really what you think?"

"I—" I shook my head, not sure what to think.

"Yes, it's good for business to have a cop on my arm. And yes, that's part of how it started with you. But that's not how it is now. It's not why you're here." His voice went soft and he shook his head, as if to clear away his thoughts. "You're here for only one reason, and that's because I want you beside me."

I swallowed, my breath hitching a bit.

"What's between us may have started as an arrangement, a deal. But I think we both know that it's becoming a hell of a lot more than that. As far as I'm concerned, that's just an excuse to be with you. To have you close, when and how I want."

He ran his palm over my shoulder, bare in the sky blue dress. "I don't know where this is going, Sloane, or where it will end. All I know is that you're in my head, you're inside me, and that I will lose a piece of myself the day you go back to Indiana."

"Tyler." I knew I should say something. Tell him I was relieved. Tell him I felt the same way. Tell him that I'd never in my life felt around anyone the way I felt around him. But I couldn't seem to find the words.

So I did the only thing I could do. I folded myself into his arms, and I kissed him.

His arms went around me, and he held me tight. Our bodies

molded together, and his hands stroked my bare back. I felt warm and safe and complete, as if I'd been living my life with a piece missing, and now that I'd found Tyler, everything clicked into place.

I was falling in love with this man. Fast and hard, maybe, but I was certain. What was it he'd said? The speed of us? And he was so right. But love was only part of the equation, and right then, I had to hold tight to the faith that somehow we could make it work. If he really was clean—if everything he'd done was truly in the past—then maybe we could find a way to move forward.

"I'm sorry," he said, when we broke apart. "I didn't think. I should have told you before. I didn't—"

"I know. It's okay." I kissed him again, this time soft and quick before pulling away with a suggestive smile. "Do you need to show me off to somebody else? Or do you think maybe you could take me home and take me out of this dress?"

I could see the answer in his eyes, but before he said it out loud, his phone rang. He glanced at it; mouthed, *Cole;* and answered the call.

He said one word—"Hello," and then he simply listened as Cole spoke.

I watched the change come over him. That relaxed, calm expression turning into hard, cold rage.

When he ended the call his eyes were blazing, and though he looked at me, I wasn't entirely sure he saw me at all.

"Tyler?"

"He tried to rape her," he said. "Lizzy woke up, and she told Cole that bastard Franklin tried to rape her. That's why she was in a hurry. That's why she crashed the car."

"I'm sorry," I said, then put a hand on his arm. "But don't. I can see what you're thinking, and don't."

He just looked at me, and then he stalked back into the rotunda.

Shit.

I hurried after him, scouring the crowd. I saw Franklin on the far side by an exit, and breathed a sigh of relief. If I could just get Tyler out of here before he saw the man . . .

But it was too late. Tyler swooped in, grabbed Franklin by the arm, and as I watched helpless from the far side of the rotunda, Tyler forced him out of the room.

Dammit all to hell.

I hurried in that direction, trying not to run and knowing I couldn't really manage it in these shoes anyway. I paused only when I saw Angie.

"What is it?" she asked when I grabbed her hand.

"Get Evan."

"Why?"

"Get him," I called back, already on the move again.

I kicked off the damn shoes, hiked up my skirt, and picked up my pace.

They weren't in the closest gallery, and I turned in a circle, cursing, trying to figure out where the hell they could have gone, when I heard the crash of metal. I ran forward, then skidded to a stop when I entered a darkened room filled with small aquariums with glowing sea life. All around me, jellyfish floated like angels on a starlit sky, and at my feet, Tyler was pounding his fist into Franklin's face as the man cowered beside a toppled trash can.

"Tyler! Get off him!"

He didn't even react, and I bit out another curse, then dove into the fray, moving in to restrain his hands—wishing I had a pair of goddamn cuffs—and yelling at Franklin to stay the fuck down and not move a muscle.

Naturally, the bastard didn't. He kicked out twice, first knocking me backward, and then catching Tyler in the jaw.

Fuck.

Tyler retaliated by snatching Franklin up by the collar, then slamming him back with a fist to the face.

"Enough," I said, this time managing to get Tyler's arm behind him and hold him fast. He was bigger than me and stronger than me, and I knew he was pissed off enough to do something about it, but I damn sure hoped he wouldn't. "Take a breath," I said. "Take a breath before you kill the bastard."

I heard footsteps, and looked up to see Angie and Evan rushing in. Evan came straight to me and Tyler, and I passed him off, figuring that Evan was better prepared to handle Tyler than I was. "Back it down," Evan said. "Back it down or it's going to get a lot worse."

"He tried to rape Lizzy," Tyler said, when he was finally calm and motionless. "He said that he'd seen her dancing at Destiny. He thanked me—he fucking *thanked* me—for sending him such a tight little piece of ass. That I sure knew how to pick them."

"Oh, Tyler, no," I said.

"And when I told him he was an ignorant prick, he told me that she wanted it. That she wore short skirts. That she teased him. That she asked for it."

I saw the same fury bloom on Evan's face, then watched as he stalked to Franklin, who still sat on the floor, breathing hard and looking like he was having the worst day of his life. He glanced up, then flinched when Evan spat on him.

I met Angie's eyes, and knew she also was fighting the urge to applaud.

Moments later, the security guard joined the fray, which really got the party started. He took initial statements and contact information, then cleared Angie and Evan to leave.

"Do you want us to stay?" Angie asked me.

"Go on back to the party. I'll make sure Tyler calls tomorrow."

"Okay," she said, then pulled me into an impulsive hug. "Take care of him."

"I will," I promised.

I moved toward Tyler, but the guard insisted that Tyler, Franklin, and I remain separated, so I sat on the floor beneath the jellyfish until I saw the detectives arrive. One went straight to Franklin. The other headed toward Tyler.

I stood, then walked toward the second detective, meeting him halfway. Then I reached into my purse and pulled out my badge. "Detective," I said. "Could I have a word?"

twenty-two

"*Self-defense, Detective,*" I said. "*Mr. Sharp had told Mr. Frank-lin that he had evidence that Franklin had sexually harassed an employee. Franklin attacked, and Sharp defended himself.*"

"*And you saw that?*"

"*I did. I'm not telling you how to do your job, but if it were my case, I'd just have everyone walk away.*"

The memory played in my head, over and over like a broken record, blocking out everything else.

"You did the right thing," Tyler said as we stepped inside his suite at The Drake.

They were the first words we'd spoken since leaving the ben-efit, and they sounded far away. "It doesn't feel that way."

"He files charges for assault, and the only way to defend is to drag Lizzy into this mess," he said as he headed into the living room. "Would you want that for her?"

"You didn't have to pound his face in," I said. "What the hell were you thinking?"

"I was thinking that he attacked an innocent girl who'd already suffered enough."

"Yes, I know. Of course." I drew in a breath. "But, Tyler, there are laws against rape, even attempted rape. Lizzy could testify. Bring assault charges, attempted rape."

"That's bullshit, and you know it," he said. "A former stripper crying rape? What cop would believe her?"

"I would," I said, and I saw the flicker of warmth in his eyes.

"Fair enough," Tyler said. "But even if the DA did believe her, Franklin would get a slap on the wrist and no cage time, and we both know it. Justice doesn't always go hand in hand with the law."

I shook my head, knowing I needed to just drop this. That it was becoming too damn personal. "That doesn't mean you can take it into your own hands."

"Why not?"

I just looked at him, willing myself to stay silent.

"I'm serious," he repeated. "Why not?"

"Because you can't," I snapped. "There are rules. There are codes." I thought of my mother. Of my stepfather. And in my mind, I heard the sharp crack of a shotgun.

I shivered, turning away from Tyler. "Don't you get it? There's an entire foundation built around those rules and codes, it's what makes us civilized."

He came to me and put his hands on my shoulders. "That foundation is full of cracks, and you know it."

I shrugged him off, took two steps forward. "Yeah? Well, it's not your job to fill them."

"Christ, Sloane, you know better than that. The rules don't always work. Even a cop should know that."

I whipped around, spitting out my words as the memories pummeled me. "You think that because I'm a cop I don't know about crossing the line? That I don't know about getting dirty? About paying a price?"

I held my hands out in front of me, my breath hitching because I knew that they were covered in blood. "I killed him," I yelled. "I killed my own stepfather, you son of a bitch, and I pay the price every goddamn day."

I gasped the moment the words were out of my mouth, a sharp sound, like I was trying to suck them back in. But they weren't coming back. Instead, they seemed to hang in the air between us.

I stood frozen, staring at him, expecting to see shock, revulsion, even surprise.

I saw none of that.

"Oh, god," I said, collapsing to the floor. "You knew." My voice was dull. Pained. "I've never told that to anyone. I don't know why I told it to you. How did you know?"

He was on the floor, holding me, stroking me, making soft, soothing noises. And I realized I wasn't entirely sure when he'd done that. "Because I see you," he said simply. What I heard was, *Because I love you*.

I blinked, and tears spilled down my cheeks.

"You mess me up, Tyler."

"Yes, well, the feeling is mutual." He pressed a kiss to my head. "Will you tell me what happened?"

I didn't want to go back, but at the same time I wanted him to know. Wanted to share the horror with someone who knew me. Someone I trusted. So I drew in a breath, and started slowly. "You know some of it," I said. "It was like living a nightmare. He beat her. He raped her. He was a monster."

I drew in a breath, clutching his hand tight. "When I was fifteen, he tried to rape me. He was drunk, and I fought him off, but I was done with him. I was so very done."

"What did you do?"

"My dad's a cop, and even though my parents had been divorced for forever, we're close. So I knew things about evidence. And I knew things about my dad. Like the fact that he had a crappy old shotgun in his garage. It used to be his father's, and it was a filthy mess. My dad wasn't a hunter, but he wasn't going to get rid of a gun. It just stayed there in the garage, unloaded, tucked behind the spare fridge."

"You took it."

"Took it, cleaned it. Left it there until the night I'd picked, then I spent that night at a friend's house—to this day my friend thinks I left her place to sleep with Tommy Marquette—and drove to my dad's. He was working nights, so it was easy to get in the garage, get the gun, and get out."

I drew in a breath, trying to push away the visual memories. "It was summer, and Harvey always slept with the light on. He was punishing my mother for something—I don't remember what—and had her locked in the bathroom. So I just got myself set up outside the window as far away as I trusted my aim. There was a rock wall, and I used it to keep the gun steady. I watched, got him in the sights. And then I pulled the trigger. After that, I tossed the gun in the lake and went back to my friend's house."

"And it was easy," Tyler said.

I nodded. "It was."

"That's because it was justice."

I shook my head. "No. No, I snapped, and I took it too far. Justice would have been him in a cage for the rest of his life. It wasn't my right to take him out." I looked at him, held his eyes so that maybe he would understand. "That made me the same as him."

"The hell it did. You protected yourself. You protected your mother. The police had already failed you. What the hell else were you supposed to do?"

"You asked me once why I became a cop. Harvey Grier is one of those reasons. It's like redemption. It's like a second chance."

He shook his head. "No. No, you're wrong. You think you crossed a line, but you didn't. He was vile. He was a monster. There's nothing wrong with killing a monster."

He took my hands and held them tight. "You did the right thing. Back then to protect yourself. Even tonight to protect me. You're one hell of a cop. And I promise you that justice is safe in your hands."

I managed a thin smile. "That's a nice compliment," I said, "coming from a criminal mastermind."

"I'm squeaky clean," he countered with a grin.

I stroked his cheek, suddenly extraordinarily tired. "I wish I could believe that," I said. "Because that's the fundamental gap between us. And there's nowhere we can go from here."

"Bullshit," he said, then kissed me so deeply I thought I might drown in it. "I already told you. I get what I want. And I don't do things halfway. You're already mine, Sloane. The rest is just making the pieces fit together."

Warm hands stroked my back, easing me out of sleep.

I started to turn over, but Tyler whispered in my ear, "No. Close your eyes and drift. I have to get up early for meetings. But you're too tempting to pass up. Just stay there."

I did, moaning as his hands gently spread my legs, then explored me fully. Soft, feather touches. Gentle kisses. Caresses designed to soothe, not tease.

Gently, he stroked my sex until I was wet and ready. I made a small sound of pleasure, my hips moving in pleasure at this treat, this morning wake-up call.

Then he was over me, his hands spreading me so his cock could slip inside me. He thrust rhythmically, and I could sense his climax coming.

Each thrust moved me against the sheet, sending soft strokes over my clit, teasing and firing my body so that I bumped close against the chasm, but never quite reached that edge.

Tyler leaned forward then, grabbing my shoulders as he levered himself deeper and then, with a low moan of male satisfaction, exploded inside me before lowering himself to the bed, his arm and leg draped over me.

"I couldn't resist your temptation," he said, when I turned my head to smile at him. "Turn over and let me touch you. I'll take you the rest of the way."

I shook my head. "No, I like it. Still sleepy and aroused. I'm going to go back to sleep and dream of you."

His brow lifted and he bent down to kiss me. "In that case," he said, "have very sweet dreams."

I drifted off to the sound of the shower. And lost myself in those sweet dreams until fingers of sunlight sneaked into the room to tickle my nose. I sat up slowly, feeling gloriously used, then laughed when I saw the Hershey's Kiss that Tyler had left on the pillow beside me.

I knew that he had a full plate today, and so we'd planned to meet at Destiny after my shift. Now I stretched in bed, feeling warm and happy and feminine.

Last night had been both good and bad, but in the end, I couldn't deny that I felt closer now to Tyler than I'd ever felt to anyone. And when we'd gone to sleep, my exhaustion so overwhelming that he'd carried me to bed, he had spooned against me, his strong arms holding me close and keeping me safe.

It had felt romantic and sensual.

It had felt like love.

I stretched across the bed, grabbing my phone to check the time, pleased to see I didn't have to rush. I slid out of bed, then decided to forgo the fluffy Drake robe for one of Tyler's button-down shirts. Foolish perhaps, but I liked being wrapped in his scent.

I found frozen waffles in the freezer and popped one in, then sat down at the kitchen table with the paper Tyler had left there. But I couldn't concentrate on the news. Last night was too fresh in my mind, and my thoughts were a jumble.

Squeaky clean.

That's what he said, and I desperately wished it was true. Hoped it was true. I could imagine a life with Tyler, though I told myself not to think like that.

Thinking like that only led to disappointment.

Still, there was no denying that we fit together in so many ways. And now—now that he knew about my stepfather, I had no more secrets from him.

It felt good. It felt honest.

The waffle popped and I pulled it out of the toaster with two fingers, then searched the fridge for syrup. When I didn't find any, I settled on peanut butter. I slathered it on thick, then took a bite, remembering the look in his eyes when I'd blurted out my secret.

He'd known. I still didn't understand how, but I guess what he said was true—he really did see me.

I took another bite, only this time it felt too thick to swallow. I spit it out into a napkin, then went to the sink. I turned on the faucet and just stood there, looking at the water draining away.

He'd known.

True, we had a connection—there was no denying that.

But still, he'd known. And in such a short time.

If he'd known after only a few days and even fewer facts, then how the hell could my father have missed the truth?

Unless he hadn't missed the truth.

I stumbled back to the table and fell into the chair, the thought enough to make me go limp.

Did he know?

I licked my lips and, before I could talk myself out of it, picked up my phone.

He answered on the first ring. "Hey there, daughter o' mine. How's the hip?"

"It has a hole in it," I said. "Otherwise it's fine."

"Funny girl. What's up?"

"I—Daddy, I wanted to ask you something."

"All right," he said, his voice softer now. "Go ahead."

"It's . . . about when I was a kid. Living with Mom. Did you know—" I sucked in a breath. "Daddy, Grier abused her."

He was silent a long moment. When he spoke, his voice sounded far away and very sad. "I realized that later."

"I should have told you. Maybe it would have helped."

"No—no, sweetheart. You were a kid. You were living in hell and doing your best. You did just fine."

"He was a monster," I said. "I wanted him dead every single day."

"I bet you did."

"And then—and then someone killed him."

"Yes, they did," he said, and I knew—because I knew his voice, just like he knew me. My father had held my secret, too.

"Sloane?"

"Yes, Daddy?"

"It's like I always say—justice wins out."

"Did it, Daddy?"

"You bet it did, sweetheart."

When I hung up, I realized I was crying, but I was smiling, too. And for the first time in a long time, I let the weight of my secret drop away.

I wanted Tyler, but he was off at meetings, and so I did the next best thing. I got dressed, got in my car, and headed to Destiny.

I would be early, but I didn't care. I could mingle with the customers, maybe see if there were any more who knew Amy.

I frowned, realizing I hadn't asked my dad about the run on

her license. Then again, it hadn't been that long, and I knew he'd call if and when he got something.

I did, however, want to give Candy an update to let her know I had even more confirmation that Amy had skipped to Vegas. I put the phone on speaker and dialed her number as I maneuvered onto the highway to head toward Destiny.

"I was going to call you today," she said, right off the bat. "Guess who called me last night?"

"Amy," I said.

"Yes! She sounded terrible, but she said she's doing great—she did meet a guy, so we were right about that. She'd lost her phone. I almost just deleted the voicemail—I figured it was a wrong number—and she said not to worry about her."

"How did she sound bad?"

"Just tired," Candy said. "I tried to call back on the number, but it said it wasn't working. Not sure what's up with that. I wanted to tell her to chill. And to lay off the guy if he was wiping her out so much. Anyway, it's good news, huh?"

"The best."

"She said she'd be here for the baby. Well, she said next month, but I'm sure she meant next week. If not, I'll chew her ass out for being late."

"I bet you will."

I hung up, smiling at the relief in Candy's voice. I thought of Sapphire, and her frustration at not knowing what had happened to Emily, and her impression that the police weren't doing enough.

I could hardly help on the investigation, but maybe I could help gather some facts. I scrolled through my contacts and put a call in to Detective Louis Carson, one of the Chicago homicide detectives I'd called to ask about Tyler and the guys when I'd first rolled into town.

"Hey, Watson," he said. "You still in our fair city?"

"I am," I said. "And I have a favor." I told him about Emily and about wanting to help Sapphire and asked him if there was anything more I could pass on to her.

"I know a bit about that case," he said. "I can give you some info, but you need to keep it to yourself. Chief wanted a tight wrap on this case, and he hasn't yet authorized release of the details. Should be soon, though, and you can tell your girl."

"I'll keep quiet until you say," I promised, then listened as he told me about how she'd been found in an abandoned warehouse—that was public knowledge—and that she'd been the victim of torture.

"Not sexual, as far as we can tell. But starved and beaten. Some sick fuck did a number on her."

"Shit."

"I know. We're hoping we don't have a serial killer on our hands."

"Anything useful from forensics?"

"Adhesive residue and POE oil," he said, spelling out the last for me. "That's the angle we're working now, but both are pretty damn common."

I thanked him and we chatted some more until I hit my exit, then I said goodbye and pulled into the Starbucks that was just a few doors down the street. I'd done the same the last two times I'd come, and when the barista knew I wanted a venti nonfat latte before I even asked, I realized I was feeling like a regular.

I bought a scone for later and took it and my coffee back to the car, then continued on to the club. I was about to pull behind the building to park when I saw the back door open and Tyler step out—and Michelle was with him.

I pulled over and watched as they got into Tyler's Buick and pulled out onto the road. And then, though I felt prickles of guilt for doing it, I followed them.

Despite what I knew about Michelle, I wasn't expecting them to lead me to a love nest. On the contrary, because of what I knew about Michelle—including Tyler's comment that first day in his office that he wanted to use her for some project—I had a feeling I was about to see the kind of thing I really didn't want to see—proof that Tyler Sharp wasn't anywhere close to squeaky clean.

The thought almost made me turn back around.

But I couldn't. I needed to keep going. I needed to see.

They pulled up at The Drake, and as I took a spot on the opposite side of the street, the valet opened the car for Michelle. She got out, looking classy in a red business suit with a straight skirt. I waited for Tyler to get out, but he continued on, pulling back into traffic.

I frowned, and was about to follow, when I noticed the white van two spots in front of me with a BAS sticker in the back window.

Okay, then.

Apparently I'd stumbled on a BAS Security operation. And I figured I might as well pop in and see what they were up to.

I was about to get out of the car to do just that when my phone rang, the caller ID showing that it was Kevin. I considered ignoring the call, but succumbed to curiosity and answered.

"I keep hoping to hear from you."

"Kevin, I told you. You're chasing rainbows. These are good guys. Trust me."

"No," Kevin said. "It's there. Those three don't operate clean. Everything they touch snakes back to dirty. Smuggling, forgery, extortion, you name it. Did you know they supposedly run a private security company? But I'll be damned if that's not just a front for them to gather intel."

I glanced out my window at the BAS van and frowned. "Jesus, Kevin. Do you have even a shred of evidence that isn't completely circumstantial?"

"I know what I know," Kevin said.

"Yeah, well, I don't." I ended the call, too frustrated and distracted to let it linger.

Once again, I glanced over toward The Drake, and then to the van in front of me.

I thought of Tyler and hoped I hadn't been a fool to let him shatter my walls and slide in through the cracks. But even as I hoped, I couldn't forget what Kevin had said—*Everything they touch snakes back to dirty.*

And I couldn't help but think that Tyler had touched me.

I'd told Kevin the absolute truth—I had nothing on these men. But while that was true, it wasn't the whole truth.

The whole truth was that I hadn't looked because, dammit, I was afraid of what I might see. And if I saw, would I lie? As I'd lied last night to the detective?

Shit. Who was I?

I'd been closing my eyes where before I would have been poking a flashlight into shadows.

That had to stop now. If for no other reason than I was falling in love with Tyler. And I had to know if the man I loved was dirty.

Before I could talk myself out of it, I exited the car and marched to the van. I drew in a breath, grabbed the sliding door handle, and tugged.

Inside, Cole whipped around to look at me, then slammed his palm down on a console, making a row of five video monitors go to black.

But it didn't matter—I'd already seen. Michelle, in full dominatrix regalia, holding a whip over a man I recognized from the Chicago papers. Alderman Brian Bentley, decked out in a ball-gag and cuffs.

"Sloane, wait—"

I slammed the door, cutting off Cole's plea. Then I ran for my car. I heard the van open, heard him call for me again. I didn't care. I started the car, slid into traffic, and floored it.

I cranked the music up loud, and hoped that the beat would drown out my thoughts, but it wasn't working. My thoughts were filled with Kevin's accusations and with the images I'd seen in that van. Extortion, I assumed. Bribery. What had Evan called it? A protection plan?

God. What the hell were they into?

And what the hell was I doing?

A year ago, a month ago, hell, a week ago, I'd be calling the local PD. Now I wasn't sure what to do.

I was twisted around because of love—but didn't that make me as guilty as they were?

I didn't know. All I knew was that Tyler filled my head, bigger and bolder than even the music my dad sent me.

Tyler, who had held me, teased me, touched me, fucked me. Whose heart had beat in time with mine.

I thought about his humor. About his compassion.

I drove on auto-pilot, my thoughts churning wildly, and it wasn't until my dad's music was looping for the fourth time that I tuned in to where I was—which was no longer in Illinois. I'd not only crossed the line into Wisconsin, but had just hit the Kenosha city limits.

I may have been on auto-pilot, but my subconscious had definitely had a plan all along.

I'd only been to the Victorian style house on Fifth Street once before, but it wasn't any trouble finding it. The lawn had been a mess the last time I was there, but now it was neat and tidy, with colorful flowers in pretty clay pots. The dingy paint had been spruced up, at least on the street-facing side. I saw buckets and two ladders around the side of the house, and assumed I was facing a work-in-progress.

I pulled up in front, killed the engine, and sat there for a while, debating. I could go in . . . or I could turn around and drive the hour and a half back to Chicago.

I decided to go in.

The house was quiet, and I saw no sign of life as I walked to the front door. I wasn't sure if I should be annoyed I'd come so far for no reason, or relieved.

I rang the bell, got no immediate response, and rang again. A good three minutes passed, still with no answer, and I finally decided that all I'd gotten out of this day was a relaxing drive and too much thinking.

I turned to go—and heard the lock click behind me.

I spun around, and found myself staring into the hangdog face of Oscar Hernandez.

He wore a coffee-stained undershirt and flannel pajama pants that had seen better days. Sleep creases lined his face, crisscrossing under his puffy eyes.

"Gee, Lieutenant," I said. "You're taking this retirement thing seriously."

"Watson?" His red eyes crinkled in delight as a wide smile split his face. "Goddammit, Detective, what in the name of the devil's younger daughter are you doing here?"

"Guess I got a little lost."

He cocked his head, and I saw the sharp mind behind the bloodshot eyes. "You're not talking about streets and maps."

"Guess not." I lifted a shoulder. "Needed a beer. Figured this was the place to find one."

"Damn right it is," he said. "Or it was last night. Wife's back home with Joey," he said, referring to their oldest daughter. "Had some of the guys over."

"A calm night of cigars and literary discussions?"

"Fuck that. We got pissed and talked about our misspent youth. Get your tiny ass in here," he said, stepping back and holding the door open wide.

I followed him into the kitchen, then hung back as he opened the fridge and stared inside. "I got Heineken and Heineken. Might have some flavored vodka in the freezer. Wife likes that whipped cream stuff."

"I'll take Heineken," I said. "And if you've got a bag of potato chips hiding around here somewhere, I'll love you forever."

"After what we've been through, you should love me anyway." But he crossed to the pantry and came out with a bag of Lay's and a bag of Ruffles.

"You're a good man, Lieutenant."

"Don't you forget it."

Fifteen minutes later we were sitting on the back porch steps, breathing in the summer air and looking out at the water. I'd never seen my partner as the Mr. Fix-it type, but I had to admit that for a house like this—big and sprawling with a huge backyard, trees, and a view of the lake—maybe being domesticated would be worth it.

"You gonna tell me what's on your mind? 'Cause as much as I enjoy your company, I don't think you drove all this way just for beer and chips."

"It's really good beer," I said, and clinked bottles with him. "But no. Honestly, I'm not sure why I came. The car sort of drove itself."

"All the way from Indiana? You must really be going out of your mind on this medical leave."

"Chicago," I said, and that was as good a lead-in as any. I gave him the basic rundown, leaving out the more titillating details. If we ended up going there, I'd need more than one beer in my system.

"Last time I looked, kid, you didn't have a Chicago badge."

I eyed him sideways. "So?"

"So whatever these guys are up to doesn't have anything to do with finding your missing friend, right?"

"Right."

"And the girl was the reason you went to Chicago."

"Yes."

"So leave it alone."

I blinked. "Leave it alone?"

"Jesus, Watson, you live and breathe this job more than any-one I know. You don't have to right every wrong, you know. So unless those guys are killing folks in Indiana, their crimes and misdemeanors aren't your problem."

"Even if I'm banging one of them?"

He drew in a loud, noisy breath. "Well, shit, Watson. Now I'm gonna have that in my head all day."

I leaned forward, my elbows on my knees and my head in my hands. "I'm all twisted up, Oscar."

"Aw, shit. Aw, hell." His big hand came down on my back and rubbed. "You'll get untwisted."

"How?"

"No idea."

I laughed. "You're a big help."

"Okay, try this. The heart knows what the heart knows."

I turned to him. "That's some flowery shit coming from you."

"Courtesy of the wife. It's what she used to tell me whenever Joey dragged home some yahoo I didn't like the looks of. Like the idiot banker who followed her home one day like some de-termined puppy."

"What's it mean?"

"I think it means if you fall, you're fucked. So you might as well enjoy yourself."

"You know, that's not bad advice, actually."

"That's me, always dispensing the knowledge. You want to hang around? Meredith'll be home in time for dinner."

"Nah. I should get back. But thanks." I stood up, then con-sidered him. "What happened with the idiot banker?"

"Turned out not to be such an idiot, after all. Gave me three of the most precious grandkids on the planet." He stood, too, then walked me around the house to my car. "You take care of that hip. And if this guys sticks, you bring him by. If there's a man out there can trip you up, I want to meet him."

twenty-four

I didn't go to The Drake when I got back to Chicago. Instead, I went to my tiny apartment. I wanted time to think. To be alone. To let all the pieces come together in my head. What I knew. What I wanted.

And how there was no way over, around, or under the giant impasse that was cop versus criminal.

Even if Hernandez was right and I didn't need to be slapping on the cuffs or ratting the guys out to Kevin, that didn't change the fundamental nature of the problem—I'd fallen for a man I couldn't have.

I wanted time alone.

I should have known that was too much to ask.

I opened my door, and found myself staring at Tyler, standing in my tiny kitchen brewing coffee, looking nine kinds of sexy in a white button-down and jeans.

"You broke in?" I said. "Well, why not? Just another crime to add to the list."

"A minor one, all things considered." His voice was smooth and held a hint of humor. I knew him well enough to know he was trying to keep a lid on my temper.

I wasn't entirely sure it was going to work.

"I thought Cole was the one with the lock-picking skills."

"No, I said it was one of Cole's two skills. I don't believe I discussed my many and varied skills at all." He held up a mug. "Coffee is on the list."

"Why are you here?" I asked wearily. I moved to the bed and sat on the edge, exhausted. I wanted to be angry, truly I did. I wanted to yell and rant and scream and rave. But I was just too damn tired and sad.

"Cole told me what happened."

"Yeah, I kind of guessed that."

"I never lied to you," he said.

I exhaled. "No," I said, "you didn't. Skirted around the truth, but never lied. And I never looked. I was like one of those monkeys with their hands over their eyes, their mouth, and their ears. I only saw what I wanted to see."

"You were only really looking at Destiny," he said. "And it's scrubbed clean. Evan insisted on that if he was going to remain a partner."

I shook my head. "No. It wasn't Destiny I was looking at." I drew in a breath. "It was you. You filled my vision. Larger than life. Bold and sexy and exciting, and I lost myself in the shine. And now I'm afraid that I see you way too clearly."

"So you're punishing me because I am what you thought I was all along?"

"Don't," I said, feeling my temper rising. "Don't play games. Not now. Not with this. I'm a cop, and you know it. Maybe I've been living in a fantasy with you, but that doesn't change the fact that I'm sworn to uphold the law."

"You became a cop to punish yourself, Sloane. You made a cage out of the rules and the laws. But you don't have to do that. You don't need to be punished. Justice won that night, I promise you."

I shook my head. "No. This isn't about Harvey Grier—it's not," I said, though he had raised no protest. "It's important to me, those rules, those codes. It's my life."

"And if I wanted you to be my life?"

His words, said so simply and plainly, were nothing more than a sucker punch. And I had to work not to shake. Not to cry out. Not to shout for him to please not say that again, because just the mere idea of it was too damn tempting—and I couldn't afford to be tempted.

Slowly, when I thought I could manage it, I shook my head. "We both know that's never going to happen." I felt the tears behind my eyes, and as I sat with ramrod posture, I kept my eyes wide open, determined not to cry.

He stood by the sink, his eyes firmly on my face. "I have never wanted a woman the way I want you," he said, his voice so full of promise and raw emotion that it almost broke me. "And I've never let a woman see into my cracks the way I have you. I understand your hesitations. I respect them. But know this. I'm damn well going to push against them."

I ran my fingers through my hair. "I'm tired. And I'm confused. I want to be with you, but I don't know how. I told you. This is the chasm, and I don't see a way across. I mean, Christ, Tyler. You're running an extortion scheme."

"No," he said. "Not extortion. Those tapes weren't for money, but for protection."

"What do you mean?"

"You might be surprised to know that not all politicians are fine, upstanding citizens. As it happens, the newly elected Alderman Bentley used to be a cog in a wheel that the guys and I ran."

"The kind of wheel that I'd disapprove of?"

He hesitated only a second, then said flatly, "A money laundering scheme. Bentley was right in the thick of it. And that means he knows too much about our operation. And now that he's an elected official, he may be inclined to try to use that information to gain pull."

"Use it and he exposes himself."

"Maybe. But it might be worth it to him."

"But it wouldn't be worth it if those pictures got out," I said.

"That's the plan. He stays quiet, the pictures are never released."

"That doesn't make it any less illegal."

Tyler shrugged. "Not really my main concern."

"What is?"

"Lately? Lately, it's you."

"Tyler . . ." I felt like a hand was squeezing tight around my heart.

"It's true. It's why I'm here running off at the mouth. Do you know how much I'm risking letting it out in the open? Because when you get right down to it, what I've told you could destroy us. And I've never been so careless before."

"Why now?" I asked, both dreading and craving the answer.

"Because I'm an idiot," he said. "I'm an idiot for falling in love with a cop."

"Tyler." Just one word, but it was full of passion and apology and, yes, love.

He moved from the kitchen to kneel in front of me. "This is more than a game to me, Sloane. And you're more than just a prize. I want a woman who burns with me. Who melts into me. Who fits into all my hollow places. That's you, Sloane. Do you see that? Do you know it? You're my everything. You're my whole world."

I swallowed, overwhelmed with emotions—confusion, fear, love.

He rose up and brought his mouth to mine, his kiss both possessive and tender.

"I told you once I want no secrets between us," he said, as he trailed his fingers up and down my arm. "I meant it. I want to tell you everything. I won't bore you with a laundry list, but if you have questions, just ask."

I had so many, but I didn't know where to begin, or even if I wanted to ask them all. "You said Destiny was clean. But it wasn't always, was it?"

"No," he said.

"And it is now because of Evan. He gave it up for Angie, didn't he? Because what he does could damage her father."

"Yes. And I think the thrill was fading. He likes business, plain and simple. I like taking a different approach."

"Could you do that, though?" I asked, realizing how much hope was lacing my voice. "Could you give it up?"

He was silent so long I thought he wasn't going to answer. When he did, it wasn't the response I'd expected. "Could you give up being a cop?"

"It's not the same. I'm enforcing the law. You're twisting it around to your liking. And you can't do that. You can't push the envelope and not expect to pay." I licked my lips. "That's the crux of it. I love you, too, Tyler. Desperately. It amazes me because it's hit me so hard and so fast. But it's true." I sighed. "Even so, it's not enough, because I don't know how to get past this."

"Then we don't get past it," he said. "Not yet. We've been living in a bubble, sweetheart. Let's stay in it for just a little longer."

I drew in a breath and considered. I only had a few more days before I had to report back, anyway. And the truth was, I would do anything for a few more days with this man.

"All right," I said as I glanced around my crappy apartment. "But can we stay at The Drake?"

twenty-five

The condo that Angie and Evan shared was about the most amazing place I'd ever seen. It was huge, and one side of the living room was made up of a wall of windows that looked out over Lake Michigan, and the boats lit up on the water at night made it look like there were stars both below and above us.

"It was my uncle's," Angie explained. "I inherited it. And since Evan loves the place as much as I do, we mostly live here."

They had invited Tyler and me over for drinks, along with Cole and Kat. Kat had arrived before us, so I got a good look at her face when Cole entered. Attraction, fascination, and then—when Cole told Angie that someone named Bree wouldn't be joining him—disappointment.

I liked Cole—he had a straightforward manner that I appreciated, and a deep-seated passion that I admired. I'd seen some of his art, and had been shocked by its beauty and power, the imagery in contrast somehow to the burly man with the dragon tattoo. I thought also of what I knew about Cole and Michelle and the dungeon. And then I said a little prayer for Kat. But whether it was for her to figure a way into a complicated man like Cole, or for her to just move on, I really didn't know.

"Got any beer, Dragonbait?" Cole asked Angie.

"You know we do. Help yourself."

He paused by me on the way to the kitchen. "I'm glad you and Tyler got clear," he said. And then he surprised me by pulling me into a quick, tight hug.

While Cole went to the kitchen, the rest of us followed Evan and Angie through a living room filled with art, most in the kind of frames that each had their own spotlight.

One piece, however, stood out. It was a handmade quilt, framed and hung just off the living room in an adjoining hallway. "Isn't that like Tyler's quilt?"

"The same woman gave them to all three of the guys," Angie said.

I glanced curiously at Tyler. "Really? How interesting."

Kat snorted, but Tyler only rolled his eyes. "Mind out of the gutter, Detective. They were handmade by the grandmother of the very first girl we pulled out of the trafficking scheme."

"They're very special," Evan added.

"They are," I agreed. "You've touched a lot of lives."

Evan turned to Angie. "Why don't you girls head to the patio. We'll bring the drinks up."

The patio turned out to be a massive outdoor living area on the roof of the high-rise. Angie and I sat on two of the plush outdoor sofas, and Kat plunked herself down on the ground. "I thought you were running a con," Kat said to me. "When I first saw you, I mean."

"A con?"

She shrugged. "I knew the guys were keeping an eye on you, and I couldn't figure out why. I didn't know you were a cop, so

I figured you were trying to scam them. I couldn't believe that anyone would be stupid enough to think they could pull a con on those three and get away with it. Trust me, I know."

"Yeah? How?"

"Well, not personally," Kat amended. "My dad did a real estate deal with Tyler years ago, but I wasn't involved. I got to hear about it from Dad's end, though." She grinned. "That's how I know you don't play mind games with Tyler Sharp."

"He took your dad?"

"Let's just say he didn't let my dad take him."

"That sounds like Tyler," I said, and couldn't help but wonder which side of the line Kat's father fell on.

The guys were back soon with the drinks, and the evening fell into an easy rhythm. They talked about work and various projects, all of which sounded legitimate, and it occurred to me to wonder just how much Kat knew about what these men did.

As for Kat and Angie, they asked me all sorts of questions about being a cop and about stripping at Destiny. I had to admit, it made for an interesting mix of topics.

I was on my second glass of wine when Kat stood up and said she had to go. "Work," she said, then pulled a face. "There really needs to be an easier way to make a living."

She headed out, and Angie and I moved to the glass barrier that shielded the patio from the abyss below. "He's gone on you," Angie said, as soon as we were out of earshot of the men.

"It's mutual," I said. "But it doesn't matter. Our lives just don't intersect, you know? And I'll be back in Indiana by the end of the week."

"Maybe it'll work out," she said. "I didn't think it would for Evan and me, but here we are."

I shifted to look at her better. "Can I ask you something? I know your dad's a senator," I began after she nodded. "And I know the guys are into a few things that are less than legitimate."

She cocked her head. "You figure?"

"Tyler told me," I said.

"Oh." Her eyes widened. "Well, that is interesting."

I grinned wryly. "Yeah, well. I imagine Evan's clean. What with your dad being who he is. Am I right?"

She nodded.

"So he changed. Evan, I mean. He changed for you."

"He changed," she said. "But it was for himself. I don't think I could be with a man who was someone other than himself. Could you?"

"No," I said, "I couldn't."

But I also couldn't be with a criminal.

When we returned to the guys, they were still talking work. This time, the gallery space.

"You mentioned it before," I said. "You're opening an art gallery?"

"We are," Cole said. "And it's an amazing space. You should check it out, Evan."

"You know I'm not signing on with you."

I raised a brow as I looked at Tyler. "Something shady going on under the layers of paint?"

As soon as I spoke, Evan and Cole glanced sharply at Tyler.

He just shrugged. "I told her," he said. "Everything."

I saw them tense, and then relax at his next words: "I love her," he added, holding out his hand for me.

The other men said nothing, but I saw the acceptance in their eyes. That was all it took, I thought, as I rested my head on Tyler's shoulder. They were family.

"Come take a look," Tyler said to Evan. "It's not like we'll make you sign in blood. And who knows," he added. "Maybe we'll end up going legit. Stranger things have happened."

We stayed another two hours, and then Tyler pulled me away, making our excuses to the others. Angie gave me a hug, and Cole and Evan both kissed my cheek. I felt, I realized, like I belonged.

"I like them," I said. "We can hang out longer if you want to."

"Can't," he said, checking the time on his phone. "We're on a schedule."

"We are?"

"We are," he affirmed, with mischief dancing in his eyes.

"Will you tell me why?"

"Nope," he said, but when we stepped out of the building, I saw my first clue—a stretch limo, complete with liveried driver holding the door open.

I turned to Tyler to ask, but he just shook his head. "In," he said, and I complied.

He followed me in, only now he held a single, blood-red rose. He gave it to me, followed by a long, slow kiss.

"I like this," I said, when he drew away. "Mysterious and romantic. How far are we going?"

"Not far," he promised, as he put his arm around me and pulled me close.

The watch that Jahn had given him brushed my shoulder and that, coupled with the fact that we'd just left a condo that had been owned by Jahn, made me remember what I still hadn't asked.

"Will you tell me now why you won't get the watch fixed?"

He turned, looked at me, and nodded. "Howard Jahn was an incredible man. Brilliant. Engaging. Entrepreneurial. He taught Evan and Cole and me everything we know," he added, with a meaningful grin.

"He wasn't, however, good with women. He kept too many secrets, and they always left. Apparently one of his earlier wives got so fed up with him that she threw the watch at him. And then another one did the same. Instead of fixing it again, he decided to wait until he found the woman of his dreams."

"He never did," I said, thinking of the broken watch. "That's so sad."

"I know, it really is. But when he got sick, he wrote notes to the three of us. And in mine he said that he thought he and I had a certain spark in common. That we each needed to find the right woman to make us whole, and he hoped that I would find her soon, so that I wouldn't be lonely like he was."

His eyes were on me as he spoke, and my pulse quickened.

"He said that time could start again once I found her." His smile was quick and just a little winsome. "I'm hoping to have the watch fixed soon."

"Are you?" I said, smiling.

"I am," he said, and had just enough time to kiss me before the limo came to a halt and the driver pulled open the door.

I peered outside. "The aquarium? Weren't we just here?"

"I thought we should try again. I like this place. I want you to have good memories."

"But it's the middle of the night. It's closed."

"Not for us," he said, then led me to the entrance. Sure enough, we were allowed in, then led back to the Caribbean Reef Rotunda again.

"Tyler," I said, the word little more than breath.

The room was set up with just one table, draped in a white tablecloth. A violinist played off to the side, and a private chef stood at the ready.

A single candle lit the table, and there was an empty bud vase for my rose.

I looked at the room, at him, and felt tears prick my eyes. "Why?" I asked.

"Because I look at you and all I want is to be inside you. To touch you. To throw you down and take you, any way and anywhere. It overwhelms me."

"It overwhelms me, too."

"But even with all of that," he said, "I don't want to forget to romance you."

He took my hand and pulled me into his embrace. "I've gone

out with a lot of women, Sloane, but I've only fallen in love with one. I want to make this work."

"So do I," I whispered, though I'm not sure how I managed to speak through the roar of emotion. "But I don't know how."

"We'll figure it out together."

twenty-six

"Venti nonfat latte, right?" the barista asked, and I cringed, just a little.

"I should probably cut back," I said. "But yes."

I paid, then scooted over to wait for my drink. And as I did, Kevin came up to me.

"I need to talk to you," he said.

I gaped at him. "What the hell? Have you been following me?"

"I just need two minutes."

"Jesus, Kevin. You're going off the rails."

"I'm not," he said, then shoved an envelope into my hands. "That's everything I have on them, a laundry list of the operations I think they're involved in."

My heart pounded in my chest with the rising fear that

Tyler—that all of the knights—were in trouble. I worked to stay steady. To not let Kevin see my reaction. Or, if he did, to think it was the thrill of the chase.

"All right," I said. "I'll look it over."

And I would, I thought. Carefully, and with Tyler. And if their asses were hanging out in any way, they could use Kevin's list as a blueprint for getting clear.

Tyler wasn't at Destiny when I got there, so I left the envelope in the top drawer of his desk, then headed in to get ready for my shift.

I had on the short shorts and was getting ready to do a circuit, when Cole's hand clutched tight on my upper arm.

"What the fuck, Sloane?"

"Excuse me?"

"Tyler's a good man—he trusted you. And that meant we trusted you, too. But dammit, girl, none of us take kindly to being played, Tyler most of all."

I jerked my arm free. "What are you talking about?"

I had no idea what had sparked this, but it was clear that Cole had a tight rein on the temper I'd seen before. Right then, he looked like he could put a hole through me the same way he put his fist through the hospital wall.

I didn't know if any of the three had ever killed someone, but in that moment, I was damn sure that Cole was capable.

"Just watch yourself," he said, then walked away.

"Cole!"

He turned back, his finger held up, his expression so tight I knew he was fighting an explosion.

And then he turned away again and stalked off.

I couldn't decide if I was pissed that he hadn't told me the problem, or relieved that he hadn't pummeled me into dust.

Either way, I wanted to ask Tyler what was going on. I knew that he'd arrived about a half hour before, so I hurried to his office and pushed through the door. "What the hell is up with Cole?" I began, but the dark expression on Tyler's face chilled me.

"What's up with Cole?" Tyler repeated, bursting to his feet, his face a portrait of anger and hurt. "Maybe the better question is what the hell is up with you."

"Jesus, you too?" I snapped as confusion and a sick feeling pounded over me. "What the fuck are you talking about?"

"Cole saw you," he said. "You're working with Kevin Warner, that goddamn prick. I trusted you. Hell, Sloane, I love you. How the hell could you—"

"You son of a bitch." I was beyond furious, and my words came out low and harsh and cold. "You goddamn son of a bitch. You really believe I would betray you? That I was working with Kevin? He's been dogging me, Tyler. Trying to get me to find dirt on you. And all I've done is tell him that you're clean. I compromised my own fucking values to tell him you're clean."

I stalked to his desk and ripped open the drawer. I pulled out the envelope and tossed it in his face. "There. That's what he has on you. I thought you might find it useful in case you wanted to clean up whatever goddamn mess you've gotten yourself into. *Fuck,*" I added, then slammed my fist down on the desk. "I'm not Amanda, Tyler. I didn't run to the cops. I'm not betraying you."

But I couldn't stay, and without another look back, I ran from the room, grabbed my purse from my locker, and headed back to The Drake, not even bothering to change my clothes.

The shorts and bra-top got a few stares, but I barely noticed, I was still seething too much.

And it wasn't until I reached the penthouse and was in the bedroom, digging workout clothes from my drawer, that I realized the irony. I'd come here. To the penthouse.

I'd been pissed, and I'd come home. And to me, home was where Tyler was.

I sighed. I loved the man desperately—had given him all my trust—and this is what I got in return. How fucked up was that?

I changed into leggings and a sports bra, then called down to the front desk to find out the location of the fitness center. As it turned out, the tenth floor had its own, and I found it easily enough, and was grateful to see it had a punching bag.

I quickly taped my hands, then shoved on some gloves. I started to beat the shit out of a bag while a skinny man in headphones jogged on the treadmill, occasionally shooting me concerned glances. I wasn't surprised. If that bag had been a man, he'd have been dead, several times over.

I'm not sure how long I tortured the bag before the door opened and Tyler eased inside. I saw him approach in the mirror. I didn't turn. I wasn't ready not to be mad.

"Want to take a few swipes at me, too?"

"Hell, yes."

"We need to talk."

"We really don't."

He moved closer, then reached out and held the bag steady. "We can talk here with an audience or we can go back to the suite. But we are going to talk."

"Fine." I headed toward the door, then waited for him to open it, as I was still wearing the gloves.

He glanced at them as we walked down the hall. "Planning on punching me?"

"Depends on what you say."

"I'm apologizing," he said, and the fist around my heart loosened. "There may even be some groveling."

I crossed my arms and tilted my head as he opened the door to the suite. "All things considered, yeah. I think groveling is in order."

"I'm sorry," he said again once the door closed behind us. "This thing between us—I want it so desperately, but it scares me, too. I told you, I don't trust easily. And when Cole told me what he'd seen, it was Amanda all over again. I fucked up."

"You sure did," I said, then used my teeth to tug off the gloves. I drew in a breath. My anger was fading now. I understood—I did. But that didn't make it hurt less. "Trust has to be mutual. You don't trust because she betrayed you. But she didn't trust you, either. She didn't believe you knew how to handle yourself.

"I don't trust easily, either," I said as I uncoiled the tape around my hands. "But I trust you, Tyler. I may not agree with what you do, but I trust you."

"I trust you, too," Tyler said. "I do. Despite my very royal fuckup."

I looked at him and my heart stuttered. This man was my everything; he had become my entire world. And I wanted—needed—him to understand just how deep that trust ran.

"I know you trust me," I said. Slowly, meaningfully, I handed him the tape. "I love you, Tyler, and I trust you more than anyone. I need you to know that. To truly understand it."

He cocked his head, obviously unsure. "Sloane. Are you sure?"

"I want it," I said. "All these years, it's been in my head. He tied her up. He hurt her. I don't want that there anymore. I want you. Bind me, Tyler. Bind me, and make love to me, and make the bad stuff go away."

He scooped me up as if I weighed nothing at all, then carried me to the bedroom and gently laid me on the bed. He got on beside me, then leaned over and kissed me. Soft and gentle at first, and then harder, until the kiss was almost a punishment.

"I want you," he said. "I need you."

"I know." I tightened my arms around him, clutching him tight, wanting more of his kisses, deeper and hotter. "I need you, too."

"I was afraid, you know. For a moment I was afraid that I'd fucked up beyond repair. That I'd lost you."

"Never," I said, and my voice trembled with the truth of it.

Slowly, he peeled off the sports bra, then took my breasts in his mouth, one and then the other, suckling each until I felt those sparking threads of sensation shoot all the way from my breasts to my sex. I arched up, wanting more. More of him. Of his touch, of everything.

"Sit up," he said. "And scoot back."

I did, and ended up sitting upright against a pillow that Tyler had placed against the wrought-iron headboard.

"Cross your wrists around one of the bars," he said.

I hesitated. I'd imagined he'd tie me down, arms out to the side.

"It's okay," he said, as if understanding my hesitation. "You'll like it. We both will."

I nodded, then complied. I breathed deep, as if that would keep the ghosts at bay.

"Are you doing okay?" Tyler asked once my hands were secured behind me.

"Yeah," I said, surprised by the truth of the words. I tilted my head up for a kiss. "So far, I'm doing fine. More than fine," I added, because the truth was I was getting excited. Knowing I was going to be bound. Taken. Knowing that I was about to surrender totally, to submit completely.

I should be terrified. Should be writhing in a desperate attempt to get free.

Should be kicking Tyler in the balls.

But I wasn't. Just the opposite. Instead, I was looking forward to what came next with potent anticipation. And all because I trusted this man.

He turned away from me, then opened a drawer at the bottom of the dresser. When he came back, he held two coils of red rope.

I frowned. "I'm not sure if I should be glad you're experienced at this or irritated that I'm not the first woman you've done this to."

He sat beside me, then kissed me gently while his fingers played with my breasts. It was an intimate, casual moment, and reminded me again that right now, more than before, I was truly his to do with as he wished.

"You are the first," he said, his voice low and full of meaning. "The first. And the only."

"Tyler—"

"I know," he said. "I know it can't last. You've made it clear, and I get it. But that doesn't change the truth. I love you, Sloane," he said as he eased my leggings off. "And that will never change. Now," he said, with a quick change in tone, "bring your knees to your chest."

I bit my lower lip, but complied. Then I held my breath as he wrapped the cord around my left leg just below my knee, effectively binding my calf to my thigh. Then he took the loose end of the cord and tied it to the post beside my hand, pulling it taut to take up the slack, and in that way holding my leg up, knee at my chest, my sex completely exposed.

He ran his fingers over me. "Your cunt is so wet, Sloane. I think you've been thinking naughty thoughts."

"Very," I said.

"Like what?"

"That I like this," I whispered, as he sank three fingers deep inside me. "That I like being at your mercy," I said, forcing the words out past a moan of deep pleasure. "That I like knowing that I'm yours. And not knowing what's coming."

"Good. Very good," he said, then repeated the process with the other leg. "Nice," he said, when he'd completed the task. "Now close your eyes."

I did, then jumped as he took hold of my knees, lifted me just a little, and spanked my ass.

"Not the best position for that," he said. "But I recall the lady liked the sensation. I wonder how far she'd like to go."

"Very far," I murmured. "All the way," I said, and he chuckled.

"All the way it is," and then I felt the smack of his hand again—not on my ass, but on my sex. I cried out, the sensation unfamiliar and strange, and yet arousing, too. And when he did it again, the sting lingered, making my clit so sensitive that I thought a single burst of air might make me come.

"So sweet," he murmured, and I opened my eyes to see his mouth close intimately over me, and just the sight of him, laving me like that, made my body quiver with the need to draw him in.

Tyler complied, first with his tongue—thrusting it so deep I arched up, at least as much as the restraints allowed, and then bucked against him, in silent demand for more.

He gave me that more, his mouth sliding up to my breast as his hand teased and tormented my sex, sending waves of sensation swarming through me. I wanted to writhe, to move, but the minuscule amount of movement I was allowed did little to deflect the onslaught, and I was overwhelmed by the sensations, certain I was about to burst.

"I'm close," I said. "Oh, god, Tyler, I want you inside me. Please, I want to feel you in me when I come."

He stripped quickly, then knelt between my legs. He lifted me up just slightly with one hand as he took his cock in the other and positioned it against me.

"Yes," I said, the pleasure so acute I almost came at that moment. Then Tyler held my legs for leverage and thrust inside me. "Watch," he said. "Don't close your eyes."

I did, mesmerized by the way he thrust in and out of my body. Torn apart when I watched him take one hand off my leg so that he could tease my clit, sending me spiraling even higher.

"You're close," he said. "I can feel how tight you are. How close you are. Come on, baby. Come on, and let's go over together."

I listened to the sound of his voice, as if it could carry me all the way.

"Now, Sloane, now," he cried, and I exploded with him, my body reaching out for the heavens even though I was so thoroughly tied down to the bed.

The shudders ripped through me for what seemed like forever, and Tyler left me like that, his fingers slowly stroking me as if to draw out every last bit of pleasure.

"Stay with me," he murmured, as he touched me so intimately. "Don't go back to Indiana." He stroked my cheek, kissed my lips, teased my sex. "Stay."

I closed my eyes, wishing things were different. "I want to. Tyler, you have to know that I want to. But I can't. I'm a cop. I can't give it up. It's part of who I am. You know that."

"So be a Chicago cop. Or even in private security. Hell, you could work for BAS."

I laughed. "Because it's so up and up?"

"I just want you to stay. At the moment, I don't care how."

I tilted my head and glanced down at my arms, still bound behind me. Then at my legs, spread wide and his hand still stroking me. "Right now you could make me."

"Tempting," he said. "Very tempting."

"You know, this trust thing has to be mutual. Maybe I should tie you up."

His grin was pure, wicked sex. "Maybe you should. I think I'd enjoy being at your mercy."

As he reached to untie me, my phone rang. "Dammit," I said. "Just send it to voicemail."

He reached for it, and I saw him hesitate. "It's your dad. Answer it?"

"Put it on speaker," I said, since I was in no position to hold a phone. "It might be important."

"Hi, Daddy," I said, once Tyler laid the phone on the bed. "Listen, this isn't a good time. I'm kind of tied up right now."

Beside me, Tyler rolled his eyes.

"I won't keep you. But I wanted to let you know that I heard back from my friend in the Vegas PD. Amy was cited. For solicitation."

I met Tyler's eyes. "Shit. Thanks for letting me know."

"Wait. There's more. They booked her. I had him compare the mug shot with the license. Honey, they don't match."

"Say again?"

"Whoever's using her ID isn't Amy."

Shit. Shit, shit, shit.

I had a bad feeling. A very, very bad feeling.

"Daddy, I have to go." I nodded to the phone and Tyler ended the call. "Untie me," I said urgently. "Untie me now."

"What's going on?"

"I'm not sure." I sat up and ran my fingers through my hair. "*Shit*. It's right there. This feeling. Something's off and it all ties back to Vegas."

"The fact that she's not there."

I met his eyes as the word that was eluding me surfaced. "Emily."

He cocked his head. "Back up. Slow down. What are you thinking?"

I stood up, then started to pace, the motion helping me think. "I don't think Amy went to Vegas. I don't think she ever did. Okay," I said, then held up a hand to silence him before his words erased my thoughts. "Emily was supposed to have been heading for Vegas, but she was found dead in Chicago. And Amy was supposed to have gone to Vegas, but we never heard from her."

"Darcy got a postcard," he pointed out. "And you said Candy got a phone call."

"A postcard with no return address. A phone call that went straight to voicemail—and had the wrong month in it."

His brow furrowed. "The wrong month?"

"Hang on. I'm getting there. I need to check something." I snatched my phone, then did an Internet search on POE oil. A second later, I knew that POE oil was used with refrigerants. "Fuck," I said. "Fuck, fuck, fuck."

"Fill me in," Tyler said.

"Call Sapphire," I said. "You have her cell number, right?"

He nodded, then dialed, putting his phone on speaker. As he did, I started to explain what I was thinking.

"If my hunch is right, Amy never sent that postcard. Someone else did. And the call was made from a burner. And in the call, she sounded terrible, Candy said. And she said she'd see Candy next month. Amy knows when Candy's due. She wouldn't get it that far off. She gave the wrong date on purpose. She was giving us a clue, and I fucking missed it—Sapphire," I added, when the girl answered the phone.

"Hey." She sounded confused. "Tyler?"

"His phone," I said. "This is Sloane. Listen, do you know who offered Emily the job? The one she turned down when she decided to go to Vegas?"

"Um, yeah. That was Big Charley. You know, the nice quiet guy who—"

"I know him," I said. "Thanks."

I clicked the button to end the call, and saw from Tyler's face that he was on the same page as me.

"Refrigerant oil," he said. "He's in the vending machine business. And he offered both girls a job."

"Lizzy, too," I said. I was already climbing into my clothes. Tyler was as well.

"He offered Lizzy a job?"

"I didn't catch it at first," I said, hurrying toward the service door. "She said she should have taken the pop job. Soda pop. Vending machines."

"Blond hair and bangs," Tyler mused. "All three of them."

"We're taking my car," I said, as I jammed the button for the elevator. I wanted my gun.

We took my car, but I let Tyler drive. Not only did he know where Big Charley's office was, but he was a hell of a lot better at navigating Chicago.

"We know that Amy's alive," I said. "Or she was pretty damn recently." I kicked at the dashboard. "The guy had her call Candy right after I talked with him. Guy's got serious balls, the fucker."

"How are we handling this?"

I took my Glock out of the glove box and checked the magazine. Then I pulled the slide back and put one in the chamber. "We can't get a warrant. I'm not local and there's no time, anyway. So we're going to go into his office and politely ask where she is."

"And if he doesn't tell us?"

I met Tyler's eyes. "Then we'll get nasty."

Charley's warehouse was near Destiny, and Tyler got us there at near the speed of light.

"I have the gun," I said. "So when it gets down to it, you stay behind me."

"If I'd known our agenda, I'd be armed, too."

I glanced at him, then shook my head. I should have assumed he'd have a weapon somewhere. "No time to get it now. And we're starting this party like it's just a regular business day. Okay?"

"I know what to do," Tyler said.

There was a buzzer on the front door of the warehouse, and Tyler pressed it, and I was relieved when Big Charley himself answered the intercom. I'd expected to have to deal with staff. But maybe we'd gotten lucky.

"Hey, Charley, it's Tyler Sharp. I've got a proposition for you."

"Yeah? What kind?"

"The kind I don't want to discuss by shouting in an intercom. Buzz me in."

There was a pause, then the door clicked open. We entered a warehouse that resembled a maze constructed of vending machines. Tyler'd been here before, though, and he led us through to the far corner and a dingy office with a cheap wooden door.

Inside, Big Charley sat behind a cheap wooden desk. I caught Tyler's eye, hoping he could read my mind. I wanted Charley out from behind that desk, because who knew what he had mounted under there.

Tyler took a seat on the ratty sofa, then pulled out his phone. "Got a new gig we're working," he said, tapping at the phone. "Come here. I've got some photos and specs. Should be lucrative."

Charley narrowed his eyes and looked at me.

"She's cool," Tyler said. "Won't say a word. Will you, baby?"

"No, sir."

Charley's brows rose and he joined Tyler on the couch. "Okay, what do you have?"

"Amy Dawson. Emily Bennett," I said, watching his face. "It's not about what we have, but about what you do."

"I don't know what the fuck you're talking about," he said, but I'd already seen the truth on his face.

"Where, goddammit?" I said, and this time I aimed the Glock at his chest. "Where are they?"

"I told you, I don't know what the fuck you're talking about."

"I'll look for keys. Something," Tyler said, going to Charley's desk. And then, "No keys, but this is interesting." He raised a 9mm Beretta, then walked over to me.

"Tyler . . ."

"You know, Charley. This all feels very personal to me. And I think I can be much more persuasive than the lady."

"Fuck. You."

"I thought you might say that," Tyler said, then shot the bastard in the kneecap, making my ears ring.

"Where?" Tyler asked, sounding as though he was at the end of a tunnel. "Tell me now or lose the other."

"Vault," Charley said, his voice laced with pain. "Far side of the warehouse."

"Bring him," I said to Tyler, as I started toward the door. "It's probably padlocked."

Tyler hauled Charley into the rolling desk chair, and we raced across the warehouse, the sick fuck crying and moaning about how much he hurt.

"Yeah, I'm guessing Emily Bennett didn't feel so good, either. And if Amy is dead, you are going to never feel right again."

We reached the vault door and, sure enough, it was locked with a heavy duty combination lock. Tyler and his new Beretta managed to persuade the combination out of Charley.

We yanked open the door. "Amy! Amy, it's Sloane," I called. I went in low, just in case, but I didn't really think anyone else was there. This wasn't a trafficking operation. This was just one perverted bastard.

"Sloane?"

I barely heard it, what with her weak voice and my still-ringing ears. But I did, and I raced across the small room to find her shoved into a dog crate hidden under a moving blanket.

While Tyler checked the rest of the room to make sure there were no other girls, I opened the crate. "Come on, sweetheart. It's over now. You're safe."

I put the furniture blanket around her, keeping her warm from the shock, and watched as she crawled back into a corner, as far away from Big Charley as she could get.

"What's this fucker's last name?" I asked Tyler.

"Dodd."

"Charles Dodd, you're under arrest for the murder of Emily Bennett and the attempted murder of Amy Dawson. You have the right to remain silent," I began, then finished Mirandizing him. I wasn't Chicago PD. But right then, I figured I'd do.

"You ain't gonna arrest me," Charley said.

"Seems to me I already did."

"Not if you're with him. Because I've got a lot of paperwork on him and his buddies. Lots of documentation. I'm careful that way. Careful to keep records. Make notes. I write down everything. And I'm a very sharing kind of guy."

My stomach turned over, and I felt bile rise in my throat. I knew how this would go down. Charley was a murderer, but he'd cut a deal. Because the knights were a much bigger and flashier feather in the cap of the local PD and FBI office. Charley would maybe get sentenced to a dime, get out in three. And the knights would end up in a minimum security facility for the rest of their lives.

Shit. Shit, fuck, damn.

"Oh, yeah. The lady knows what I'm saying," Charley sang.

There was, however, one way out.

I lifted the Glock. I'd done it with Grier, and this guy was at least as bad. I could do it. Take him out, and save Tyler the way I couldn't save my mother.

I started to depress the trigger, stopping only when Tyler very firmly said, "No."

"It's the only option. He's right. You'll do time. All of you."

"We've always known that was a risk," Tyler said. "I don't like to lose, but the possibility is inherent in the game. That's part of the thrill."

I felt the tears streak my cheeks. "Let me do this. Let me do this so you can stay with me."

"And destroy you in the process? Do you think I don't know how much Grier cost you? I'm not letting you add to that. Sloane," he said gently. "Put the gun down. Call the cops. Whatever happens, happens."

Slowly, I lowered the gun. And I knew in that moment that I would never love anyone more than I loved this incredibly brave man.

"Oh yeah, that's what I'm saying," Big Charley said. "This way's good, isn't it, Amy-doll. She's one of my favorites, and I've had so many. So pretty, and then they get thin and they're just for me. I let them eat off my boots. Lick them clean. Let them suck me off if they're really good. I don't fuck them—don't do that. But I've got to keep them under control. Make them supple. Make them touch themselves for me. And if they don't come, well, they don't get food. They just get thinner and thinner."

He droned on, and I wasn't sure if it was blood loss or if he believed so firmly that he'd get off easy or if he was just plain crazy. All I knew was that I couldn't take it. All those girls. All that torture.

Amy.

And the thought that he might be out on the street again in thirty-six months. Maybe even less.

My finger twitched on the trigger. I met Tyler's eyes, then looked at Charley.

I have to. This time, it really will be justice.

I didn't wait to see if he understood. I just lifted my gun and then, knowing that I was perfectly justified, I blew the devil back to hell.

The paramedics assured us that Amy would be fine, then whisked her off to the hospital. Tyler and I were separated, each giving a statement to a different detective. I didn't know how this would shake down, but I wasn't too worried. Tyler had found another gun in Charley's office, and after firing off a round in the vault, he'd given it to the dead man, making what happened look remarkably like self-defense.

When the cops were finished with us, I went to Tyler, who was waiting for me in the warehouse. I fell into his arms, and we sank to the floor, leaning against a Coke machine. "I love you," I said, then kissed him.

He rose, and held out a hand for me. "Come on, Detective. Let's go home."

twenty-seven

"Stay."

We were in Grant Park, walking among the Agora, and I felt as lost as they were.

Tyler tugged me to a stop. "Stay," he said again. "I love you, Sloane Watson. I don't want to lose you." He cupped my face with his hand. "I told you once that I always get what I want. That's you. Don't make a liar out of me."

I managed the tiniest of smiles. "I want you, too," I said. "But I love my job. And maybe you're even right. Maybe I went into it in part to punish myself. To use the rules and the laws and all the strict procedure as a cage of sorts to punish myself for what I did. I don't know, but it doesn't matter."

"It does matter," he said, but I shook my head.

"No, because however I came into it, I really do believe in what I do. In finding justice for people who've been wronged."

I drew in a breath, then laid out the horrible truth. "You're right. I can push the envelope. I can bend the rules. And, yeah, I can break a few. God knows I proved that. But I can't say that I'm sworn as an officer of the law when the man in my bed is breaking it at every turn. And not to save girls, but for profit."

"Sloane—"

I pressed a finger to his lips. I heard the anguish in his voice, but I had to keep going, because if I didn't finish this, I was afraid that I would back away from the decision. And I couldn't do that. So long as he and I did what we did, this was the right decision. It was the only decision.

In the end, I think we both knew it.

"Please," I said. "Let me finish. I love you. Dear god, I love you with a length and breadth I never even thought possible. And I will keep your secrets until the day I die. But if we're together—if it's the cop and the criminal—and I'm living that lie, it will chip away and chip away at me until I am no longer the woman you love."

"Then don't live it," he said. "Quit."

"You know better than that. It's who I am. You say you love me, and I know it's true. But, Tyler, you see me better than anyone, so you know I'm right. You know this is who I am."

I managed a smile, thin and a little sad.

"That's why I can't ask you to quit, either. You are the man you are—I'm not in love with some polished version of you. And I *am* in love with you. Desperately. Hopelessly."

"You're breaking my heart, Sloane. Before you, I never thought it was possible."

"I'm sorry," I said, as a tear traced down my cheek. "But I have to leave. I have to go home."

Before I could stop him, he drew me close and pressed his lips to mine, soft yet firm. Possessive, yet tender.

When he drew back, I saw the familiar fire in those ice blue eyes. "I won't try to change your mind. Not right now, anyway.

But I want to say something, and I want you to listen. To really hear me. Okay?"

I nodded.

"You're right," he said. "I do see you. I see everything about you. The good, the bad, the courageous, the bold. I see a woman who fights for what's right. And, sweetheart, you don't need a badge to do that."

He lifted my hand and pressed a gentle kiss to my palm. "This may be goodbye," he said. "But it isn't the end."

twenty-eight

"Isn't she the most beautiful thing ever?" Candy said, cuddling her new baby daughter close. "My sweet little Brianna."

"She's amazing," I said sincerely, and beside me Amy nodded agreement, still a bit shaky, but doing well after more than a week of recovery.

"I didn't think I'd get to meet you," Amy said, bending over to stroke the infant's head. She turned to look at me, and I saw the gratitude in her eyes, now brimming with tears.

"Do you want to hold her?" Candy asked Amy.

"Oh, yes."

"I'll get a chair," I said, then scooted one of the uncomfortable blue guest chairs closer to the bed.

Amy took the baby, holding her as if she were glass, and started to softly sing. I watched them, then turned to smile at

Candy. She gestured me over, and I moved to sit carefully on the side of her bed.

"And how are you feeling, Mommy?"

"Good. Tired. Although this one gave me less trouble than Sam."

"Is he excited about having a little sister?"

"Over the moon. Jim took him out to the store," she added, referring to the bartender she'd married, who was the love of her life. "Gonna buy little sis a stuffed rabbit. And maybe something for himself, too," she added with a wink.

"I'm glad," I said, feeling foolishly sentimental. And trying very hard not to think of Tyler. Considering he seemed to be in my mind constantly, that wasn't an easy task.

"So here I am, in this comfy bed with a television and my new baby and friends and people to wait on me. I'm doing fine," Candy said. "How are you doing?"

"Great," I said, then conjured a perky smile.

"She misses Tyler," Amy said, and I shot her a withering look. She just smiled. "Well, you do. When we drove back here after they let me out of the hospital, he saw us off. It was sappily romantic."

Not romantic, I thought. *Torture.*

I'd walked away. I'd left him behind. And though I'd been absolutely certain that was the right thing to do, now I was haunted by regret and memory, loneliness and loss.

I moved to Candy and gave her and the baby quick kisses. "I'll come back tomorrow, okay? I have to run. I'm still on duty."

That was a lie—I actually had the rest of the day off—but I wanted to get out of there. I loved Candy, but I needed to be alone.

I'd been spending a lot of time alone. Alone and quiet, moving like a ghost through my own life. A life I used to love, but now it just seemed empty.

My apartment seemed empty, too, I thought a half hour later

as I approached my familiar blue door. I sighed, then slid the key into the lock. Maybe I should get a hamster. Just so there was some life to come home to.

I started to push the door open—and heard the sharp snap of a drawer being shut.

Shit.

Immediately, I was on alert. I'd come off duty before I went to see Candy, and I was still wearing my weapon harness under my light linen jacket. I reached for my Glock, immediately more at ease with its weight in my hand.

I checked my perimeter, then went in low—and found myself facing Tyler.

A thousand emotions battered me—joy, confusion, even anger because I was trying so hard to get past him, and here he was making me stumble.

Most of all, I felt love.

I wanted to run to him and toss my arms around him. I wanted to cover him with kisses. I wanted to run my hands over every inch of him simply to prove to myself that he was real.

I did none of that. Instead, I calmly put my gun on the entry-way table, then looked at him. "Dammit, Tyler, I could have shot you. You can't just break into people's apartments."

"I was hardly going to wait in the hall," he said, his voice perfectly reasonable, though there was amusement dancing in his eyes.

He crossed the distance to me in three long strides, then stood just inches from me. "I missed you," he said, and the power of those words seemed to hum between us. Dear god, I missed him, too. Missed the way he looked at me. The way we fit together.

I looked down at the floor. "Don't," I said. "You're not making this easier."

"I'm not trying to," he said. "I told you it wasn't over."

I stood there, my heart twisting painfully, and tried unsuccessfully to find words.

"I brought you something," he said, then pulled a small flat box out of his jacket pocket. Out of reflex, I reached for it, only to be stymied when he pulled it back. "It's contingent," he said.

"On what?"

"On you agreeing to my proposition."

"Tyler . . ."

"I want you, Sloane. And we both know that I get what I want."

I shook my head. "Please, I can't do this again. It's too hard to walk away from you."

"Then don't."

I felt the tears prick at my eyes. Damn him—damn him for making this harder than it had to be.

"I had a long talk with Evan and Cole about BAS, and we're going legitimate. Well," he amended with a lift of his shoulder. "We're spinning off a new company. Private investigations. Very specialized. There are a lot of people who get screwed by the system. Emily wouldn't have had anyone to stand for her if it wasn't for you. Amy wouldn't have met her godchild if it wasn't for you."

I licked my lips, letting the truth of what he was saying roll over the need in my heart.

"You can be who you are, Sloane. You just don't have to be it with a badge. Of course, if you need a badge . . ." He trailed off as he handed me the box.

I opened it, and nestled among pink tissue paper I found a shiny silver sheriff's star, and for the first time in a long time, laughter bubbled out of me.

"I told you once I would always give you what you need. Please, Sloane, I think we both need this. Will you come to work with us? Will you stay with me?"

I looked at the badge, then looked at the man I loved. The man who knew me so intimately and loved me so completely.

The man who'd come to me, all sexy and gorgeous and charming and brilliant and handed me not only a solution but a little silver star.

How could I say no to that?

I couldn't.

And so I did what I had to do. I threw myself in his arms and kissed him.

When I broke the kiss, he smiled down at me.

"Is that a yes?"

"Yes," I said, my heart full to bursting. "It is."

I kissed him again, and this time the kiss was deep and long. A kiss celebrating things lost and found again. A kiss that held the past and the promise of the future.

A kiss that stole my breath and made my knees go weak.

"Tyler," I whispered. "If you don't make love to me right now, I just might have to arrest you."

He laughed. "In that case, Detective . . ." He trailed off as he very efficiently peeled me out of my clothes. "Dear god, Sloane, I've missed you," he said as his hands roamed every inch of me.

"Yes," I said, because I couldn't manage anything more than that simple thought. One single word that somehow expressed everything that had been missing in me since I'd walked away, and everything I'd found in Tyler.

He led me to my bed, then gently laid me down and covered his body with mine. Our kisses were wild and claiming, his hands were gentle but demanding.

"Mine," he whispered as his hands stroked me, exploring and teasing.

"Yes," I answered, arching up to meet his touch. I was hot and ready and when he brushed his thumb over my lower lip, I drew it in, suckling him until he groaned with soul-deep satisfaction.

"In me," I said. "I need you inside me. I need to feel us together. Please, Tyler. Please, now."

"I love you, Sloane," he said as I spread my legs wider and he thrust inside me. "I love you," he repeated, as we pistoned together, deeper and faster, the sweet storm rising higher and raging harder. "For now," he said, his voice right on the edge. "For always," he said, and exploded inside me.

My own release was like the crescendo of a symphony, rising up and up, and then higher still until there was nowhere left to go and there was no choice but to burst free in color and light and music.

He held me tight while I came back to myself, and I curled against him. "I love you, Tyler," I said. "I always will."

He sighed, the sound full of warmth and pleasure, then stroked his fingers lightly over my bare shoulder.

"There's one other thing I have for you," he said. "I don't want to move, but I want you to have it now." He grinned, revealing his dimple. "Don't go away."

"Never."

He left the bed just for a moment, then came back with another wrapped package. This one in red, and not nearly as professionally done. I glanced at him. "You wrapped it?"

He lifted a shoulder.

I narrowed my eyes, then tugged out the card—and looked at him with genuine confusion. "The card says this is a gift from me to you."

"Yes," he says. "It does."

"I'm giving this gift to you? This mysterious thing I've never seen before?"

"You are," he said, holding out his hand.

With a baffled laugh, I gave him the package. He held it up to his ear and shook it gently. From his expression, I could almost believe he didn't have a clue.

"Go ahead," I said, playing my role. "Open it."

He peeled off the paper, then opened the box. Slowly, he tilted the box to show me what was inside.

"Jahn's watch," I whispered, pulling it out of the box and holding the now-ticking timepiece up to my ear.

"You fixed it," I said.

"No," he said, his voice full of love. "You did."

I blinked back tears of understanding and joy. Then I shook my head, smiling easily. "We did it together," I said.

"Yes," he agreed. "We did." He put the watch on, strapping it on his wrist with something close to reverence.

"We're going to make a hell of a team," I said.

He drew me close and wrapped his arms around me. "Sweetheart, we already do."

If *Heated* stoked your fire, the explosive finale of J. Kenner's scorching hot Most Wanted series will have the flames fully

Ignited

Read on for a special sneak peek!

Coming soon from Headline Eternal

one

Cons and games, lies and deceit.

Those aren't just words to me, but a way of life.

I've tried to escape—to be other than my father's daughter—but I have failed.

Because the truth is, I never tried too hard. I never really wanted to get out. Why would I? I like the rush. Like the challenge.

I have twenty-six years of the grift behind me, and I thought I knew it all. Thought I understood risk. Thought I knew the definition of danger.

Then I saw him.

Raw and carnal, dark and dangerous.

I didn't know risk until I met him. Didn't understand danger until I looked into his eyes. Didn't comprehend passion until I felt his touch.

I should have stayed away, but how could I when he was everything I craved? When I knew that he could fulfill my darkest fantasies.

I wanted him, plain and simple.

And so I set out to play the most dangerous game of all . . .

I stood in the middle of the newly opened Edge Gallery, my heels planted on the polished wood floor and the brilliant white walls of the main exhibit space coming close to blinding me.

A sparkling gala reception thrummed all around me. Guests buzzed from one painting to the next like bees around a flower. Male waiters in sharply creased tuxes carried wine-topped trays with purpose, while their similarly attired female counterparts offered tasty morsels to anyone in the gallery who was either hungry or wanted something to do with their hands.

I fell into the latter category, and I stopped a svelte, dark-haired waitress, then debated between a spring roll and sushi. I ended up taking one of each. Apparently, the indecisiveness that had been plaguing me all night extended to my appetite as well.

Great.

I'd come here tonight ostensibly to help celebrate the opening with two friends who co-owned the gallery, Tyler Sharp and Cole August. "Ostensibly" because—although I truly did want to celebrate their accomplishment—I'd really come here for one purpose, and one purpose only: To finally and completely get Cole August's attention—and then get him in my bed.

But damned if I hadn't already been here for ninety minutes, and I hadn't made the slightest inroad toward that goal. Primarily because I kept second guessing myself as to what would be the best approach.

And that really wasn't like me. I'm my father's girl, after all. Planning and focus have always been second nature to me. I'd grown up in the grift, and I'd known the ins and outs of designing a long con even before I knew my multiplication tables.

Tonight wasn't about a con, though. Tonight was about me.

I swallowed the sushi, then waved down a waiter, trading my used-up napkin for a glass of chardonnay.

I held up my finger as I downed it, silently signaling the waiter to stay. Then I replaced my empty glass for a full one. "Liquid courage," I said, though he was well-trained enough not to have asked.

To the waiter's credit, his lips only twitched slightly. He tilted his head in both acknowledgment and dismissal, then slid off into the crowd. I watched him go, knowing that I should go after him. Because Cole was somewhere in that throng, too.

Right then he was working the room, discussing art with the guests—both serious buyers and casual friends—who'd come to the gallery's opening. Art was his passion, and it was easy to see how much tonight meant to him. The two featured artists—a local street artist who Cole had found and pulled out of the ghetto, and a well-renowned painter who specialized in hyper-realism—worked the crowd alongside him.

He moved with a raw power and casual arrogance that both suggested his South Side upbringing and also defied it. He'd pulled himself out of the muck to become one of the most powerful men in Chicago, and as I watched him, it was easy to see the confidence and grace that got him there.

I stared, a little mesmerized, a little giddy, as Cole continued through the room. He was dressed simply in black jeans that showed off his perfect ass and a starched white shirt that accented the smooth caramel of his mixed-race background. He wore his hair short, in an almost military style buzz cut, and the style drew attention to the slightly tilted eyes that missed nothing, not to mention the hard planes of his cheekbones and that wide, firm mouth that seemed molded to drive a woman crazy.

He was sex on a stick—and all I wanted was to taste him.

I don't do relationships, and I rarely craved men. But I couldn't deny that I craved Cole. That he'd filled my senses. That he'd snuck into my thoughts. Over the past few months, he'd become an obsession, and if I wanted to get clear of him, I had to have him. And I'd come here tonight determined to get what I wanted.

"Careful, Kat," my friend Sloane Watson said as she eased up beside me. "Any minute now you're going to drool."

I smirked, but I also dabbed at the corner of my mouth with my napkin, making Sloane laugh.

"So is tonight the night?" she asked.

I shifted, abandoning my view of Cole to turn my attention to Sloane. "What are you talking about?"

"Cop, remember? I know how to read people. And you, Katrina Laron, are plotting something. I can only imagine it's something to do with Cole." Her mouth curved in a wicked grin. "Something naughty, perhaps?"

I scowled, because I'm usually better at hiding my emotions and my plans. But Sloane was right—as a former cop, she's used to watching people and noting the details. More than that, it wasn't that long ago that she'd been in a similar position, plotting out a way to seduce Tyler Sharp. Considering she and Tyler were now desperately in love and deliriously happy, I had to figure she understood the game.

"You're right about the intentions," I admitted. "But I'm doing a piss-poor job on the execution." I scowled again, this time at myself. "He's driving me crazy, and what makes that really pathetic is that he hasn't even looked at me once tonight."

"The hell he hasn't," Sloane said, the response whipping out so fast and so sure I knew it was the god's honest truth.

I narrowed my eyes. "When? How?"

Sloane laughed, undoubtedly amused by my eagerness. It's no secret—at least not to her and my best friend Angelina Raine—that I have lusted after Cole for months. This, however, is the first time that the prospect of me doing anything about that has been on the table. "Every time his eyes skim over you," she said. "At least, every time you're not looking back." Her mouth quirked up. "You know as well as I do that Cole doesn't give anything away that he doesn't have to."

I did know that. And it was that uncertainty that was making me hesitate. Yes, I thought that he was attracted to me—I'd felt his eyes on me in the past. Felt that zing when our hands brushed and the trill of electricity in the air when we stood close together. But I had no real assurance that it wasn't all me. Maybe I was projecting attraction where none existed and, like a moth, I was going to get singed when I fluttered too close to the flame.

"Tell me what you saw," I demanded, shamelessly eager for whatever tidbit that Sloane could throw my way.

"That dress, for one. If you came here hoping to catch his attention, I'd say you nailed it."

"Really?" I asked innocently, though inside I was cheering.

"Are you kidding? If Tyler looked at me the way Cole was looking at you, I would expect a very long night at home, with very little sleep."

"That's something," I said, unable to keep the smile out of my voice. "And makes me feel better about the abuse I put my credit card through to buy this thing," I added, indicating the dress. It was fire engine red, had a plunging neckline, and hugged every one of my curves. And while I might sometimes think that my curves are more appropriate for a 1940s film noir wardrobe, I can't deny that I filled out this dress in a way that was designed to turn male heads.

I'd worn my mass of blonde curls pinned up, letting a few tendrils dangle loose to frame my face. My red stilettos perfectly matched the dress and added four inches to my already ample height. If you looked up *fuck me heels* in the dictionary, these shoes would be right there.

Sloane was eyeing me with something that almost seemed like sisterly concern.

"What?" I demanded.

"Nothing. I just—" She cut herself off with a shrug.

"No," I said. "No way are you pulling that with me. You've got something to say, and it's about me or it's about Cole. And I want to know."

"It's just— Are you sure about this? And why now?"

"Yes," I said, because I'd never been more sure about anything. I took her arm and steered her to a far corner, where there were no paintings displayed on the walls and therefore no guests to overhear us. "And as for now, I don't think I have a choice anymore. I can't get him out of my head," I admitted. "He's getting into my dreams. I've never had a guy get this far under my skin, and it's driving me a little bit crazy."

"So this is an exorcism?"

I had to laugh. "Maybe. Hell, I don't know. Why?"

"Because we're friends, Kat. All of us. Me and Tyler, Angie and Evan. And even you and Cole. I don't want it to get weird, and I don't want—" She shook her head. "Sorry, that's none of my business. Shouldn't go there."

No way was I letting her get away with that. "Go where?"

"I just don't want you to get hurt," she said.

"What are you talking about?"

She dragged her fingers through her hair. "I just happen to know that Cole doesn't date. But I've seen the way you look at him, and you've got stars in your eyes. I don't want you disappointed. And—to be perfectly selfish—I don't want to lose the dynamic between the six of us."

"I don't either," I said, truthfully. "But I need to do this." I didn't try to explain that if I didn't, the dynamic between us would change anyway. I'd crossed a mental line, and no matter what, I couldn't go back to being Friendly Kat, the girl with the secret crush on Cole. Because this wasn't a crush. This was a need. This was a hunger. I'd opened Pandora's Box, and even if I'd wanted to, I couldn't shove everything back inside.

"What do you mean he doesn't date?" I pressed.

"That's what Tyler told me. He fucks," she said with a quirk of her brow. "But he doesn't date."

"That's part of what makes him perfect," I admitted, because although I hadn't known for sure, I'd watched him long enough and intently enough to guess that Cole was at least as fucked up as I was. "I'm not looking for a relationship, Sloane. I just want to scratch an itch. And if you're right, then Cole has the same itch, and this should work out just fine."

"So you're just looking for a fuck buddy?" She narrowed her eyes, looking dubious.

"Yeah," I said, though I hadn't really put it in those terms before. "Yeah, I guess I am."

"Kat . . ." She trailed off, and there was no way to miss the censure in her voice.

"What?"

"That's a load of total bullshit."

"No," I said firmly, "it's not." And it wasn't. I'd admit—at least to myself—that the attraction I felt for Cole pulsed hard and drove deep. But that didn't mean I wanted to date the man—or, more specifically, it didn't mean that I *would* date him, no matter how much I might want it.

Not that I could explain all of that to Sloane. We might have become friends over the last few months, but no way was I opening my closet so she could see all of my skeletons.

I didn't need a degree in psychology to know I was fucked up, and I didn't need a degree in human sexuality to know that I wanted Cole's hands on me. The second one I could do something about. The first one I just had to live with.

"Trust me, Sloane," I said, hoping that I wasn't about to screw up royally. "I know what I'm doing."

For a second she didn't answer, then she nodded. "It's your life. Go get him."

I laughed, then passed her my empty wineglass. "Here goes nothing," I said, then moved away from her and back toward the throng. This time, I was determined to see this through.

I saw Cole amidst the guests, his expression perfectly professional as he pointed out the various elements within one of the wall-sized street art paintings. I stood a few feet away from the edge of the group, just listening, letting his smooth voice roll over me and give me courage.

After a moment, he wrapped up his spiel and left the guests to contemplate the painting on their own. When he did, he turned and saw me, and I felt the impact of that first connection all the way to my toes. He stood motionless, his lips curving up in greeting even as his gaze traveled over the length of me, making my entire body tingle with delight. And though I knew it might only be my own desire reflected right back at me, when I looked in his eyes, I saw a lust equal to my own.

Go. Now.

I drew in a breath for courage. Yeah, it was time to do this thing.

And so I took one step, and then another and another. Each taking me toward Cole August. Each fueling that fire inside me that raged for him—a fire that had the power to either raise me up or reduce me to ashes.

I could only hope that tonight I would capture the man, and not destroy myself in the trying.

J. Kenner's fast-paced, erotic novella

Take Me

introduces Evan Black, the enigmatic man at the center
of *Wanted*, the first book in J. Kenner's new
Most Wanted series, and continues the story of
Damien Stark and Nikki Fairchild after the events of her
bestselling Stark Trilogy came to a close.

**Read the full novella now, in print for the first time
exclusively for this edition!**

White.

It is all around me. Soft and billowing. Gentle and soothing.

I am standing in a room, though I can see neither walls nor windows. There is only the endless flow of material. The sensual caress of silk against my body as I move through the drapes that fill the space before me. Hundreds, maybe thousands. They are beautiful. They are perfect. And I am not afraid.

On the contrary, I am perfectly calm. And as I move forward, my bare feet padding softly on the cool floor, I realize that I am heading toward a light. It shines through the diaphanous panels that flutter as I pass, as if struck by an ocean breeze.

I know that I am traveling toward something—*someone*—and I can feel the wellspring of joy rising up inside me. *He* is there. Somewhere beyond this forest of sensuality. Somewhere in the light.

Damien.

I quicken my step, my pulse increasing as I move faster and faster.

I am desperate to see him. To feel his fingertips upon my skin, as gentle as the brush of these curtains against my body. But though I hurry forward, I don't seem to be getting anywhere, and now the soft flutter of the drapes has taken on a menacing quality. As if they are reaching out, clutching me, holding me back.

Panic bubbles inside me; I have to get to him. I have to see him, touch him, and yet no matter how hard I try, I do not seem to be moving forward at all. I'm stuck, and what had only a moment ago seemed like the welcoming beauty of a curtain into heaven now seems like a trap, a trick, a horrible nightmare.

A nightmare.

My pulse quickens as the truth settles over me. I am not in a room; I am in a bed.

I'm not running; I'm sleeping.

This is a dream, a dream, and only a dream. But it is one from which I cannot seem to wake, even though I am moving faster now, clawing my way through these damnable drapes because I am certain—with the kind of certainty that comes only in the world of dreams—that if I can just get through them then I will be free. I will be awake. And I will once again be safe in Damien's arms.

But I cannot get through.

Though I push and shove and beat my way through the gauzy silk—though I run and run until I am certain that my lungs will burst with the exertion—I can get nowhere other than where I already am, and I collapse, defeated, onto the cool ground, my skirt billowing out around me like the petals of a flower.

I tentatively stroke the material. I had not realized when I was running that I was wearing a dress, but this is a dream and

I know better than to think too deeply about the odd parameters of this version of reality. Instead, I focus on gathering myself. On staying calm. On breathing deep. I am no longer moving forward, and that is good, because now that I have come to a stop, the curtains are falling away, drifting gently to the ground, only to disappear like cotton candy touching water until there is nothing left but me and this room with white walls that seem to press in around me, moving closer and closer with each breath that I take.

My chest is tight, and when I look down, I realize that my hand is fisted in the silk skirt. There are small yellow and gold flowers embroidered against the white silk at the hem, and the flowers are inset with shimmering white pearls that now feel hard beneath my palm. I glance down at the fitted bodice, the perfection of the silk, the gentle pressure of the stays.

I am in my wedding gown, and for a moment, that reality soothes me. *Damien,* I think again. He is not beside me, but I know that he is with me. This man—this incredible man who will soon be my husband.

Just the thought of him calms me, and I am able to breathe more easily. I can continue, I can move. I can stand and go forward and leave this room.

I can go into Damien's arms.

I start to do exactly that, shifting my weight so that I can rise to my feet.

That's when I see the stain.

A blur of pink rising up from the pure white silk of the skirt. It is so faint that at first I think it must be a trick of the light. But then the hue deepens, shifting from pink to red as it spreads out, tainting the purity of my beautiful dress.

Blood.

Frantic now, I scramble backward, as if I can somehow escape the stain despite the fact that I am wearing it. But of course there is no escape, and I claw at the skirt, trying to yank it up, trying to see beneath it. Trying desperately to find the source of the blood.

I can't. My hands are too slippery. Red and wet and stained. I rub them on the skirt, trying to clean them. My breath is coming in gasps, my pulse pounding so loudly in my ears I can hear nothing but my own blood flowing through my veins. That same blood that is coating me, escaping me.

No, no, oh, god, no.

But it is true—I am certain of it. The blood on the skirt is mine, and with one final, desperate jerk, I draw the material up, tugging at the silk and satin and lace until it is gathered around my waist and I can see my legs, bare and slick with blood.

I hear a noise—a gasp. It came from me, and I'm rubbing at the blood, searching for the source. I'm on my knees, my thighs pressed together, but now I separate them, and I see the scars that have for so many years marred the soft flesh of my inner thighs. Self-inflicted wounds made by the pressure of a blade held tight in my hands.

I remember the sweet intensity of that first slice. The glorious heat when steel penetrates flesh. The relief that comes with the pain, like the screech of a boiling kettle when it finally releases steam.

I remember the pain, but I no longer need it. That is what I tell myself. I don't need the wounds; I don't want the pain.

I don't need to cut anymore.

I'm better now. I have Damien to hold me tight. To keep me centered and safe and whole.

But there is no denying the blood. And as I look down at the open wound—at the raw and mangled flesh, and at the blood that pools around me, so sticky and pungent—I feel the tightness building in my chest and the rawness in my throat.

Then, finally, I hear myself scream.

two

I come awake in Damien's arms, my throat raw from the violent sound that had been wrenched from it. My face is pressed to his bare chest, and I sob, my breath coming now in gasps and gulps.

His hands stroke my shoulders, the movement both strong and soothing, possessive and protective. He is saying my name, "Nikki, Nikki, shhh, it's okay, baby, it's okay," but what I hear is that I am safe. That I am loved.

That I am his.

My tears slow and I breathe deep. I concentrate on his touch. On his voice. On his scent, sexy and familiar and desperately male.

I focus on all the little things that make up the bits and pieces of this man I love. All the things that make him who he is, that give him the power to calm me. To look my demons in the face and send them scurrying. He is a miracle, and the biggest miracle of all is that he is mine.

I open my eyes, then lean back as I tilt my head up. Even thrust out of sleep as he was, he is exceptional, and I drink in the vision of him, letting the beauty of this man soothe my parched soul. My breath hitches as I look into his eyes, those magical dual-colored eyes that show so much—passion, concern, determination. And most of all, love.

"Damien," I whisper, and am rewarded with the ghost of a smile upon his lips.

"There she is." Gently he strokes my cheek, brushing my hair back from my face. "Do you want to tell me about it?"

I shake my head in the negative, but even as I do, I hear myself say a single word, "Blood."

Immediately, I see the worry prick in his eyes.

"It was just a dream," I say, but I don't completely believe it.

"Not a dream," he corrects. "A nightmare. And this isn't the first."

"No," I admit. When the nightmares started, they weren't even truly nightmares. Just a vague sense of unease upon waking. More recently, I've jerked awake during the night with my heart pounding in my chest and my hair damp with sweat. This, however, was the first dream with blood.

I pull back more and sit up straighter, clutching the sheet around me, as if it offers protection from the nightmares, too. I twine my fingers with his and our legs are still touching. I do not want to think about the dreams, but if I must, then I need Damien's touch to anchor me.

"Did you cut?"

I shake my head. "No. Except—except I must have. Because it wasn't scars on my legs, but wounds. And they were open. And there was blood everywhere and—"

He silences me with a kiss, so deep and firm and demanding that I cannot hold on to my fear. Instead, he fills my mind with a raging heat so intense that it destroys everything except Nikki and Damien and the passion that is constantly smoldering between us, ready to ignite at the slightest provocation. Ready to burn away anything that threatens this life that we are building together, be it the ghosts of our pasts or my fears of the future.

My fears of the future?

I turn the words over in my head, and realize with a violent shock that they hold the weight of truth. The realization baffles me, because I am not afraid of being Mrs. Damien Stark. On the contrary, I think that being Damien's wife is the thing in this world that scares me the least. It is what and who I am meant to be, and I am never more certain of that than when I am in his arms.

Is that it, then? Am I afraid of the span between now and "Do you take this man"?

His thumb gently brushes my lower lip, and I see the knowing glint in his eyes. "Tell me," he says, in the kind of voice that allows no refusal.

"Maybe they're portents," I whisper. "The dreams, I mean." The words feel foolish on my lips, but I must say them. I can't hold the fear inside. Not when I'm certain that Damien can turn it around.

"Portents?" he repeats. "Like a bad omen?"

I nod.

"Of what?" His brow rises. "That we shouldn't get married?"

I hear the tease in his voice, but even so, my response is both violent and firm. "God no!"

"That I will hurt you?"

"You could never hurt me," I say. "Not the way you mean." We both know that there have been times when I have needed the pain—when I would have once again taken a blade to my flesh if Damien had not been there. But he is here, and he is all that I need now.

"Then what?" he asks as he gently lifts our joined hands to his lips. Softly, he dots kisses along my knuckles, and the sweet sensation distracts me.

"I don't know."

"I do," he says, and there is such certainty in his voice that I feel calmer. "You're a bride, Nikki. You're nervous." He presses a playful kiss to the end of my nose. "I think you're supposed to be."

"No." I shake my head. "No, that's not—" But I go no further. Because the truth is that he may be right. Bridal jitters? Could it really be as simple as that?

"But there's nothing to be nervous about," he says, even as his hands go to my shoulders, even as he gently slides his palms down my arms, making the thin sheet drop away.

I am naked, and I shiver. Not from the slight chill in the air, but from the longing in Damien's eyes. A longing to which I so willingly surrender.

"What is it they say about marriage? That the bride and the groom are becoming one?" He trails a fingertip lightly over my collarbone, then down slowly, the touch butterfly soft, until he reaches my breast. "That isn't true for us, baby. It's not true because we already are one, you and I, and this wedding is just a formality."

"Yes," I say, my voice little more than breath.

His hand cups my breast as his thumb rubs idly over my hard, tight nipple. The touch is so soft, and yet I feel its echo throughout the whole of my body. Just one simple brush of flesh against flesh, but it is not simple at all, because it holds the power to destroy me. To rip me apart and put me back together.

I close my eyes in surrender and in welcome, then lie back as Damien guides me down onto the bed. He pulls the sheet away, leaving me exposed, and then I feel the bed shift as he moves to straddle me. He is naked and the hard steel of his erection presses against my thighs, hot and needy. I reach for him and cup my hands on his tight, firm ass. He is not inside me—he is not even stroking my sex—and yet I am awash in awareness, my muscles clenching with desire for him, my hips writhing in wanton, unashamed need.

"Damien," I murmur, then open my eyes to see him above me, his eyes soft as he gazes upon my face.

"No," he says. "Close your eyes. Let me give this to you. Let me show you just how well I know you. How intimately I know your body. Because it's not just yours—it's mine, too. And I intend to show you how very well—and how very thoroughly—I take care of what is mine."

"Do you think I don't already know that?"

He doesn't answer with words, but the soft brush of his lips over mine is all the response I need. Slowly, he trails gentle kisses down the arch of my neck, then lower still until his mouth closes roughly over my breast. My nipple is already tight and hard and so very sensitive, and he drags his teeth over it.

I arch up as little shock waves shoot through me to pool like warm liquid in my womb. The muscles of my sex clench with longing. I want him inside me—I want it desperately. But he is not even touching me there. He's not touching me anywhere except on my breast, where he is suckling and biting, tasting and teasing. He is erasing everything—thought, worries, fears—until I am reduced to that one point of pleasure that seems to fill me, dazzling me from the inside, sparking and singing until I am certain that I am going to come simply from the sensation of his mouth upon my breast.

Slowly—so painfully slowly—he moves his mouth away from my breast and then kisses his way down my midline. He pauses at my navel, his tongue teasing me, the touch almost a tickle, but far more sensual. He slides a hand under my lower back, and I arch up as he nips at me, tiny bites and the scrape of teeth against the soft skin of my belly.

He has moved down the bed, and my legs are spread wide.

He is between them, but he is not touching my sex. He's not even stroking my thighs. He has one hand beneath my back and the other on the mattress beside my hip for balance. But there is heat coming off of him, and the triangle made up of my thighs and sex seems on fire. I am alive with need, with desire, with want.

And yet Damien makes no move to satisfy me. He is content to tease and torment, and as he slowly traces the shape of my navel with the tip of his tongue, I moan in both pleasure and frustration.

"You like that?" he asks.

"Yes," I murmur.

"So do I." His voice is low and reverent. "You taste like candy."

"Candy is bad for you," I tease.

"In that case," he says with a low growl, "I like being bad."

"Me, too," I whisper, even as my hips rise in unspoken demand. "But, Damien—"

"You want more," he says, finishing my thought. He kisses the top of my pubic bone, then trails his lips over the bone of my hip, following it down to the juncture of my thigh.

"Yes, oh, god, yes."

"And if I'm not done tasting you? If I want to kiss and suck and tease every inch of your body? If I want to have my fill of you before I thrust myself deep inside of you? Before we get lost together? Before I let you come?"

He lifts himself up, then bends over me, so close that I am certain he will kiss me, so near that we are breathing the same air.

Then he shifts away, moving his mouth to my temple. His lips brush lightly over my skin before he whispers, "I will always give you more, baby, but first I want you ready, I want you hot, I want you desperate."

"I am." The words are wrenched from me, and as Damien pulls away, I see the smug smile tug at his mouth.

"You are," he says. "But you also asked for more. And that, my darling Nikki, is a demand I'm always happy to satisfy. The question is, more what?" His mouth closes over my breast, and I cry out as he bites my nipple. "More pain?"

I cannot answer, my body is reeling from the erotic storm he is conjuring inside me.

"More pleasure?" he asks. He slides farther down my body, and this time skin does touch skin, the contact making the embers within me burst into raging flames. His lips move down between my breasts, then lower and lower until he reaches my clit. He blows gently on my sex even as he places his palms firmly on my inner thighs, spreading me wide. He takes one hand away, then strokes his finger gently over my slick, hot sex. I tremble, so close I think that if he breathes on my clit, I will come.

"More anticipation?" And then his mouth is moving again, tracing down my leg, over the scars on my inner thigh, to that sensitive spot behind my knee. I am lost, melting. I am his to control, to command, and I can do nothing but absorb the pleasure with which he is bombarding me.

He continues on, lower still, until he reaches my ankle, then the sole of my foot. He drags the tip of his finger from heel to toe, and my foot arches in response, along with my back. My sex clenches greedily, and I am astounded at the reaction from a simple touch upon my foot. Then again, how can I be astounded by my reaction to any touch rendered by Damien? I can't. I can only surrender, which was of course Damien's plan all along. To take me away from myself and bring me to this place that we share, a place where there is only Nikki and Damien and the pleasure we find in each other.

He is not done with me, and he slowly trails kisses up my leg until I am squirming, my hips gyrating in both pleasure and need. I want more. I want it all. And, miracle of miracles, Damien finally gives it to me. His tongue flicks gently over my clit, just the tiniest of touches, but he has primed me so thoroughly that I explode, shock waves shooting out to my fingers and toes, pleasure spiraling through me.

A tiny touch, yes, but also just the beginning. He closes his mouth over my sex, sucking and teasing. He holds my legs wide so that I cannot shift or move. He doesn't relent, making my orgasm grow and grow until there is torment behind the pleasure, until I am ripped open and needy, desperate for him to come to this place with me, to find me in the stars.

"Now, Damien. I need you inside me now."

This time, thank god, he doesn't hesitate, but neither is he gentle. He is on his knees, and he turns me onto my side. He straddles one of my legs, but hooks my other over his opposite hip, then holds me steady with his palm on my outer thigh. His other hand is cupped on my ass, but he slips down so that he teases the rim of my anus even as he thrusts deep inside my cunt.

This is not a position he's taken me in before, and the sensation of my legs being scissored, of his hand and cock so intimately on me, of the way he is kneeling against me, his body as erect as his cock while I lie prone like a vestal offering, is astoundingly exciting, and as he moves inside me, I feel the orgasm rise within me again.

I close my eyes, letting the sensations flow through and around me. It is magical, this feeling. Being so open to Damien. Being so joined with Damien. *Joined*. In sex, in life, in marriage.

A shiver runs through me, and I hear Damien moan as the muscles of my vagina tighten around him, drawing him deeper and deeper into me.

"That's it, baby. Open your eyes."

I do, and see him looking not at me, but at the juncture of our bodies. I am watching his face—watching the passion build—and when he moves his gaze and meets my eyes, the storm I see building there nearly does me in. I am breathing hard in time with the waves of pleasure that crash through me. The same pleasure I see on his face, driven by the same heat I see burning in his eyes.

A heat that is melting me.

That is ripping me apart.

That is going to shatter us both, I think, as the climax breaks over me and I arch back, held in place by Damien's body and hand as my sex clenches tighter and tighter around him, milking him to his own fantastical release.

Reality returns slowly, like stars appearing in a newly dark sky.

For a moment I have to wonder if I have melted, but it is only the limbless feeling that comes with a release born of pure pleasure.

Damien pulls out, and I mourn the loss of our connection, at least until he lies beside me, our arms and legs a tangle, our faces close. "Thank you," I murmur.

"For what?"

"For distracting me. From my nightmare."

He laughs. "I didn't realize I was that transparent."

"Only to me. Like you said, we know each other."

He kisses the tip of my nose. "You have nothing to be nervous about."

I nod, but the truth is that he is wrong. I realize it now. I want this wedding to be a reflection to the world. An outward manifestation of what he and I are together. Beauty and grace and something special and unique. I want it for him. For us. And for the whole damn world.

And so yes, I am nervous.

"I want the wedding to be perfect," I confess.

"It will be," he assures me. "How can it be anything else? Because no matter what happens, the wedding will end with you being my wife. And that, my darling Nikki, is the only thing that matters."

I brush a kiss over his lips, because he's right. I mean, I know that he's right.

But I also know that he's forgetting about the cake and the dress and the band and the photographer and the tents and the tables and the champagne and on and on and on.

Men, I think, and then snuggle close, reluctantly acknowledging that for tonight, at least, he's distracted me.

For tonight, I care only about this man who will soon be my husband—and who already is my life.

three

I awake to an empty bed and the smell of frying bacon. I roll over to find my phone on the bedside table, then glance at the time. Not yet six.

I groan and fall back among the pillows, but I don't really want to go back to sleep. What I want is Damien.

I slide out of bed, then grab the tank top and yoga pants I'd left draped across a nearby armchair. I head barefoot out of the bedroom and move the short distance down the hall to the third-floor kitchen.

We're in Damien's Malibu house, and the wall of windows that faces ocean is wide open, the glass panels having been thrust aside to let in the breeze. The smell of the ocean mingles with the scent of breakfast and I breathe deep, realizing that I am content. Whatever demons had poked at me during the night, Damien effectively banished them.

I glance toward the windows and out at the darkened Pacific. Waves glow white in the fading moonlight as they break upon the shore. There is beauty there, and part of me wants to walk to the balcony and stare out at the roiling, frothing water. But the siren call of the ocean is nothing compared to my desire to see Damien, and so I turn away from the windows and head straight to the kitchen. It is larger than the one in the condo I used to share with my best friend, Jamie, and it is not even the primary kitchen for this house. That is on the first floor, and could easily service a one-hundred-table restaurant. But this—the "small" kitchen—was installed as an adjunct to the open area that serves as a venue for entertaining, and since it is just down the hall from our bedroom, Damien and I have gotten into the habit of cooking our meals and eating in this cozier, more informal area. Usually we're joined by Lady Meow-Meow, the fluffy white cat I took custody of when Jamie moved out. I know Lady M misses Jamie, but she's also enjoying having the run of this huge house, and Gregory—the valet, butler, and all around house-running guy—spoils her rotten.

Now I lean against the half wall that marks the break from hallway to kitchen. Damien is standing at the stove cooking an omelette as if he were nothing more than an ordinary guy. Except there is nothing ordinary about Damien Stark. He is grace and power, beauty and heat. He is exceptional, and he has captured me completely.

At the moment, he is shirtless, and I cannot help the way my breath stutters as my eyes skim over the defined muscles of his back and his taut, strong arms. Damien's first fortune came not from business, but from his original career as a champion tennis player. Even now, years later, he has both the look and the power of an elite athlete.

I let my gaze drift down appreciatively. He is wearing simple gray sweatpants that sit low on his narrow hips and cling to the curves of his perfectly toned ass. Like me, he is barefoot. He looks young and sexy and completely delicious. Yet despite his casual appearance, I can still see the executive. The powerful businessman who harnessed the world, who shifted it to his own liking and made a fortune in the process. He is strength and control. And I am humbled by the knowledge that I am what he values most of all, and that I will spend the rest of my life at his side.

"You're staring," he says, his eyes still on the stove.

I grin happily, like a child. "I enjoy looking at pretty things."

He turns now, and his eyes rake over me, starting at my toes. "So do I," he says when his gaze reaches my face, and there is so much heat in his voice that my legs go weak and my body quivers with want. His mouth curves into a slow, sexy smile, and I am absolutely certain in that moment that I am going to melt. "You spoiled my surprise," he says, then nods toward the breakfast table where a tray sits with a glass bud vase displaying a single, red rose. "Breakfast in bed."

"How about we share breakfast at the table?" I move to him, then stand behind him with my arms around his waist. I gently kiss his shoulder and breathe in the clean, soapy scent. "Early meeting?" Damien is hardly a slacker, but he usually doesn't go into his office until after nine. Instead, he works from home, then showers after a brief workout before heading downtown. Today, apparently, we're operating on a compressed timeline.

"Not early," he says. "But also not here. I've got a meeting in Palm Springs. The helicopter's coming in twenty."

"I've got an appointment in Switzerland," I counter airily as I step back so he can finish putting our breakfast together. "The jet's coming in an hour."

His mouth twitches with amusement. The omelette is already on a plate, and now he adds the bacon. I follow him to the table, pour us both orange juice and coffee, then sit across from him. Putting a napkin in my lap, I realize I'm smiling like an idiot. And the best part? Damien's smile matches mine.

"I love this," I say. "Breakfast together. Domesticity. It feels nice."

He sips his coffee, his eyes never leaving my face, and for a moment there is nothing between us but contentment. Then he tilts his head, and I see the question rising in his eyes. I should have expected it. Damien wouldn't leave for a meeting without being absolutely certain that I am okay. "No more shadows this morning?" he asks.

"No," I say truthfully. "I feel good." I take a bite of the omelette we're sharing, and sag a bit in my chair in ecstasy. I'm a lucky girl in so many ways, not the least of which being that my fiancé can cook. "How could I not with you taking such good care of me?"

As I hoped, my words bring a smile to his lips. But worry still lingers in his eyes, and I reach across the table to squeeze his hand. "Really," I say firmly. "I'm fine. It's like I told you—I want this wedding to be perfect, which is ironic considering that I've spent my whole life trying to escape from my mother's plan to mold me into Perfectly Plastic Nikki." I immediately regret mentioning my mother. After years of playing the good and dutiful daughter, I've finally come to terms with the fact that my mother is a raging bitch—one who also happens to despise my boyfriend. She made my childhood miserable, and while I am fully prepared to accept the responsibility for my cutting, there's not a shrink in the world who wouldn't agree that the causative threads of that particular vice lead back to Elizabeth Fairchild and her various quirks and neuroses.

"You're not your mother," Damien says firmly. "And there isn't a bride in the world who doesn't want her wedding to be everything she's dreamed of."

"And the groom?" I ask.

"The groom will be happy if the bride is. And so long as she says 'I do.' And when he can call her Mrs. Damien Stark. And once we get to the honeymoon."

I'm laughing by the time he finishes. "Thank you."

"For putting up with your wedding jitters?"

"For everything."

He stands and refills my coffee before clearing the table. "Is there anything you need my help with today?"

"Nope."

"We're getting married on Saturday," he says, as if this was news to me, but the words make my supposedly nonexistent jitters start jittering again. "If you need Sylvia's help, just ask," he adds, referring to his supremely efficient assistant.

I shake my head and flash him my picture-perfect smile. "Thanks, but I'm good. Everything is on track."

"You've taken on a lot," he says. "More than you had to."

I tilt my head, but stay silent. This is a conversation we've had before, and I don't intend to have it again.

We'd traveled across Europe for a month after he proposed, and while we were there, he'd suggested we simply do it. Get married on a mountaintop or on the sands of the Côte d'Azur. Return to the States as Mr. and Mrs. Damien Stark.

I'd said no.

I want nothing more than to be Damien's wife, but the truth is that I also want the fairy-tale wedding. I want to be the princess in white walking down the aisle in my beautiful gown on my special day. I may not agree with my mother about much, but I remember the care that she and my sister put into Ashley's wedding. I'd envied my sister a lot of things, not really understanding that she'd had her own demons to battle, and when she walked down the aisle on a pathway of rose petals, my eyes filled with tears and my one thought had been, *Someday. Someday I will find the man who will be waiting for me at the end of that aisle with love in his eyes.*

And it wasn't just my own desire for the fantasy wedding that made me insist we wait. Like it or not, Damien is a public figure, and I knew that the press would be covering our wedding. It didn't need to be the fanciest affair—in fact, I wanted it outside on the beach—but I did want it to be a beautiful celebration. And since I knew the paparazzi would be pulling out all the stops to get tacky pictures, I wanted a collection of portraits and candid shots that we controlled. Fabulous pictures that we could give to the legitimate press, outshining—I hoped—whatever ended up in the tabloids.

More than anything, though, I wanted the story and photographs to overshadow the horrible things printed just a few months ago, when Damien had been on trial for murder. I wanted to see the best day of our lives on those pages in sharp counterpoint to and in triumph over the worst days.

I have said all of this to Damien, and while I know he doesn't fully agree with my reasons for needing this wedding, I also know he understands them.

As for me, I understand his fear that I've taken on too much. But this is my wedding we're talking about. The nightmares are only my fears; they are not my reality. I can handle it; I can handle anything if the end result is walking down that aisle toward Damien.

"Everything is going great," I say to reassure us both. "I've got it all under control. Really."

"You found a photographer?"

"Are you kidding? Of course." It is a lie. And that's a risk, because Damien can read me better than anyone. I force myself not to hold my breath as I wait for him to ask me details—name, studio, credentials. Those are questions I can't answer because the truth is, I *haven't* found a photographer to replace the one Damien fired last week after we learned the man had made an under-the-table agreement to sell unapproved candid photos of the wedding and reception to TMZ.

And that's not even our only problem. I found out yesterday that the lead singer for the band I'd lined up had decided to drop everything and move back home to Canada, which means we are now entirely without entertainment.

I need to get off my ass and find someone—and I need to do it fast. As Damien had so kindly reminded me, the wedding is just a few days away.

But, hey, it's not like I'm feeling stressed or anything.

I frown, realizing that maybe there is a solid explanation for my nightmares, after all.

"What is it?" Damien asks, and I fear that despite all my efforts to keep these minor ripples in the wedding planning out of his hair, it's about to get gnarly.

"Nothing," I say. "Just thinking about my massive to-do list."

I can tell by his expression that he doesn't buy it. But I am a bride, and like most grooms, he knows innately that "handle with care" is standard operating procedure. "In case it escaped your notice, we have the cash to pay someone to help you. Use it if you need it."

"What? Like a wedding planner?" I shake my head. "For one thing, the wedding's too close for that. For another, as I keep telling you, I want to do this myself. I want it to reflect us, not the latest fad in weddings."

"I get that," he says, "but you've taken on a hell of a lot."

"You've helped," I respond.

He chuckles. "As much as you've let me."

I lift a shoulder. "You have a universe to run."

It's a simple fact that I have more time than Damien. I'm juggling only one small business, which has exactly one employee—me. He's running Stark International, which has about as many people as an emerging country. Maybe more. And, yes, I have been busy, but that's partly because Damien didn't want a long engagement. And since I didn't think I could stand waiting, either, I was happy to agree.

It's been three months since he proposed, two months and twenty-nine days since I started diving into planning and prep, balancing my software development business against the business of my wedding. I'm proud of what's come together, and I'm even more proud that I've done so much of it on my own. Hell, I've actually been getting some use out of all those etiquette classes my mother forced me to sit through. Imagine that.

I aim an impish smile at him. "Maybe you're right. I mean, it is a bit stressful doing everything so fast, but I'm actually having a lot of fun working out the details of decorating the beach and organizing the caterer and pulling all the pieces together. I suppose we could push the wedding back a few months to make things even easier on me."

His eyes narrow dangerously. "Don't even joke about that. Not unless you want me to scoop you up, toss you on the helicopter, and elope to Mexico. Which, for the record, I still think is a fantastic idea."

"Vegas would be easier," I tease.

"There's no beach in Vegas," he says, his expression going soft. "Even if I'm kidnapping you, I won't deny you the surf or the sunset."

I sigh and fold myself into his arms. "Do you have any idea how much I love you?"

"Enough to marry me," he says.

"And then some."

He hooks his arm around my waist and tugs me close, then brushes his lips over mine. The kiss starts softly, a feather-touch, a tease. But there's no denying the heat between us, and soon I am moaning, my mouth open to him, his lips hard against mine, taking and tasting. He pulls me closer to him, my name like a whisper on his lips, and the embers that are always burning between us burst into white-hot flames.

His hand slides along my back, then under my tank top at its base. The sensation of skin upon skin is delicious, and I sigh with pleasure, then gasp with longing as those clever fingers slip beneath the waistband of my yoga pants and curve over my rear. He tugs me closer, his erection hot and hard between us, as his fingers slip inside me. I'm liquid heat, and I want nothing more than to strip us both bare and let him take me right here, on the hardwood floor.

Passion thrums through me, and I swear I can feel the house vibrating around us.

It takes me a moment to realize that the thrum isn't entirely the result of my lust for my fiancé—it's the arrival of his ride, the helicopter approaching from the north to settle on the helipad that Damien installed on the property.

I pull away, breathless. "You're going to be late, Mr. Stark."

"Sadly, you have a point." He kisses the corner of my mouth, and the pressure of his tongue at that sensitive juncture is almost as enticing as the feel of his erection hard against me. "Are you sure you don't want to come with me today?" he asks. "I don't think I've ever fucked you in the helicopter."

I laugh. "It's on my bucket list," I assure him. "But today's not the day. I'm meeting with the cake lady." Rather than a regular wedding cake, I'd decided to go with tiers of cupcakes, with only the top layer being the traditional cake with fondant icing. The baker, a celebrity chef named Sally Love, came up with an exceptional design for the icing on each individual cake, and she's going to incorporate real flowers on the tiers, making the overall design both elegant and fun. Not to mention tasty. Damien and I went together to pick out the flavor for the top layer, and also selected ten possible flavors for the cupcakes. Today, I'm going back to narrow the ten finalists to the final five.

"Do you need me?" he asks.

"Always," I say. "But not at the bakery. You did your part, I'm just finalizing the cupcake choices."

"Don't ditch my tiny cheesecakes," he says.

"I wouldn't dare."

"Is Jamie going with you?"

"Not today," I say. My best friend and former roommate recently moved back home to Texas for the express purpose of getting her shit together. She'd come back three days ago determined to be the best maid of honor ever—which meant that I'd had to field a full hour of apology when she explained to me why she might not make it to the bakery today. "She drove up to Oxnard last night, and she's not sure when she'll get back today. She did a play there a few years ago, and the director's a friend who now does commercials, and . . ." I trail off with a shrug, but I'm sure Damien understands. Jamie's still trying to land a gig.

"And if she gets a job?" he asks.

I shrug again. I'm torn between wanting her to be cast and wanting her to take as much time as she needs to get her head back on straight. I miss Jamie, but Hollywood pretty much ate her up and spat her out, and although my best friend likes to pretend like she's tough enough to take it, underneath the careless sex kitten veneer is the heart of a fragile woman. And it's a heart I don't want to see broken.

Damien kisses my forehead. "Whatever happens, she has you. That makes her one step ahead of the game already."

I smile up at him. "Will you be back tonight?"

"Late," he says, then trails a fingertip over my bare shoulder. "If you're sleeping, I'll wake you."

"I look forward to it," I say, then tilt my head up for a quick kiss on my lips. "You better go get dressed, Mr. Stark," I say, then push him off toward the bedroom. He's back remarkably fast, securing his cuffs as he walks toward me, then taking my hand as he tugs me onto the balcony with him. I follow him down the staircase and along the path toward the helipad.

We pause at the edge, and he kisses me gently one last time. "Soon, Ms. Fairchild," he says, but what I hear is *I love you.*

I watch as he bends over and hurries under the spinning

blades to board the helicopter, which has *SI* emblazoned on the side. Stark International. I grin, thinking that *SU* would be more appropriate—Stark Universe. Or Stark World. Damien is, after all, my whole world.

I shield my face from the wind, then watch as the bird rises, taking Damien away from me. I know he'll be back tonight, but already I feel hollow.

I consider going inside to get dressed, but instead I follow the flagstone path that cuts through the property until it reaches the beach. I walk along the sandy shore, imagining my wedding. We've planned it for sunset, with a party to follow. Considering who Damien is, the guest list is relatively small. We've invited our mutual friends as well as a number of key employees of Stark International, Stark Applied Technology, and the rest of Damien's subsidiaries. Also, some of the recipients of grants from Damien's various charitable organizations.

The ceremony itself is going to be short and simple, with Damien and I having only a best man and a maid of honor, respectively. Since my father ran off ages ago, I don't have a man to walk me down the aisle. I considered asking one of my best friends, Ollie, but even though he and Damien have negotiated a truce, I didn't want to risk marring my wedding day with drama.

And there's no way I'm having my mother do it. How could I stand to have her give me away when I've spent the last few years running from her? I have not, in fact, even invited her to the wedding. Which means I have no parent to give me away. So I'm going to walk myself down the aisle, a journey on a pathway of rose petals, with Damien Stark standing tall and elegant at the end of it.

We've written vows—short and sweet—and we both agree that what is important is getting to the meat of the ceremony: *Do you take this man? Do you take this woman? I do, I do, dear god, I do.*

The reception is a different story—*that* we expect to go on all night. Maybe even into the next day. After Damien and I head out on our honeymoon after the appropriate socializing and cake-eating interval, Jamie is taking charge of the Malibu house and she, with the help of Ryan Hunter and the rest of the Stark International security team, will make sure that anyone who needs a place to crash has one, and anyone who needs a lift home gets one.

Even though we'll be off on our honeymoon for most of it, it is the details of the reception that have been occupying most of my time. I've arranged for tents, dance floors, lanterns, and heaters. There will be a buffet, three bars, and a chocolate fondue station provided by Damien's best man, his childhood friend Alaine Beauchene. I'm a little flummoxed by my music conundrum, but I'm revved up and eager to solve it, and I tell myself that by the end of the day I will have arranged both the music and the photographer. I am nothing if not optimistic.

Other than that, the only major things still needing to be wrapped up are finalizing the cake—which I'll do in a few hours—and then the final dress fitting. The dress is a Phillipe Favreau original that we purchased in Paris after hours of conversation with Phillipe himself. It is insanely expensive, but as Damien reminded me, there's very little point in having gazillions of dollars if you don't enjoy them. And I really did fall in love with the design.

Phillipe is custom-making it for me, and it is being shipped from his Paris studio. There were some nerve-wracking delays, but I've been assured that all is on schedule now, and it is set to arrive at his Rodeo Drive boutique tomorrow morning. His most trusted associate will make any final alterations tomorrow afternoon and deliver it the next morning—Friday—so that it will be locked up safe in the Malibu house, all ready to transform me into a bride on Saturday.

All in all, things are going reasonably smoothly, and I can't help but smile. So what if I've had a few nightmares? For the most part, I'm kicking serious wedding butt, and I don't intend to stop.

I breathe deep, content, then fling my feet through the surf, sending the water sparkling. *Mrs. Damien Stark.*

Honestly, I can't wait.

"Ms. Fairchild!"

I look up to see Tony, one of Damien's security guys, hurrying down the beach toward me.

"What's wrong?"

"I'm sorry, Ms. Fairchild, I tried your phone but there was no answer."

My phone, I remember, is by the bed. "What is it?" I ask, alarmed. "Is it Damien?"

"No, no, nothing like that. But there is a woman at the gate," he says, referring to the gate that Damien had installed at the property entrance after the paparazzi got all crazy during his murder trial. "Ordinarily, I would simply send her away and insist that she make an appointment, but under the circumstances . . ."

"What circumstances?"

"Ms. Fairchild," he says, "the lady says that she's your mother."

four

My mother.

My mother.

Holy shit, my mother?

My knees go watery and I have to force my arms to stay at my sides so I don't reach out automatically for Tony. There's nothing on the beach that I can use to steady myself, and right now I really need steadying, so I stand perfectly still and smile and hope Tony doesn't yet know me well enough to pick up on the fact that I'm totally and completely freaking out.

"I wasn't expecting my mother," I manage to say. "She lives in Texas."

"I knew she was from out of state, Ms. Fairchild. I checked the lady's ID. Elizabeth Regina Fairchild, address in Dallas. I assume she's here for the wedding."

"Right. I just—she's not supposed to be here until Friday," I lie. I conjure what I hope is a bright smile, but I fear it looks like something out of a low-budget Halloween thriller. "So, right. I guess tell her to drive on up to the house. If you could buzz Gregory and ask him to settle her in the first-floor parlor, I'll run in and get dressed," I add.

"Of course, Ms. Fairchild." If he has picked up on my nerves, he is either kind enough or well trained enough not to say anything.

I hurry back up the path and take the stairs to the third floor. I want to ensure that I don't see my mother until I'm dressed and made-up and looking polished and pretty enough that maybe—*maybe*—she'll wait an hour or two before she starts in on me.

Once I'm in the bedroom, the first thing I do is grab my phone off the table and dial Damien. The second thing I do is end the call before it has the chance to connect.

I sit on the edge of the bed and suck in air. My heart is pounding so hard, my chest hurts, and I am holding my phone so tightly in my right hand that it is making indentations into my palm. My left hand is curled in on itself, and I concentrate on the sensation of my fingernails digging into my palm. I imagine my nails cutting through skin, drawing blood. I focus on the pain—and then, disgusted with myself, I hurl my other arm back and toss my phone across the room. It shatters from the impact, an explosion of plastic and glass, a smorgasbord of sharp edges now glittering on the floor, tempting and teasing me.

I rise, but I am not heading toward those shards. I will not touch them, not even to sweep them away. They are too tempting, and despite the fact that I've grown stronger in my months with Damien, I do not trust myself. Not now. Not with Elizabeth Fairchild just two floors below, waiting like a spider to draw me in, wrap me up, and suck the life right out of me.

Shit.

My mother.

The woman who locked me in a dark, windowless room as a child so that I had no choice but to get my beauty sleep. Who controlled what I ate so meticulously that I didn't make the acquaintance of a carb until college.

The woman whose image of feminine perfection was so expertly pounded into her daughters' heads that my sister committed suicide when her husband left her, because she'd clearly failed at being a wife.

The woman who said that I was a fool to stay with Damien. That once you passed the ten-million-dollar mark one man is pretty much like another, and I should move on to one who came with less baggage.

The woman who said that I'd ruined the family name by posing for a nude portrait.

The woman who'd called me a whore.

I didn't want to see her. More than that, I wasn't sure I *could* see her and manage to stay centered.

I needed Damien—I *wanted* Damien. He was my strength, my anchor.

But he wasn't in town and my mother was downstairs. And while I knew that one phone call would have him returning within the hour, I couldn't bring myself to go to the kitchen, pick up the house phone, and make that call.

I could do this on my own—I had to.

And with Damien's voice in my head, I knew that I'd survive.

At least, I hoped I would.

"Well, look at you!" My mother rises from the white sofa, then smoothes her linen skirt before coming toward me, her arms out to enfold me in a hug that is capped off by her trademark air kiss. "I was beginning to think you were going to leave me down here all alone." She speaks lightly, but I can hear the indictment in her words—I left her unattended, and broke one of the cardinal rules from the Elizabeth Fairchild Guide to Playing Hostess.

I say nothing, just stand stiffly in her embrace. A moment passes, and I decide to make an effort. I awkwardly put my arms around her and give her a small squeeze. "Mother," I say, and then stop. Honestly, what more is there to say?

"Married," she says, and there is actually a wistful tone in her voice. For a moment, I wonder about her motive for coming. Is she here because she honestly wants to celebrate my marriage? I'm not quite able to wrap my head around the possibility, and yet I can't help the tiny flame of hope that flickers inside me.

She steps back and looks me up and down. I've taken the time to shower and change and put on my makeup, and I know exactly what she sees as she looks at me. My blond hair is still short, though it has grown out since I took scissors to it and violently whacked off large chunks after the last time I saw her. I like this new shoulder-length style. Not only is it nice not to have the weight of all that hair, but the curls are bouncier and frame my face in a way that I like.

I'm wearing a simple linen skirt that hits just above my knees and a peach sweater over a white button-down. My feet are in my favorite pair of strappy sandals. The three-inch heels are wildly impractical for an afternoon of running wedding errands, but these are the shoes I was wearing the night I met Damien at Evelyn's party so many months ago, and as I stood in my closet a few moments before, I was certain I'd need the extra bit of magical shoe confidence they impart if I was going to survive my mother.

The truth is, I know that I look good. It's not possible to have entered and won as many pageants as I have and still hem and haw and pretend not to know how you look. Objectively, I'm pretty. Not movie star gorgeous—that's Jamie—but I'm pretty, maybe even beautiful, and I know how to hold myself well. Under other circumstances, I'd be standing tall, knowing that I passed the inspection of anyone who took the time to look me over. But these are not ordinary circumstances, and I am suddenly feeling like an awkward teen, desperate for my mother's approval. And the thing I hate the most? That soft look in her eyes only moments before. She'd knocked me off kilter, and now I don't know what to expect. My defenses are down, and I'm left hoping for affection, like some lost puppy that followed her home looking for a handout.

It's not a feeling I like.

"Well," she finally says, "I suppose if you're going to wear your hair short, that style is as good as it's going to get."

My rigid posture slumps ever so slightly, and I look down so that she can't see the tears pricking my eyes. I really am that puppy, and she's just kicked the shit out of me. I can either cower, or I can bare my teeth and fight back. And damn me all to hell, but the cowering almost wins out.

Then I remember that I'm not Elizabeth Fairchild's pretty little dress-up doll anymore. I'm Nikki Fairchild, the owner of her own software company, and I'm more than capable of defending my own damn haircut. I suck in a breath, lift my head, and almost look my mother in the eyes. "It's shoulder-length, Mother. It's not like I've been shaved for the Marines. I think it's flattering." I flash my perfect pageant smile. "Damien likes it, too."

She sniffs. "Darling, I wasn't criticizing. I'm your mother. I'm on your side. I just want you to look your best."

What I want is to tell her to turn around and go home. But the words don't come. "I wasn't expecting you," I say instead.

"Why would you be?" she asks airily. "After all, it's not as if you invited me to your wedding."

Um, hello? Did you really think I would after the things you said? After you made it clear that you don't like Damien? That you don't respect me? That you think I'm a slut who's only interested in his money?

That's what I want to say, but the words don't come. Instead,

I shrug, feeling all of ten, and say simply, "I didn't think you'd want to be here."

I watch, astonished, as my mother's ramrod straight posture sags a bit. She reaches a hand back, then takes hold of the armrest and lowers herself onto the couch. I peer at her and am astonished at an emotion on her face, one I'm not sure I've ever seen there before—my mother actually looks sad.

I move to the chair opposite her and sit, watching and waiting.

"Oh, Nichole, sugar, I just—" She cuts herself off, then digs into her purse for a monogrammed handkerchief, which she uses to dab her eyes. Her Texas twang is more pronounced than usual, and I recognize that as a sign of high drama to follow. But there are no tears, no histrionics. Instead, she says very softly and very simply, "I just wanted to spend some time with you. My baby girl's getting married. It's bittersweet."

She reaches out, as if she intends to take my hand, but draws hers back into her lap. She clasps her hands together and straightens her posture, then takes a deep breath as if steeling herself. "I think about your wedding, and I can't help but remember your sister's. I want . . ."

But she doesn't finish the sentence, and so I do not know what she wants. As for me, I don't know when, but I've risen to my feet, and have turned away so that she can't see the heavy tears now streaming down my cheeks.

I squeeze my eyes shut, determined not to think of Ashley, and even more determined not to think of the hand that my mother had in her suicide. But these thoughts are hard ones to banish, because they have lived inside me for so long. And now—well, now I can't help but wonder if this is my mother's way of showing remorse.

Or am I simply being a fool and wishing, perhaps futilely, that there is a detente to be had between my mother and me.

five

"Cupcakes." My mother's voice is flat, but her smile is perky and falsely polite. She's speaking to Sally Love, the owner of Love Bites. It's one of the most popular bakeries in Beverly Hills. Sally has catered dozens of celebrity functions, has been featured in every food and dessert magazine known to man, and is a longtime friend of Damien's. She's also an artist with icing and a pleasure to work with.

I am terrified my mother is going to offend her.

Mother's smile stretches wider. "What a perfectly charming idea. And was that your suggestion?" she asks Sally.

"I believe in working with my clients to figure out exactly what they want, to make their event not only special but uniquely theirs."

"In other words, you don't feel bound by tradition or societal expectations?" Her words are venomous, but her tone and manner are so polite that it's hard to tell if she's being deliberately offensive or making genuine conversation. I know the answer because I know my mother, and I step in and flash my own perky smile.

"I'm completely in love with the cupcake idea. I saw it in a magazine and it seemed like the perfect way to combine tradition and whimsy." I turn to Sally, purposefully excluding my mother. "So we're good to go on the top tier, right?"

Sally grins, displaying rosy cheeks that make me think of Mrs. Claus and Christmas cookies. She's probably only ten years older than me, but there's something maternal and soothing about her. I can understand why she does so many wedding cakes. She can calm a nervous bride with nothing more than a look.

"We're all set," she assures me. "But we do need to narrow down the choices for the cupcakes." The plan is to have five different flavors of cupcakes—one for each of the tiers—so the guests can pick their favorite. Additional cupcakes—in case anyone wants seconds—will be scattered artfully on the table, mixed with the fresh wildflowers I have on order from the florist. Daisies and sunflowers and Indian paintbrushes that remind me of the incredible arrangement Damien sent me after the night we first met.

Sally nods to the table set up at the back of the storefront, elegantly draped in white linen. It's topped with a row of ten tiny cakes. "I thought you might want to refresh your memory."

I laugh. "Even if I'd already decided, you know I'd have to sit down and taste those." I glance at my mother as I head toward the table. "Do you want to try, too? They're all amazing."

Mother's brows lift sky high, and I wonder when she last had a carb that didn't come from a lettuce leaf or a glass of wine. "I don't think so."

I shrug. "Suit yourself," I say, and see my mother's lips purse as I settle behind the table. "More for me."

The first cake is a tiny cheesecake. It's Damien's favorite, and I restrain myself from taking a bite because I'm going to ask Sally if I can take it home for him. I can think of all sorts of interesting negotiations we could have if he's bargaining for cheesecake.

I smile as I taste the next cake, not because I'm a fan of red velvet, but because I'm imagining all those possibilities. The next is a deep, delicious chocolate that I savor with a moan that is almost sexual. Sally laughs. "That cake gets that a lot."

"It totally stays," I say, then grin wickedly at her. "In fact, let's have a dozen packed up to take with us on the honeymoon."

We're laughing, and Sally's asking me about the honeymoon, and I'm telling her that it's a secret even from me—a Damien Stark surprise—when my mother clicks her way over on her nail-point heels. She stops in front of me, effectively ending my moment of bridal bonding with Sally.

"Chocolate, yellow, white," she says. "A pound cake. A cheesecake. If you insist on doing cupcakes at least stick with traditional flavors."

"I don't know," I say, taking a second bite of the cupcake I'm working on. "This one—butternut?—is to die for."

"It's very popular," Sally says. "But try the strawberry."

My mother reaches over and snatches the fork out of my hand. For a moment, I'm fool enough to think that she's going to get in the spirit and try the cake. But all she does is point the tines at me. "Honestly, Nichole," she says, in a tone that leaves no doubt that I have committed some heinous sin. "Are you trying to ruin your wedding? Have you thought about your waist? Your hips? Not to mention your skin!"

She turns to Sally, who is clearly struggling to wipe the expression of appalled shock off her face. "Bless her little heart," my mother says, in a tone that practically drips sugar, "but my

Nichole isn't a girl who can eat cake and then get into something as form-fitting as a wedding gown."

"Nikki is a lovely young woman," Sally says firmly. "And I'm sure she's going to look stunning at her wedding."

"Of course she will," my mother says, her voice sounding farther and farther from me. It's as if I'm sliding back, moving down some tunnel, away from her, away from Sally, away from everything.

"That's why I'm here," Mother adds, her tone entirely reasonable. "My daughter knows she has no self-control about things that are bad for her—*cakes, candy, men,*" she adds in a stage whisper. "I've always been there to help her keep her eye on the prize."

"I see," Sally says, and I have a feeling she sees more than my mother wants.

As for me, even from the depths of this well into which I've fallen, I am seething. I want to leap out of my chair and tell my mother that she's never helped me, she's only manipulated me. That she's not interested in what I want, but only what I look like and how I act and if I'm presenting an image that stands up to the Fairchild name—a name that's not worth what it used to be since she took over—and decimated—the oil business that she inherited when my grandfather passed away.

I want to say all of that, but I don't. I just sit there, my plastic smile on my face, hating myself for not moving. For not telling her to get the hell back to Texas.

But what I hate even more is the fact that I'm now clutching the second fork in my hand, and it's under the table, and the tines are pressing hard into my leg through the thin material of my skirt. I don't want to—I know I need to stop, to stand up, to simply get the hell out of there if that's what it takes—but whatever strength has been building in me over the last few months has scattered like dandelion fluff under the assault of a ferocious wind.

"Nikki," Sally begins, and I can't tell if the concern in her voice is because of my mother's speech or if she sees some hint of my struggle on my face. It doesn't matter, though, because her words are cut off by the electronic door chime.

I look up, then draw in a breath. The tunnel disappears and my vision returns. The fork tumbles from my hand to the floor, and I realize I've stood up.

It's Damien—and he is moving like a bullet toward me.

I head around the table, unconcerned about anything else. He stops in front of me, his face hard, his eyes warm but worried. "Turns out I could work the cake thing into my schedule, after all."

I try not to smile, but the corners of my mouth twitch, and I feel tears of relief prick my eyes. "I'm glad."

He reaches out and strokes my cheek. "You okay?"

"I'm perfect," I say. "At least, I am now."

The worry fades from his eyes, and I know that he believes me. He takes my hand, then turns to face my mother. "Mrs. Fairchild. What a pleasant surprise," he says, in the kind of overly polite voice that suggests there's nothing remotely pleasant about this particular surprise.

"Mr. Stark—Damien—I—" She stops abruptly, and I am amused. My mother is very rarely rendered speechless, but the last time she and Damien met he sent her away, effectively getting rid of her by flying her back to Texas on one of his jets. And that was before she'd said the variety of nasty things she's since uttered about the two of us. I have to wonder if she doesn't now fear that her ride out of California this go-round will be significantly less pleasant.

Damien, however, is the picture of cultured politeness. "It was so kind of you to come with Nikki today. I think we both know how valuable your opinion is to her." My mother's eyes widen almost imperceptibly. I can tell that she wants to reply, to lash out with the sweet sting of words that she'd want to cut him as deeply as a blade has cut me, but they clearly don't come. I'm not surprised. My mother is formidable, but Damien is more so.

Her expression shifts from consternation to surprise when Jamie bursts into the bakery like a tornado. "I'm here! I'm here! Big ticky mark for the maid of honor!"

For a moment I think that she really is here simply because she promised me she'd try to make it to Love Bites on time. But when I see that it is not me she looks to first, but Damien, I realize that he called her—and that she is part of the cavalry, too.

A moment later, Ryan Hunter, Damien's head of security, hurries inside as well, only to stop short when he sees Damien, then fall back toward the door, his eyes on my mother, as if she is a bomb about to go off. Laughter bubbles in my throat. I never felt loved by my mother. Damien not only makes me feel loved, but also cherished and protected and safe.

I understand what has happened, of course. Tony called Damien. Since Damien was in Palm Springs, he called both Jamie and Ryan in order to ensure there was someone with me to run interference. I squeeze his hand, then mouth, *Thank you.* The words are simple; the emotion is not.

He squeezes back, but his attention is focused on my mother. I look toward her, too, and as I do I realize that Sally has gracefully exited, leaving the drama of the showroom for the relative calm of the kitchen.

Damien's voice is firm as he addresses my mother. "Between Jamie and me, I think we have it covered. I'm sure you have unpacking to do. Why don't you let my security chief drive you to the hotel?"

"Don't be silly," my mother says. "I'm happy to stay." She smiles at me, and my stomach curls. "I want to spend time with my daughter."

"Awesome," Jamie says. "Today's her bachelorette party." She glances at her watch. "In fact we're supposed to meet the others girls at Raven in about half an hour. It's a strip club," she adds in a stage whisper. "It's going to be awesome. Wanna come?"

My mother goggles at her, and it takes all my power not to laugh. I know Jamie is joking—I specifically told her I didn't want to do the bachelorette thing—but in this moment it would almost be worth going through with it.

"Um, no. Thank you. I—" Her eyes cut to Damien. "I suppose I should get settled."

"I keep a suite at the Century Plaza hotel," Damien says. "I insist you stay there."

"Oh, no. I wouldn't want to be any trouble."

He doesn't say what I know he is thinking—*You've already been that*. Instead, he graces her with his most formal corporate smile. "No trouble at all. In fact, your car is already there. You're all checked in."

I see the confusion on Jamie's face—*she's* been staying at the Century Plaza suite.

"Oh. I see. Well, then." My mother turns her attention to me. "I'll go with you tomorrow to the dress fitting," she says, and I remember with regret that I'd nervously prattled off my schedule for the week as I drove us from Malibu to Beverly Hills.

"Sure," I say, though what I really want is to scream that there is no way in hell I want her in my head as I try on my wedding dress. "That would be great."

Damien is looking at me questioningly, and I shrug in reply. Part of me wants him to step in and send her packing. But she *is* my mother, and another part of me—the secret, buried part that I don't like to take out and examine too closely—wants to have her at my wedding. Wants to have her hold me and tell me she's sorry for all the years of horror and drama.

I want it, but I do not expect it. Yet still that flame of hope is alive, and I feel it flickering inside me.

"Ryan will take you," Damien says to my mother. I glance at

Ryan and watch as he turns his attention away from Jamie to this new assignment. I turn to look at my best friend. Her expression suggests that she's oblivious to Ryan's attention, but there's an unfamiliar color to her cheeks, and as she watches him lead my mother out the door, I can't help but wonder.

Jamie crosses the room to join me at the table, then picks up the red velvet cake with her fingers and takes a huge bite. "You realize that there's no way I'm sharing a suite with your mother."

I laugh. "Neither of you would survive."

"I had Tony pack your things when he delivered Mrs. Fairchild's car," Damien says. "You're staying in Malibu with us."

Jamie does a fist pump. "Score!"

My smile is so wide it almost hurts. "Thanks for having my back," I say to Damien.

"Always." The softness in his eyes hardens a bit. "Do you want me to send her back to Texas?"

I almost say yes, but then shake my head. "No. I'm getting married, and she is my mother. I'm strong enough to handle it," I say, in response to his reproachful look.

"You are," he agrees.

"And there was a moment—" I shake my head, thinking about the way she'd talked about Ashley's wedding, and the vulnerability that I'd seen in her eyes.

"What?" Damien is looking at me intently.

"I just think that, despite all the Elizabeth Fairchild nonsense, part of her really does want to be here for me on my wedding day."

For a moment, Damien only looks at me, his hands on my shoulders. Then he leans forward and captures my mouth with the sweetest of kisses. When he pulls away, I expect an argument. I expect him to recite an itemized list of every horrible thing my mother has done to me, to us. I expect him to point to his own father, whom neither of us want at this wedding. Hell, I expect him to talk some sense into me.

Instead, he says simply, "Be careful."

I swallow and nod, because I know that he's right to be concerned.

Once again, the door chimes, but this time I do not know the man who enters. He is drop-dead gorgeous, with dark hair highlighted by gold and red. He carries himself with a Damien Stark kind of confidence, and when his gaze sweeps the room, I see both calculation and intelligence in his sharp, gray eyes.

"We should finish up with Sally and get going," I say to Damien. "She's got other customers to deal with."

"I'm sure she does," he replies, "but Evan isn't one of them. He's with me."

"Holy crap," Jamie says, "do you travel in packs?"

Damien frowns, and I almost laugh. There aren't many people who can knock him off kilter. "What are you talking about?" he asks.

"Never mind," Jamie says, waving her hand as if wiping the words away. But she turns her attention to me, and I nod slightly. I have understood her perfectly, because this guy is hot. Maybe not Damien Stark hot, I think loyally, but he's got some serious sizzle going on.

"Evan Black, let me introduce you to my fiancée, Nikki Fairchild, and her best friend, Jamie Archer."

Evan strides across the room to join us. He shakes my hand, then Jamie's. I can't help but notice that she holds on a moment longer than is necessary.

"Congratulations," Evan says to me. "I knew the first time he talked about you that one day you two would be married. I wish you all the best."

"Thank you," I say, looking curiously at Damien. He's never mentioned this man before.

"I've known Evan for years," Damien says. "He lives in Chicago—we had a drink when I flew out there a few months ago," he adds.

"We met when we were both looking to acquire a failing business," Evan adds.

"Who got it?" I ask.

"Damien," Evan says, without regret. "But today it's my turn."

That I don't know what he means must be obvious by my expression. "Evan's acquiring the galleries," Damien says, referring to the art galleries that Giselle Reynard recently transferred over to him. "We were in Palm Springs examining the items in storage, and Evan's going to come to Malibu tomorrow to take a look at the main property."

"I have a few other things to take care of while I'm here," Evan says, "but I'm honored to have been invited to the wedding. I'm very happy for both of you."

"Thank you," I say, noticing that Jamie is still peering at him with interest. This is something that needs to be nipped in the bud. Not only is Jamie supposed to be backing away from men, but considering Evan is Chicago-bound, he could be nothing more than a fast fuck. And that is *so* not what my best friend needs.

Jamie pulls out her phone and makes a face, then looks at me. "We need to hurry," she says. "We're going to be late."

"Late? For what?"

She rolls her eyes. "I told you. We're meeting the girls at Raven," she says, referring to a male strip club in Hollywood.

"Raven," Damien says, his brows lifting.

"Um, hello?" Jamie says. "Bachelorette party. Alcohol. Mostly naked gorgeous men." She looks him up and down. "Not that she doesn't already have that in her life, but still. This is the night to be naughty."

"It's only barely past lunchtime," I say stupidly.

"I know," Jamie says. "That's when there's less of a crowd. More attention for us."

Oh my.

I glance toward Damien, but this is one of the few times when I cannot read his expression. My gaze shifts toward Evan. He is easier to read, as he's not even trying to hide his amusement.

"I told you I didn't want a bachelorette party," I say. "And I have stuff to do today. The music. The photographer," I remind her, then grimace when I see Damien's brows rise again. *Damn.* My little lie earlier has been soundly caught out.

"And I need to make sure the flowers are confirmed," I add, rushing on. "I need—"

"To chill with your friends," Jamie says. "Come on, Nick. Music or not, pictures or not, come Saturday night you're going to be married. You'll never, ever, ever get to go out as a hot single girl again. So we're doing this. I'm your maid of honor and I'm insisting." She glances at Damien. "Sorry, dude. It's in the best friends rule book."

"I'm certain it is." He turns to me, his expression implacable. "I need to speak with you alone."

I shoot Jamie the kind of look that could bring down an army, then follow Damien to the far corner of the showroom. We're standing beside a case filled with gorgeous, decorative wedding cakes. I glance at them, then wish that I hadn't, because all they do is remind me of how quickly Saturday night is barreling down on us. And while Damien's entry only moments ago might have felt like the cavalry, now those prickles of stress and nerves are starting up again. Because Jamie is right—this is my last chance to cut loose with my girlfriends.

But I don't want to irritate Damien, and though it has never actually come up between us, I feel confident he is not going to graciously accept the idea of another guy getting up close and personal. And we both know that even if we insist on ground rules, Jamie will make sure that they are soundly ignored.

"It's not my idea," I say.

"But you want to go." His voice is low, sensual—and it's making me nervous, because I can't figure out his angle.

"I didn't even know about it," I say.

He twines a strand of my hair through his fingers, then releases it as he brushes his thumb over the curve of my jaw, then over my lower lip.

My mouth parts, and I feel my body go soft and needy. There is no one in the world who has ever had the effect on me that Damien does, and right then I want nothing more than to fold myself into his embrace and lose myself in his kisses.

That, however, isn't where the moment is going.

"Go," he says. "Have fun with your friends."

I blink. "Really?"

He chuckles. "Would I deny you the full wedding experience?"

"I—well, no, but Raven . . ." I trail off, because really, what is there to say about buff men dancing in thongs?

"Mmm, yes, about that." He moves closer, his heat so palpable I feel the sizzle. "You go. You have fun. And you come back and tell me all about it."

I lick my lips. "All about it?"

He leans forward so that his lips brush my ear. "Every last thing, baby. Have as good a time as you want. And when you get home," he adds, his hand sliding down to cup my ass, "I'll decide whether I need to simply spank this beautiful ass, or whether you need a more thorough punishment so that you remember just how much—how thoroughly, completely, and irrevocably—you belong to me." He pulls back so that he is looking straight into my eyes, and the desire I see there almost makes me come on the spot.

"Do we understand each other?"

I nod.

"What's that?"

"Yes," I say, and then meet his eyes defiantly. "Yes, sir."

The corner of his mouth twitches. He takes my hand and pulls me close, then brushes a gentle kiss over my lips. "Just so you know, Ms. Fairchild," he whispers, "I'm secretly hoping you spend this afternoon with your friends being very, very naughty."

six

Jamie lets out a laugh as a guy in nothing but a thong and a cowboy hat gets up close and personal in her face. I'm sitting right beside her and am listing toward the left—away from him—but Jamie is eating it up, gleefully tucking ones and fives into the elastic band of his thong. Elastic that, from the stretched-out look of it, is going to snap at any moment.

Which probably wouldn't bother Jamie at all.

But even though the guy's not bad-looking, the only naked man I'm interested in anymore is Damien. And this guy is no Damien.

Jamie pulls out a fifty, and I roll my eyes, thinking that I'm about to witness a new level of hip-gyrating entertainment. That's when Jamie hooks her thumb toward me, nods, and very deliberately sticks the fifty right over the guy's package.

"Jamie!" I squeal, but I'm laughing now, because she's laughing and so are Lisa and Evelyn and Sylvia. I try to squirm away, but Jamie holds me in place, grinning wickedly.

Beside me, Evelyn takes a shot of straight Scotch. "Honey, you know I love your boy—and I am quite fond of my own man's attributes, too—but you need to relax and appreciate this from an artistic perspective." As if in illustration, she leans back, takes another drink, attaches her eyes firmly on the cowboy, and sighs.

Evelyn Dodge is brassy, opinionated, and often inappropriate. She says what she thinks, takes no shit off anyone, and has conquered Hollywood and then some. A former-actress-turned-agent-turned-patron-of-the-arts, Evelyn has been friends with Damien since his early days on the tennis circuit. She's known his secrets for longer than I have, and she loves him as much as I do. Damien lost his mom when he was just a kid, and I've always been grateful that Evelyn was in his life. Now I'm grateful that she's in mine.

But this isn't the time to be sappy, and I flash her the kind of smile that would make my mother proud. "Evelyn," I say sweetly, "you are so full of shit."

"It's the years in Hollywood, Texas." She cocks her head at Jamie. "At least this one already has the mouth for it."

"Fuck, yeah," Jamie says. Then she waves another bill and points at me. "Come on, John Wayne," she says. "Don't stop now."

The dancer obviously knows which of us is shoving bills down his pants, because he does as she says, gyrating closer and closer, and I'm squirming out of reach and laughing so hard that I almost pee my pants.

And all the while I'm wearing a fake diamond tiara that says *Virgin Bride* in equally fake red gemstones.

"It's no use," Jamie finally announces, then waves the dancer away, but not before giving him one more fifty. "She only has eyes for Damien."

"Can you blame her?" Sylvia says. I turn to her, eyebrows raised. Sylvia is Damien's assistant, and we've spent so much time together as I've planned the wedding that we've become pretty good friends. "What?" she says, holding her hands up in a sign of innocence. "Just because I work for him doesn't mean I'm blind to him."

"What happens in Raven stays in Raven," Jamie says wisely, then points a finger at me. "And don't even pretend to be jealous of her. You'd have to be jealous of the whole world, because every straight female out there thinks he's the most fuckalicious thing on two legs. Besides, you know Damien's only got eyes for you."

"I do," I say happily. At the moment, I'm very happy. It may not even be five yet, but I've had a Happy Hour buzz going for the last couple of hours, and have imbibed more than my fair share of Manhattans, because Jamie says that the little cherry garnish is appropriate for a bachelorette party, even though my cherry was popped long ago.

My best friend has a way with words.

The waiter comes with another round of drinks, but before I can snag a fresh Manhattan, Lisa snatches it off the tray. "I think it's about time we get you home to Damien," she says. "You're getting glassy-eyed."

I squint at her. "No way."

She laughs. "He will be so mad at all of us if we send you back tonight only to pass out. Especially since you're going home with a goodie bag."

"I am?" I'm beginning to think that Lisa's right and I'm a little wasted, because even if she's talking in euphemisms, I have no idea what she means by a goodie bag.

"Instead of each of us buying you a present, we went in together and got you a Bag O' Fun from Come Again," Jamie explains, referencing a local sex toy shop.

"You didn't," I say, not sure if I should be amused or mortified. "What's in it?"

"You're just going to have to wait and see," Jamie says, while the rest of them grin.

"I promise it's good," Lisa says. "I may have to re-create a bag for Preston and me." Lisa is a business consultant who has done some work with me, and her fiancé, Preston, is one of the top executives at Stark Applied Technology.

"You're supposed to save it for your wedding night," Sylvia adds.

"But we won't think less of you if you dig in tonight," Jamie says. She shares a mischievous grin with Evelyn. "She's going home to Damien, after all, so how could we blame her?"

The limo parked outside of Raven is one of Damien's insane stretch numbers that the company keeps primarily for impressing competitors and rewarding employees. Since this isn't the greatest neighborhood in the world, a crowd of gawkers have gathered. I think some of them are drooling. A few must recognize me, because about ten feet from the car I start to hear my name called out. I see phones being thrust into the air, and a flurry of shouts and camera flashes surround me.

I walk faster, flanked by my friends.

I'm surprised that Edward isn't on the sidewalk holding the door open for me, but it doesn't matter, because Jamie and Evelyn have taken the lead, and they bundle me into the limo, tell me that they hope I had a great time with them and that I have an even greater one with Damien—wink, wink—and then slam the door, effectively blocking the paparazzi and tourists who are determined to get in my face.

I lean back against the soft leather and take deep breaths. Dealing with the paparazzi is part and parcel of dating and marrying a multi-bazillionaire who owns half the world, and I know that. But once the press got hold of the fact that Damien had paid me a million dollars to pose for a nude portrait—and once Damien was indicted for murder—the press went a little nuts. Now it's a good day if we go out in public with only a small swarm.

I've learned to live with it, but I don't like it. It makes me tense and uncomfortable, and if there was a way to avoid it, I would.

What I hate the most is that I know they will be out in full force for the wedding. Although all of the Stark International security force will be at the house to make sure we don't have party crashers on the perimeter, the beach itself is public—and I'm certain that it will be crowded with paparazzi with long lenses and lots of determination.

Since I can't do anything about that except move the wedding inside or to another location altogether, neither of which are options that appeal to me, I have come to terms with the fact that I'm going to have to simply deal with the paparazzi and all the pictures that will surface afterward.

Yay.

That realization was one of the reasons we fired the photographer that we'd hired to do our wedding day portraits. I really didn't need one more underhanded person trying to snap a picture of someone who is having just a little bit too good a time at the champagne fountain after the wedding.

I frown, remembering that I still have to find a photographer, and it's already Thursday and the wedding is Saturday. *Shit*. If it weren't my own wedding, I could take the pictures myself. For that matter, I suppose I could take my Leica to the ceremony . . .

I shake off the ridiculous thought. Honestly, the black camera strap would totally clash with my dress.

Still, I should use this time in the limo to be productive. Maybe call some of the folks on my initial list of maybes and see if they're booked for the day. But my head is too light from my Manhattan indulgence, and all I want to do is sit back, enjoy the ride, and think about seeing Damien again in just a few minutes.

The fact that I tossed my phone across the bedroom and broke it also puts a crimp in my plan to manage a little work.

Frustrated at being without Damien, and irritated about my own foolish temper, I glance out the window and frown, because this isn't the way that we usually go home. I am about to hit the button for the intercom when a phone rings, which is odd because there is no permanent phone in the back of the limo, and, as I have just reminded myself, my iPhone is toast.

The ring comes again.

I lean forward, cock my head, and decide the sound is coming from the bar. I get off the leather bench and move carefully in that direction. Another ring, and I narrow the source down to the ice bucket. I pull off the lid, glance down, and find a phone in the otherwise empty container.

With a grin, I answer the call. "Hello?"

"Ms. Fairchild," he says—his voice is low and enticing and flows over me like warm chocolate.

"Mr. Stark," I say, unable to hide my amusement. "Funny you were able to call me, since I have no phone."

"I told you—I will always take care of your needs."

I smile, feeling warm and satisfied. "Where are you?"

"I'm not with you," he says. "Other than that, does it matter?"

My mouth curves into a smile. "No, but you're wrong. You are with me. You're always with me."

There is a pause before he answers. "Yes," he finally says, and I don't think I have ever heard that simple word spoken with so much meaning and complexity before.

I sigh with satisfaction, then close my eyes. He may not be beside me, but for the moment, I am content.

"We've done this before," he says. "You, alone in the back of my limo. Me, somewhere else, thinking of you. Imagining you. Wanting you."

I swallow, my body already tightening in anticipation of where these words are going. Because we *have* done this before—and the caress of his voice upon me that night is one of my most treasured memories.

"Tell me what you did," he says.

"That night in the limo?" I ask, though I know that is not what he means.

"Tonight. At Raven."

"I watched the dancers."

"What did they do?" His voice has a hard edge, and I shiver a little, remembering his promise to punish me.

"They danced," I say. And then, because I'm feeling reckless, I add, "They stripped down to thongs. They were slick with oil. They got close."

"How close?"

I think of the way the cowboy was gyrating right in front of my face. I remember the way that Jamie laughed and Lisa and Evelyn egged him on. "Pretty close," I whisper.

"I see."

There is a pause, and I squirm on the seat. My legs feel prickly, my sex clenches greedily. I'm thinking of Damien's promise to punish me, and I yearn to be home. To feel his hands upon me.

"Did it turn you on?" he asks, with that low, dangerous tone.

I almost lie, but I can't do that. "Yes," I whisper. "But only because it made me think of you. Your body hard and naked in front of me. Your chest close to me. That thin strip of hair that leads down to your cock, so near I could lick it. And those amazing muscles that form a V as if arrowing down to heaven."

"Christ, Nikki."

I smile, pleased I can bring that ragged tone to his voice.

"Mostly, though, it turned me on because I was watching other men. Because they were nearly naked, and I knew that when I got home to you—" I cut myself off, my bravado suddenly evaporating.

"What?" he asks. "What will happen when you get home?"

"You said you'd punish me," I say, so softly I'm not sure that he can hear me.

"Did I?" There is a note of triumph in his voice, and it makes me weak. "How should I punish you?"

I lick my lips. "You should probably spank me."

"I probably should," he agrees. "Would you like that?"

"Yes." My voice is nothing more than a whisper of air.

"Why?"

I close my eyes. It's a question that I expect whenever I ask for the pain, and I know that after my dreams he will be even more careful with me. I love that he understands me so well, but it means that I have to say aloud what I want from him, and that voicing of my desires is both awkward and undeniably exciting.

"Why, Nikki? I want to hear why you want the sting of my palm."

I lick my lips, forcing them to wrap around my words. "Because of the way it feels."

"Tell me."

"Tiny pinpricks of pleasure," I say, my soft words becoming bolder even as they sizzle through my body, sparking like currents of electricity that fire my senses. "They melt into heat, into liquid desire. It makes me wet, Damien, you make me wet." I pause, knowing that my words have captured him. "Pleasure and pain, Damien, and you're the only one I trust to give me both."

For a long moment he is silent. Almost too long. And then I hear his intake of breath, followed by his slow, clear words. "There is no one else who has the power to tear me apart the way you do, Nikki. No one else who can reach in and squeeze my heart. You are my world, Ms. Fairchild, and I love you desperately."

"I know," I whisper.

"But, baby," he adds, with a lightness now coloring his words, "that doesn't change the fact that you were naughty."

"Was I?" I am breathing hard now, anticipating what is to come.

"Have you seen the Internet?"

I frown. That wasn't a question I was expecting. "Um, no."

"Your party is all over Twitter," he says, and I cringe. *That* I should have expected. "I imagine it'll be on TMZ by morning. The gentleman who was, shall we say, in your face looked quite energetic."

"I think he probably works out," I say dryly.

"You realize this puts me in a bit of a predicament."

I'm trying very hard not to smile. "Does it?"

"I'm just not sure how to punish you now. Considering your ... eagerness ... I'm beginning to think that spanking isn't quite the punishment it ought to be."

"Damien!" I'm laughing—but I'm also a little worried. Damien is nothing if not creative.

He chuckles, and it's obvious the bastard is enjoying himself.

"Maybe I should just hang up?" he says.

"No."

"No, what?" he asks, and I hear the tightening in his voice. Whatever playfulness has been between us, it's fading under the slow burn of something else. Something hot. Something dangerous.

"No, sir," I say. My breath stutters in my chest, and I know that I am already wet. I've been wet since the moment I heard his voice. "Please, sir. Please don't hang up."

"I'll stay on the line, but only if you obey. Bend my rules, and I hang up."

"Yes, sir."

"Take your skirt off. And your panties."

I unbutton the skirt and shimmy out of it. I toss it onto the floor of the limo and drop my panties on top.

"Okay."

"Are you sitting back down?"

"Yes."

"Are you wet?"

"Yes."

"I'm going to punish you, Nikki, just like you want. I'm going to make you come. I'm going to make you explode."

I close my eyes and lean my head back, lost in the power of his words.

"But it won't be fast." He pauses, then, "Tell me how wet you are."

"Very."

"No, not like that. I want you to touch yourself. Just one finger. Imagine it's mine."

"I am."

"Now slide it down the juncture of your thigh," he orders. "Let me feel how silky your skin is. How soft. How tempting."

I do what he says, trembling as much from the gentle touch as from the fantasy that it's Damien's.

"Don't touch your clit," he says, and though I desperately want to, I obey. "Now tell me."

"Like I said, I'm very wet."

He chuckles. "I'm very glad to hear it. Tell me, what's in the goodie bag?"

"I don't know. Hang on."

I tug the bag over and peek inside. "A mask, a vibrator, some sort of oil, handcuffs, a video."

"Oil?"

"Yeah." I pull out the small bottle and read the label. "Arousal oil."

"Interesting. Open it."

"I—okay." I break the seal and unscrew the cap. Immediately, I can smell the spices. "It's a bit minty. There aren't instructions."

"Dab a little on your finger," he says. "Then stroke it onto your clit."

"Are you kidding?"

"Should I hang up?"

"Right. Okay. No problem." I'm not at all sure what this stuff is, but I figure if it's in a bag from Jamie, it must be fun. I put a drop on my finger and ease my finger over my clit. I'm so sensitive that even that tiny sensation makes me shiver.

"Well?" Damien asks.

I cock my head, expecting some sort of new sensation. "Nothing."

"Hmm. All right, then, we'll move on. Does the vibrator have batteries?"

I test it out, and find that it purrs nicely in my hand. "It does," I say, and immediately cringe. I sound far too eager, and I know from Damien's chuckle that he both heard and understood.

"And the mask," he says. "Go ahead and put that on."

"All right." I slip it over my eyes, and the world goes dark. "Okay, I—holy fuck." The oil that I thought did nothing is now doing considerably more than nothing. "That oil, it's . . . well, it's very wow."

"Tell me."

"It's like mint, I guess. Like if you sucked on one of those really strong mints and then went down on me. Oh, wow. It feels amazing, sensitive—oh, god, Damien, please."

"Please, what?"

"Everything. Anything." I squirm, wanting simply to relieve this growing pressure, this demanding sensation. "Please, sir, can I touch myself?"

"Oh, yeah. We're going to use the vibrator. Your fingers. I'm going to tell you how to touch yourself, baby. And you're going to let me hear you come."

I am awash with gratitude. I've been holding the phone, but now I put it on speaker and set it beside me, peeking out from under the blindfold just long enough to make sure I push the right buttons.

"Slide your hand up your thigh," he says, "then gently stroke your clit. Are you doing it?"

"Yes." I can barely speak.

"Can you turn on the vibrator?"

"I—I think so."

"Fuck yourself with it, baby. I want it inside you. I want you imagining it's me. Holding you, fucking you, burying myself deep in you."

Oh my god. I fumble, turned on, frantic, weak with longing. I switch to my right hand, and stroke my clit with my left. The oil is amazing, and . . . "I'm close," I say. "God, Damien, I'm so close."

"I know, baby. Come the rest of the way for me. Let me hear it."

"I—" But I can't talk anymore. I've done as he asked with the vibrator, and it fills me, the dual sensation of the vibration and my finger stroking my clit coupled with my fantasy of Damien, and his voice on the phone telling me to "Come for me, baby, come for me," is too overwhelming. I let my head fall back, and grind my hips, lost to everything now but the need for release that is close, so close, so very close, and then—

I explode, and as I do, I cry out Damien's name.

"That's it, baby," he says. "That's it. Keep touching yourself. Don't stop. Don't stop, baby, you can come again."

I've turned off the vibrator and tossed it onto the seat, but I do as he says and stroke myself. I'm so desperately wet. Wet and wide open and wishing that Damien were right here.

I still have the mask on, but I can hear the mechanical sound of the privacy screen starting to descend.

What the fuck?

"Damien!"

"I hear it, too. It's just the privacy screen. Don't stop. Don't put your legs together. Stay like that, baby. Open and wide."

"Are you crazy? *Edward.*"

"I believe we agreed that you needed to be punished."

"*No.*" I pull my legs tight together and rip off the mask even as I slide sideways, out of the line of sight of the driver.

And when I do, I realize that it isn't Edward behind the wheel, it's Damien.

He turns to glance, and I take deep, gasping breaths as I try to reconcile fear and relief and anger.

"Bastard," I finally say, though that hardly covers it.

"Slide back to the middle."

"And if I don't?"

"Suit yourself." He starts to raise the privacy screen.

"Fine." I'm pissed, but I'm not stupid. And, yeah, I'm still turned on.

As he drops the screen, I slide back to center.

"Spread your legs," he says, and as I do, he adjusts his mirror. "Now, that really is a beautiful view." There is awe in his voice, and it makes me feel beautiful. Despite being exposed, despite the scars on my thighs. Damien makes me feel like the most beautiful woman in the world, and that is just one of the things that makes me love him.

"Wider," he says. I comply, and I hear Damien's sharp intake of breath. He may be playing with me, but there's no denying that he's turned on, too.

"Are you excited, Ms. Fairchild?"

"Yes," I admit. "Except for that one moment of terror, yes."

"You should know me better. And you should listen better."

"Listen?" And then it hits me. "The bag. How would you know about the goodie bag if you weren't in the car?"

"Exactly. I gave you that clue. It's not my fault if you were too distracted to pay attention."

I manage a smirk. "Actually, I think it was your fault."

He chuckles again. "Maybe so."

I start to bring my legs together.

"Oh, no, Ms. Fairchild. That's how you sit for the rest of the ride. It's your punishment—and my reward," he adds, tapping the rearview mirror.

"In that case," I say, and strip off my sweater, shirt, and bra.

"Jesus, Nikki," Damien says, as I sit naked on the backseat, feeling suddenly very smug.

"I thought you needed to be well rewarded. After all, you earned it. I mean, you've been sitting in an empty limo all afternoon while I was inside drinking and watching hot guys."

"Best not to remind me of your infractions," he warns. "And the truth is, I wasn't just sitting in the limo."

"Oh?" I lick the tip of my finger and slowly circle my nipple. I'm pretty sure I hear a low growl come from the driver's seat. "What were you doing?"

"You were with the girls," he says, his voice unnaturally tight. "I was with the guys."

"Were you?" I let my finger trace down, down, down. Slowly, I stroke my sex, thrusting my finger deep inside, then withdrawing it to tease my clit.

I started this little show to torment Damien, but I'm also tormenting myself. "So, um, who were you with?" Honestly, it's getting hard to think.

"Alaine, Charles, Preston. Jesus, Nikki, do you have any idea how hard I am?"

I allow myself the pleasure of a satisfied smile. "Anyone else?"

"Ryan, Evan, Blaine. A few others."

"Mmm." I force myself not to drift, not to let myself come. I want him hard and hot. I want to turn the punishment around on him.

I want to keep control.

"So, um, tell me about Evan. Jamie was certainly checking him out."

"Tell her to stay away," Damien says sharply, and my hand pauses.

"Why?"

"Actually, I take it back. Don't tell her anything. Knowing Jamie, telling her to stay away would just make her more determined."

"All right," I agree. "But why? What's wrong with him?"

"Not a damn thing. I like him, a lot. But he has an edge."

"An edge? What kind of edge?"

"The dangerous kind."

"Oh." I want to ask more; however, I know better than to try to get information out of Damien that he doesn't want to give. "To be honest, I think Jamie's appreciation is more aesthetic than active. I'm pretty sure she's got her eye on another guy."

"Who?" Damien asks.

I shrug. I don't answer, but I'm thinking of Ryan.

For a moment I think Damien will press the point, but all he says is, "We're here."

I glance out the window and see that we've entered a drive-in movie lot. I laugh out loud. "Where are we?" I ask, tugging my skirt and shirt back on. I don't bother with the bra or underwear. At the moment, they seem superfluous.

"The Vineland Drive-In. City of Industry."

"Don't you have to pay?"

"I called ahead and made arrangements."

"You planned this all along," I say, which is pretty much stating the obvious. "Why?"

He opens his door, gets out, then joins me in the back.

"Why?" I repeat.

"So we could make out in a car at the drive-in," he says simply.

I laugh, because as corny as it sounds, the idea is also exciting. "Interesting. I think I'd like that."

"Would you?" He reaches over and begins to unbutton the shirt that I just put back on. I lean toward the console so that I can raise the privacy screen.

"No," he says as he peels the shirt off.

"Damien!"

His fingers unbutton my skirt, then tug down the zipper. "Do you really think that someone is going to lean on the hood, press their face to the glass, and peer all the way back here?"

"They might," I say, though I agree it's doubtful.

"They won't. But doesn't the possibility make you wet?" He slides his hand up my skirt. "Yeah," he says. "I think it does."

I lick my lips, refusing to admit the excitement that's building inside me. "I was already wet," I say.

"Mmm-hmm."

I feel my cheeks heat. "I thought you didn't do public sex."

"I don't. And I'm not going to. We're in a limo. No one's looking in. But I like the fantasy," he admits. He leans forward and kisses me, even as he slides two fingers deep inside me. "And so do you."

"I do," I admit, both because it's true and because I don't want to have secrets from Damien. "You are my fantasy, Damien. You know that, right?"

"And you are mine," he says, after kissing me softly. "We're lucky, you and I. There were so many places where our lives made wrong turns. And yet all those turns, all those horrors, all those days that we want to forget—they all add up to this moment. To you in my arms." He strokes my hair, his expression tender. "I have no regrets for the past, Nikki. And when I'm with you, the only thing I can see is the future."

"Damien," I say, the word soft like a prayer.

"Yes?"

"Kiss me."

"Whatever you want, sweetheart," he says before his mouth closes over mine and I slide down into the bliss of his arms.

seven

I sit in the silence of the Malibu house, sipping a sparkling water as I work at a small desk in the library. The library is my favorite room in this house, and it's not really a room at all. Instead, it's a level—a mezzanine—broken into a variety of sections. The comfy chairs and coffee tables are by the wall of windows overlooking the ocean. The bookshelves line the area that is visible from the massive staircase leading up from the entrance hall. The work areas are farther back, hidden from view, and it is in one of those quiet corners that I now sit.

It is late—barely three in the morning—and Damien is asleep in our bed.

I couldn't sleep, and though I stayed in bed for hours, warm in Damien's arms as I drifted in and out of a hazy dream state, I never managed to fall into slumber. I'm not sure if it was nerves or too much bourbon or the persistent thoughts of my mother, but in the end I gave up and came down here. Now I am sitting in the light of my laptop monitor putting the finishing touches on the gift I intend to give Damien on our wedding day—a scrapbook of our time together.

I've been working on it for months, even before we were engaged, and have managed to gather and edit photos ranging all the way from our very first meeting at a Dallas pageant to the present. I had originally intended it to be entirely electronic, but once he proposed and I realized that this was the perfect wedding-night gift for the man who owns everything, I decided that it needed to be tangible. I bought a leather-bound scrapbook with thick, archival paper, and have been carefully pasting in the images and writing captions and notes to him with my very best effort at penmanship.

Right now I am searching the computer for a picture of the Vineland Drive-In, because that is a memory I want him to keep, though I don't think either one of us had any idea what movie was playing. Instead, we made out like teenagers in the backseat, kissing and exploring, touching and groping. And when Damien finally thrust hard inside me—when I came in sudden release and exultation—I am certain that my cry was at least as loud as the movie soundtrack.

The hairs on the back of my neck prickle, and I know without turning around that Damien is here. His walk, his scent, his presence—I don't know what it is, but there is something in him that calls so profoundly to me that I am never unaware of him. If he is in the same room, my body knows—and wants.

I gently close the scrapbook, then tuck it into a drawer before turning to him.

"I don't like waking up without you," he says.

I smile. "Now you know how I feel." Usually it is me who wakes up to find the other side of the bed cold and empty.

"What are you doing?"

"Just working on something." I lift a shoulder. "I couldn't sleep."

"Oh, really?" He lifts a brow and eyes the desk.

"Don't even think about it, mister. You'll see it on Saturday."

"Saturday," he murmurs, the hint of a smile playing around his mouth. "Seems like there's something I'm supposed to be doing on Saturday."

I laugh, and fly out of the chair to smack him playfully on the chest. He pulls me into his arms and kisses me, gently at first and then with increasing fervency. "I reached for you," he says. "You weren't there."

The words are matter-of-fact, but to me they seem thick with meaning. I lean back so that I can see his face more clearly. "What's wrong?"

"I could ask you the same thing," he says, deflecting my words but not my worry. There is something on Damien's mind. He tucks my hair behind my ear. "Tell me what's keeping you awake."

"Bourbon," I say. "Bridal jitters."

"Not your mother?"

"That, too," I admit.

"Whatever you want to do, you know that I support it. All I ask is that you remember this is your wedding, and it's the only wedding you're going to have." He strokes my cheek, the touch melting me as much as the words. "Consider that when you decide how to handle your mother."

I nod. "You're right." I take his hand. "And you? Is it wedding jitters that are bothering you? Is something going on at work?"

He turns, looking out toward the rows of polished bookshelves now standing like sentries in the dark. He doesn't answer right away, and I'm starting to suspect he isn't going to answer me at all. Then he says, "It's Sofia."

I try not to react, but I have no control over the quickening pace of my heart, and I'm certain that my eyes have gone unnaturally wide. "What about her?" I ask carefully. Sofia is so far off my list of favorite people, it isn't even funny. Still, she was important to Damien when he was growing up, and despite a lot of recent shit, I know that she's still important to him.

"I got an email from her. I saw it right after we got home. She wants to come to the wedding. She thinks that it could be arranged."

The words hang in the air, like one of those cartoon anvils that is defying the laws of gravity and simply hovering, waiting for the moment when it will drop and crush the hapless coyote.

I open my mouth, close it, then try again. "Oh," is all I can manage.

"That pretty much sums it up," he says. He's wearing pajama bottoms tied loosely around his waist, and he slides one hand into a pocket. With the other, he massages his forehead with his thumb and finger.

"Do you want her to come?" I finally ask.

He lifts his head, looking at me as if I've gone insane. "No."

A moment passes, and then he lets out a soft curse. "No," he repeats, "and the not wanting makes me sad." He meets my eyes. "But I meant what I said in the limo, about our choices and the people in our lives leading us to this point. To each other." He steps closer to me. "It saddens me—hell, it angers me—but I have no regrets."

"I don't, either," I say, thinking of my mother. Of who she is, what she's done, and what I want. It's all a turmoil inside me. A storm. I know what I should do, what I want to do. But I'm not certain it's what I can do.

And though he hides it better than I do, I know that a similar storm is raging within Damien. How can it not be? He thrives on control. It is his lifeblood, his sustenance, and yet just the mention of Sofia's name conjures the specter of everything that spun out of control, cutting a path of destruction through his life as effectively as a spinning propeller breaking loose from its axle.

"Damien," I say, and I hear both longing and helplessness in my voice.

I see the heat flare in his eyes as he moves even closer to me. I take an automatic step backward, but am foiled by the desk. I stop, breathing hard, as he cages me in. I am wearing the button-down shirt that he abandoned on the floor when we went to bed. The tail hits me mid-thigh, and he uses his finger to trace the line of the hem, slowly easing it up, higher and higher.

My pulse quickens, and I feel the effects of his touch shimmering through me, hot and electric and alive.

Without thinking, I shift my stance, widening my legs. I want his hands upon me. I want his cock inside me. I want everything he has to give, and I want him to take everything he wants.

His hand slides between my legs and cups my sex, finding me desperately wet. "Tell me you want me," he says, sliding his fingers inside me. I almost melt with pleasure.

"Always," I say truthfully, and I know with absolute certainty that there will not ever be a time when I don't respond to Damien's presence. To his proximity, his heat. When I won't open like a flower to him. When my body won't crave his touch.

He thrusts another finger inside me and I grind down, shamelessly wanting more. But he denies me, and I hear myself whimper as he pulls his hand away. And then my whimper changes to a gasp when he grabs either side of the shirt and tugs it open, baring my breasts and sending buttons flying.

"Beautiful," he murmurs, and I close my eyes in expectation of his mouth on my nipple. But the touch doesn't come. Instead, he turns me around, then pulls the shirt the rest of the way off so that I am naked in front of him. I am facing the desk, my ass pressed against his erection, now hard steel beneath the thin pajama bottoms.

"I wanted you in the limo," he says. "But I need you now. Do you understand what I'm saying?"

"You know I do." I turn to look at him as I speak, but he shakes his head.

"Eyes forward. Bend over. Hold on to the far side of the desk."

I do as he says. I feel vulnerable. I feel *him*.

"I don't think we ever took care of that little issue of punishment," he says.

I lick my lips, my body already tight with anticipation and my sex clenching with desire.

"Is that what you want, Nikki? Shall I spank your ass? Shall I punish you with the sting of my palm, turning your ass pink and sweet, making you hot?"

"I'm already hot," I say honestly. "And yes. Please, yes." We both want this. Hell, we both need it. He needs to take back some of that control, and I so desperately need to give it to him. Because I need the storm to settle inside me as much as he needs my submission.

I do not turn around, but I can hear the soft rustle of material as he slips off the pajama bottoms. He steps closer, and the tip of his cock rubs along the crack of my ass. "Maybe I should just take you, fast and without warning."

"Yes." There is no hiding the need in my voice, and Damien chuckles.

"Soon," he says, and then lands his palm sharply against my rear.

I cry out, more from surprise than pain, and then brace for the second blow. It comes fast, and then Damien's palm is caressing the point of impact, smoothing out those brilliant red sparks, making them flow inside me, shifting from pain to a vibrant pleasure that pulses through me.

"More?" But he doesn't wait for an answer, just spanks me again, and again. Eight more times, until my rear is red hot and sensitive and my cunt is so wet that I can feel my desire coating the inside of my thighs.

I am bent over the desk, my breasts rubbing against the wood with every impact, and now my nipples are as tight and hard and sensitive as my clit. I'm awash in sensation, my entire body sparking like a live wire, and with the right touch, I know that I will shatter.

I expect another smack, but this time his hands grab my hips instead. With his knee, he roughly shoves my legs apart. One hand comes down on my back, holding me in place over the desk. The other strokes my sex, opening me, readying me, though that is hardly necessary—as I am so ready for him to be inside me, I can barely stand it.

"Damien, please," I beg. "I need you in so many ways, but right now, I just need you to take me."

He does, thank god. Gently at first, just the tip of his cock sliding into me as my muscles clench greedily around him. He withdraws, and I moan, immediately regretting the loss of him. Then, without warning, he slams into me, our bodies coming together brutally, violently, and I can feel his body tightening as his climax draws close. "Come with me, baby," he says, his hand snaking around to stroke my clit.

It is that touch in combination with the sensation of being filled by Damien that sends me spiraling off the cliff, then grabbing on to the edge of the desk as Damien thrusts into me, faster and faster until he explodes as well, then collapses onto the carpet, clutching me around the waist and pulling me down with him.

I land on top of him, and he grins. "Again, Ms. Fairchild?"

"I could be convinced," I say, though I am still breathless.

He lifts himself just high enough to kiss me. "Marry me," he says, then grins.

"Yeah," I say happily. "I think I will."

* * *

"All I am saying is that there is a reason that tradition exists," my mother says as we enter Phillipe Favreau's Rodeo Drive boutique.

I am regretting not only having her come along today, but also that I answered her questions about my flower choices for the wedding. She has been harping on it ever since I explained that the cupcake tower would be decorated with wildflowers because that was the overall floral theme.

Wildflowers, in the world of Elizabeth Fairchild, are an epic fail where weddings are concerned.

"Orchids, lilies, gardenias. Darling, those are all lovely and elegant and classic."

"I like what I've picked out, Mother." I glance around the studio. There are only three gowns on mannequins and one very thin woman working behind a tall glass table that doubles as a desk. "Now, would you drop it?" I glance at the woman. "I'm Nikki Fairchild. I have an appointment with Alyssa for an alteration on a gown that arrived this morning."

"Nikki Fairchild?" she repeats, looking a bit more flummoxed than is usual for store clerks on Rodeo Drive. "The Damien Stark gown?"

I frown. "Um, well, I'm going to be the one wearing it, but Damien ordered it, yes. Why? Is there a problem?"

She smiles an overly perky smile, and little knots of dread form in my stomach. "I'll just get Alyssa. One moment."

"Even magnolias," Mother says.

"Would you stop it?" I am practically snarling, and Mother's eyes go wide.

"Nichole! You need to learn to control yourself."

I suck in both a breath and my temper, and refrain from telling her that she needs to learn to shut up. "I'm a little nervous," I say. "I think there may be something wrong with the dress."

"Nonsense. I'm sure it's lovely. Do you have a picture?"

I glance sideways at her, thrown off kilter by the fact that she's actually being soothing. "Um, sure." I pull out my phone and call up the photographs we'd taken in Paris, both of Phillipe's sketch and of the basted-together version that I wore for the initial fitting. Just seeing it makes me smile. It has a fitted bodice with a low neckline that reveals a hint of cleavage. The sleeves are slim and hug my arms. The skirt is not a traditional princess style, but is instead sleek in the front and over my hips, showing off my curves. The back has a modified bustle that supports a train.

The neckline and the hem and the lower line of the bodice are embroidered with tiny flowers accented with pearls, giving the pure white dress a touch of the whimsical. I think it's an exceptional dress, and I cannot wait for Damien to see me in it.

I glance over at my mother, expecting to see approval in her eyes. I should have known better.

"Well," she says with a sniff, "I suppose this is to be expected, considering your choice of flowers and cake."

"I—" I snap my mouth shut. I have no idea what to say. No idea what insult to hurl that will cut her as deeply as she is cutting me, each word like a new wound.

All I want is one tiny crumb from my mother. Approval, compassion, respect. But there is nothing there, and there never has been.

And yet I have been foolish enough to let that flame of hope keep burning. God, I'm an idiot.

I turn away so as to not let her see that my eyes are bright with tears.

"A longer train," she says. "And a fuller skirt. This is one of the few times you can completely hide those hips, Nichole. You should take advantage of it."

I cringe, wanting to scream at her that just because I'm no longer a size four does not mean that I have to start wearing caftans. I'm young, I'm healthy, I'm pretty, and if she's too god-damn stupid to see that—

My wild thoughts are interrupted by the door to the back room bursting open and a tall red-haired woman hurrying in.

"Nikki," she says, holding out her hand. "I'm Alyssa."

I start to hold my hand out as well, only to discover that I've clenched it so tight that I've left indentations from my nails in my palms. I flex it, then extend it to her. "Is there a problem?"

"I'm afraid so," she says. "This is terribly embarrassing, but your dress is missing."

"Missing," I repeat stupidly.

"We hope it's just a clerical error in customs, and we're doing everything we can." I halfway tune her out, still stuck on that one word: "missing." My dress is missing, and my wedding is Saturday. Tomorrow.

". . . have been other shops with items missing . . ."

What the hell am I going to do? This is my dress. My *wedding* dress. I mean, I can't just run to Target.

". . . customs or the shipper, but we're looking into it, and . . ."

And it's not even just a wedding dress. It's the dress I bought during my trip to Europe with Damien. It's the dress we bought during our days and nights in Paris. The dress made by the designer who assured Damien that he would go faint with awe when he saw me in the gown. This is not a dress I can lose, nor is it a dress I can replace, and I can feel the panic, the anger, the futility rising inside me.

One goddamn thing after another, and I can't even lash out. Because it's not this poor girl's fault—hell, she's mortified, too. But everything is just piling on: the photographer and the music and the flowers. Those goddamned flowers that my mother has been talking about for the last hour.

"Ms. Fairchild?" Alyssa says, her voice ripe with concern. Her fingers brush over my arm, and I use the touch as an anchor to draw me out of my thoughts and back to reality. "Ms. Fairchild, are you okay?"

"She's fine," my mother says firmly. "This can only be considered a good thing. It gives her a chance to find a dress that might actually flatter her figure."

Alyssa's eyes are wide, and she's staring at my mother like she's never met such a creature before. Hell, she probably hasn't.

"Come on, Nichole. This is Beverly Hills. I'm sure we can find you a gown."

"Get the hell out of here." I did not plan the words, but I know the moment that they are out that I mean them with all my heart.

"Excuse me?"

"Texas," I say. "Go back to Texas, Mother. Go now."

"Texas! But, Nichole, how—"

"It's *Nikki*," I snap. "How many times do I have to tell you? You don't listen."

Beside us, I see Alyssa lick her lips and then fade into the background. At the glass desk, the thin girl seems overly interested in the single piece of paper on the surface.

I really don't give a shit. Right then, decorum is the last thing on my mind.

"I can't possibly go to Texas now. I'd miss the wedding."

"That's the idea," I say. "I'll have Grayson fly you. You'll need to leave today so that he can be back in plenty of time. He is invited," I add, my voice syrupy sweet.

"Darling, I'm your mother. You can't ask me not to be at your wedding."

I hesitate for just a moment, just long enough to hear Damien's voice in my head talking about choices and paths and where they lead. And this choice leads to my wedding day. To a day of celebration. Or to a day with my mother harping in my ear. The woman who has, in so many ways, gone out of her way to steal the joy out of so many moments in my life.

"Nichole, don't do this. I need—" She cuts herself off, her lips clamping tightly shut.

I take a deep breath, suddenly realizing that I've been more of an idiot than I thought. My mother didn't come here because my impending wedding spurred her to repair our relationship. And she didn't come because she wanted to apologize for the horrible things she said to Damien.

She came because she spent every dime our family had a long time ago, and she sees a new cash cow in me. I don't know what it is she needs—a new house, a new car, investment capital. I don't know, and I don't care. She's not getting a dime of my money, and she's sure as hell not getting Damien's.

"Goodbye, Mother."

"Nichole, no. You can't do this."

"You know what, Mother? I can." I head for the door, my heart feeling lighter and my step springier. I glance back at her and smile. "And for that matter, why don't you go ahead and find your own way home?"

eight

"You're amazing," Damien says that night when I tell him what I did. "You once told me that you didn't have the balls to stand up to your mother." We're in the swimming-pool-sized bathtub, facing each other, our legs touching.

"I still don't have balls," I say with a laugh.

"Sure you do." He reaches for my hand and tugs me toward him, then very deliberately cups my hand over his package. "These are all yours."

"Damn straight," I say, then capture his mouth in a kiss.

His arms go around me and he pulls me close, until I have no choice but to straddle him if I want to sit in any sort of comfortable position.

Not that straddling Damien is a hardship, especially when his erection is rubbing against my folds in a way that is very effectively taking my mind off the day's drama.

"I'm proud of you," he says, trapping me in the circle of his arms.

"I'm proud of me, too," I say. "I took control of the situation. I decided what I wanted for this wedding, and I did what had to be done." I kiss him. "I think I'm going to make a habit of going after the things I want."

"Haven't you always?"

I press a finger over his lips. "That's not the point."

"What is?" he asks.

"This," I say, reaching between us to cup my hand around his erection. Slowly, I stroke the length of him. "Taking control can be very rewarding," I say.

"Oh, yes." His voice sounds raw.

"Something wrong, Mr. Stark?" I ask innocently. "You seem distracted."

"On the contrary," he says. "I'm very focused. Very aware."

"Are you?" I increase the pressure on his cock, then tease the tip with my thumb.

He sucks in air, and I see the shudder cut through him and the heat in his eyes.

He looks at me, and I smile, slow and easy and with all sorts of promise.

"Kiss me," he says. "Ride me."

Now it's my turn to shudder in anticipation. I rise up, capturing his mouth in a kiss that is hot and deep and demanding. His tongue wars with mine, thrusting and teasing. I lower myself onto his cock and ride him, lifting myself up and down in a frantic rhythm that sends water sloshing around the tub.

Over and over, deeper and deeper, until I have no choice but to break the kiss, because I have to arch back simply from the weight of the pleasure that is shooting through me.

When I do, his mouth closes over my breast, and his teeth nip at me, the pain sending hot wires of pleasure down through my body to my cunt, to that deep place inside me that he's touching, thrusting against with every stroke, building a delicious pressure that grows and grows until finally we explode together, sending water flying out of the tub and me collapsing back against Damien's chest in utter satisfaction and release.

We stay that way until we fear that we will shrivel in the tub, then Damien lifts me out, dries me off, and carries me to the bed, tucking me gently under the cool sheets.

"You haven't told me what you're doing about your dress," Damien says moments later as we twine together in the bed, half drifting off to sleep.

"I went back inside after Mother left," I tell him. "It's not perfect, but they had a dress that was my size in the back."

"Do you like it?"

I shrug. The truth is that it's a lovely dress that any bride would be thrilled with. But it's not *my* dress, and what girl is happy with sloppy seconds?

"I'm sorry, baby," he says, kissing my bare shoulder.

"It's okay, really. I promise you'll think I'm stunning."

"I always do."

I smile, and I'm still smiling as I start to drift off. I'm just about to slide into the sweet oblivion of sleep when I remember one other thing. "You still awake? I have a brilliant idea."

"I'm always awake for brilliance," he says.

"I got the idea from those tweets of us from Raven."

"Us?"

"Us girls," I clarify.

"Uh-huh. If this is about inviting the Raven men to the wedding, I'm going to exercise my veto power."

"Very funny. No, I was thinking about our photographer problem. I know I told you I wanted to make sure we had wedding portraits, but we can sit for a portrait anytime. Besides, I want to remember the day, not a pose. And I was thinking that we could do the same thing all those folks did in tweets."

"Which is?"

"Candid shots. We give each guest a camera as a wedding souvenir. And then we have them drop the memory cards in a bowl before they leave. We'll get a ton of fabulous pictures of our friends, us, dancing, eating. They won't be professional, but they'll be fun. And they'll be *us*. And not the kind of tacky pictures that the paparazzi will snap from the beach. What do you think?"

"I think you're brilliant," he says. "Brilliant and beautiful. And I cannot wait to be your husband."

I smile in contentment and love. "Me, either," I say, and then, finally, I close my eyes, snuggle closer to Damien, and let sleep tug me under.

Damien is already gone when I wake up on Friday. He's left word with Grayson that he has some business to attend to before we leave on our honeymoon and that he will either be at the office or looking at various properties with Mr. Black.

I put a waffle in the toaster—which pretty much sums up my culinary skills—and eat it without syrup on the patio while I make some morning phone calls. The first one is to Sylvia, and I explain my plan about the cameras. She thinks it's brilliant, and swears that she has plenty of time to handle it.

"I'll make sure they're delivered by morning. Seriously, Nikki, don't worry about it. Rest a little today. You deserve it. And you'll need it for your honeymoon."

I roll my eyes, but since she's right, I don't argue. Instead, I actually do the delegation thing and email her the names of three bands I auditioned, liked, but rejected. It's not a perfect solution, but it is a low-stress one. She promises to call them, see who's still available, and to pick the best one.

I thank her and sign off, then try to decide on the appropriate form of pre-wedding relaxation. I actually managed to finish

Damien's scrapbook last night, so that's out. And while my own work has been stacking up, somehow the idea of getting onto the computer and programming just doesn't appeal.

About the only thing that does, actually, is a walk along the beach. And since I don't want to go alone, I head downstairs to the first-floor guest suite, knock, and then head into Jamie's darkened room.

Normally, I'd let her sleep. But since this is my last day as a single best friend, I figure an exception is in order. I pull the covers back and give her a little shake.

"Mmm, Ryan . . ."

I lift my brows, because that's a very interesting development, but Jamie doesn't indulge me by talking in her sleep again. Instead, she bolts upright, springing awake.

"Holy fuck, Nikki," she screeches. "What the hell are you doing?"

I shrug. "Wanna take a walk on the beach?"

Fortunately, Jamie is easygoing. She shoots me a couple of dirty looks for good measure, throws in a curse, but gets dressed. We're down at the beach within fifteen minutes.

"So, do you have anything to tell me?" I ask.

She stares at me like I'm a loon. "The moon isn't made of green cheese. Masturbation doesn't make you go blind. Jethro Tull is a band, not a guy. How do those work for you?"

"Not bad," I say. "I was thinking more along the lines of Ryan."

She slows her step. "What about him?"

"Ever since Damien had him take you home that time, you've had this thing."

I expect her to deny it. Instead, she shrugs. "So?"

"So there really is a thing?"

"Not as far as he's concerned," she says, her tone frustrated. "As far as I can tell, I'm invisible to him."

I hook my arm through hers. "I can't imagine you being invisible to anyone."

"I know, right? I mean, what's up with that?"

I laugh. "So what are you going to do?"

"About Ryan?"

"About you."

She slows her pace. "I don't know. I didn't get that commercial that Caleb is directing, but it felt nice doing the audition thing again. But I don't want to get back on the same hamster wheel, you know? And I'm—" She glances at me, then clams up.

"What?"

"Nothing."

"James . . ."

"Fine. Whatever. It's just that everything changes with you getting married."

"I'm still your best friend." I stop walking, and tug her to a stop, too.

"Well, duh," she says, in a way that sends a shock of relief running through me. "I just mean that I don't think I'd do that great living by myself. In case you hadn't noticed, I have a tendency to run a little wild. And you're off the roommate market. I thought about living with Ollie, but that might be weird."

"Ya think?"

She waves a hand. "Nah, that's over," she says, referring to their romps between the sheets. "But it still might be weird. Where is he, anyway? He's coming to the wedding, right?"

"He's supposed to be at the dinner tonight." Since we're not doing a big wedding, we're not having an official rehearsal dinner. But we are getting a whole slew of our friends together. "He's been in New York. Depositions, I think he said."

"And Damien's cool with him coming tonight?"

"Like you said, it might be weird, but on the whole it's okay. They aren't ever going to call each other up to go have a beer at the corner pub, but I think we can manage the occasional dinner and social event."

"Good." She crosses her arms over her chest. "Change sucks."

I think about the changes in my life since Damien entered it, and the ones that are coming. A wedding. Hopefully a family. I smile, then start walking again, tugging Jamie along beside me. "No," I say firmly. "You'll see. Change doesn't have to suck at all."

Le Caquelon in Santa Monica is closed tonight for our private party. Alaine, Damien's childhood friend and best man, owns the fondue-style restaurant, and has graciously offered it for this evening's party.

I love the place, with its funky decor and wild colors. The last time I was here, Damien and I shared a very private booth. Tonight, everyone is gathered in the main restaurant. We are laughing, talking, and toasting. And, of course, indulging in the various fondue pots that Alaine has scattered throughout.

He has turned off the restaurant's normal New Age music in favor of piping Rat Pack tunes from the speakers. Apparently he is aware that Damien and I share a love of Sinatra, Dean Martin, and the rest.

I smile at Damien, who is talking to Ollie and Evan across the room. He leaves them, then strides to me and pulls me close, easing me around the makeshift dance floor before dipping me, much to the amusement of the other guests. "I am a genius," he says.

"So I've been told."

"I also own a stereo," he adds.

"This is also a fact that I'm aware of. I assume there's some sort of connection coming."

He points to the speakers. "We don't need a band tomorrow. We just need a DJ."

I gape at him. "You are a genius. Except I already told Sylvia to hire a band."

"She didn't have the heart to tell you, but they've all been booked." He leans closer, nips my earlobe, then whispers, "I think you may be exhibiting signs of stress. My assistant was trying to protect you. I can't say I blame her."

I laugh and push him away, then immediately pull him back into my arms. "You're in a good mood."

"Of course I am. Haven't you heard? I'm getting married tomorrow."

"Lucky man," I say.

"Very," he replies, and the intensity of his gaze acts like an underscore to the word.

"I have something for you," I say, tugging him to the far side of the restaurant where all the women have piled our purses. I had brought a huge tote, and now I pull out the present wrapped in silver paper.

He takes it, his expression so much like a boy on Christmas morning that I laugh with delight. "Go ahead," I urge.

He peels off the paper, studies the book, then slowly opens it. I know the first image he sees—a snapshot of the two of us in Texas six years ago. It was an offhand shot by a local news reporter and it never even made the paper. I lucked into it after a call to the paper's morgue. "Nikki," he says, and there is awe in his voice. He flips through the pages, and the love I see in his eyes makes my knees go weak.

I watch as he examines every page, every memory. When he is finished, he closes the book with reverence, sets it gently on the table, and then pulls me close. "Thank you," he says, those two words holding a lifetime of emotion.

He kisses me gently, then leads me back to the crowd. "I have a gift for you, as well," he says, then looks at his watch. "I need about fifteen more minutes."

My brow furrows as I wonder what he could be up to, but I

nod. "That gives me plenty of time to make the circuit and eat more chocolate. Come with?"

"Of course," he says, then follows me to the chocolate fondue station. Alaine is there, and we chat for a while. Then Alaine and Damien go off to talk with Blaine and Evelyn. Since I have something to ask Evelyn, I almost follow them, but Ollie approaches, and I pause to give him a hug.

"Hey, deposition guy. How goes the wild and woolly world of civil litigation?"

"Wild and woolly," he replies with a grin. "And over. At least for a few weeks." He waves to Charles Maynard, his boss, then leads me into a corner. "Charles asked if I wanted a transfer back to New York."

"Really? Why?"

"Courtney, I think. I asked for the transfer to LA originally to be closer to her. Now that we're not a couple . . ." He trails off.

"Are you going to take him up on the offer?" Ollie and I haven't been as close lately, but I know that I will miss him if he moves.

"Thinking about it. But I'm on the fence. I love Manhattan, but LA has its perks, too." He looks at me as if there is something else he wants to say.

"What?"

He hesitates, then barrels forward. "Do you think there's any chance of repairing the damage with Courtney?"

I feel my shoulders sag. "You fucked up, Ollie. Big time. We all love you. Hell, she loves you. But I don't know if that's enough."

"No," he says. "I don't, either."

I squeeze his hand. "I'm here if you need me."

"I know," he says, then hugs me. "I'm glad."

I return the hug tightly, thinking that this is another nice thing about weddings—it lets you clear out the last of the ghosts lingering in your past.

I make the circuit, chatting with Ryan and Edward, with Steve and Anderson. Charles and Blaine come up and I try to get some sense of where Charles stands on Ollie's move, but he's saying nothing.

Sylvia and Ms. Peters and others on Damien's staff are here as well. And, of course, there's Evelyn.

"I've been trying to corner you all night," I say to her.

"Funny, I was just thinking that you were the popular one." She steps back and examines me in that sentimental way folks have of looking at brides before the wedding. "You're good for him, Texas. Hell, you're good for each other."

"Yes, we are," I say. "Did Damien tell you about my mother?"

"I heard some of it from him," she admits. "I think I heard the rest from Jamie."

I grin. That doesn't really surprise me.

"I sent her packing," I say. "And I never asked her to walk me down the aisle, even though she's the only parent I've got."

"Parent?" she repeats. "You know better than that, Texas. Family's what you make of it, and that woman may have given birth to you, but she's not your family, not really."

I look around this room filled with friends, and have to nod. "I know," I say. "But you're family, and I love you." I take a deep breath. "Would you walk me down the aisle?"

I think I see tears in her eyes, but I don't say anything. I just give her a moment to gather herself, even while I'm holding close to my heart the knowledge that my request moved her. "Hell yes, Texas," she finally says. "You better believe I will."

Moments later, Damien calls me over to where he stands chatting with Evan. He pulls a flat silver-wrapped box out of his pocket, and hands it to me.

"I can open it?"

"Of course."

I rip the paper off. I lift the top off to reveal a beautiful necklace with a silver chain and sunshine-yellow gemstones. "Damien, it's lovely." I glance down at the emerald ankle bracelet I always wear, feeling spoiled.

"I remembered the flowers on your wedding gown. I thought this would match them."

My heart twists at his thoughtfulness. "But that was the first dress," I explain.

"I know," he says, as Evan reaches over and grabs a large box off the floor. He sets it on the table, and I look between the two men with curiosity. "Go ahead," Damien urges. "Open it. I think you'll find the necklace appropriate, after all."

Wary, I pull off the lid, and find myself gazing down at my beautiful, missing wedding dress.

"How—?"

"I have a few friends who have a unique ability to track down internationally shipped items that have gone missing," Evan says.

"Oh." I glance at Damien, wondering if that means what I think it does. But his face reveals nothing. To be honest, I really don't care how or where he found my dress. I'm just glad it's arrived.

"Alyssa's coming to the house in the morning. She'll take care of any alterations on-site," Damien adds, and I lean over and kiss him impulsively, this man who takes such exceptionally good care of me.

"Thank you," I say to Damien, then turn to include Evan. "Thank you both. You saved me."

A sense of relief sweeps over me, and for the first time since I started this wedding planning thing, I'm truly stress-free. It feels nice.

I reach out and hold tight to Damien's hand. *This,* I think, *is the only thing that's important.*

The party continues until well into the night, and it's almost two by the time we get home. I'm about to strip and fall into bed when I realize that I've missed a call. I put the phone on speaker and listen as the message plays.

"Hi, Nikki, this is Lauren with the flowers for tomorrow. I just wanted to let you know that we're all set. It was last minute, but we were happy to make the change."

I frown and glance at Damien, who looks as confused as I feel.

"So we'll be there in the morning to set up, this time with the lilies and gardenias. And we're sending a selection over to Sally, too, for the cake. Thanks again, and we can't wait to see you tomorrow. Congratulations again to you and Damien."

The call ends, and I stare at the phone like it is a serpent.

What the fuck?

What the bloody fuck?

"She switched them," I say. "My mother actually fucked with my wedding." I meet Damien's gaze. I know mine is angry. His is murderous. Not because of the flowers—I sincerely doubt he cares about sunflowers versus gardenias—but because of what that woman has done to me over and over and over.

"It's like she's reaching out from Texas and twisting the knife. Like there is no pleasure in her life unless she's screwing with me."

I stalk around the bedroom, trying to get my head together. I feel cold and angry and out of control. Whatever pleasure I'd felt when Damien and Evan presented me with my wedding dress has been swept away. It's as if this wedding will never truly be my own. And now I either have to endure a wedding with my mother's stamp upon it, or I have to spend my wedding day sorting out this mess.

"Dammit," I howl.

"It will be okay," Damien says, pulling me into his arms.

"I know it'll be okay. It's not like we're talking about curing cancer. But that's not the point. She just went and turned the whole thing around on me."

"And at the end of the day, we'll still be married," he says reasonably.

I am in too bitchy a mood to listen to reason, but it's still there. Inescapable and true and hanging in the air between us.

I stalk around the room a bit more, while Damien eyes me with trepidation, as if I'm a bomb about to go off.

Smart man.

Finally, the bubbling anger cools, leaving calm calculation.

I feel the prickle of an idea, and slowly it grows. After a few more laps around the room, I stop in front of Damien.

"I can fix this," I say.

"What do you mean?"

"I can howl and complain that she fucked up my wedding. Or I can turn it around on its ear, flip my mother the bird, and say that she didn't fuck up my wedding, she did me a favor."

"Did she?"

My smile is slow. "Yes. And I'll tell you why." I grab the collar of Damien's shirt, pull him toward me, once again feeling light and free. I kiss him hard. "I can tell you," I repeat, and then flash a smile full of wicked intentions, "but you're going to have to make me."

nine

I stand on the third-floor balcony looking out at the calm Pacific. It is a beautiful evening, perfect for an outdoor wedding.

It is almost sunset. Just about time for the ceremony to begin.

Damien is beside me, his arm around my waist. The expanse of his property, lush green fading to pale sand, spreads out before us.

Usually, the beach is empty this time of day. Right now, however, it is dotted with white tents and glowing lanterns. Guests mingle, indistinguishable from this distance, and I hear the soft strains of Frank Sinatra drifting up to us. Beyond the line of tents, the paparazzi are camped out, ready to pounce.

I can't help but smile at the thought that we're pulling something over on those vultures.

Beyond them, the Pacific glows a warm purple tinged with orange from the swiftly setting sun.

Soon, I think. *Soon I will be Mrs. Damien Stark.*

"You're sure this is what you want?" Damien asks as the air fills with the thrum of his helicopter. It swoops down in front of us to settle gently on the helipad.

I take one more look at the panorama spread out before me. "I'm sure," I say, raising my voice to be heard over the rotors.

Below us, Gregory and Tony are loading suitcases into the bird.

I rise up on my toes and kiss Damien, hard and fast and deep. I pull away, breathless, and smile at the irony—it took a shove from my mother to drive home something I should have realized all along.

I press my palm to Damien's chest, wanting to feel the beat of his heart beneath my hand. "It's not the walk down the aisle that matters—it's the man waiting for me when I get there. You said it yourself, it's the only wedding I'll ever have, and this is the way I want it." No stress, no drama, no paparazzi. No polite chitchat, no worries about music or food or flowers or unexpected relatives showing up out of the blue. Just Damien and those two little words—"I do."

"And all the work you've put into the reception?" he asks, even though we talked about this last night—about how I'd been working so hard for perfection that I lost sight of what Damien already knew—that so long as we end up as man and wife, "perfect" is a given.

Still, I indulge him by answering again. I understand he needs to be certain that I am sure I want to do this.

"The party's important, too," I say. "And they'll have a great one." I nod toward the beach. "Trust me. Jamie has it under control. If anyone knows how to make sure a crowd has a good time at a party, it's my best friend." I smile more broadly. "I asked Ryan to help her. They'll party through the night, and anyone who has a mind to can watch us get married in the morning. And Evelyn promised to spin the crap out of it for the press."

Damien's smile is as wide as my own. "I love you, Ms. Fairchild," he says.

"You won't be able to say that much longer. Soon it'll be Mrs. Stark."

He takes my hand and tugs me toward the stairs. "Then let's go," he says. "The sooner, the better."

We hurry hand in hand down the stairs, then sprint for the helicopter, heads down, laughing. Damien helps me aboard, and once we're strapped in, he signals the pilot and the bird takes off.

So, with the guests waving goodbye from the beach and the paparazzi snapping wildly, we elope into the sunset, leaving our wedding guests to eat our food, drink our champagne, and dance into the night.

Damien and I stand on a beach beside a foaming sea that is shifting away from the gray of night into a cacophony of colors with the rising sun. That was something else I'd realized: I couldn't get married at sunset. I had to have a sunrise wedding.

I am wearing my wedding dress and the necklace that Damien gave me, and when I saw the look in Damien's eyes as I walked the short distance down the aisle to him, I knew that whatever trouble it took to rescue the dress was worth it. I feel like a princess. Hell, I feel like a bride. And in Damien's eyes, I feel beautiful.

I am not wearing shoes, and I curl my toes into the sand, feeling wild and decadent and free. There is no stress, there are no worries. There is simply this wedding and the man beside me, and that is all that I need.

In front of us, a Mexican official is performing the ceremony in broken, heavily accented English. I am pretty sure I have never heard anything more beautiful.

"Do you take this man?" he asks, and I say the words that have been in my heart from the moment I first met Damien. "I do."

"I do," says Damien in turn. He is facing me as he speaks, and I can see the depth of emotion in his dual-colored eyes. *Mine,* he mouths, and I nod. It is true. I am his, and always will be.

And Damien Stark is mine.

A few feet away, a small boy who has been paid some pesos is holding Damien's phone, streaming video of our wedding back to Malibu, where Jamie is projecting the ceremony onto one of the tent walls, just in case any of the guests are still sober and awake after a long night of partying.

Here on our beach, the official pronounces us man and wife. The words crash over me, heavy with meaning, filling my soul. "That day," I whisper, my heart full to bursting. "That day when you asked me to pose for you—I never expected it to end like this."

"But it hasn't ended, Mrs. Stark. This is just the beginning." His voice sounds full to bursting, and his words are absolutely perfect.

I nod, because he is right, and because I am so overwhelmed by the moment I can manage nothing else.

"I'm going to kiss you now," he says, then captures my mouth with his. The kiss is long and deep, and all around us the locals clap and cheer.

I cling to Damien, never wanting to let go, as the sun continues to rise around us, casting us in the glow of morning.

Perfect, I think. *Because the sun will never set between Damien and me. Not today, not ever.*

RELEASE ME

He was the one man I couldn't avoid.
And the one man I couldn't resist.

Damien Stark could have his way with any woman.
He was sexy, confident, and commanding: anything
he wanted, he got. And what he wanted was me.

Our attraction was unmistakable, almost beyond control,
but as much as I ached to be his, I feared the pressures
of his demands. Submitting to Damien meant I had to
bare the darkest truth about my past – and risk
breaking us apart.

But Damien was haunted, too. And as our passion
came to obsess us both, his secrets threatened to
destroy him – and us – for ever.

CLAIM ME

For Damien, our obsession is a game.
For me, it is fiercely, blindingly, real.

Damien Stark's need is palpable – his need for pleasure,
his need for control, his need for me. Beautiful and brilliant
yet tortured at his core, he is in every way my match.

I have agreed to be his alone, and now I want him to be fully
mine. I want us to possess each other beyond the sweetest edge
of our ecstasy, into the deepest desires of our souls. To let the
fire that burns between us consume us both.

But there are dark places within Damien that not even
our wildest passion can touch. I yearn to know his secrets,
for him to surrender to me as I have surrendered to him.
But our troubled pasts will either bind us close . . .
or shatter us completely.

COMPLETE ME

Our desire runs deep.
But our secrets cut close.

Beautiful, strong, and commanding, Damien Stark fills a void
in me that no other man can touch. His fierce cravings push
me beyond the brink of bliss – and unleash a wild passion
that utterly consumes us both.

Yet beneath his need for dominance, he carries the wounds of
a painful past. Haunted by a legacy of dark secrets and broken
trust, he seeks release in our shared ecstasy, the heat between
us burning stronger each day.

Our attraction is undeniable, our obsession inevitable.
But not even Damien can run from his ghosts, or shield
us from the dangers yet to come.

Wanted

He is everything I crave, all I desperately want.
And he is everything I can't have.

Evan Black embodies every fantasy I've ever had. He is brilliant, fierce and devastatingly handsome. But he is also headstrong, dangerous and burdened with secrets.

My family warned me to stay away, that I could never handle Evan's dark dealings or scarred past. Maybe I should have listened. Maybe I should have run. But our desire is undeniable, and some temptations you just can't fight.

And from the moment we finally touch, I know that we will never be the same.